Arranging for Large Jazz Ensemble

Edited by Michael Gold

Berklee Media
Associate Vice President: Dave Kusek
Director of Content: Debbie Cavalier
Marketing Manager: Jennifer Rassler
Senior Graphic Designer: David Ehlers

Berklee Press
Senior Writer/Editor: Jonathan Feist
Writer/Editor: Susan Gedutis
Production Manager: Shawn Girsberger
Product Marketing Manager: David Goldberg

ISBN 978-0-634-03656-9

1140 Boylston Street
Boston, MA 02215-3693 USA
(617) 747-2146

Visit Berklee Press Online at
www.berkleepress.com

Distributed By

Hal•Leonard®
Corporation
7777 W. Bluemound Rd. P.O. Box 13819
Milwaukee, Wisconsin 53213

Visit Hal Leonard Online at
www.halleonard.com

Printed in the United States of America.

10 09 08 07 06 05 04 03 5 4 3 2 1

Contents

Introduction

What this Book Covers

The large jazz ensemble, or big band, has a prominent place in the history of jazz. Some of the most dynamic personalities of jazz—Duke Ellington, Count Basie, Woody Herman, Buddy Rich, Stan Kenton, Maynard Ferguson, Gil Evans, and Thad Jones—were leaders of large jazz ensembles. Their bands were instantly recognizable by the unique musical personalities of the arrangers and composers who wrote for them. Today, Bob Brookmeyer, Bill Holman, Maria Schneider, Jim McNeely, Rob McConnell, and many other great writers and band leaders keep that tradition alive, continuing the big band as an important outlet and creative challenge.

This book is your guide to creating jazz arrangements for such large ensembles. It covers the following subjects.

Basics: We quickly review fundamental concepts that all arrangers need to have under their belts.

Voicing Techniques: Starting with simple unison- and octave-writing strategies, we then spend many chapters exploring the use of mechanical voicings, spreads, voicings in fourths, upper structure triad voicings, and clusters. We also examine such specialized techniques as line writing and the use of woodwind doubling in combination with muted brass.

Soli, Background, and Shout Choruses: Separate chapters analyze and present procedures for creating each of these trademark elements of big band arrangements.

Style: This discussion examines the question of what defines an arranger's style by comparing different versions of "Happy Birthday," done in the parodied styles of Duke Ellington, Count Basie, Gil Evans, and others.

Analysis of a Complete Arrangement: The final chapter presents an annotated score of a full-length arrangement that demonstrates many of the principles presented in preceding chapters. As with most of the musical examples, the reader has at his or her disposal not only written music but also a recorded performance of this complete arrangement on the CD.

The large jazz ensembles discussed in this book are described variously as 4&4s, 5&5s, 7&5s, and 8&5s. A 4&4 has four brass (usually three trumpets and one trombone) and four saxophones (usually one alto, two tenors, and one baritone). A 5&5 has five brass (usually three trumpets and two trombones) and five saxes (usually two altos, two tenors, and one baritone). A 7&5 has seven brass (usually four trumpets and three trombones) and five saxes (usually two altos, two tenors, and one baritone). An 8&5 has eight brass (usually four trumpets and four trombones, including a bass trombone) and five saxophones (usually two altos, two tenors, and one baritone). The rhythm section for such large ensembles consists of piano, bass, drums, and, very often, guitar.

Throughout this book, we primarily focus on what to write for the horns, since they traditionally dominate most big bands. It is important to remember, however, that a successful arrangement also needs detailed and clear parts for the rhythm section players. A good arranger will facilitate their supportive "comping" role and occasionally make use of their orchestral potential, both in the doubling of horn lines and as a separate unit to contrast the horn section.

How to Use this Book and CD

If you are new to arranging, we suggest you start with the review of basic nuts-and-bolts information provided in Chapter 1. Even seasoned arrangers may want to refresh their knowledge of these key concepts. And as they progress through the rest of the book, most readers will probably find it useful to dip back into Chapter 1 for reminders about such things as the ranges of specific instruments, appropriate choices for chord scales, or the positioning of rehearsal letters on a score.

For a more thorough discussion of the basics, we recommend *Modern Jazz Voicings* by Ted Pease and Ken Pullig (Berklee Press, 2001). Beginner and intermediate arrangers will want to study its explanations of mechanical and nonmechanical voicing techniques for small ensembles. A working knowledge of these techniques is a prerequisite for grasping the arranging methods for large ensembles that are covered in this book.

As you move into the meat of the book in Chapter 2 and beyond, we suggest that you learn the material in the following way:

1. Read through the procedure or description for each arranging strategy, making sure you grasp the theoretical basis as well as the step-by-step "recipe."

2. Study the written examples to see how the strategy should be applied in a specific musical situation. Examples range in length from a few measures to entire pieces.

3. Listen repeatedly to the corresponding recorded demonstration in order to actually *hear*—and eventually internalize the sound of—the musical effect. The CD symbol 1 tells you which of the more than 60 tracks to listen to.

4. Practice the technique by completing the exercises that appear at the end of most chapters.

A Note on Range Recommendations

The range guidelines we recommend throughout the book focus on the practical range within which the average player will be comfortable. They are intended to encourage the best ensemble balance and blend. Going beyond these boundaries will put players into extreme high and low registers where it is more difficult to control intonation and tone.

When writing for professional-level players, these limitations can be extended. This is why our range charts sometimes include notes beyond the practical range. For instance, a professional lead trumpet player will be able to play a high concert *f* above high *c*, well beyond our suggested practical limit of high *a-flat*, one ledger line above the staff. But the lead player in the average high school, college, or amateur band will be unable to play that high *f* consistently—or, perhaps, at all! When you do not know the abilities of the musicians in a band, play it safe by remaining within the practical range.

Acknowledgments

Many thanks to our colleagues in the jazz composition department at Berklee College of Music for their ideas, suggestions, and musical contributions: Ted Pease, Greg Hopkins, Scott Free, Jeff Friedman, Bill Scism, Bob Pilkington, and Jackson Schultz.

About the Authors

Dick Lowell, Associate Professor in the Jazz Composition Department, has taught at Berklee College of Music for thirty years. An active composer and arranger, he has written the majority of original compositions and arrangements for three CDs released by the New York–based Dave Stahl Big Band. Trombonist Rick Stepton was featured on his arrangement of "My Buddy," written for the Buddy Rich Big Band. His arrangements can be heard on CDs by the Ken Hadley Big Band backing vocal great Rebecca Paris. He is also under contract with Heavy Hitters, a production company specializing in prerecorded music for television. Segments of his music are being used on daytime television. An active trumpeter, he has performed with a variety of entertainers including Tony Bennett, Sammy Davis Jr., Jack Jones, Shirley Bassey, Carol Channing, Ray Bolger, Jerry Lewis, and Mel Tormé. He has also played in the Harry James and Artie Shaw big bands.

Ken Pullig joined the faculty of Berklee College of Music in 1975 and was named Chair of the jazz composition department in 1985. He was awarded a Massachusetts Council of the Arts Fellowship in 1979 for his extended jazz composition, "Suite No. 2 for Small Jazz Ensemble." For many years he led his ten-piece jazz ensemble Decahedron in performances throughout New England. A freelance trumpeter, he is regularly featured with the Cambridge Symphonic Brass Ensemble. He has performed with Mel Tormé, Ray Charles, Johnny Mathis, Rita Moreno, Dionne Warwick, and many others. In recent years, Pullig has presented clinics on jazz composition and arranging in France, Finland, Germany, and Argentina. In 1997, he was guest conductor/composer with the Jazz Company in Vigevano, Italy.

CHAPTER 1
Basic Information

IN THIS CHAPTER

1-1 Transposing from concert pitch to an instrument's written part.
1-2 Range limits and sound characteristics for big band instruments.
1-3 Comparison of instruments' ranges.
1-4 Limits on lower intervals to avoid muddy voicings.
1-5 Special effects for wind instruments.
1-6 Reharmonizing approach notes.
1-7 Chord scales: which scales work with which chords.
1-8 Preparing a score.
1-9 Overview of an arrangement.
1-10 Exercise

1-1 Transposition of Instruments

Use the table below to transpose parts for instruments commonly included in large jazz ensembles. For example, in order to have an E♭ alto saxophone play a concert *b-flat* pitch, you write the note *g* on the alto's part a major sixth above what would be written in the concert score.

Instrument	Concert Pitch	Written Note	Transposition from Concert Pitch
Flute			Non-transposing
B♭ Clarinet			Up a major 2nd
B♭ Soprano Sax			Up a major 2nd
E♭ Alto Sax			Up a major 6th
B♭ Tenor Sax			Up a major 9th

Instrument	Concert Pitch	Written Note	Transposition from Concert Pitch
E♭ Baritone Sax			Up a major 13th (octave + major 6th)
B♭ Bass Clarinet			Up a major 9th
B♭ Trumpet or Flügelhorn			Up a major 2nd
French Horn in F			Up a perfect 5th
B♭ Trombone			Non-transposing
B♭ Bass Trombone			Non-transposing
Tuba			Non-transposing
Guitar			Up an octave
Bass			Up an octave

1-2 Instrument Ranges and Sound Characteristics

For each instrument commonly used in large jazz ensembles, the following charts describe the available range as well as the timbral characteristics and the useable dynamic levels within certain registers. The limits of the practical range, within which the average player will be comfortable, are shown by vertical arrows pointing to darkened note heads. The theoretical extremes are shown by open note heads; arrows pointing upward to question marks are meant to suggest that for brass instruments, the upper limit is set only by the technical skills of the individual.

Range and Sound Characteristics Chart

In all examples that follow, ● = practical range.

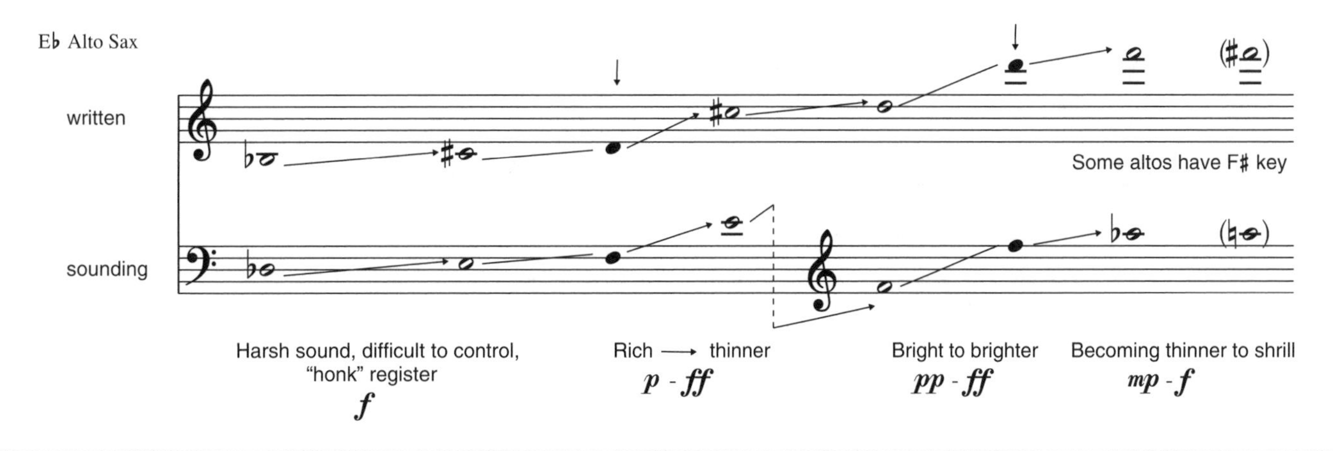

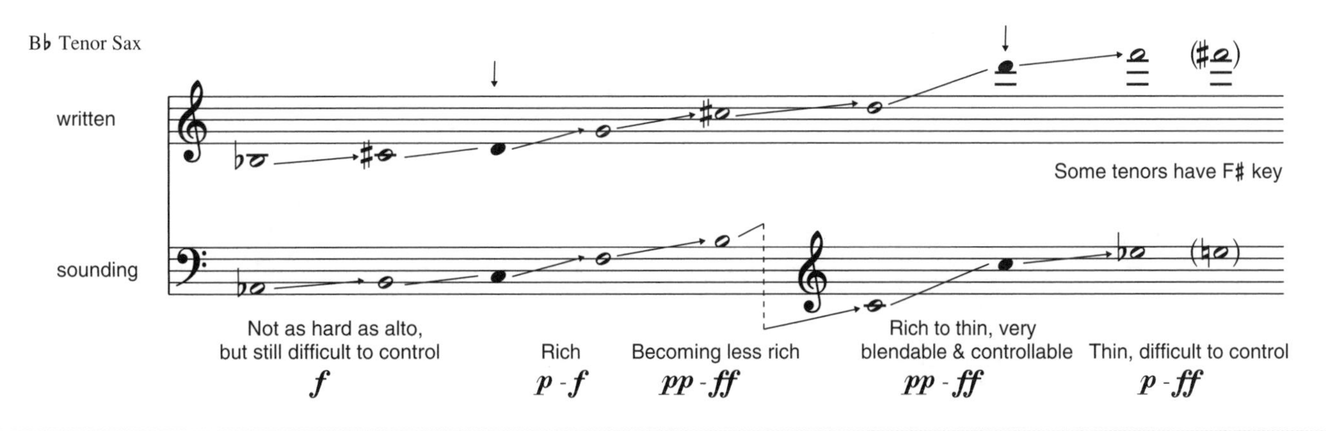

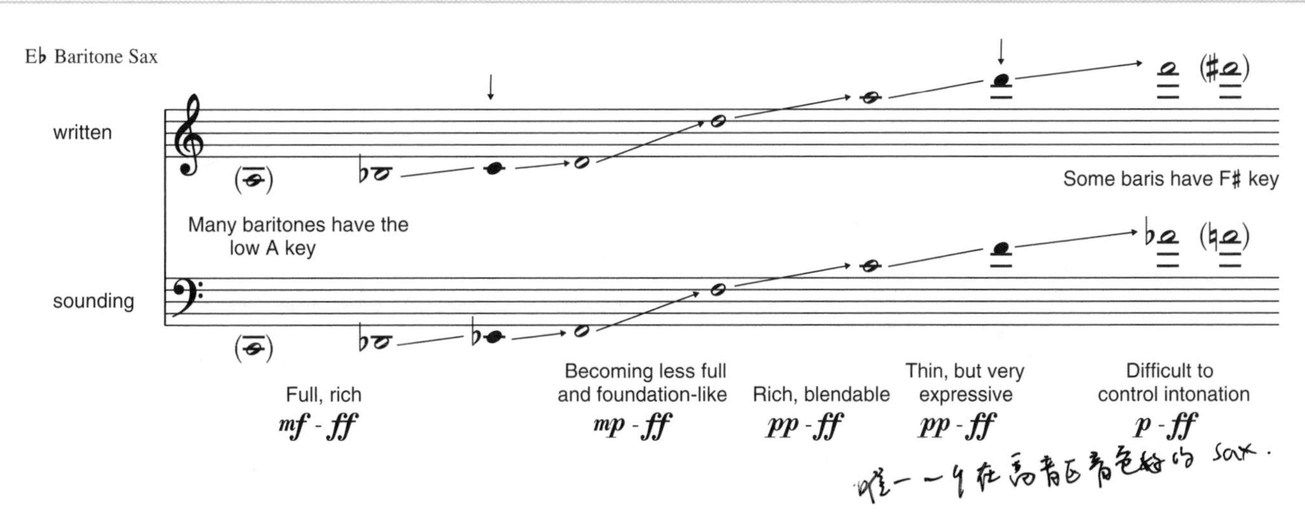

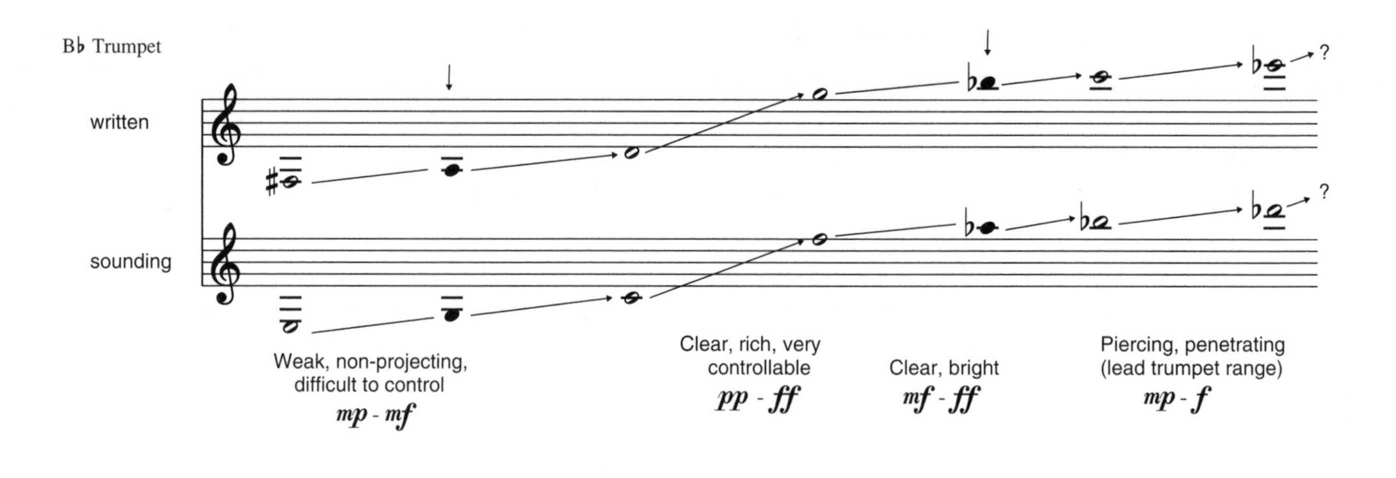
B♭ Trumpet
written
sounding
Weak, non-projecting, difficult to control
mp - mf
Clear, rich, very controllable
pp - ff
Clear, bright
mf - ff
Piercing, penetrating (lead trumpet range)
mp - f

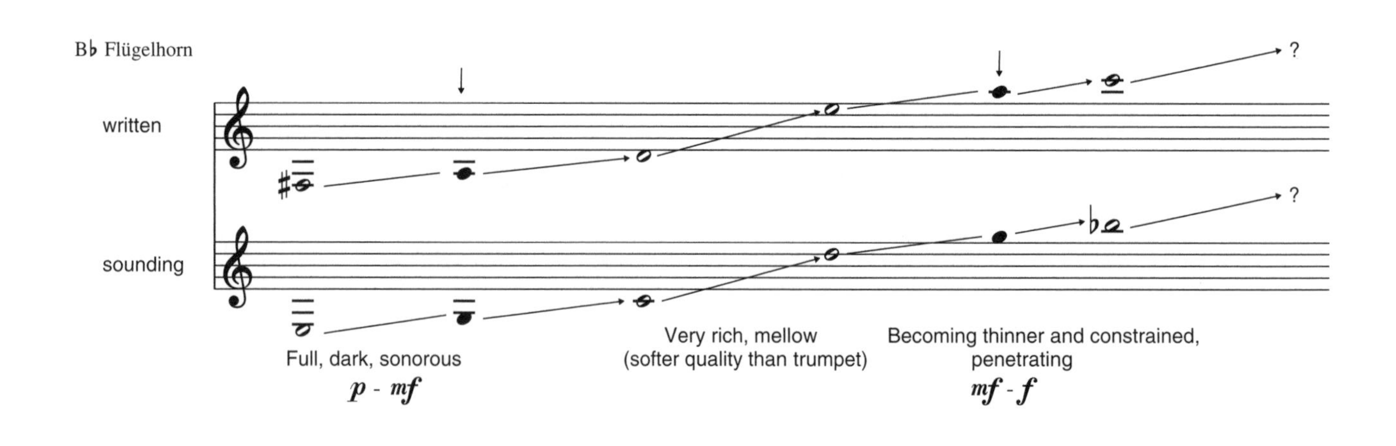
B♭ Flügelhorn
written
sounding
Full, dark, sonorous
p - mf
Very rich, mellow (softer quality than trumpet)
Becoming thinner and constrained, penetrating
mf - f

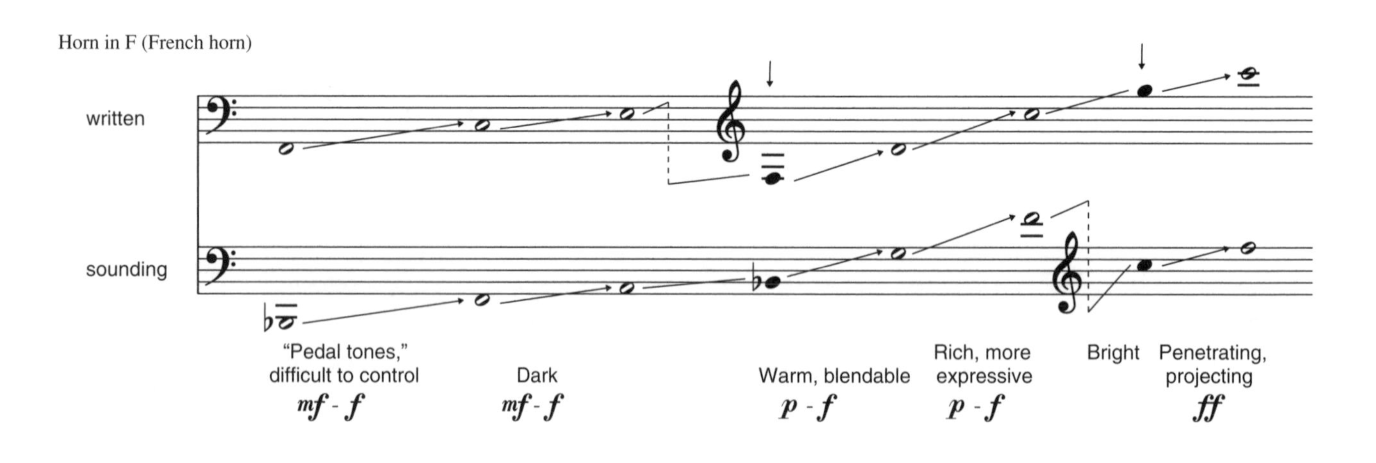
Horn in F (French horn)
written
sounding
"Pedal tones," difficult to control
mf - f
Dark
mf - f
Warm, blendable
p - f
Rich, more expressive
p - f
Bright
Penetrating, projecting
ff

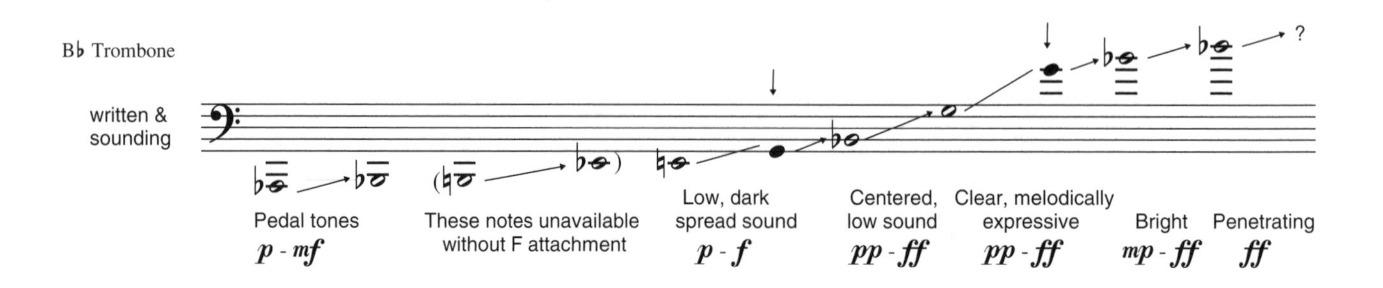
B♭ Trombone
written & sounding
Pedal tones
p - mf
These notes unavailable without F attachment
Low, dark spread sound
p - f
Centered, low sound
pp - ff
Clear, melodically expressive
pp - ff
Bright
mp - ff
Penetrating
ff

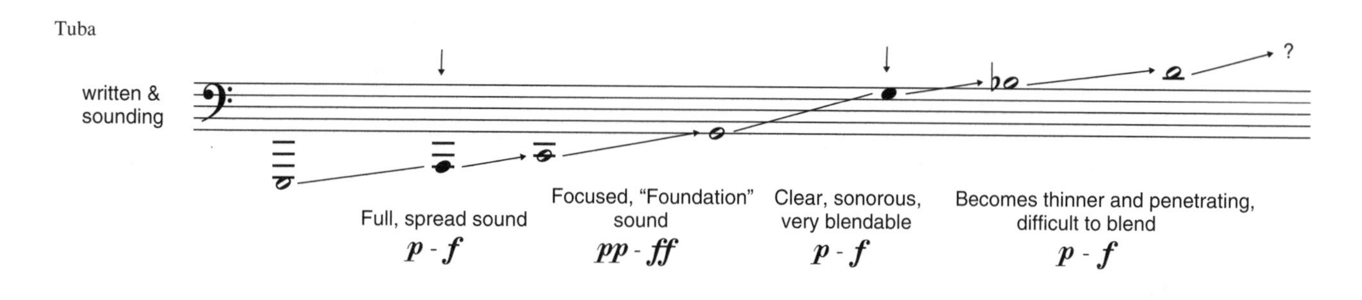
Tuba
written & sounding
?
Full, spread sound
p - f
Focused, "Foundation" sound
pp - ff
Clear, sonorous, very blendable
p - f
Becomes thinner and penetrating, difficult to blend
p - f

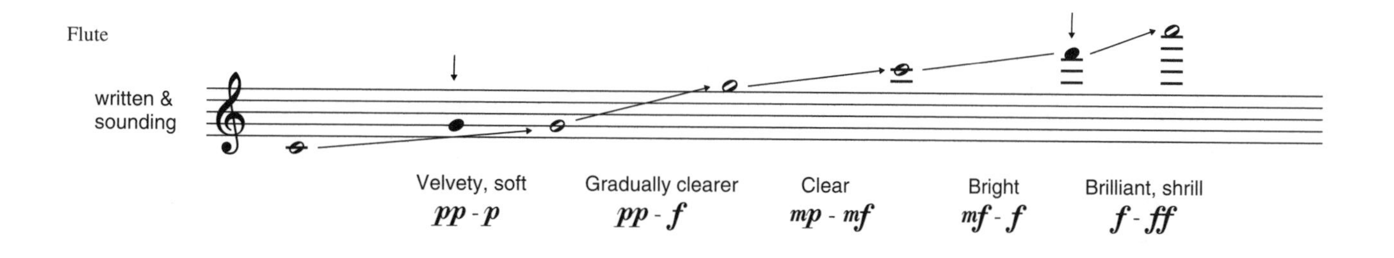
Flute
written & sounding
Velvety, soft
pp - p
Gradually clearer
pp - f
Clear
mp - mf
Bright
mf - f
Brilliant, shrill
f - ff

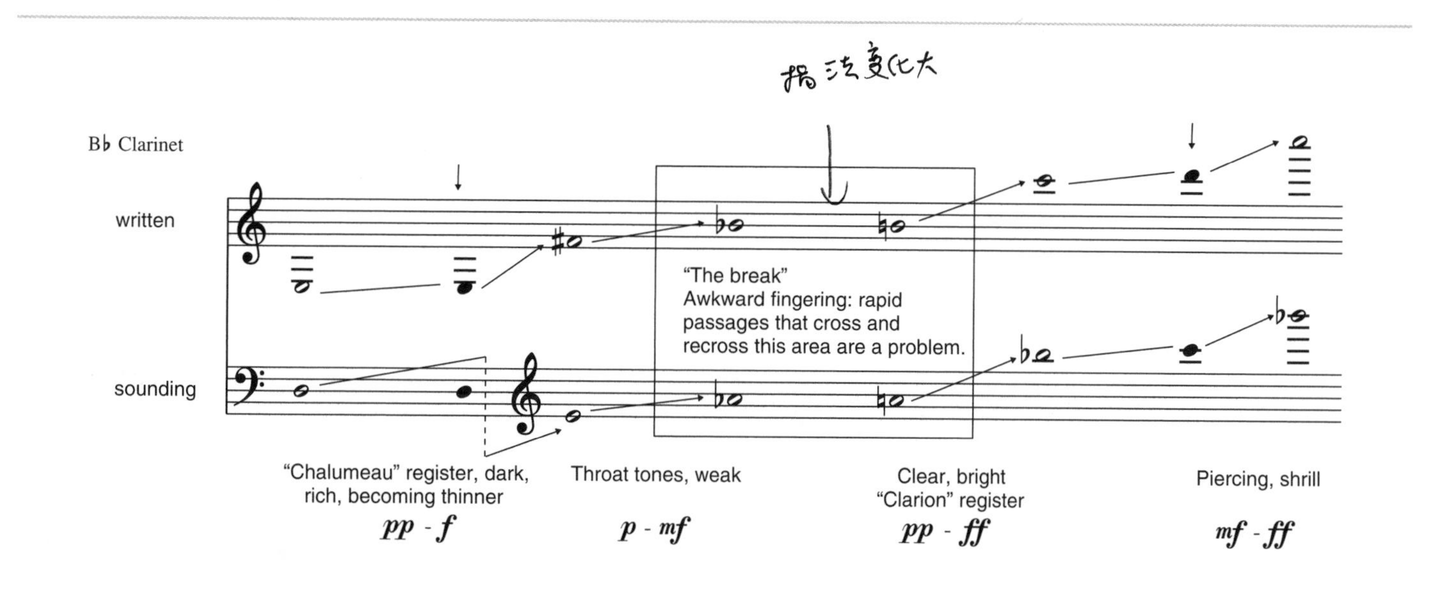
指法变化大
B♭ Clarinet
written
sounding
"The break"
Awkward fingering: rapid passages that cross and recross this area are a problem.
"Chalumeau" register, dark, rich, becoming thinner
pp - f
Throat tones, weak
p - mf
Clear, bright "Clarion" register
pp - ff
Piercing, shrill
mf - ff

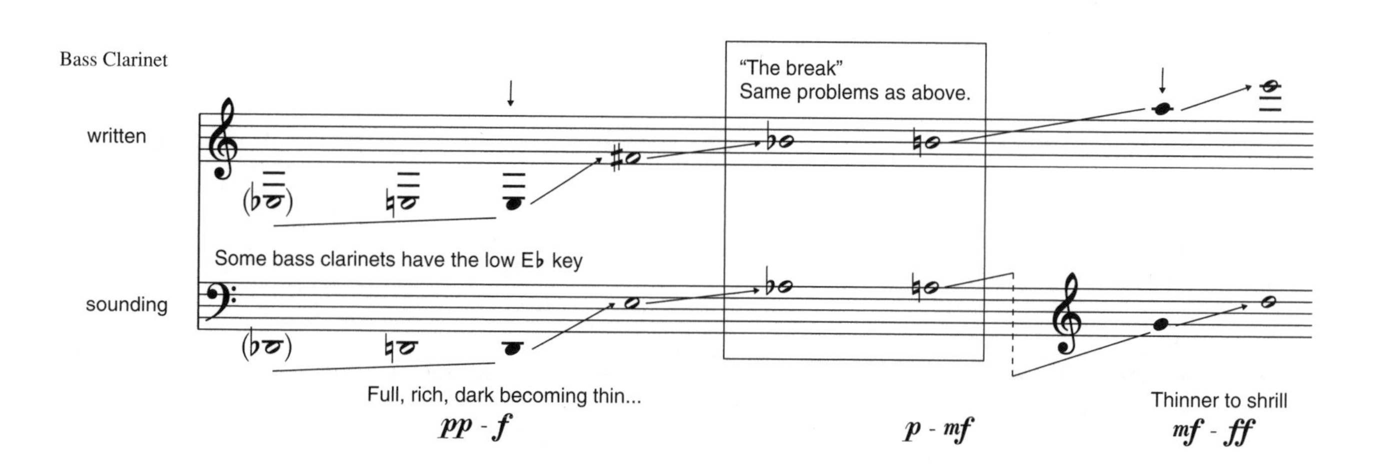
Bass Clarinet
"The break"
Same problems as above.
written
Some bass clarinets have the low E♭ key
sounding
Full, rich, dark becoming thin...
pp - f
p - mf
Thinner to shrill
mf - ff

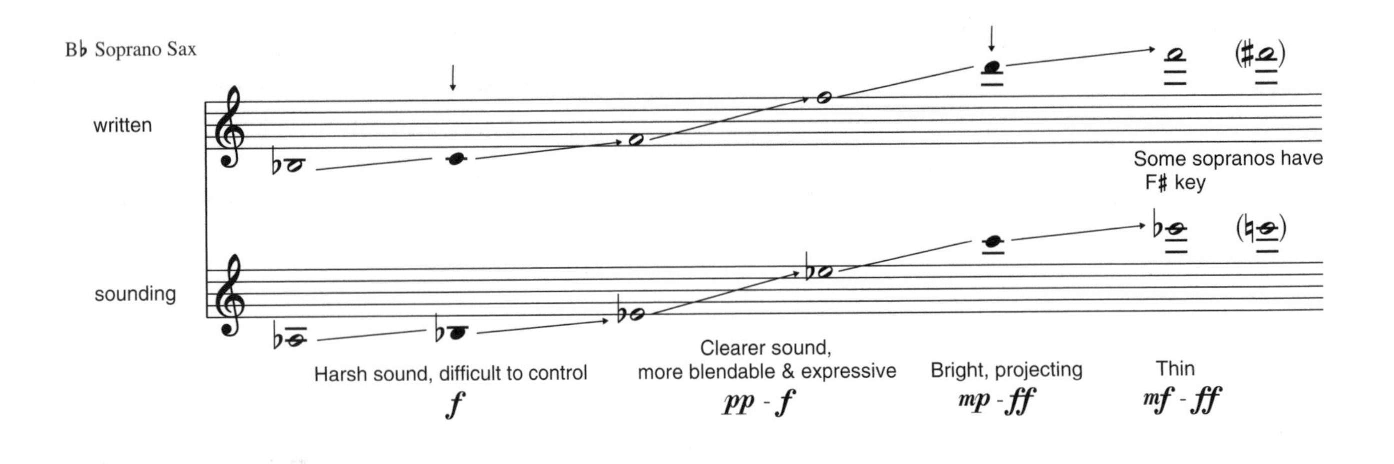

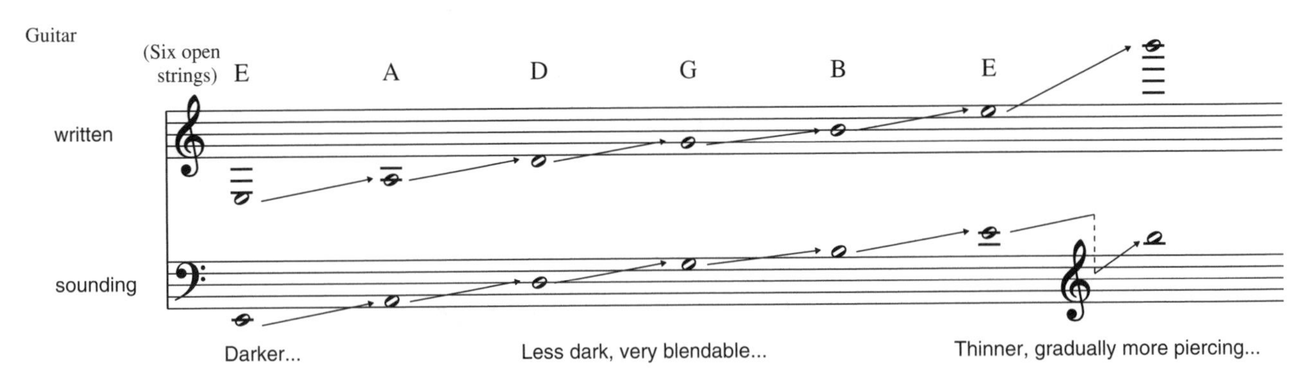

For a better understanding of the guitar's capability to play and voice chords, consult *The Jazz Style of Tal Farlow* by Steve Rochinski, *The Advancing Guitarist* by Mick Goodrick, or *Everything About Guitar Chords* by Wilbur Savidge.

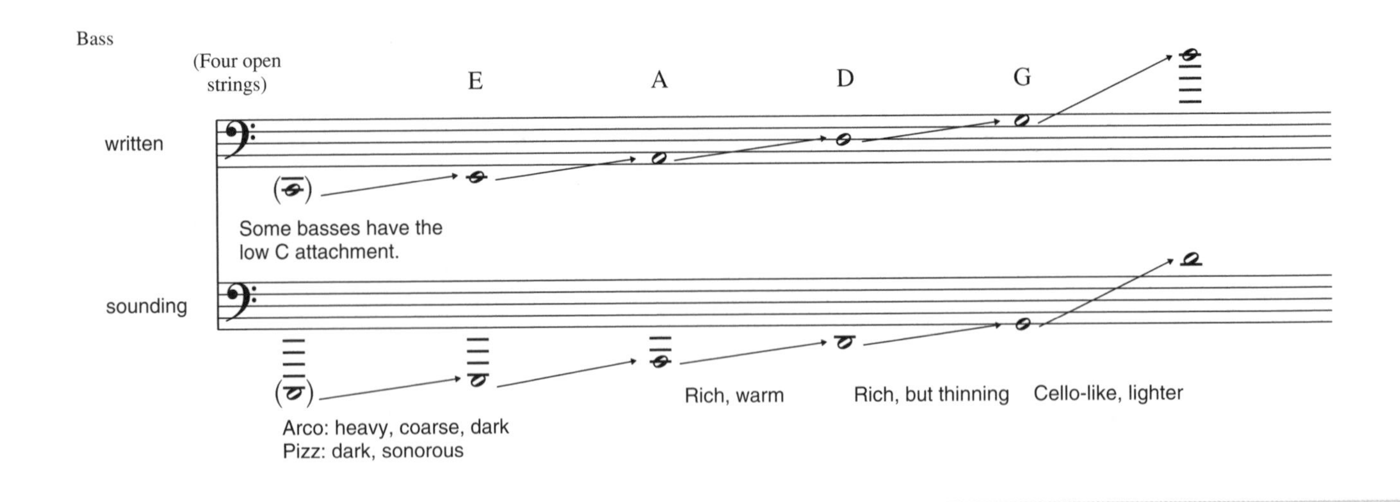

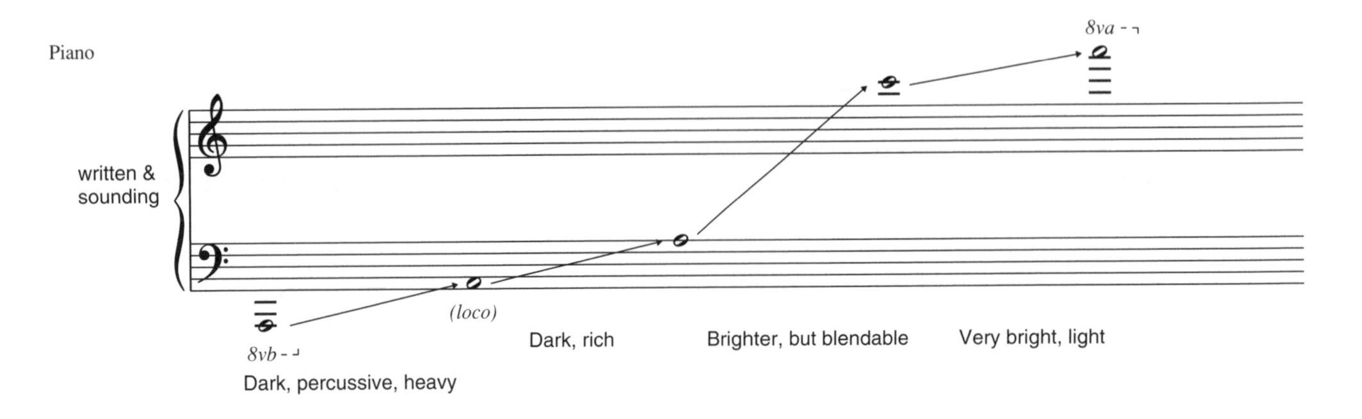

1-3 Comparison of Instruments' Ranges

By comparing the ranges of big band instruments in concert pitch, this chart shows at a glance where the instruments overlap. This is important to know as you plan your orchestration of voicings (see Chapters 3 through 7) and lines that are to be scored in unison and/or octaves (see Chapter 2).

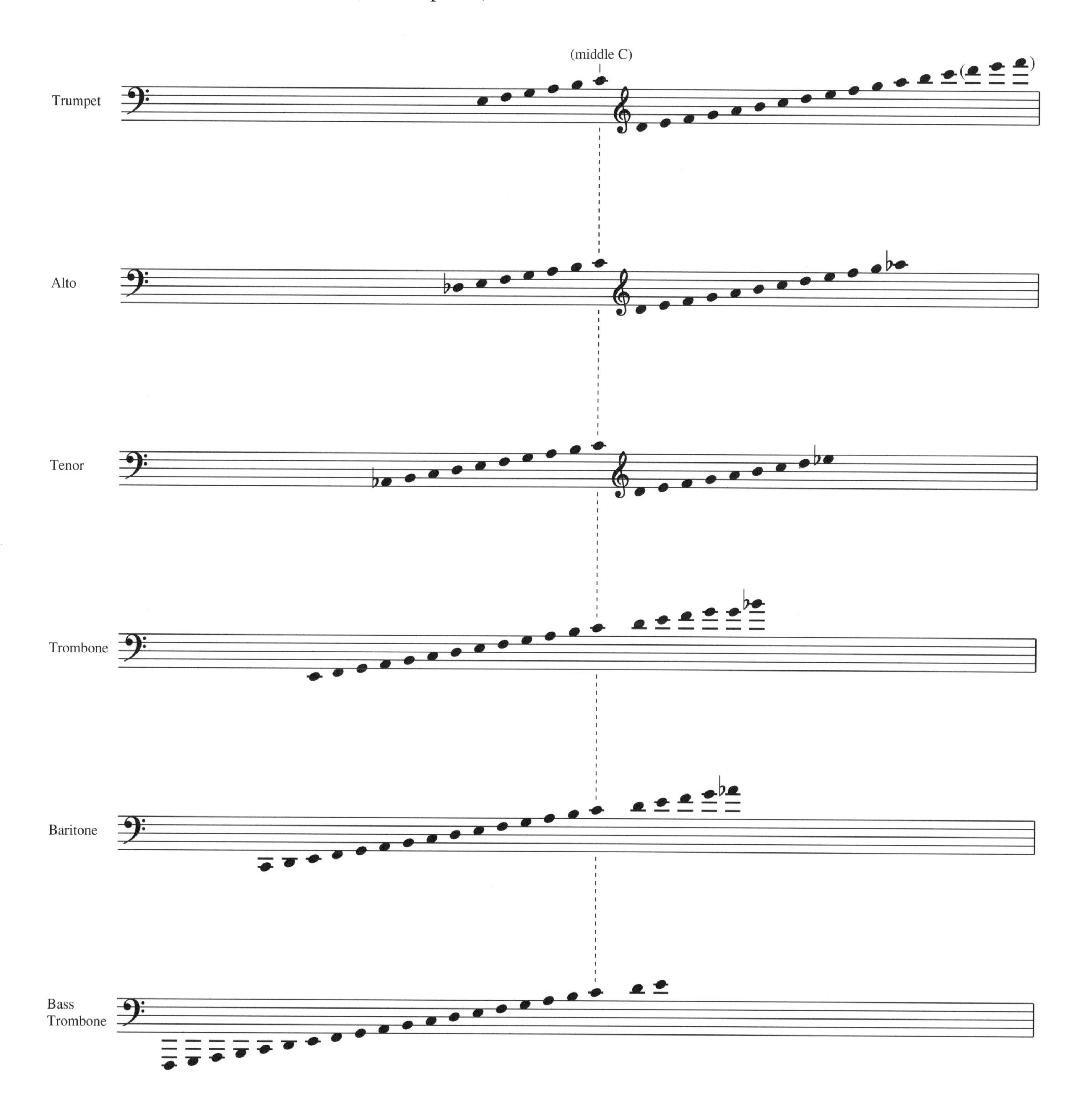

1-4 Low-Interval Limits

To ensure that your voicings create a clear impression and that the intervals they contain will be heard distinctly, do not include intervals below the limits shown in the chart below. There are always exceptional cases in which these limits may be adjusted downward. But if you follow them strictly, your voicings will never sound muddy.

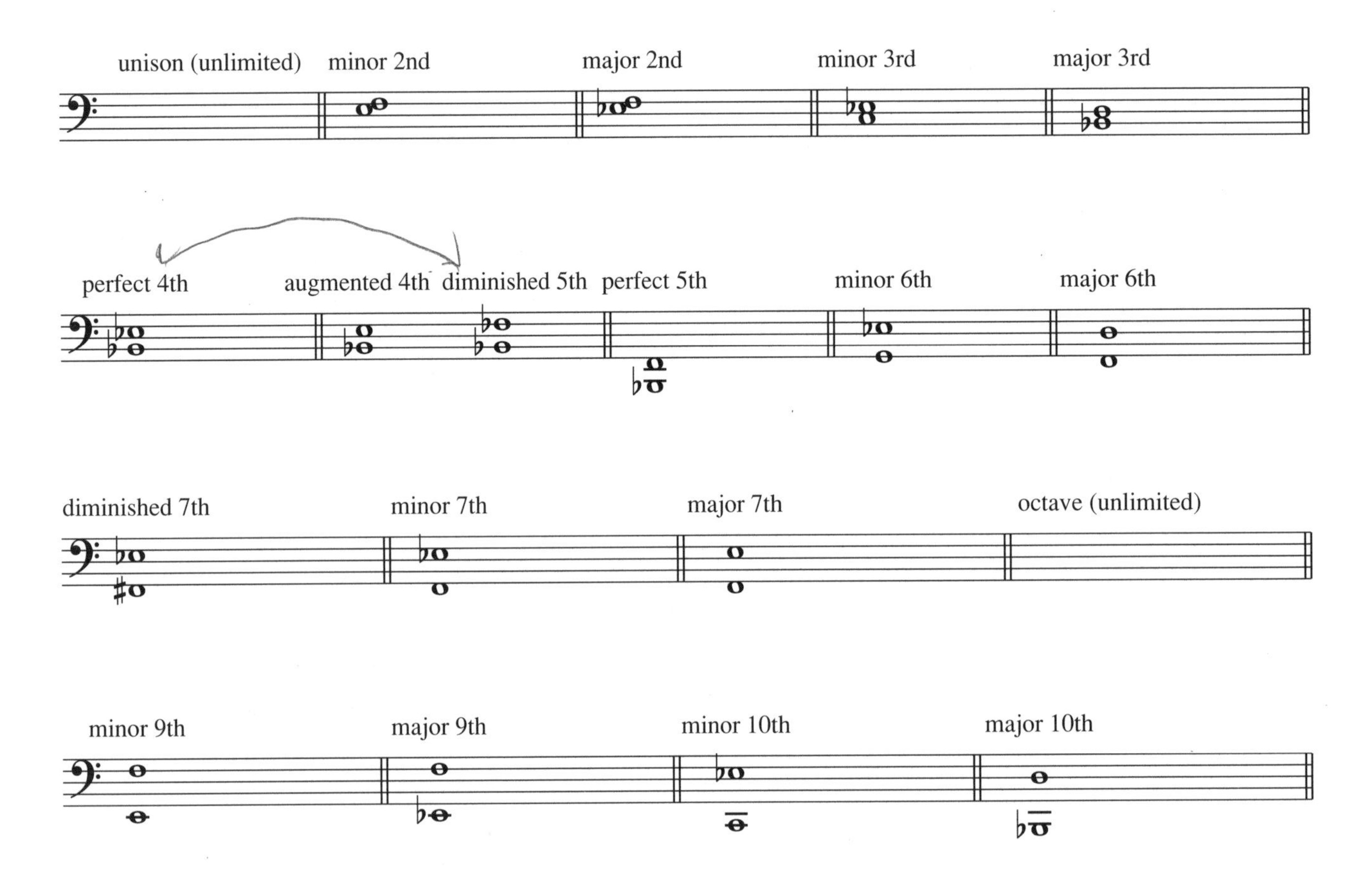

Whenever the bottom note of a voicing is not the root, "assume" there is a root and then check that the voicing follows the low-interval guidelines. In the example shown below, the C7 voicing conforms to the guidelines. But in the A–7 voicing, after we assume the root, the resulting minor third interval falls below recommended low-interval limits (LIL).

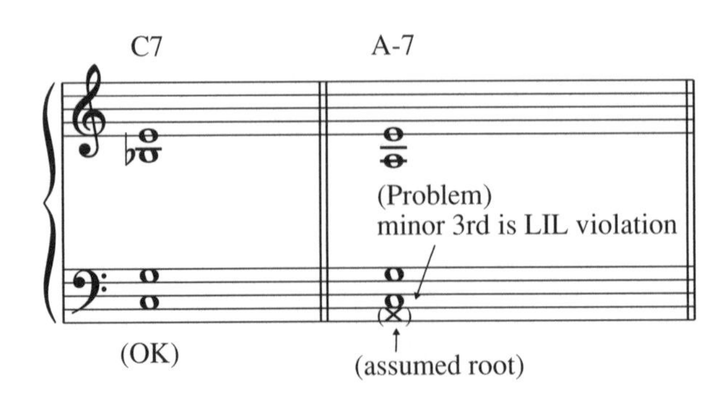

1-5 Special Effects for Wind Instruments

Arrangers for large jazz ensemble often use special effects for the wind instruments. You may use them in passages that involve the entire band, individual featured sections, or smaller mixed groups within the ensemble. The lead player dictates exactly how these effects will be performed and the rest of the band follows.

① **Shake**. Brass players rapidly oscillate upward to the next highest note in the overtone series, or sometimes to a wider interval for a more dramatic effect. Saxophone and woodwind players trill to the next highest diatonic or chromatic note.

② **Fall (or Falloff or Spill)**. A fall is a downward drop from a specific note to an indefinite ending pitch. Brass players glide down through the overtone series, smoothing the shape using half valves on trumpet or the slide on trombone. Saxophone and woodwind players lightly finger a descending chromatic scale. Falls may be short or long as indicated by the length of the curved line off the note.

③ **Doit**. Like a fall but moving in the opposite direction, this effect starts on a note and slides upward to an indefinite ending pitch.

④ **Connecting Gliss**. A connecting gliss is a rapid scalewise run or slide between two definite pitches separated by a leap. It may go either up or down.

⑤ **Flip (or Turn)**. Played when going from a higher pitch to a lower one, a flip combines an upward gliss to a neighboring tone or indefinite pitch with a downward gliss to the target note.

⑥ **Smear (or Bend)**. Players slide or bend into pitch, starting flat and moving upward to the correct pitch. A short smear sounds like a quick "scoop" into pitch; a long smear is a more extended approach.

⑦ **Plop**. This effect is used to approach a middle-register or low-register note preceded by a rest. From a higher, indefinite starting pitch, a player moves rapidly down through a scale or overtone series to end on the target note. To make the rapid descent, trumpeters use half valves, trombonists use the slide, and saxophonists and woodwind players finger a diatonic or chromatic scale.

⑧ **Rip**. Like a plop but moving in the opposite direction, a rip approaches a middle- or high-register note from an indefinite pitch below.

This example shows all these effects, identified in the score by number. Listen to the CD to hear how they sound.

1-6 Reharmonizing Approach Notes

When harmonizing a melody, an arranger needs to distinguish between target notes and approach notes. Target notes are long or emphasized chord tones and tensions. They are harmonized using chord sound. Approach notes, short notes that lead stepwise to targets, are reharmonized to keep their "undervoices" lines compatible with the melody's movement. The chords arising from this reharmonization do not disturb the primary harmony of the passage because they resolve back quickly to the harmony of the target notes.

The standard reharmonization techniques reviewed below are chromatic, diatonic, parallel, and dominant. Because the reharmonization of approach notes plays such a critical role in arranging, we will regularly draw the reader's attention to instances of it as we look at examples of voicing and orchestration strategies throughout this book.

Reharmonizing Specific Approach Note Patterns

1. **Chromatic Approach** (ch): When an approach note moves by a half step to a chord tone or tension target note, it is known as a chromatic approach: chromatic approach notes are usually nondiatonic.

Chromatic Reharmonization: Each voice moves a half step into the corresponding note of the target voicing, in the same direction as the melody, as shown below.

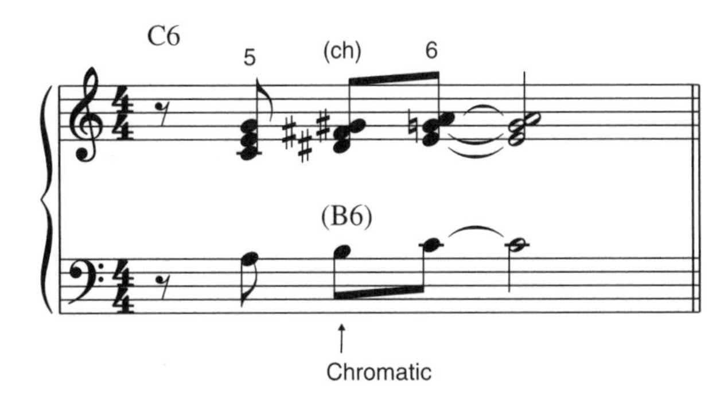

2. **Scale Approach** (S2, S4, S♭6, etc.): When an approach note moves by a diatonic whole or half step to a chord tone or tension target note, it is known as a scale approach. (The "S" labeling relates to the chord of the target note.)

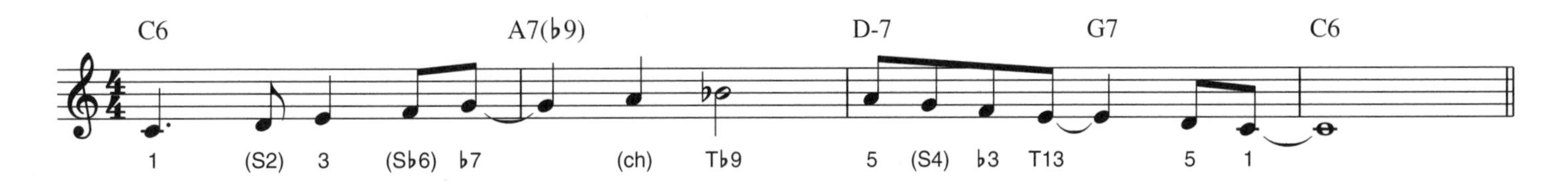

The voicings in the following example were created using all the standard techniques for reharmonizing approach notes. In addition to chromatic reharmonization, these are:

- Dominant Reharmonization: The approach note is voiced with a dominant seventh chord, either pure or altered, serving as the V7 of the target chord. The approach note must be a chord tone of that V7 or one of its tensions.
- Parallel Reharmonization: This method matches the precise motion of the lead to that of each voice below it. In other words, each undervoice moves the same number of semitones into its note in the target voicing. This technique may be used to voice any kind of approach note—including chromatic approaches, as discussed above.
- Diatonic Reharmonization: Each voice moves one diatonic step into the corresponding note in the target voicing. This works best when both melody and harmony are diatonic to the key or to the current harmonic situation as outlined by the chord progression.

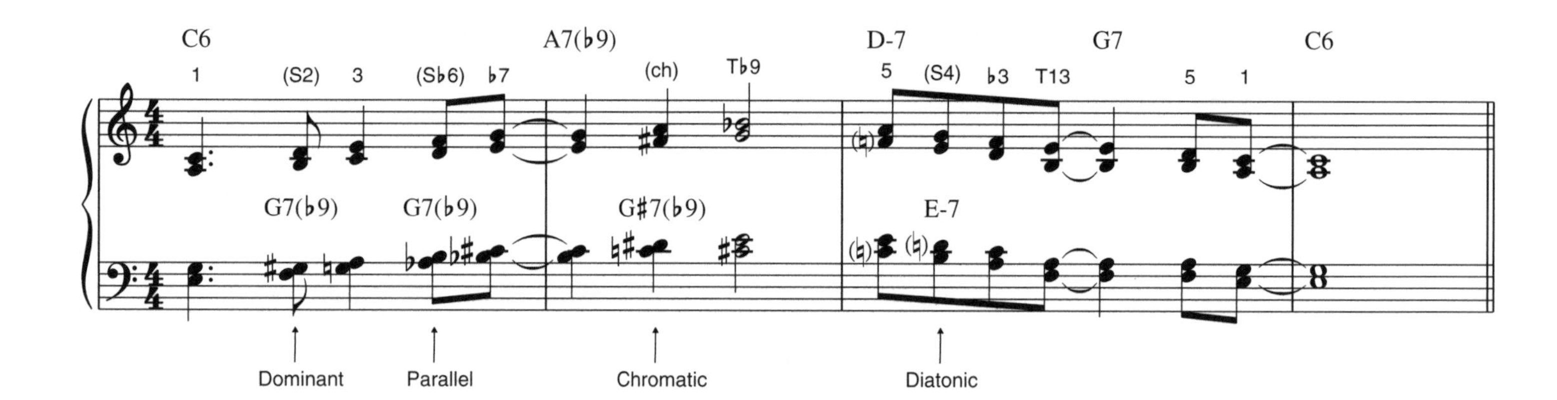

3. Double Chromatic Approach
When two notes of short and equal duration approach a chord tone or tension target note by consecutive half steps in the same direction, they form a double chromatic approach pattern.

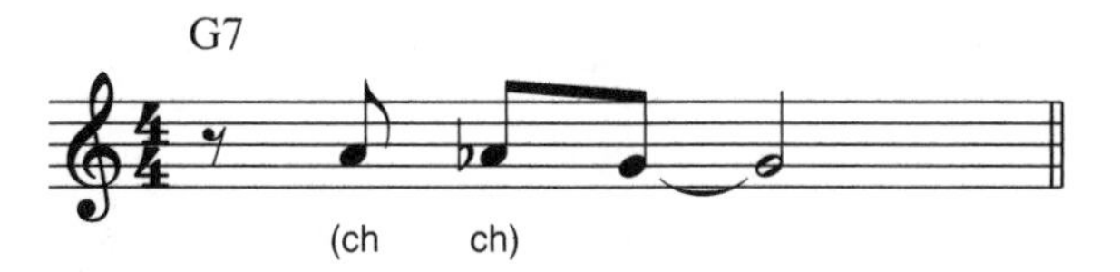

To voice double chromatic approach notes, use chromatic reharmonization with voices following the same direction as the melody.

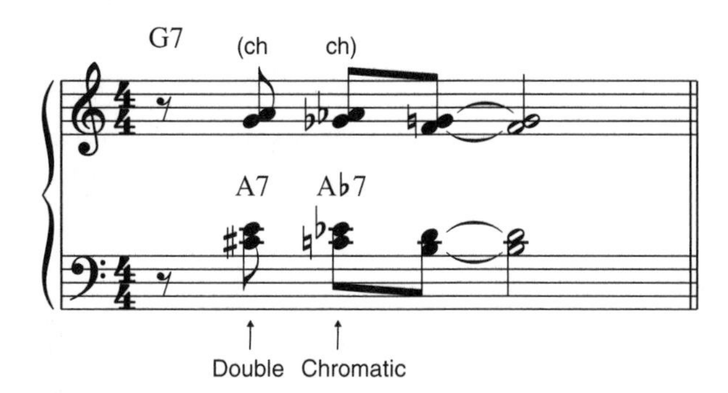

4. Indirect Resolution (SS), (ch ch), (S ch), or (ch S)
When two notes of short and equal duration approach a chord tone or tension target note by stepwise motion from opposite directions, they form an indirect resolution pattern.

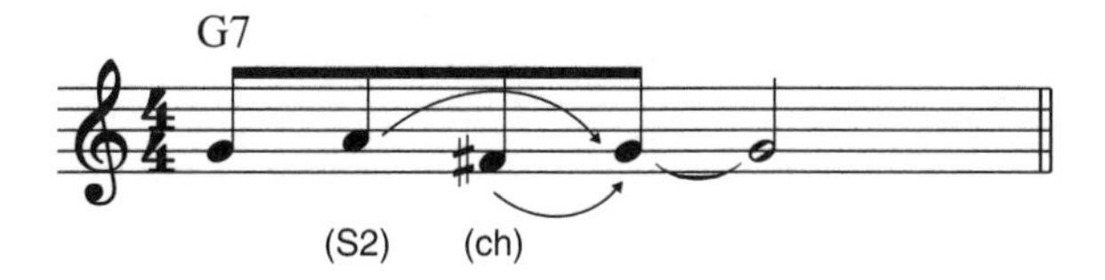

When handling indirect approach notes, reharmonize each approach note independently. The two notes may be reharmonized using different methods, as in this example.

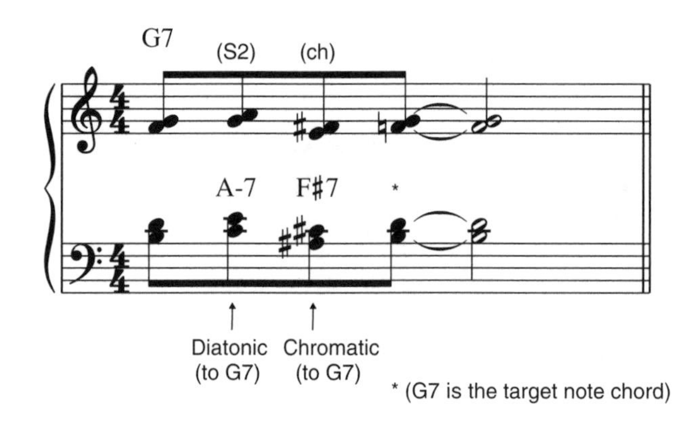

Independent Lead

The independent lead technique is an alternative to reharmonizing approach notes. In this method, the voices below the approach note simply maintain the prevailing harmony, or in some cases, the lower voices may rest. Independent lead works well where a less driving feel is acceptable, and for pickups.

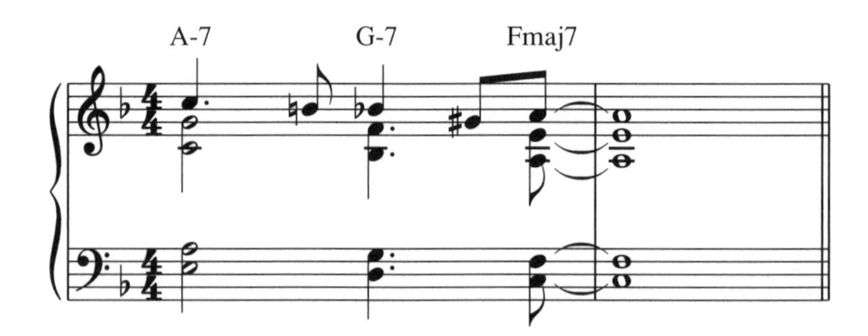

1-7 Chord Scales

A chord scale is a set of stepwise pitches related to a chord symbol that provides a supply of notes compatible with that chord's sound and its tonal or modal function. Chord scales are an arranger's raw material for writing voicings and lines that are consistent with a given harmonic and melodic context.

In the chord scales shown on the following pages, chord symbols and Roman numeral functions relate to middle *c* as the principal pitch axis unless otherwise indicated.

Chord tones and tensions are notated with open noteheads (**o**). Arabic numbers describe their interval distances from the root of the chord. Tensions are numbered as upper structure extensions (9, 11, 13) of the chord and preceded with "T."

Avoid notes are notated with closed noteheads (•). Arabic numbers describe the interval distances from the root, in the lower structure (1 through 7). Avoid notes are preceded with an "S" to indicate the "scale approach" function.

For a thorough discussion of tensions, avoid notes, and chord scale theory, see *Modern Jazz Voicings* by Ted Pease and Ken Pullig (Berklee Press, 2001).

Tonal Chord Scales

CHORD SCALES IN TONIC MAJOR

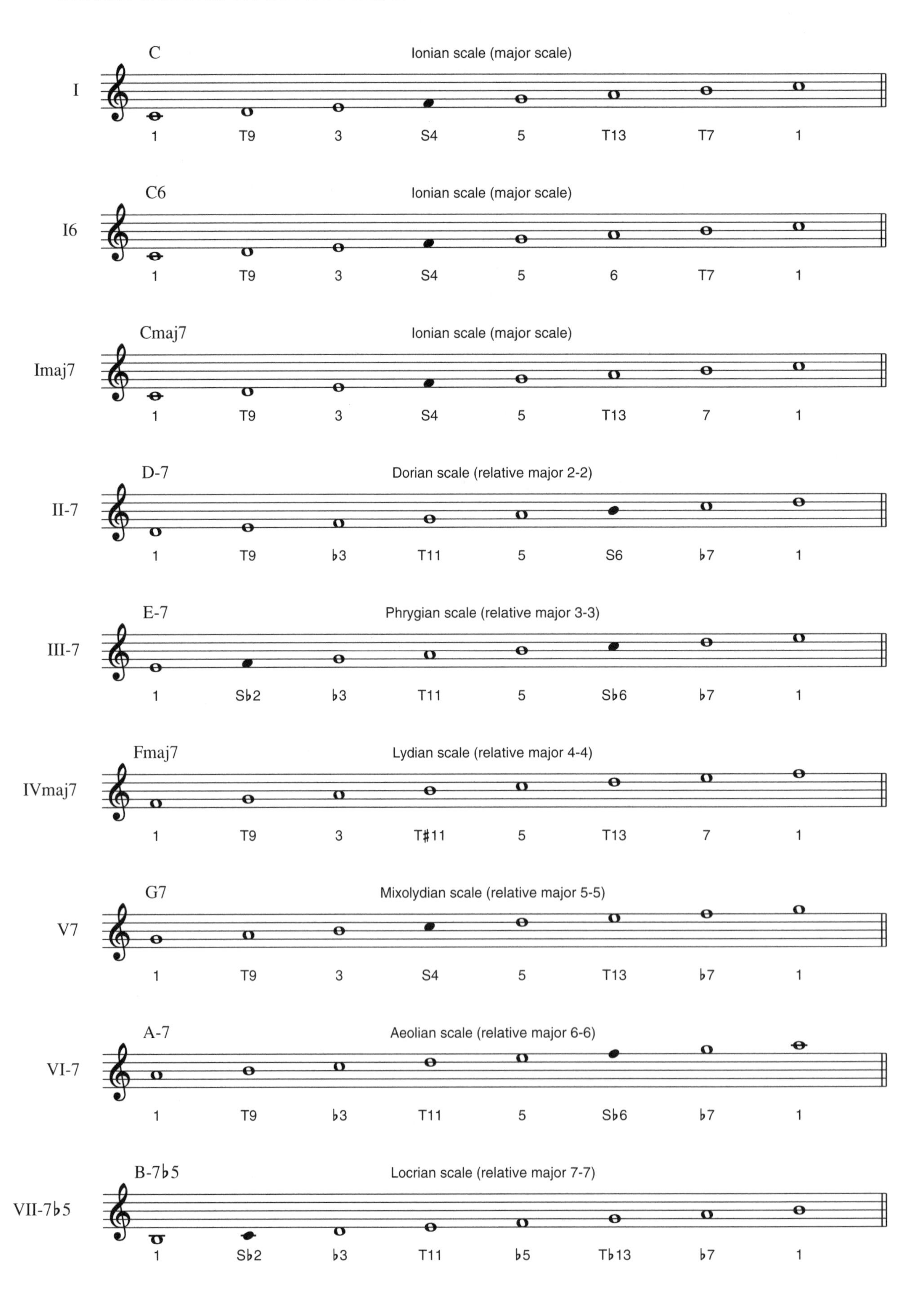

CHORD SCALES IN TONIC MINOR

These chord scales are based on three minor parent scales: natural minor (Aeolian), jazz minor (ascending melodic minor), and harmonic minor.

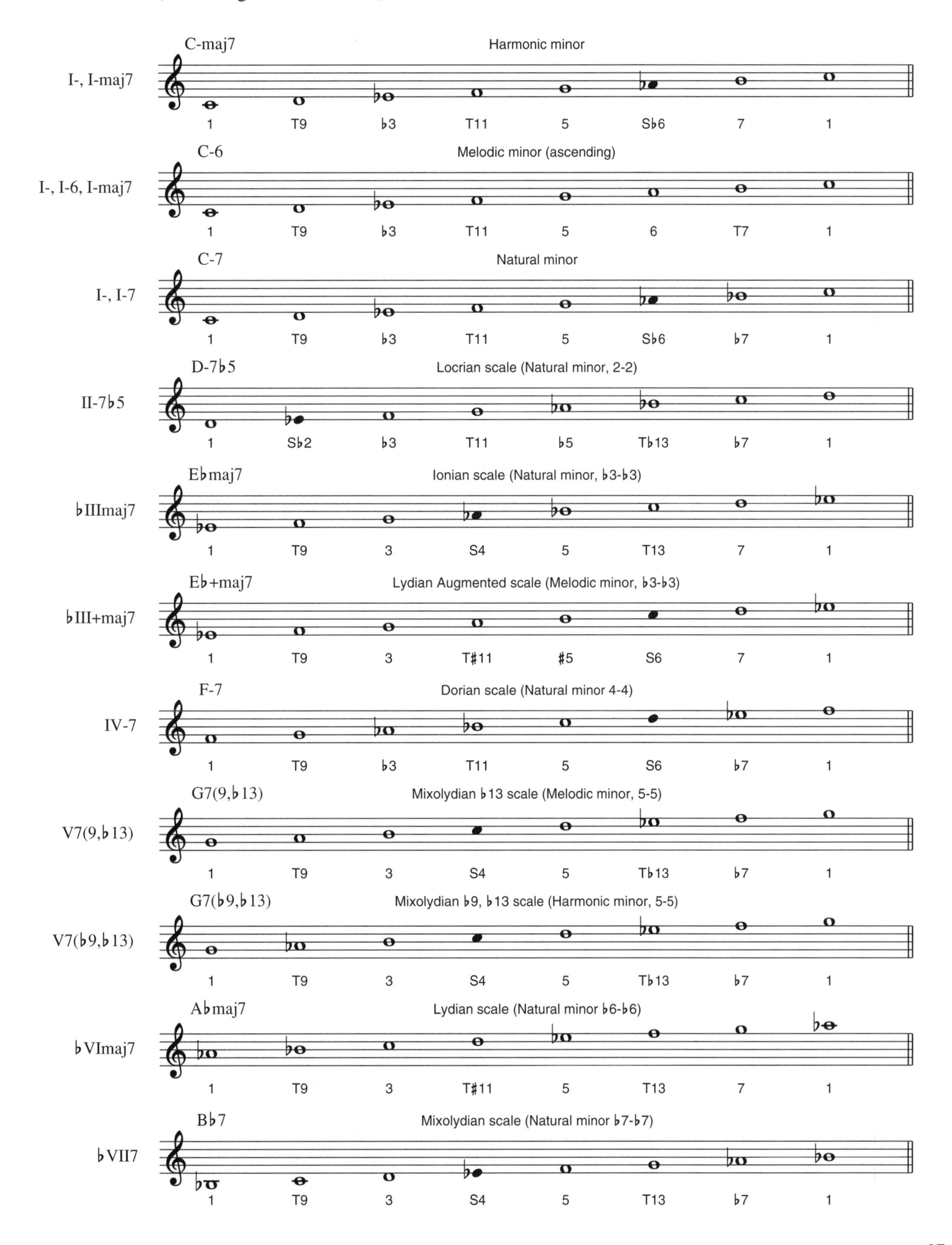

MODAL INTERCHANGE CHORDS USED IN MAJOR

Modal interchange chords and their chord scales are "borrowed" from a parallel tonality (one having the same pitch axis) for use in the primary tonality.

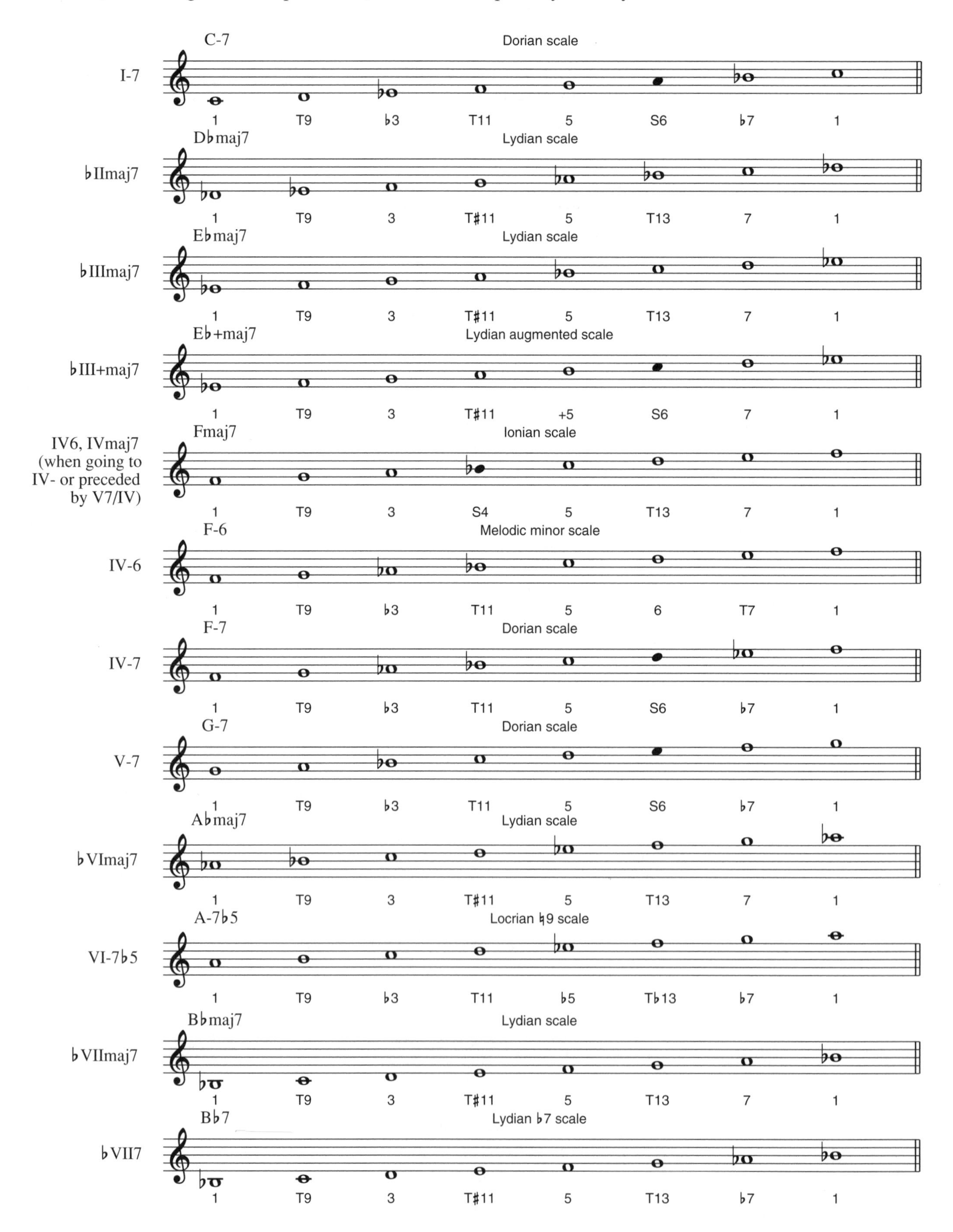

CHORD SCALES FOR THE V7 CHORD (PRIMARY DOMINANT SEVENTH)

There are many different chord scales available for the V7, the "primary" dominant seventh chord (for instance, G7 in the key of C). The appropriate choice is determined by tensions listed in the chord symbol, melody notes, musical context, and personal taste.

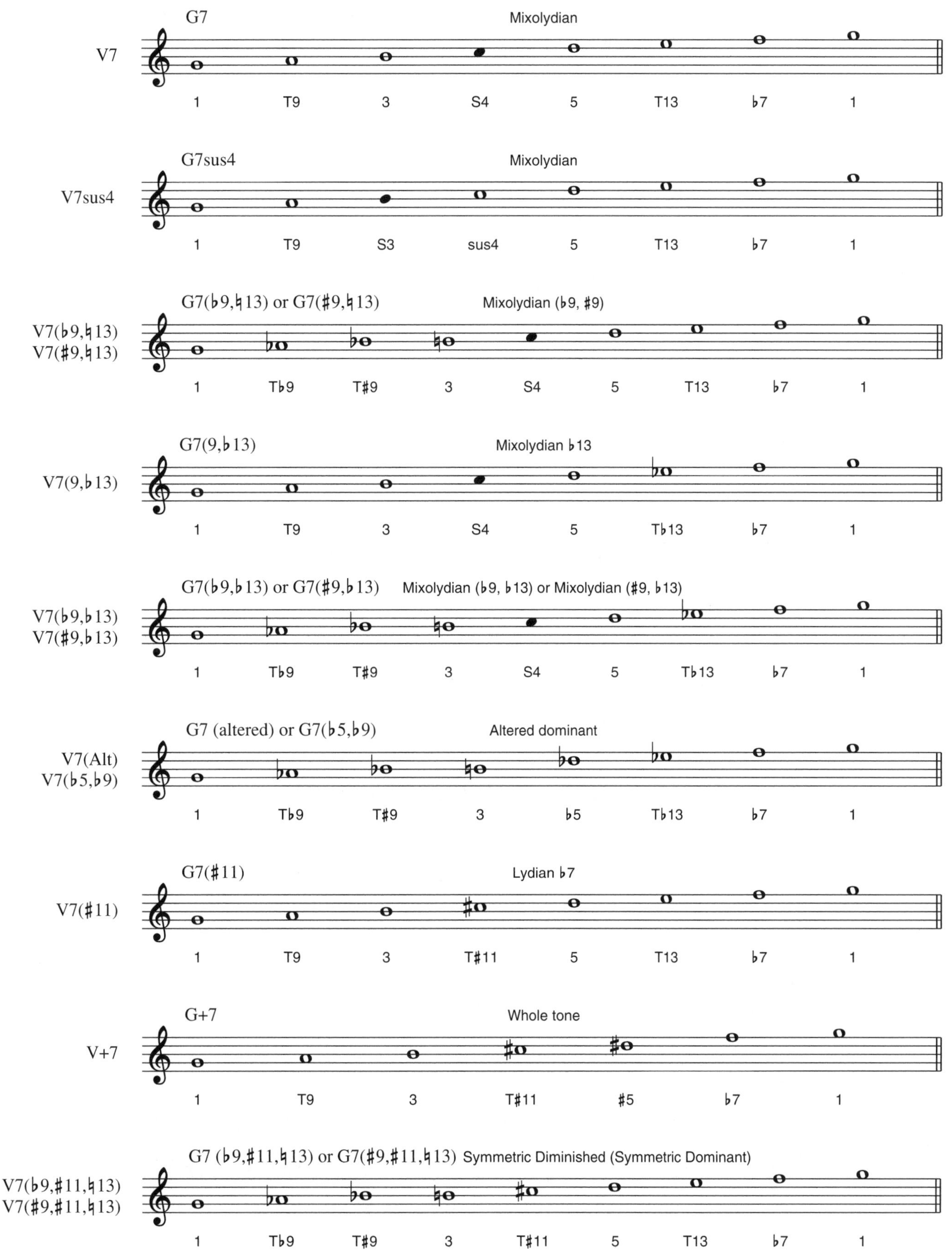

SECONDARY DOMINANT SEVENTH CHORD SCALES

A "secondary" dominant seventh chord moves directly to a diatonic chord other than the I chord (i.e., V7/II, V7/III, V7/IV, V7/V, V7/VI). When the target chord contains a major 3rd, the secondary dominant seventh chord generally takes Mixolydian as a chord scale. When the target chord contains a minor 3rd, the secondary dominant seventh chord takes a chord scale containing T♭13. The following secondary dominant seventh chord situations all relate to C major as "home."

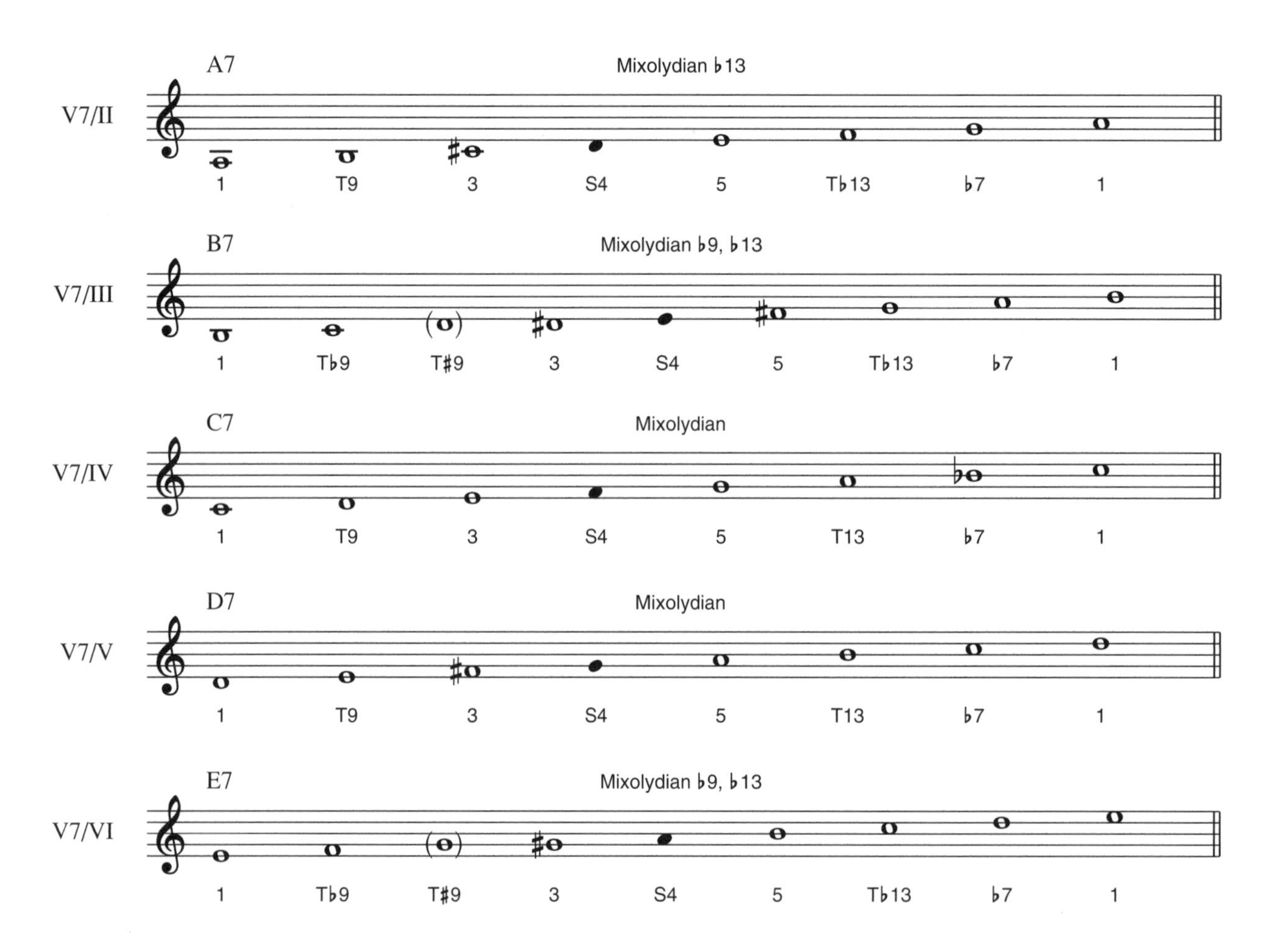

SUBSTITUTE DOMINANT SEVENTH CHORD SCALES

All SubV7s, those dominant seventh chords resolving down half a step to a diatonic target, take Lydian ♭7 as a chord scale. (Remember, C major is "home.")

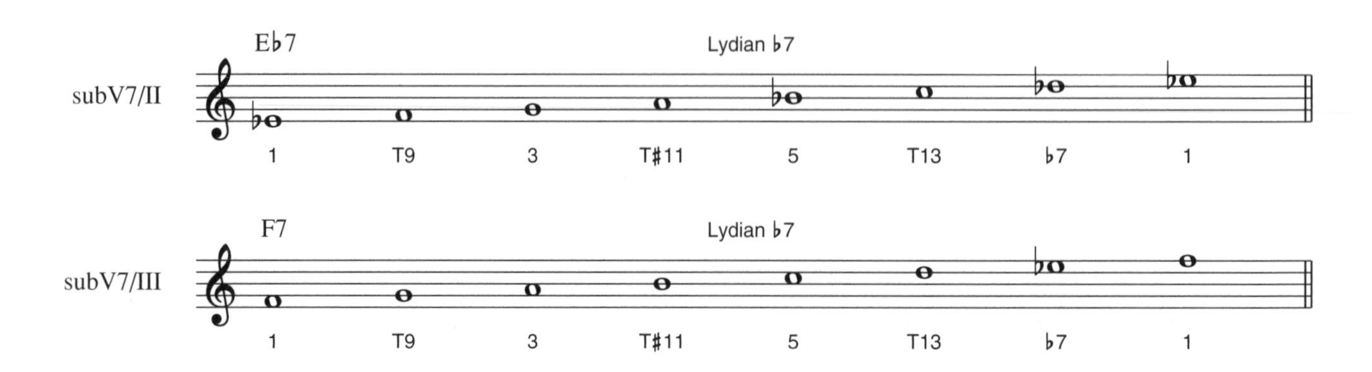

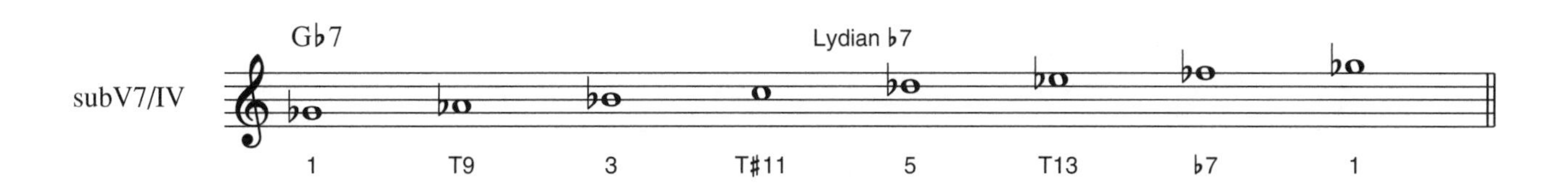

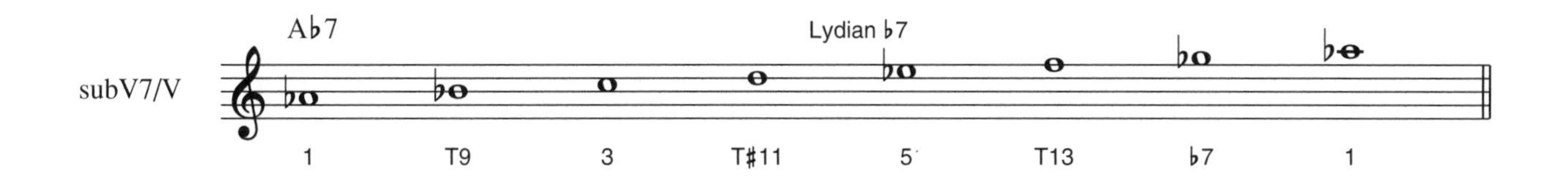

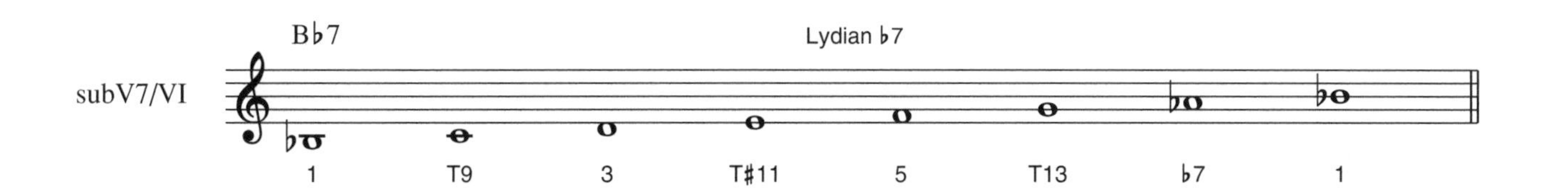

SPECIAL FUNCTION DOMINANT SEVENTH CHORD SCALES

These nonresolving dominant sevenths do not go down a half step or perfect fifth to a target. They are "color chords" usually found in a blues context and often move directly, or as part of a pattern, to the I chord.

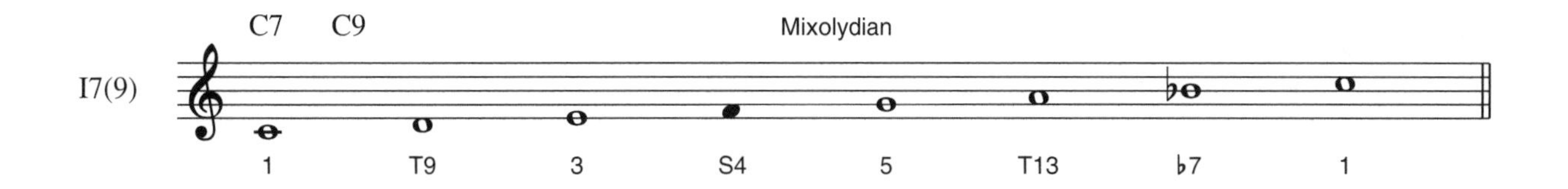

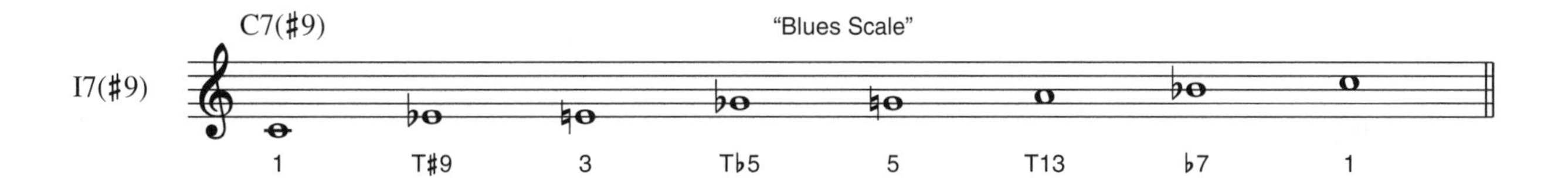

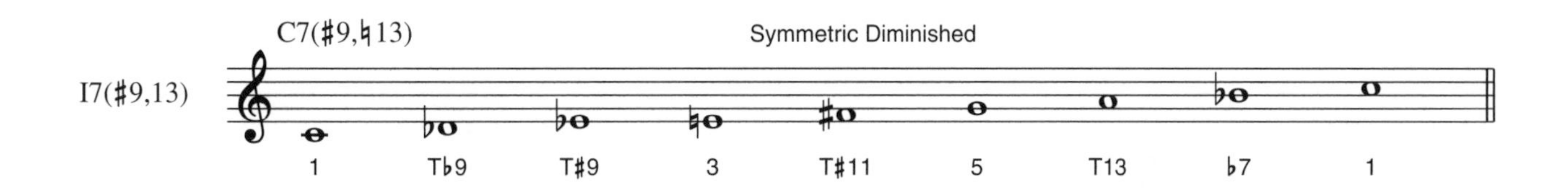

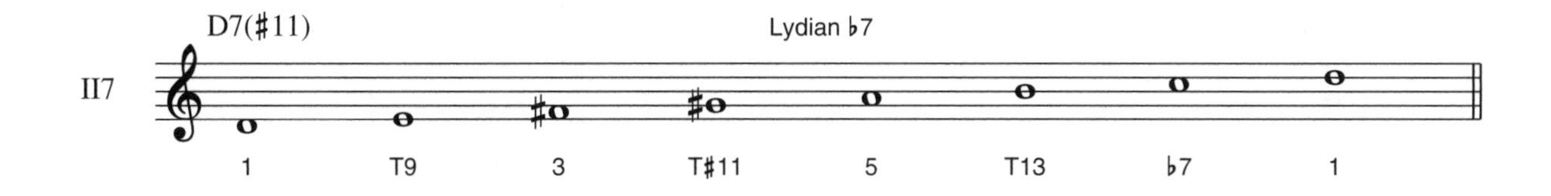

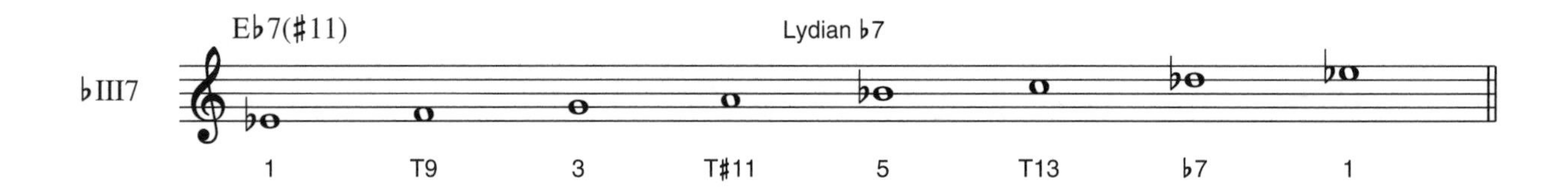
♭III7
E♭7(♯11)
Lydian ♭7
1 T9 3 T♯11 5 T13 ♭7 1

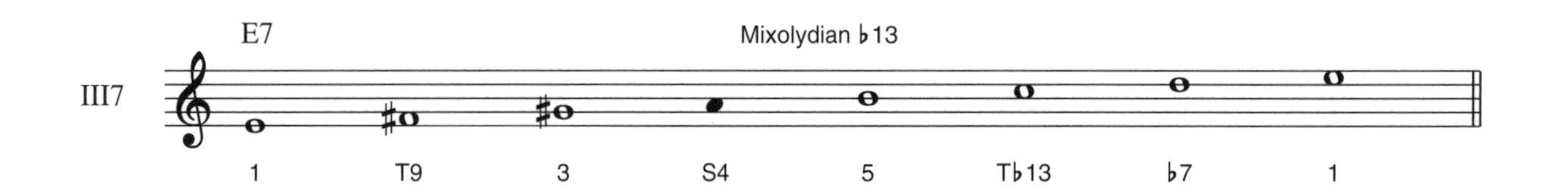
III7
E7
Mixolydian ♭13
1 T9 3 S4 5 T♭13 ♭7 1

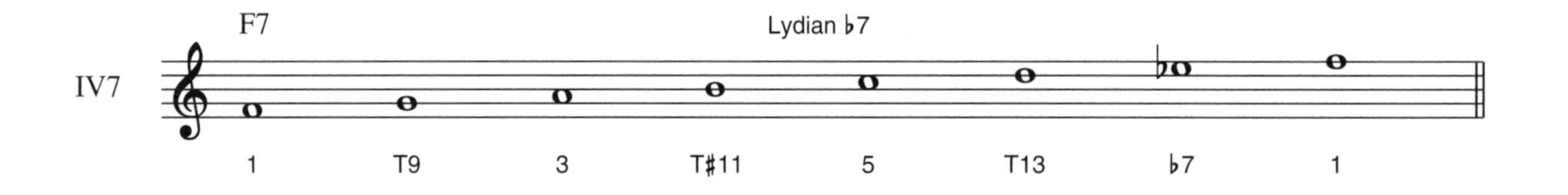
IV7
F7
Lydian ♭7
1 T9 3 T♯11 5 T13 ♭7 1

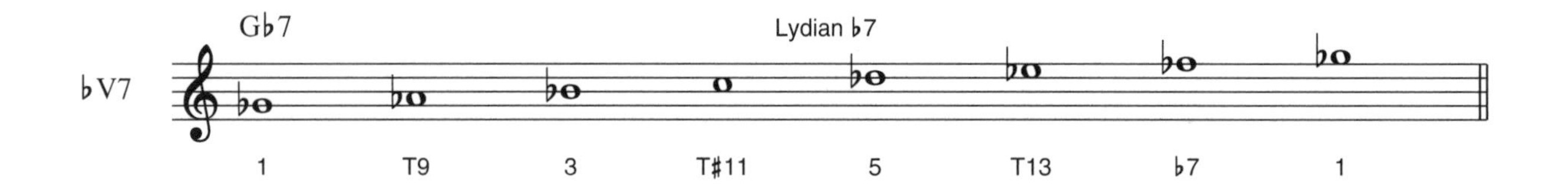
♭V7
G♭7
Lydian ♭7
1 T9 3 T♯11 5 T13 ♭7 1

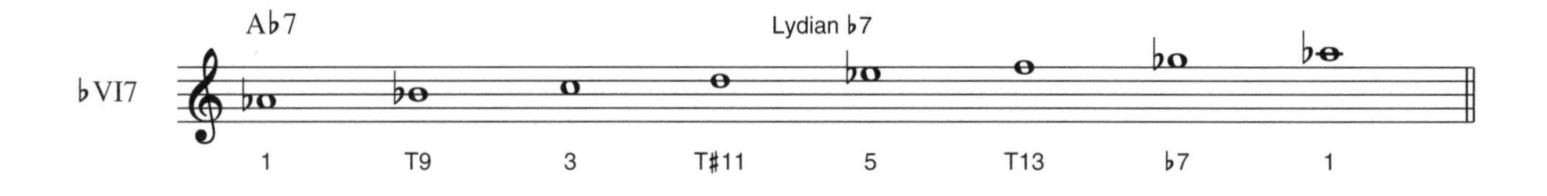
♭VI7
A♭7
Lydian ♭7
1 T9 3 T♯11 5 T13 ♭7 1

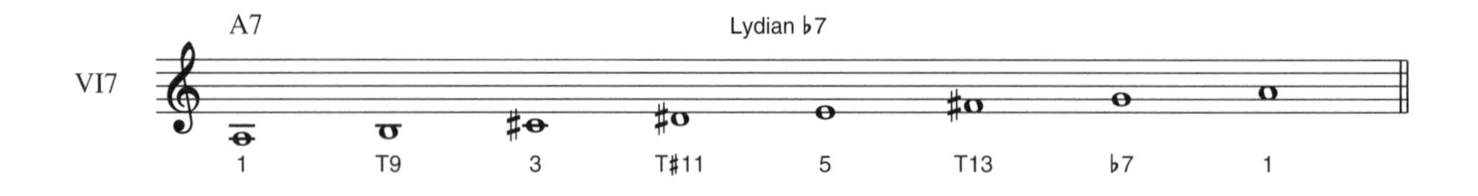
VI7
A7
Lydian ♭7
1 T9 3 T♯11 5 T13 ♭7 1

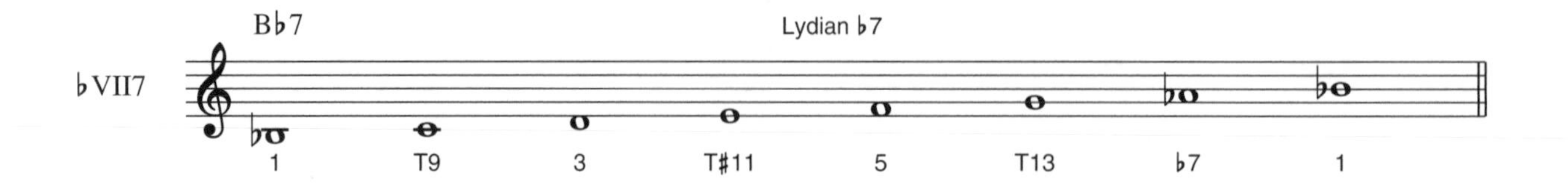
♭VII7
B♭7
Lydian ♭7
1 T9 3 T♯11 5 T13 ♭7 1

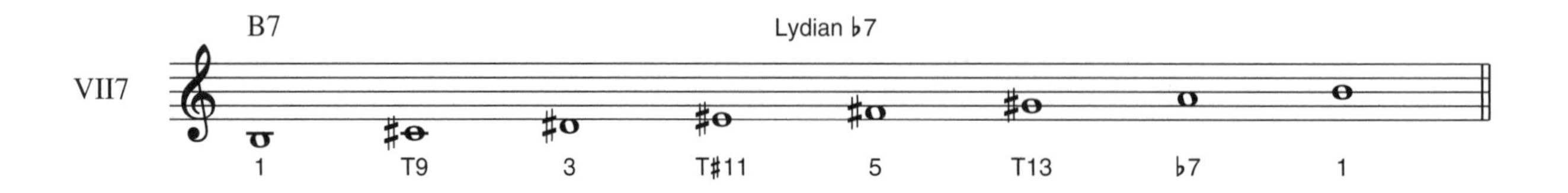
VII7
B7
Lydian ♭7
1 T9 3 T♯11 5 T13 ♭7 1

DIMINISHED SEVENTH CHORD SCALES

Passing Diminished

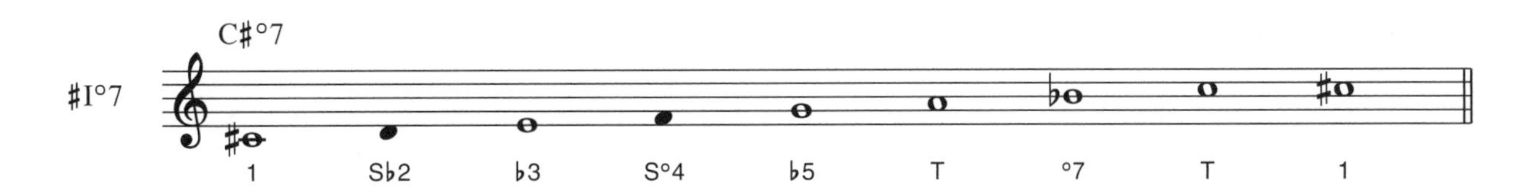

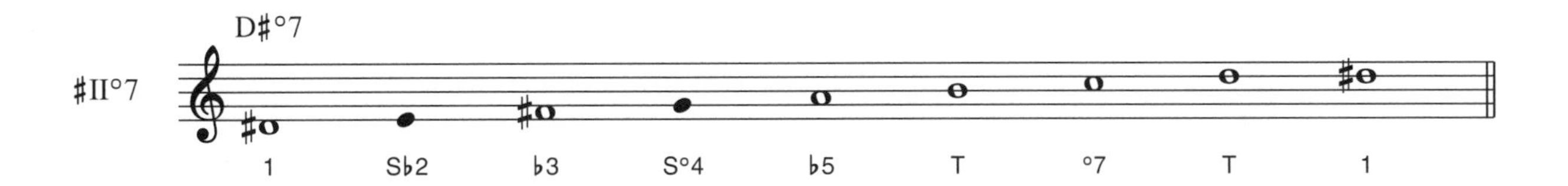

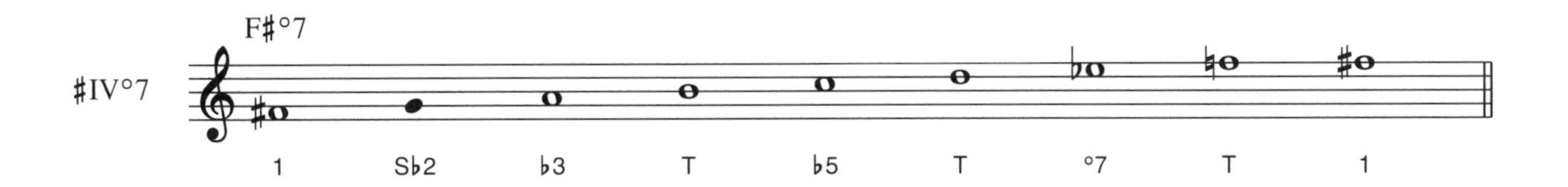

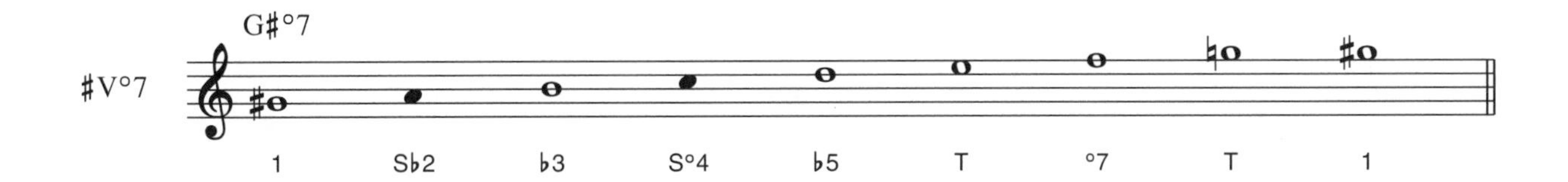

Chromatic Diminished

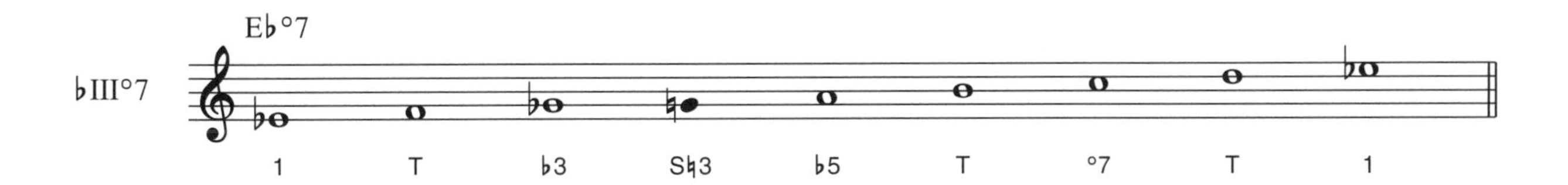

Auxiliary Diminished

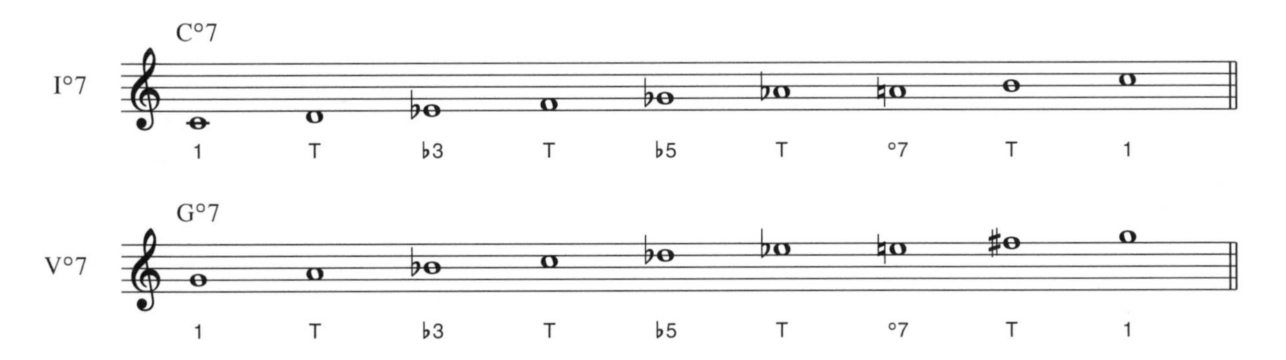

MODAL CHORD SCALES

In modal contexts there are no avoid notes. Instead, there are the so-called characteristic notes of each mode, which should be used freely. In the list that follows, these characteristic notes are indicated with a circled arrow.

The following I chords provide the pitch axis and characteristic color associated with each of the common modes below.

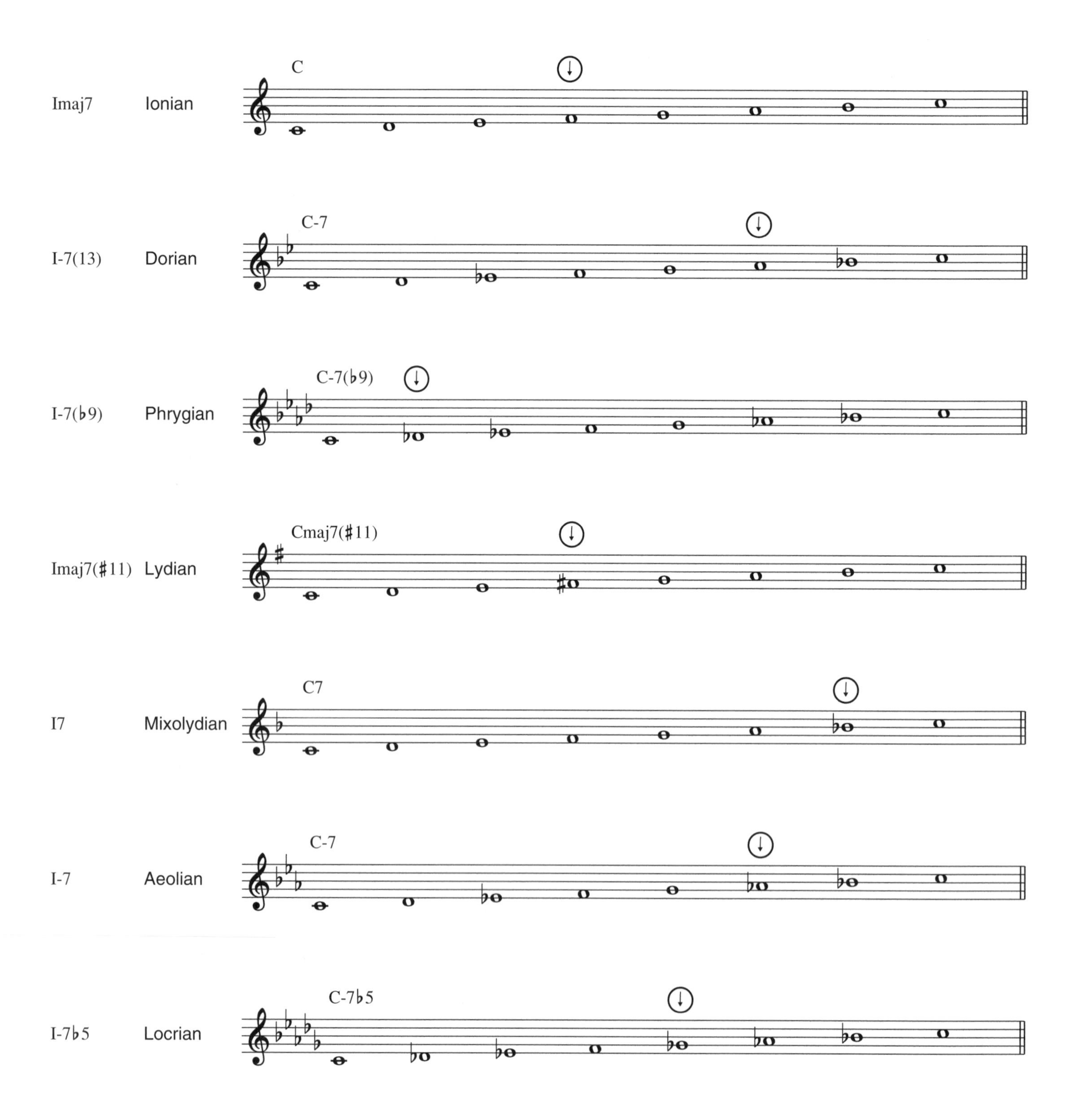

1-8 Preparing a Score

When composing or arranging for large ensemble, begin by sketching your ideas in a condensed score of four staves or fewer. You can usually omit the rhythm section from such a sketch, except perhaps for a few isolated voicing ideas or some phrases that need a specific bass line. For the rest of the band, show several voices on each stave if necessary, and keep track of instrumental assignments by penciling them in.

Once you have completed the sketch, it is time to create the full score, or "open score," in which every instrument's part is written on a separate stave. Follow the guidelines below for organizing and formatting the full score. You should also keep a book on standard notation handy; we recommend *Music Notation* by Mark McGrain (Berklee Press, 1986). And be sure to proofread your score for errors and omissions, especially if you are using computer software.

As you read these guidelines—and as you assemble your score—you may also find it helpful to consult the arrangement of "1625 Swingerama Ave." beginning in Chapter 14. It is a working model of how to put these principles to practical use.

Identifying and Positioning the Instruments

Place each instrument's part on a separate stave, beginning with the saxophones on top, followed by the brass below them, and finishing with the rhythm section on the bottom. Identify each instrument in the left margin of every page of the score. Beyond the first page, you may abbreviate the instruments' names. Use numbers to indicate chairs in the section. Chair number 1, for example, is the "lead" player. If you want some players to double on another instrument, list both the primary instrument and the double on the first page. On successive pages, just indicate the instrument being played at that time in the piece.

Here is a standard 7&5 layout, showing some typical doubles:

Alto 1/Flute
Alto 2
Tenor 1/Soprano
Tenor 2
Baritone/Bass clarinet
Trumpet 1
Trumpet 2
Trumpet 3/Flugelhorn
Trumpet 4/Flugelhorn
Trombone 1
Trombone 2
Trombone 3
Guitar
Piano
Bass
Drums

Transposed Versus Concert Score

The industry standard is the transposed score, in which each instrument's part is transposed to its particular key. Copyists prefer transposed scores because they do not have to take the extra time and care to transpose when copying out the individual sax and trumpet parts. (They charge more for copying out parts from concert scores.)

Concert scores, on the other hand, are favored by certain conductors. And teachers prefer them when analyzing arranging and composition techniques. If you do write your score entirely in concert key, it is a good idea to indicate "concert score" to avoid any possible confusion.

If you work on a computer, it is easy to generate either a transposed or a concert score. When dealing with a client, teacher, or copyist, be sure to check which type is required.

Brackets and Bar Lines

In published scores, the saxophones, trumpets, and trombones are sometimes "bracketed" by section. That is, within each section, a slightly thicker second line is drawn to the left of the bar line of the first measure of every page. Each rhythm section player gets such a bracket. Similarly, measure lines appear as continuous vertical lines within sections, but not through the vertical space between sections. This helps to highlight each section and to clearly indicate its size. Follow this practice for a professional look when generating scores with computer programs.

If you are writing out your score by hand, however, you may choose not to follow these practices. Many writers omit the brackets and draw measure lines down through the entire score. In fact many score paper pads have preprinted measure lines that go continuously down the entire page.

Rehearsal Letters and Numbers

Place these musical road signs in a box above the saxophones and immediately over measures that begin new phrases or sections. When arranging a tune that follows song form, use a different letter for each new chorus, indicating the phrases within a chorus with both the letter and measure number in that chorus. For instance, for two choruses of a standard thirty-two-measure AABA form, the rehearsal markings for eight-bar phrases would be:

[A] [A9] [A17] [A25] [B] [B9] [B17] [B25]

Some compositions do not solely rely on stating a song-form melody and then repeating the melody's harmonic progression for each new section or chorus. For these more complex, episodic forms, use boxed measure numbers instead of letters. For instance, for a composition with a first phrase of twelve measures, a second phrase of nine measures, a third phrase of thirteen measures, and a fourth phrase of nine measures going on to a new section, the numbers would be:

[1] [13] [22] [35] [44]

Key Signatures

Place the key signature in every part on every score page. This is the publishing standard. For complex chromatic pieces that are not focused in any one key center, use no key signature. Such pieces are said to be written in open key.

Time Signatures

Write time signatures in every part on the first page of the score. You need not show the time signature again, unless you change the meter. In that case, write the new time signature in every part on the page where the change occurs, but not on subsequent pages.

Dynamics

Write dynamic markings in every part to which they apply. Always place them below the staff.

Articulation Markings

Generally, place all articulations (longs, shorts, and accents) above the staff in all parts. Occasionally, they may appear below the staff or even in the staff.

Rests

When a section of the band has an extended rest, write whole-measure rests in all those parts involved. For handwritten scores, you can save time by writing the rest in the lead part only and drawing a line down through the remainder of the section indicating that those parts also rest.

Tempo, Motion, and Style Markings

Although there is no standard practice on this point, we suggest you place all markings indicating speed and style at the beginning of the score above the saxophone section only. Use additional markings only when you need to change the speed or style later in the piece. Again, place these additional markings, including *ritardando* (signaling a slowing down) and *accelerando* (signaling a speeding up), at the top of the score above the saxophone section.

Fermatas (Holds) and Caesuras (Short Pauses)

Place these markings in every part on the score.

Beat Alignment and Spacing

The location of beats must line up vertically in all parts. Within measures, beats also must be spaced evenly. If you are writing by hand, pre-lined score pads can make it difficult to abide by these rules, especially in measures with many notes. If you are trying to accommodate an extended passage of sixteenth notes, for example, you may have to shift the location of bar lines to create wider measures. If you are using computer software, check its decisions about alignment and spacing. Do not assume the computer understands the aesthetics of good notation.

Indicating Unisons and Octaves

To indicate that one player is duplicating the same melodic line as another, use the terms Col, coll', or colla (meaning "with"). For instance, if Alto 2 is duplicating Alto 1 at the unison, rather than writing out the whole line again, write "coll' Alto 1" on the second alto part and then draw a horizontal line to the end of the passage. Use *8va* or *8vb* to show that the second player's part is up or down an octave from the original melodic line. This simplifies the score, making it easier to read.

Computer notation programs require that you write out each line explicitly in order for them to "extract" and print out separate parts. If you do write out duplicated parts in full, you can still make the score easier to read by indicating when one line is in unison or in octaves with another. For instance, if Tenor 1 were playing the same line as Alto 1 down an octave, you would write "sounding *8vb* with Alto 1" above that passage on the tenor part. Or, you can produce two scores, one for the conductor showing only the coll' label for duplicated parts and the other showing all lines written out fully so that the program can extract individual parts.

In transposed scores, you may use coll' only for instruments that share the same clef and transposition. In concert scores, you may use coll' for any instruments of the same clef, regardless of differences in transposition.

1-9 Overview of an Arrangement

Before applying the detailed techniques that occupy the bulk of this book—voicings for horn sections, how to write solis, the creation of backgrounds and shout choruses, and so on—a would-be arranger needs to conceive his or her arrangement in a general way. This section briefly summarizes what you need to consider in this early stage in order to work up an overview of your musical plan.

Begin by spending the time you need to thoroughly learn the tune or thematic material. In other words, take the lead sheet out of your eyes and put it in your ears. This will help you apply melodic embellishment and reharmonization in a natural way, enabling you to alter the music to best suit the mood, style, and tempo you have chosen.

Think about overall momentum and flow. "Peaks" and "valleys" are necessary as the piece unfolds. Ideally you should have one main climax that serves as a focal point. Variety and contrast are the main elements to be controlled in order to maintain an aesthetic balance and to keep performers as well as listeners involved and excited. Consider, for example: high versus low, loud versus soft, slow versus fast, thick versus thin, reeds versus brass, concerted versus contrapuntal, ensemble versus soloists, and more.

Elements of Form (Introductions, Interludes, and Endings)

A well-conceived arrangement usually contains an introduction, interludes or transitions, and an ending.

Introduction: The "intro" sets up the character and mood of the music that follows. Generally it establishes the tempo and rhythmic style while at the same time preparing the tonality or modality of the piece's first melodic phrase. Length is flexible, but it is usually at least four measures. If the introduction is longer than sixteen measures, be sure that the lengths of other sections of the piece such as phrase extensions, interludes, and endings are proportioned. There are several common types of introductions.

- Thematic introductions contain some recognizable melodic fragment from the tune itself, very often from the last four or eight measures.
- A rhythmic introduction establishes a rhythmic motive that reappears in the main body of the arrangement.
- Vamps repeat a two- or four-measure pattern until the first chorus begins.
- Sustained introductions consist of sustained voicings against which a soloist or a small group of instruments play. When there is no pulse, this type of intro may have to be conducted.

For contrast, the introduction's orchestration is often different from that of the first melody section. Further contrast in the first chorus may result from a different time feel and tempo or from the use of "stop-time" figures, specifically notated patterns that break away from the prevailing rhythmic pulse. "Breaks," moments when the rhythm section stops playing time altogether, may also distinguish the first chorus from the introduction. During such a break, there may be melodic pickups that link to the beginning of the next phrase.

Interlude: An interlude furnishes transitional space between choruses or larger sections of an arrangement. Interludes provide the opportunity to change keys, feels, soloists, and so on. Material from the introduction may reappear in an interlude as a means of establishing continuity.

Ending: The ending dramatizes the sense of finality at the conclusion of an arrangement. Added measures can build up to an exclamation point or gradually dissolve down to a very passive finish. In either case, the sense of closure must be emotionally convincing. Try not to end with a final chord that is out of context with the rest of the arrangement. Fade-out endings work in the studio, but for live performance it is safer to have a predetermined written ending.

Like interludes, endings often draw on material from the introduction. Repeating the entire introduction as an ending is known as the "bookends" technique.

Modulation and Reharmonization

Modulating to a new key and reinventing the harmonic accompaniment for a given melody are vital techniques to a good arrangement. Both strategies add interest and prevent monotony. In addition, modulation is often used to establish a suitable range for the instruments involved in a new section.

Graphing an Arrangement

Below is a graphical outline of Dick Lowell's arrangement of "1625 Swingerama Ave.," a composition by Ken Pullig. The full score appears in the final chapter of this book. Although no notes are shown here, you can see that the arrangement contains all the critical elements. There is plenty of variety and contrast. It has an introduction and matching ending, in the bookends style. It also includes an interlude, several contrasting written textures, modulations, space for soloists, and a developed final chorus.

When creating your own arrangement, develop your initial concept fully enough to show this amount of detail in a graph. The process will greatly facilitate the next steps to musical sketch and full score.

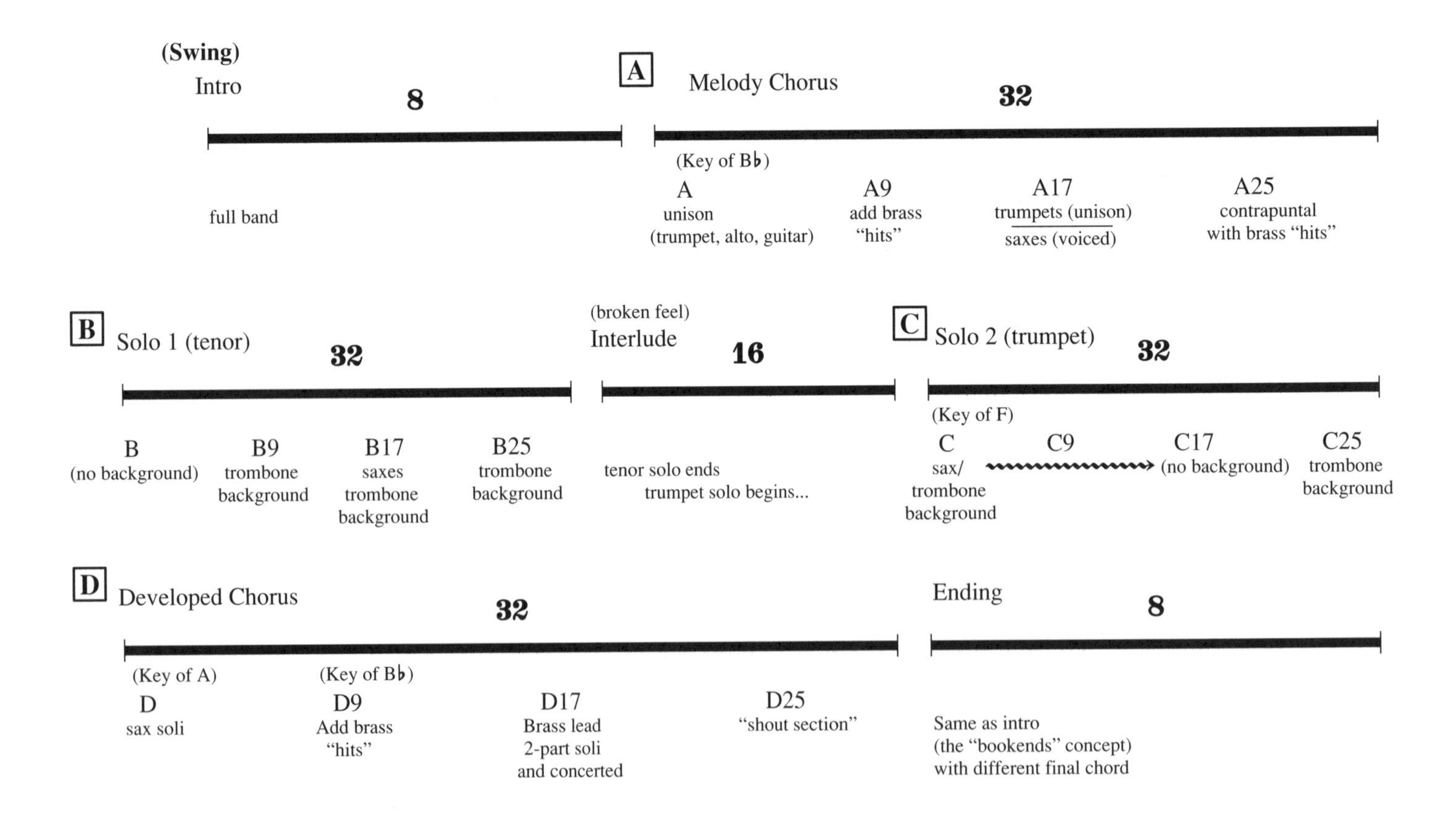

1-10 Exercise

1. Listen carefully and repeatedly to a recording of one of your favorite big band pieces. Following the example of the "1625 Swingerama Ave." graph on the previous page, graph the arrangement of the recorded piece.

2. Select a standard tune that follows the popular song form AABA. After internalizing the music, invent an arrangement of it on a large scale. Decide whether and how you will alter the melody and harmony. Determine how you will build in variety and where you will position the climax. Devise ideas for an introduction, for an ending, and possibly for interludes, shout choruses, modulations, and other major elements. When you have settled on the broad outline of the arrangement, graph your concept schematically following the "1625 Swingerama Ave." example.

This page intentionally left blank.

CHAPTER 2 Unison and Octave Writing

IN THIS CHAPTER

2-1 Procedure

We begin our discussion of arranging techniques with one of the simplest yet most powerful approaches, the use of unison and octaves. Many of the complex voicing strategies to be examined in later chapters create a dense, blended effect. Unisons and octaves offer a dramatic contrast to such textures by creating a cleaner, more clearly defined sound. More important, by scoring a passage with instruments in unison, octaves, or a combination of both, you emphasize melodic clarity, focusing the listener's ear on a single line.

A unison or octave passage needs at least two players on the line so as to distinguish it from either a solo line or an improvised line. To increase the sense of presence and resonance, you can assign additional players, though we recommend no more than a total of four for most situations.

When writing counterpoint passages, scoring in unison or octaves clarifies and strengthens each of the lines and establishes a colorful orchestral effect. It also highlights the arranger's personality rather than an individual player's. (If only one player were on a line, each would have the freedom to interpret more personally.) Accordingly, you must be sure to embellish and evolve lines in the most appropriate musical manner. Again, use at least two instruments on a line, add more to suit the desired effect, but do not go beyond four in most cases.

2-2 Orchestration and Timbral Effects

When orchestrating single lines, be aware of the difference in effect between unisons and octaves. Unisons add weight to the line; octaves help project the line. Furthermore, both effects are influenced by the timbral characteristics of the instruments involved. The big band can be thought of as being divided into three timbral areas:

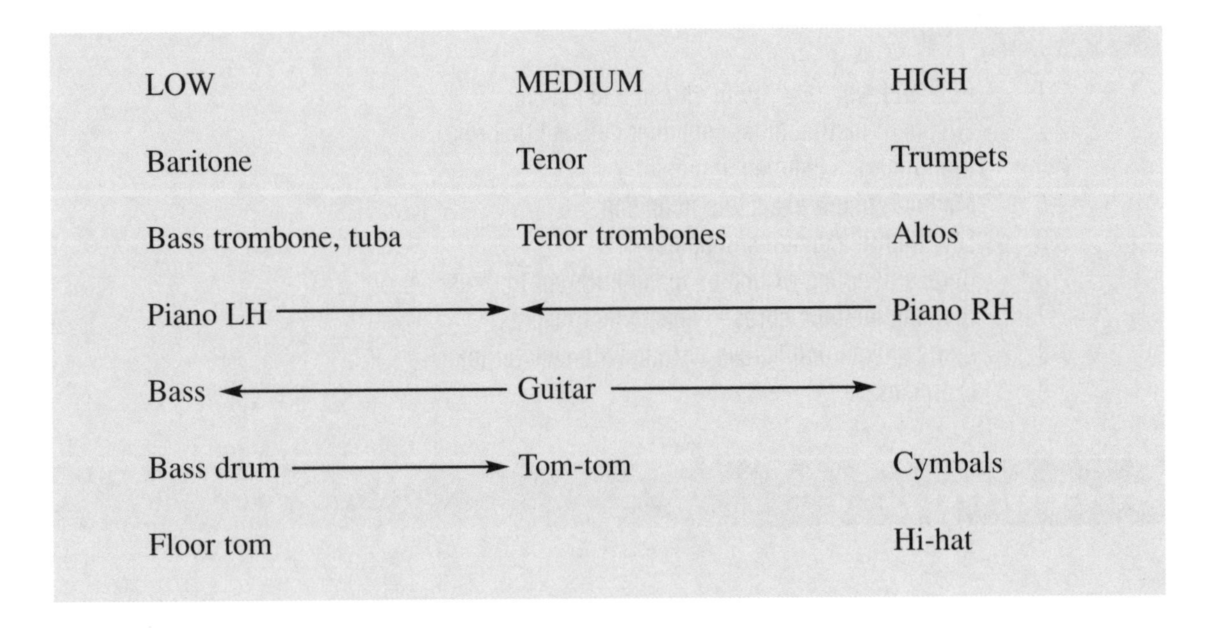

Two or more instruments on the same line create a *shared* sound. The effect of this shared line depends on how the instruments are combined according to family and timbre. Every possible assortment creates a unique effect. A combination of brass and reeds, mixing high and low timbres, yields a more complex sound than a joining of instruments that come from the same family or that have similar timbres.

An arranger needs a thorough understanding of each instrument's timbral characteristics and how they change from low to high register. Balancing the two or more instruments involved is crucial. Try not to use extreme registers; in particular, avoid high-timbre instruments in the low register and low-timbre instruments in the high register. The best way to learn how to employ the tremendous number of unison and octave possibilities available for large ensemble is through trial and error and dedicated score analysis while listening to recordings.

Sections 2-3, 2-4, 2-5, and 2-6 present examples of unison and octave combinations using various high-, medium-, and low-timbre instruments.

2-3 High-Timbre Unison

CD tracks 2 through 5 demonstrate four distinct high-timbre approaches to unison scoring of the lead line shown below. Notice the difference in sound quality between groups of instruments from the same family (the first two tracks) and groups from different families (the last two tracks).

2 High brass: two trumpets in unison

3 High reeds: two altos in unison

4 Mixed high timbre: trumpet and alto in unison

5 Mixed high timbre: trumpet, alto, guitar in unison

2-4 Medium-Timbre Unison

We scored the melody line below in unison using two different combinations of medium-timbre instruments. Compare the effects by listening to the recording.

6 Medium reeds: two tenors in unison

7 Mixed medium timbre: tenor and trombone in unison

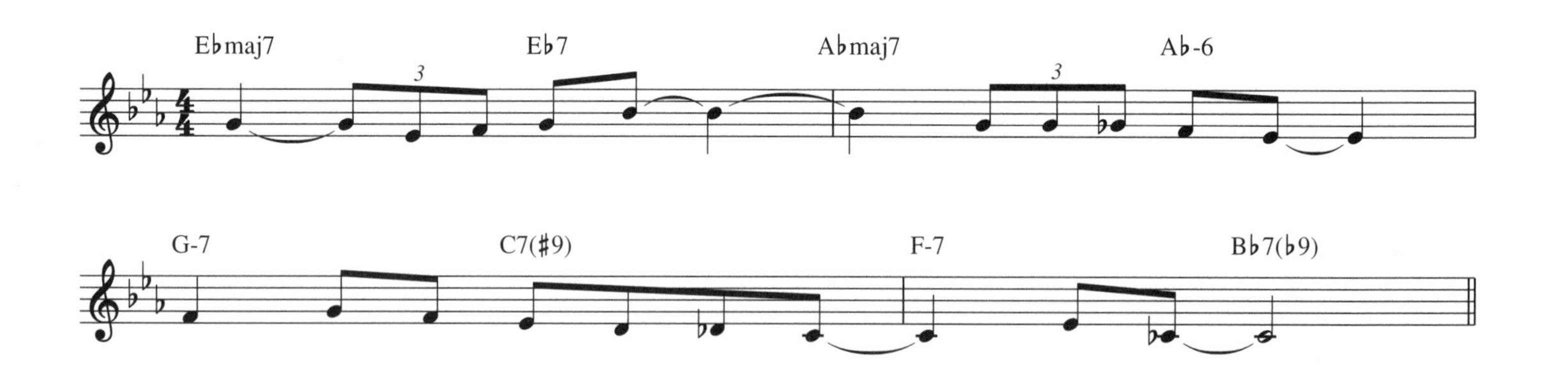

2-5 Low-Timbre Unison

Listen to the differing effects of these three low-timbre versions of unison scoring. The melody line is the same as that used for the medium-timbre examples in the previous section, except that it is an octave lower.

8 Low brass: two trombones in unison

9 Mixed low: trombone/baritone unison

10 Mixed low: trombone, bari, piano, and bass

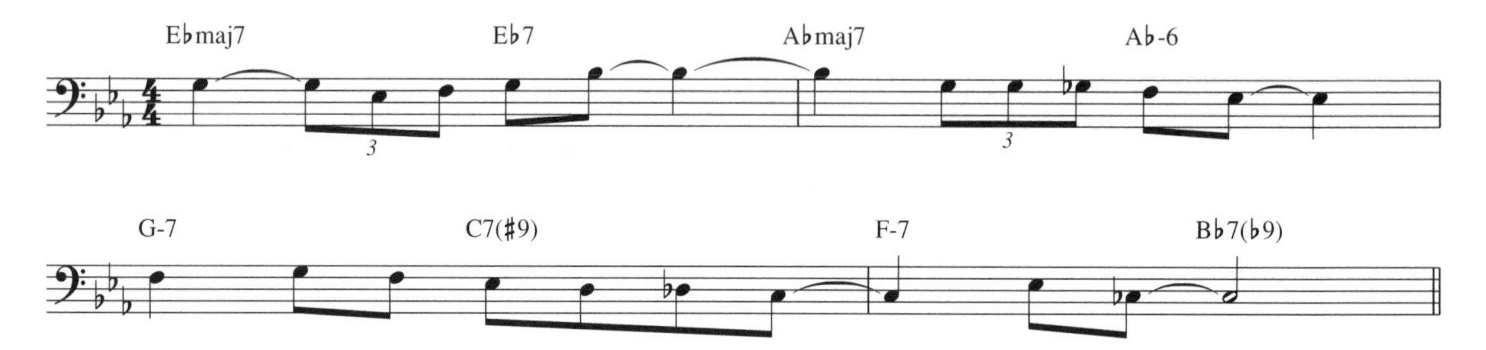

2-6 Octave Doubling

Tracks 11 through 15 demonstrate how scoring in octaves helps to clearly project a melody line. The line shown below is doubled at the octave using various high-, medium-, and low-timbre instruments. Each version is played twice. The first time, single instruments cover each line; the second time features two instruments on each line.

11 Trumpet over tenor; two trumpets over two tenors

12 Alto over trombone; two altos over two trombones

13 Trumpet over baritone; two trumpets over baritone and trombone

14 Alto over baritone; alto and trumpet over baritone and trombone

15 Trumpet over trombone; two trumpets over two trombones

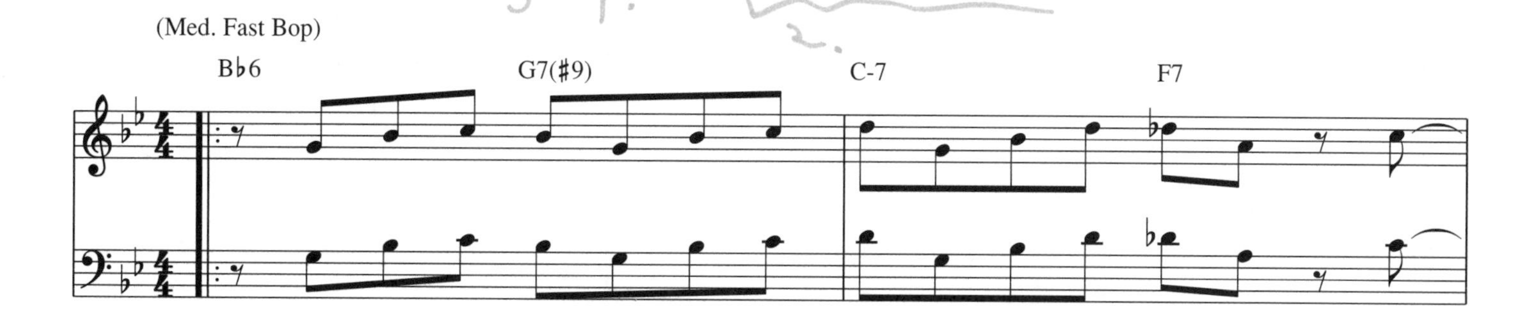

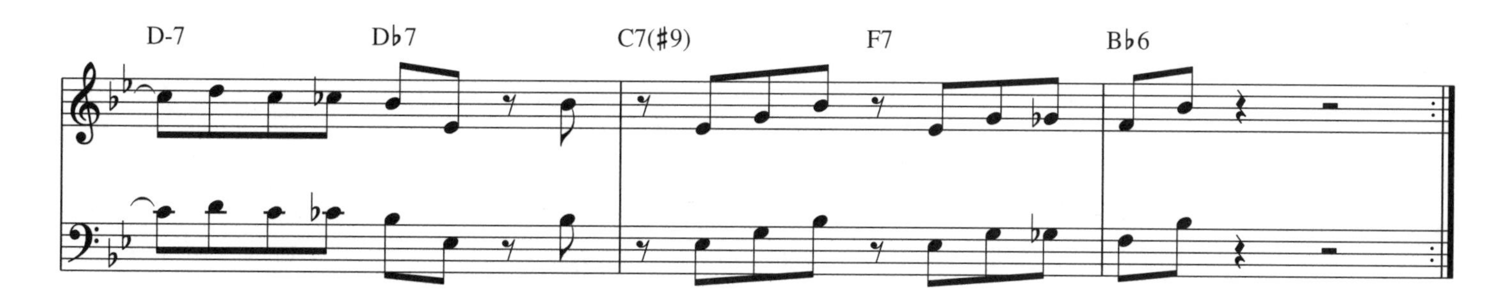

2-7 Melodic Subdivision

One method for varying and developing your material is to break the melody down into small phrases, each of which is scored for different instruments. This is known as melodic subdivision. Orchestrate these fragments with various unison or octave combinations containing different timbres and registers. The result is that as the differing combinations drop in and out, the melody will seem to change colors.

The fragments should not dart in and out every few notes; that will make the music feel chaotic and ragged. Each instrumental combination must play long enough to establish a logical melodic statement. To further ensure a smooth melodic flow, you can dovetail, or overlap, the entrances and exits of each subdivision.

We will use this melody line in the following examples of melodic subdivision.

Abrupt Fragments

In this example, the combinations change too abruptly. The melodic flow is awkward.

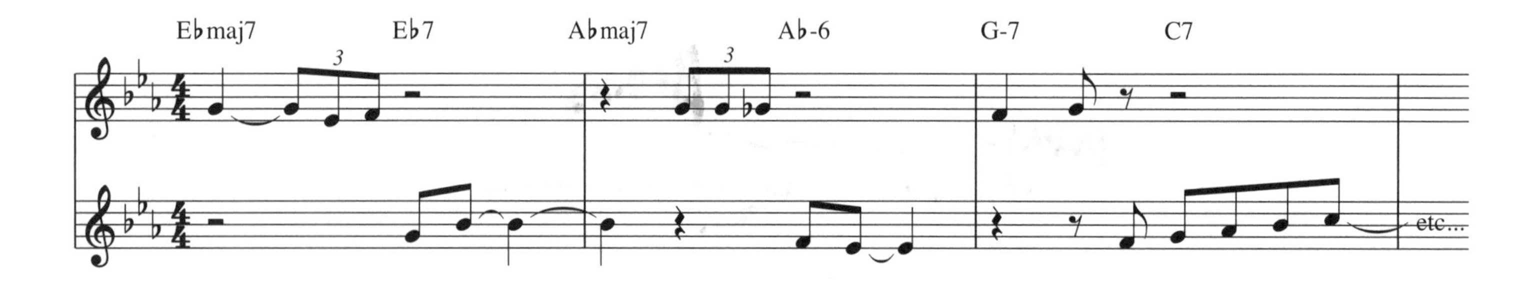

Smooth Flow

Notice how these phrases are longer than those in the previous example. In addition, the ending of each phrase overlaps with the beginning of the next. This creates a smoother and more flowing effect.

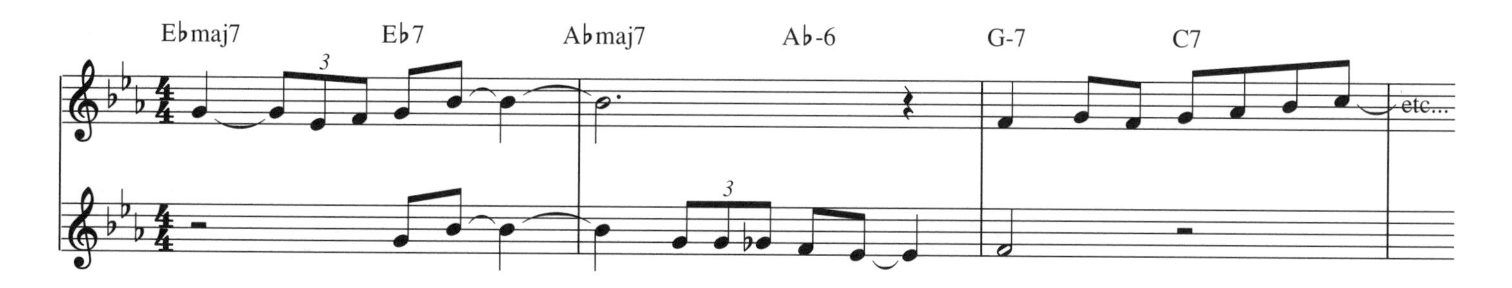

Let us look at three different applications of melodic subdivision for the following twelve-measure melody.

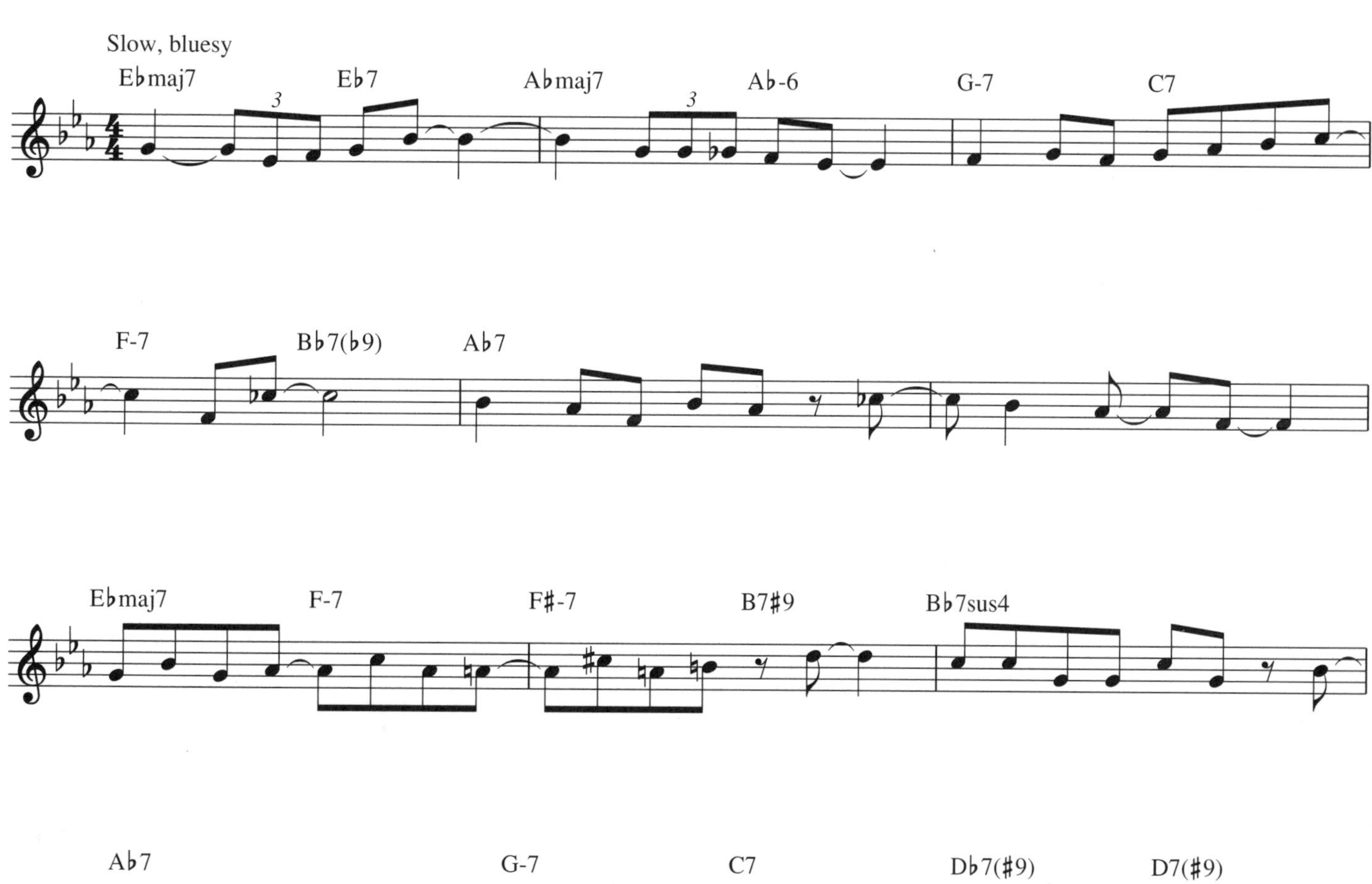

Short Subdivisions, Two Groups

This example uses short subdivisions, one- and two-measure fragments, to shift the melody from one unison instrumental group to the other. Note that when the unison middle- and low-timbre group (tenor, trombone, baritone) takes over from the unison high-timbre group (trumpet, alto, guitar) the melody is displaced downward by an octave.

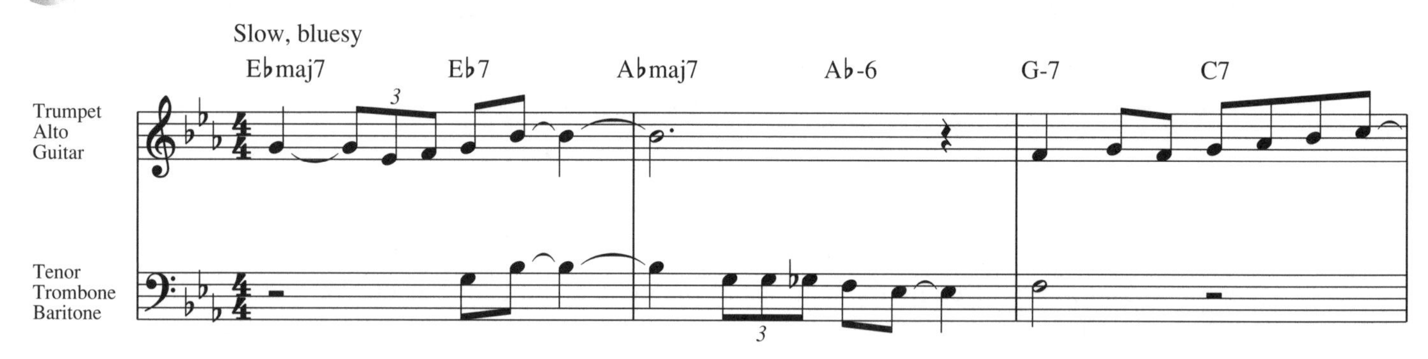

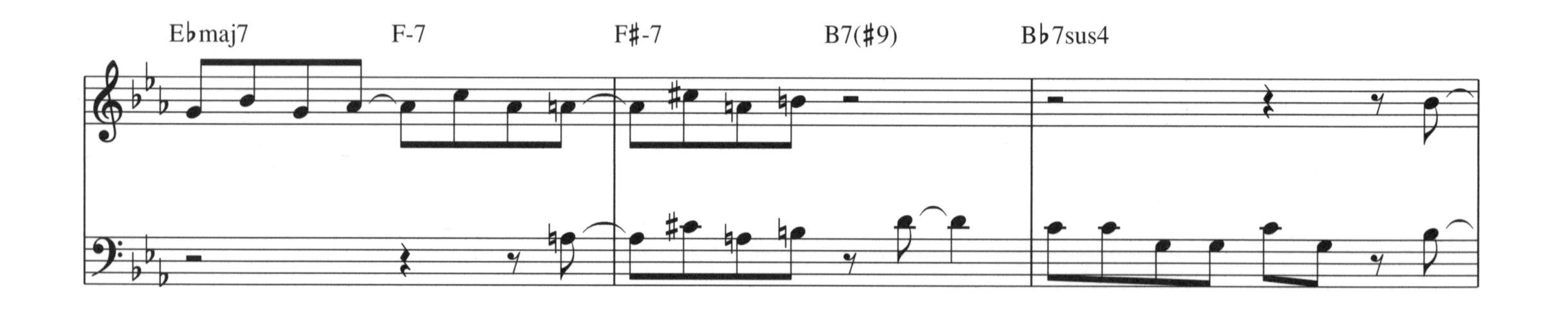

Longer Subdivisions, Three Groups

This example subdivides the melody into longer phrases, shifting every four measures among three different instrumental groups. Note the dovetailing and octave displacement as the unison high-timbre group (two trumpets, two altos, guitar) passes the melody to the unison medium-timbre group (two tenors, two trombones). For contrast in the last four measures, the low-timbre group is scored in octaves: trombone and baritone, with the left hand of the piano doubling both.

Longest Subdivisions, Two Groups

The subdivisions in this example are longer than in the previous two. There are only two fragments, each lasting six measures. The orchestration contrasts the brass section in octaves (four trumpets above three trombones) during the first six measures with the saxophone section in octaves (two altos above two tenors and the baritone) in the last six measures.

18

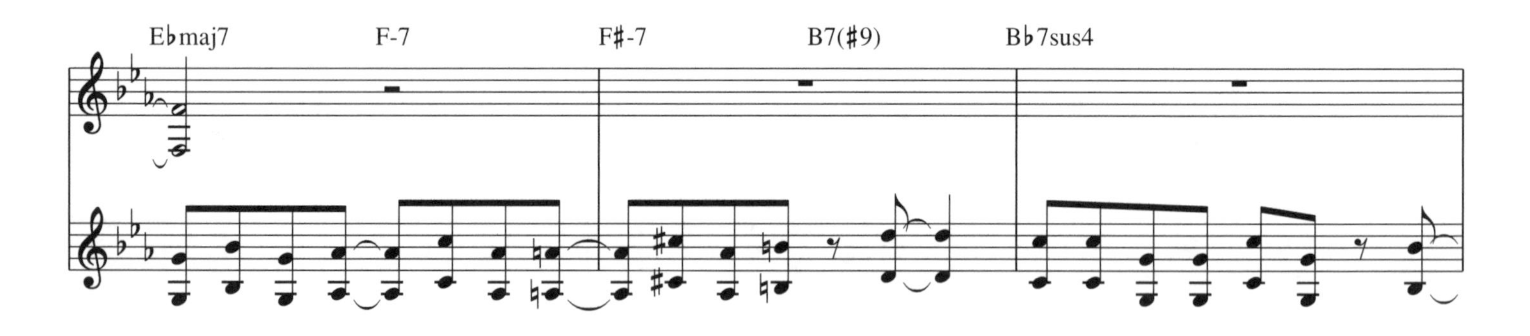

2-8 Contrapuntal Application

Counterpoint passages frequently call for orchestrating in unisons and octaves. For this arrangement of the melody used in the previous three examples, we composed a simple secondary line to create two-part counterpoint. Each line makes use of mixed-timbre unison combinations.

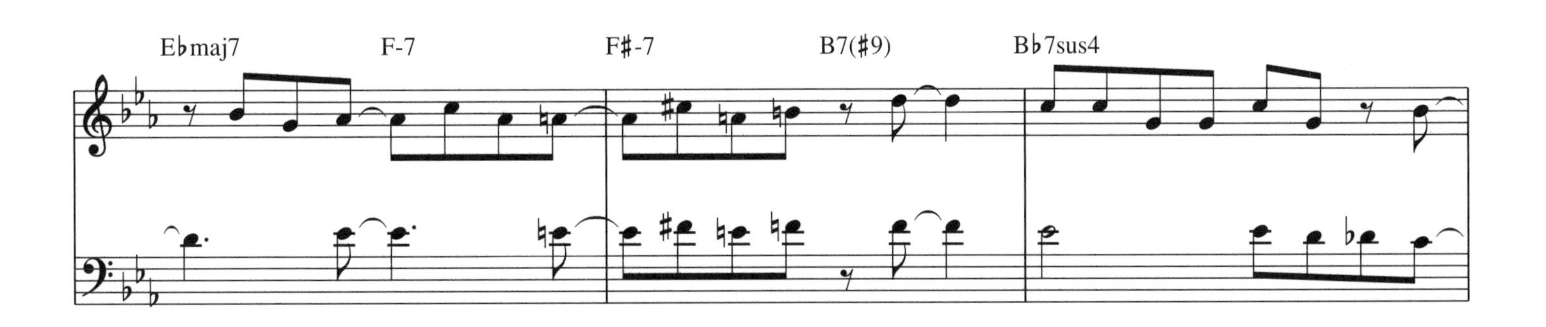

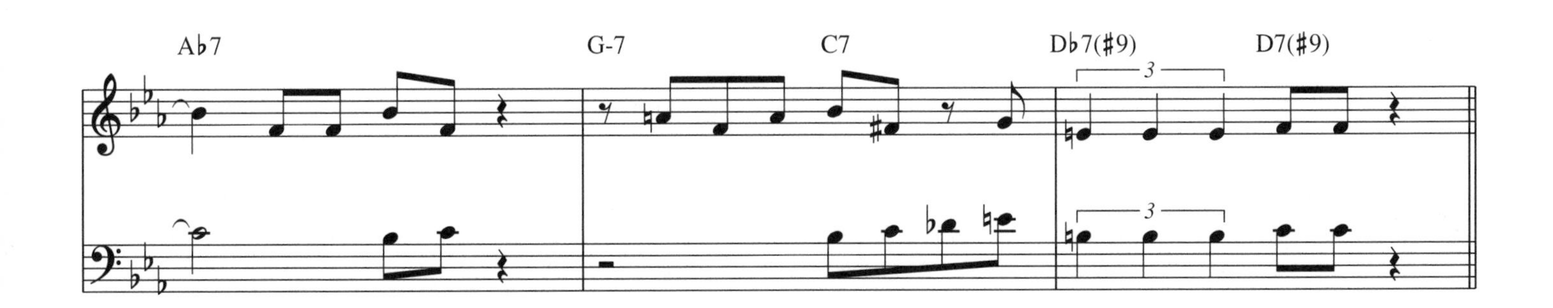

This page intentionally left blank.

2-9 Exercises

Refer to the melody below to complete the following three exercises.

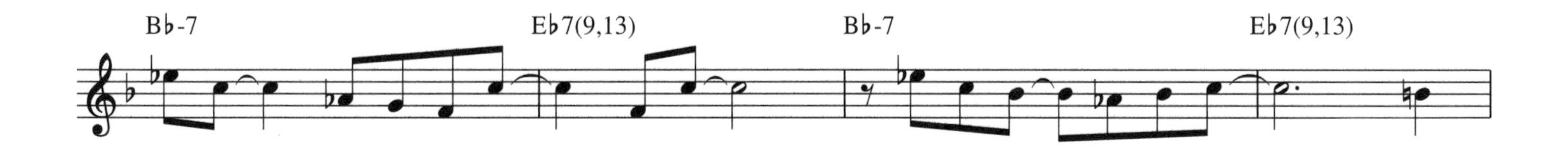

1. For a 7&5 ensemble, apply melodic subdivision to change the color of the melody every two measures. Use unisons of two to four instruments on each line. List the instruments used over each entering line. Be sure to dovetail one phrase into the next.

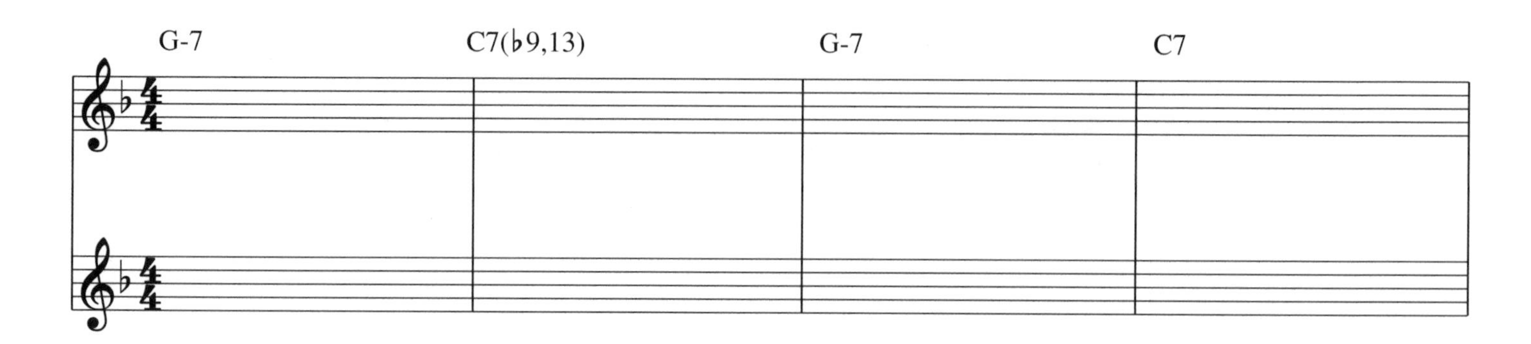

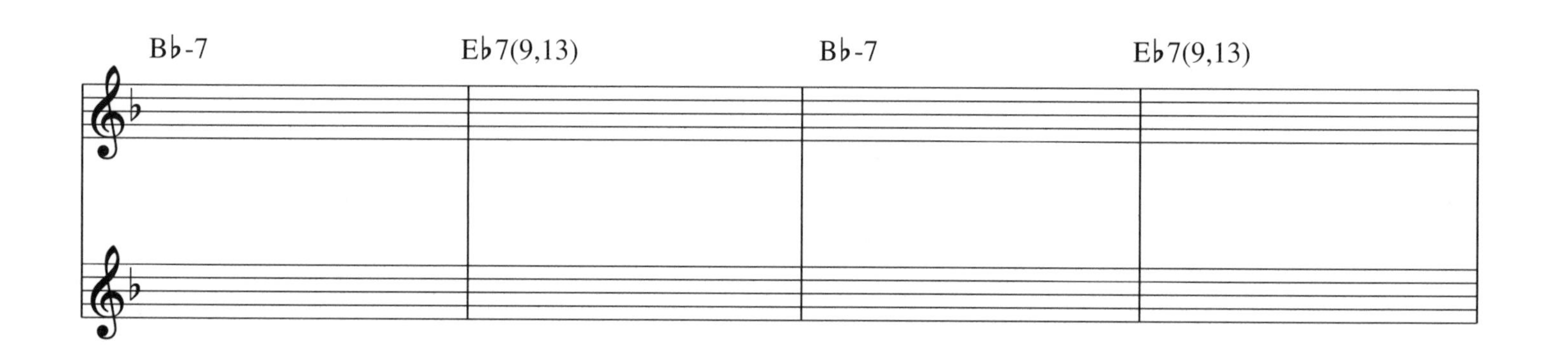

A♭maj7 A♭-7 D♭7 G♭maj7 A-7 D7

G-7 C7(♭9) Fmaj7(9)

2. For a 7&5 ensemble, change the color every four measures using unisons and/or octaves. The bass clef stave is provided to facilitate doubling a line an octave lower. Work with two to four instruments per phrase, listing the instruments used over each line.

3. For a 7&5 ensemble, change the color every eight measures using unisons and/or octaves. Include two to four instruments in each melodic subdivision and list them over each line's entrance. Although this four-stave sketch format separates the saxes and brass, employ both sectional and mixed-family combinations.

CHAPTER 3
Concerted Writing with Mechanical Voicings

IN THIS CHAPTER

3-1 Procedure

One of the most popular strategies for treating a melody and its harmonic accompaniment in large ensembles is "concerted writing." A concerted passage is one in which the melody and harmony lines all play the same rhythm (while, of course, playing a variety of different pitches). Concerted passages generally involve all the horns—brass plus saxophones and/or woodwinds—or a smaller combination of horns from within the ensemble. The rhythm section usually comps during such passages or may play the same rhythm as the horns.

In basic concerted writing, the arranger usually begins in the brass section, "hanging" chord tones below a melody line using a variety of formulaic or "mechanical" voicings. These mechanical voicings are four-way close and the three variations of open voicings that are formed by dropping the second voice one octave (drop-2), dropping the third voice one octave (drop-3), or dropping both the second and fourth voices one octave (drop-2+4). You will need a working knowledge of these voicing strategies in order to understand and apply the material covered in this and later chapters. See *Modern Jazz Voicings* by Ted Pease and Ken Pullig (Berklee Press, 2001) for a full treatment of this subject.

After scoring the melody for the brass section with the appropriate mechanical voicing technique, you then establish saxophone section parts using unison and/or octave doublings of lines from the brass section. Make sure the brass voicing contains all the notes essential to making the chord function clear. The sax section simply supports those notes by doubling them. You can greatly shape the passage's texture and depth by your choices in two areas: how open or close the spacing is in each section and how you decide to "couple" the saxophones to the brass.

3-2 Coupling the Saxes to the Brass

Precisely which of the brass section's notes the saxophone section doubles and how depends on the lead saxophone line. If the lead saxophone line doubles one of the brass harmony lines note for note, then the rest of the saxophones follow the same contour, resulting in parallel motion between the brass and sax sections. This is known as constant coupling.

But an arranger may instead create the lead saxophone line out of notes from more than one of the brass harmony lines. This is often done to create contrary motion between the brass and sax sections.

When determining the coupling for the lead alto, you may find it helpful to think of the saxophone section as a sliding unit. Putting this unit higher up in the brass voicing results in more unisons in the top of the voicing, creating a bright orchestral effect. Putting it in a lower position in the brass voicing results in more octave doublings and creates a sound with more bottom or depth.

3-3 Recommended Ranges for Lead Instruments

When writing basic concerted passages, keep the parts for lead instruments within the ranges suggested below. This will ensure good balance and intonation. These guidelines are conservative. When writing for professional bands, or when you know the capabilities of the individual players, you may exceed these limits. The highest two notes shown for the lead trumpet, for example, would be feasible for professionals. But when you do not know who you are writing for and to guarantee the best musical results, stay within the more practical boundaries.

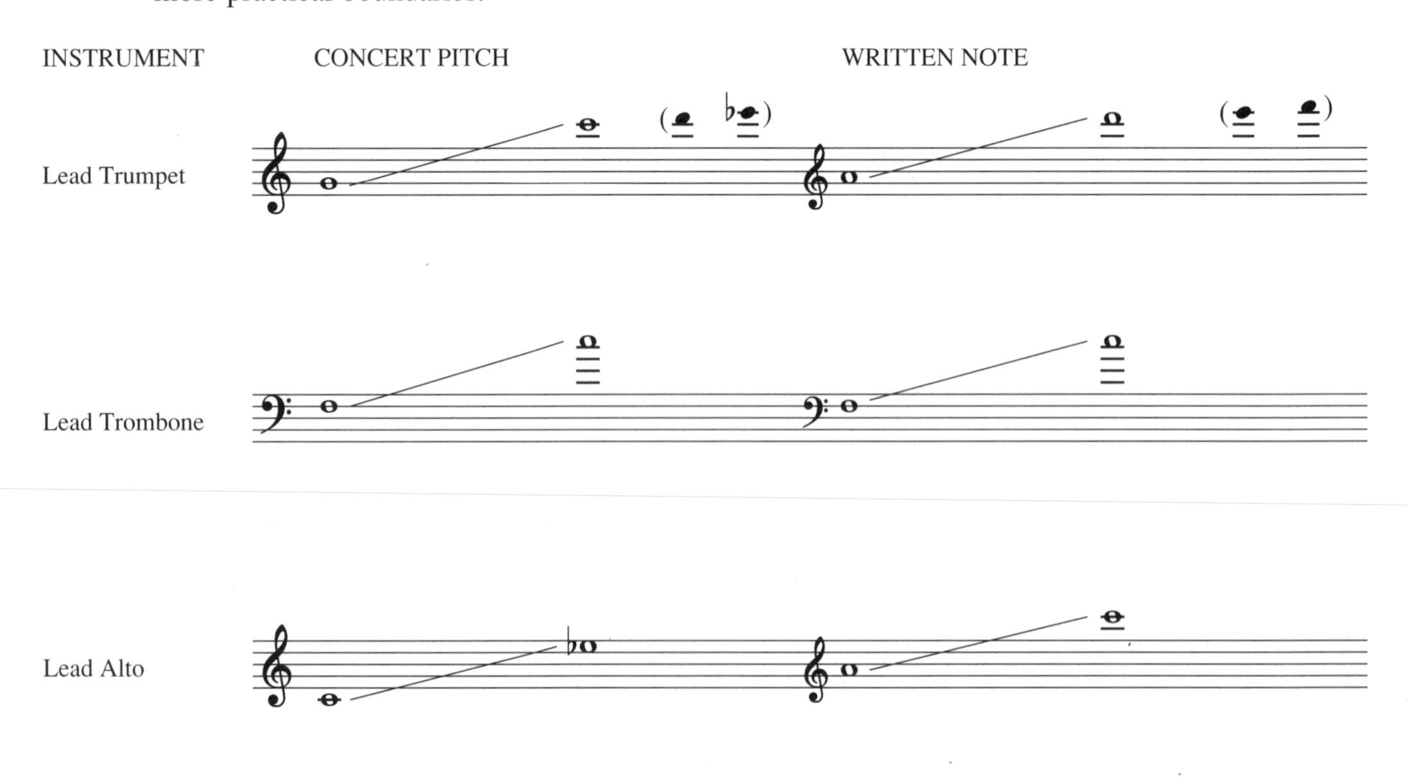

3-4 4&4 Concerted Writing

4&4 with Constant Coupling

The following example shows step-by-step how to create a basic concerted passage for a 4&4 band (four brass and four saxes).

Step 1.
Create the lead line for Trumpet 1, embellishing it to fit the style.

Step 2.
Voice the brass section, choosing an open or close voicing technique most appropriate for the lead line and its range. In this case we choose an open (drop-2) voicing. Avoid intervals of a second between the top two voices so as not to conceal the lead line. Also avoid high trombone parts (notes beyond *g* three ledger lines above the bass clef staff), which could cause balance problems.

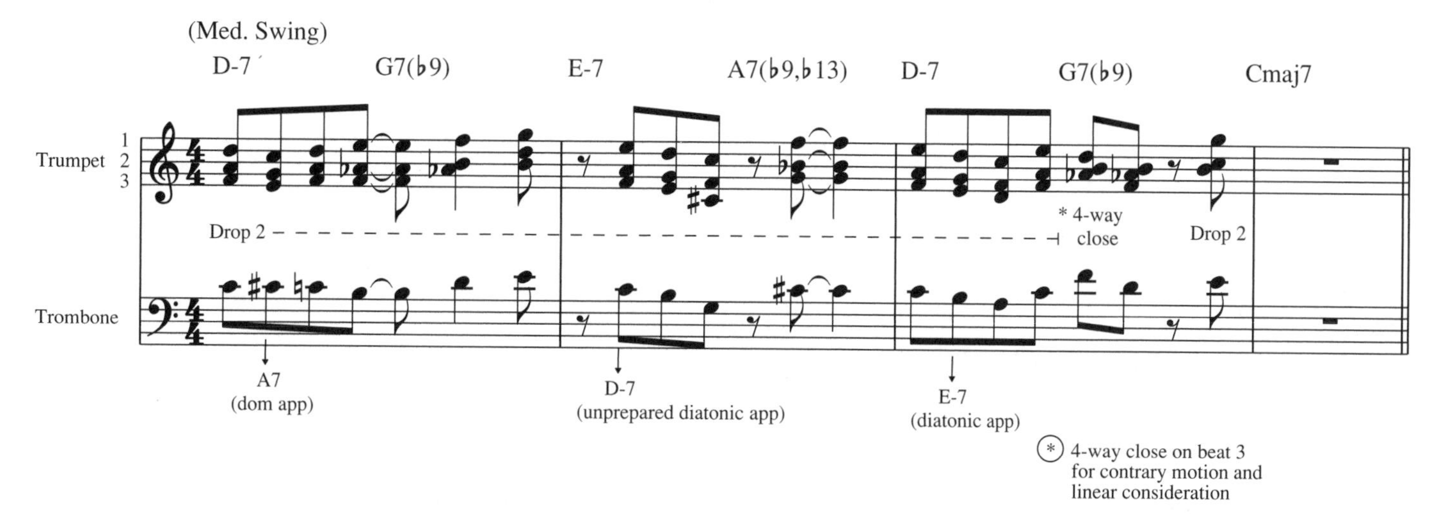

Step 3.
Decide the coupling technique, then create the lead alto part. With constant coupling, the lead alto usually doubles the second or third trumpet, depending on range considerations. Here we choose constant coupling with the lead alto doubling the second trumpet.

Step 4.
Voice the saxophone section in open or close position, being careful to observe low-interval limits (see section 1-4). In this example, we use a four-way close voicing.

20

In the variation below, we repeat the same open brass voicing with constant coupling of the lead alto, but this time the saxophone section is scored with an open (drop-2) voicing. Listen to the subtle difference in texture depth between this and the preceding example on the CD.

21

4&4 with Variable Coupling

Here we use the same lead trumpet line and the same brass voicing as in the previous example, but apply variable coupling of the saxophones in step 3. We build a lead alto part by choosing notes from the three lower brass parts (shown in grey) that result in contrary motion and a linear flow. The saxophone section is scored with a four-way close voicing. Try to hear the sax/brass contrary motion on this track; compare it to the sound of the sections' parallel movement on the previous track.

4&4 with Constant and Variable Coupling Combined

To create orchestral variety, an arranger may choose both constant and variable coupling techniques in the same phrase. In this example, the lead alto part doubles the second trumpet for the first two measures, then uses notes from the lower three brass lines in the third measure (all notes shown in grey). The saxophone section is again scored with a four-way close voicing.

4&4 with Full Doubling

24

When the brass lead line is very low, around the bottom of the treble clef, the sax section may double all four parts in unison. This will avoid any potential violation of low interval limits.

(Slow Swing)

A T

T B

F7(♯9) E♭7 D♭7(♯11) C7(♯9) B7(♯9) C7(♯9) F7(♯9)

Tp 1 2

3 Trb

(dom. app. B♭7)

3-5 Concerted Writing for 5&5, 7&5, and 8&5

In basic concerted writing for larger ensembles, follow the same four-step process given for 4&4 writing at the beginning of section 3-4. The examples below demonstrate constant, variable, and a combination of constant and variable coupling.

5&5 with Constant Coupling

25

In this example of constant coupling, the lead alto doubles the second trumpet, the brass section has an open (drop-2) voicing, and the saxophone section is scored using a close voicing.

7&5 with Variable Coupling

26

Here the lead alto line, following the variable coupling strategy, draws on notes from the three lower trumpets and the lead trombone (shown in grey). The brass section is again voiced using drop-2. The saxophone section is scored with a close voicing. Listen for the saxophones' contrary motion against the brass lines.

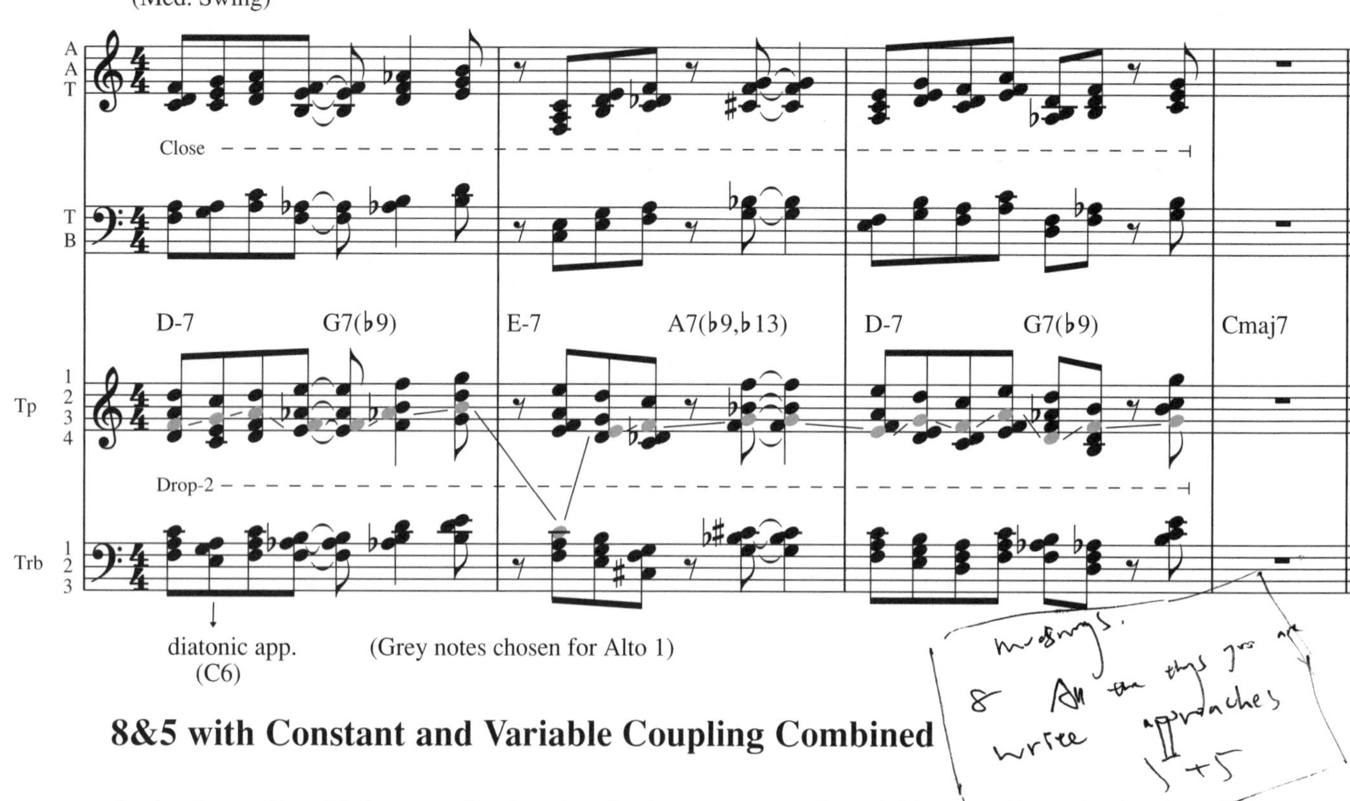

8&5 with Constant and Variable Coupling Combined

27

As in the earlier 4&4 example showing both constant and variable coupling, the lead alto line doubles the second trumpet part for the first two measures, then uses notes from the three lower trumpet parts (all notes shown in grey). The brass is scored with a drop-2 voicing, the saxophone section with a close voicing.

(Med. Swing)

constant coupling — variable coupling

A A T — Close

T B

D-7 G7(♭9) E-7 A7(♭9,♭13) D-7 G7(♭9) Cmaj7

Tp 1 2 3 4 — Drop-2 — Close

Trb 1 2 3 4

(Grey notes chosen for Alto 1)

3-6 Dealing with Repeated Notes

It is important to avoid repeating notes in the under parts of a melodically active concerted passage. A repeated note usually makes the line less fluid and creates a less interesting melodic shape. Repeated notes also present an articulation problem at fast tempos when the lead player wants to slur a passage. Obviously, a repeated note cannot be slurred. If some players are forced to articulate their lines differently from the lead, the ensemble sounds less unified.

Equally important, the playing of under parts that have no repeated notes is simply a more melodically pleasant experience for the musicians, a consideration that no arranger hoping for a good performance should overlook. Scoring a passage so that each player has the best line possible is worth the effort.

You can avoid repeated notes in the under parts of a melodically active concerted passage by choosing the spacing of your voicings wisely and reharmonizing approach notes strategically. This applies whether the whole band is playing or a smaller unit—such as a sax soli, a brass soli, or a mixed-timbre soli—is featured.

When scoring a concerted passage for large ensemble using a coupling technique, avoid repeated notes in the saxophone section by substituting an available tension or chord tone for the repeated note. You can also choose a different spacing within your voicing.

In cases where the spacing of voicings is most important, an arranger may deal with repeated notes by "crossing voices," which we discuss later in this section. This strategy provides each individual player an interesting line, while maintaining the writer's preferred spacing for the ensemble as a whole.

You will, of course, find some scores in the professional repertoire that contain repeated notes in the under parts of active concerted passages. Repeated notes are generally not a problem when the tempo is slow and the melodic flow is accented or percussive. Repeated notes are also less troublesome when they appear as the last two notes of an eighth-note or sixteenth-note passage. And sometimes players can just make repeated notes sound fine through their performance.

Editing to Eliminate Repeated Notes

Look closely at the previous 5&5, 7&5, and 8&5 examples—you will find repeated notes. Below, we show each instance where repeated notes are considered to be a problem. Next to each is a revision that avoids the repeated note. Those repeated notes that remain conform with the exceptions noted above.

Here is measure 1 of the 5&5 example from page 55. In the alternative version, we eliminate the repeated note in the second tenor line by substituting a *b-flat* (♭9) for the *c* (♯9) in the A7 (approach note reharmonization) chord (♭9 for ♯9).

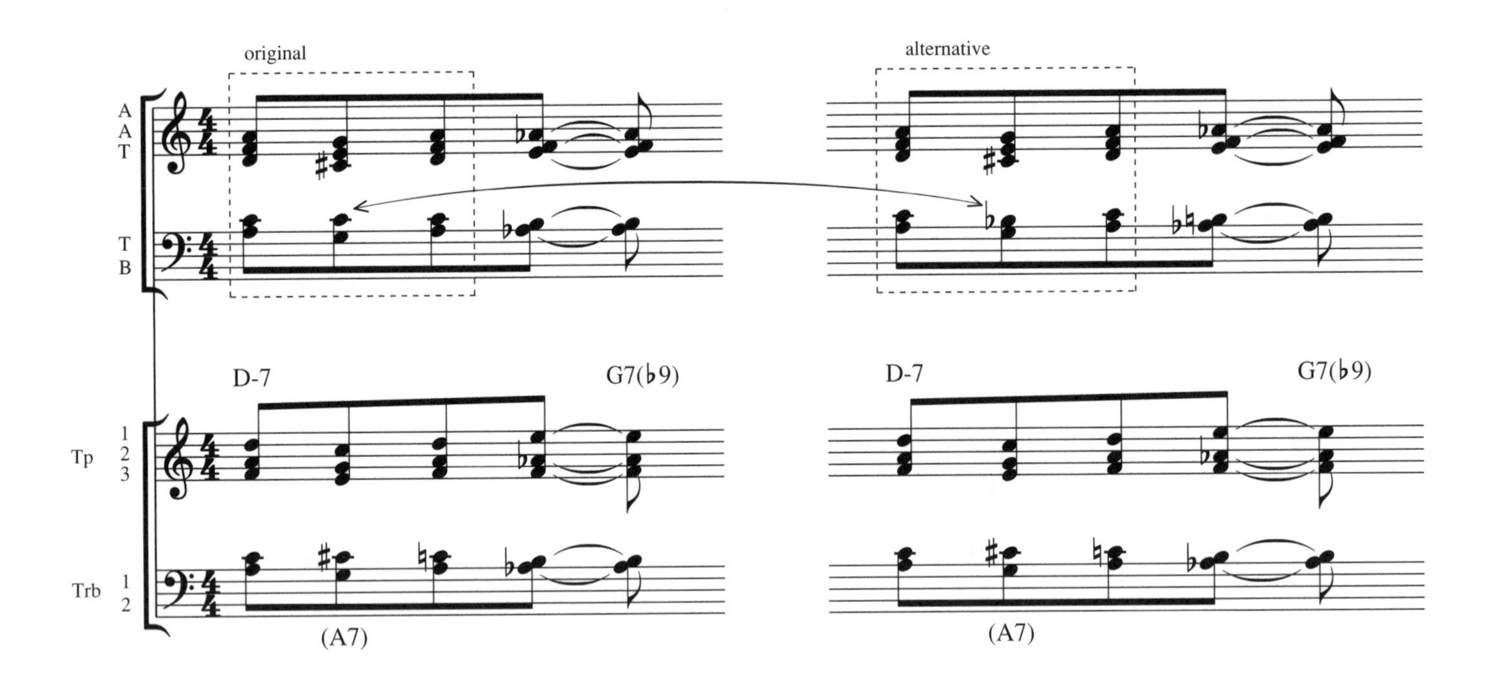

Here is measure 3 of the 7&5 example from page 56. We eliminate the repeated *f* in the third trumpet line and the repeated *f* in the third trombone by changing from an open voicing (drop-2) to a close voicing.

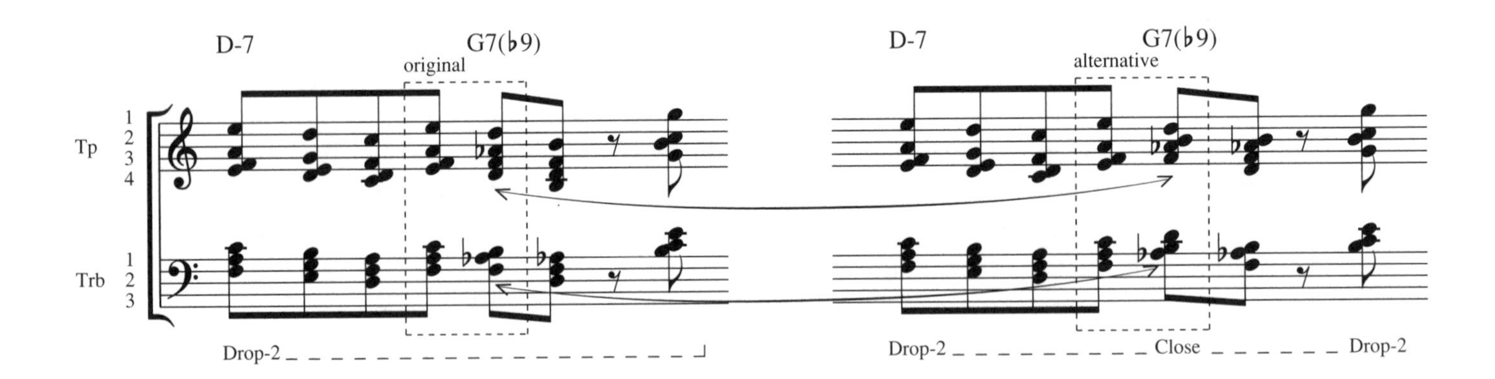

Here is measure 3 of the 8&5 example from page 56. We eliminate the repeated *e* in the second alto line by substituting 1 for 9. By replacing a close voicing with an open voicing (drop-2), we do away with Trumpet 4's repeated *f*. Trombone 4's repeated note is adjusted by substituting a *g* for the *f* in the D–7 chord (11 for ♭3).

Crossing of Voices

Another strategy for removing repeated notes from a particular player's line is to cross voices. In essence, you trade notes between two lines so that the lower voice momentarily jumps up to the upper line and the upper voice momentarily dips down to the lower. Although the repeated note stays in the same relative position in the ensemble's overall voicing, it is not played by the same player.

When you cross voices, make sure the linear flow is appropriate. The motion of any under part should be no more than a 2nd greater than the intervallic movement of the lead. Otherwise, you will overemphasize the harmony part and take attention away from the melody line.

Below we use crossing of voices, as indicated by the arrows, to eliminate Tenor 2's repeated *c* in the 5&5 example from page 55. On the second eighth note, Tenor 2 jumps up to play what was originally Tenor 1's *c-sharp*, while Tenor 1 jumps down to play what was originally Tenor 2's *c-natural*.

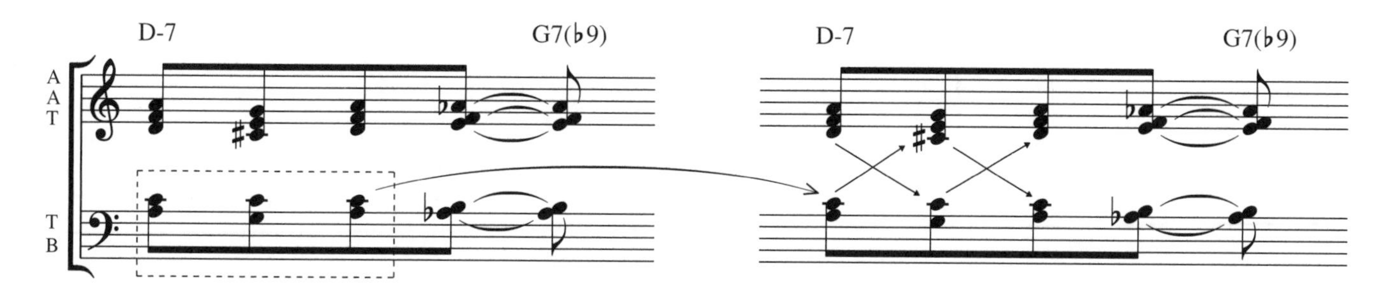

Reharmonizing Approach Notes

One of the keys to successful concerted writing is the reharmonization of approach notes. If an arranger fails to properly reharmonize approach notes in a melody line, his or her supporting lines are likely to be weakened by repeated notes. For detailed discussions of reharmonizing approach notes, see Chapter 1 of this book and Chapter 2 of *Modern Jazz Voicings* by Ted Pease and Ken Pullig (Berklee Press, 2001).

Below are two arrangements of the same lead line. The first contains no reharmonization of approach notes and is entirely in close position. Note the awkward lines and the many instances of repeated notes among the under parts.

Here we eliminate repeated notes by reharmonizing the approach notes using diatonic and dominant approach techniques. We also create contrast by scoring two melody notes with an open voicing (drop-2). Now the lines are more expressive and move more fluidly.

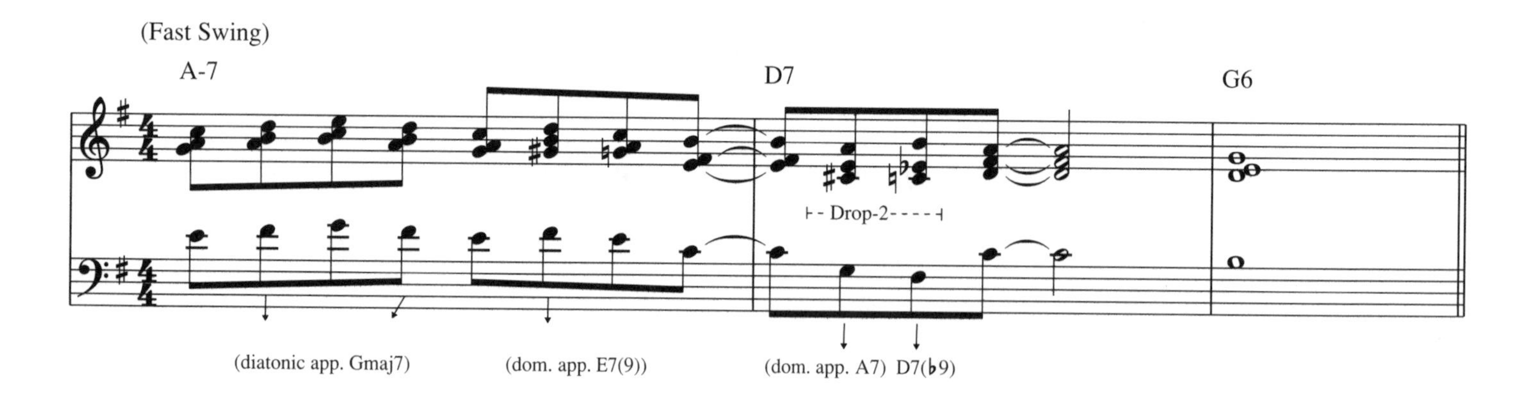

3-7 Exercises

1. For a 4&4 ensemble, voice the brass section as indicated. Then, using constant coupling, voice the saxophones in close or open position.

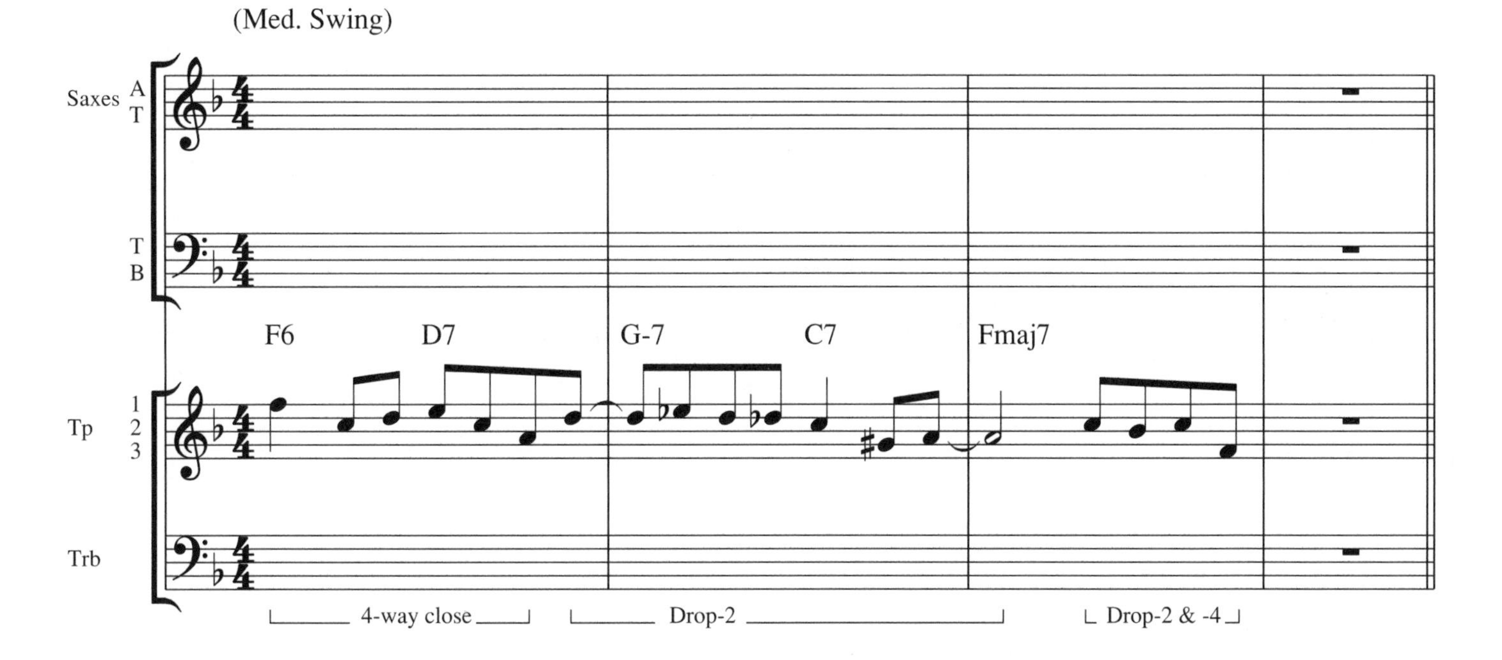

2. For a 5&5 ensemble, voice the brass section as indicated. Then, using variable coupling, voice the saxophones in close or open position.

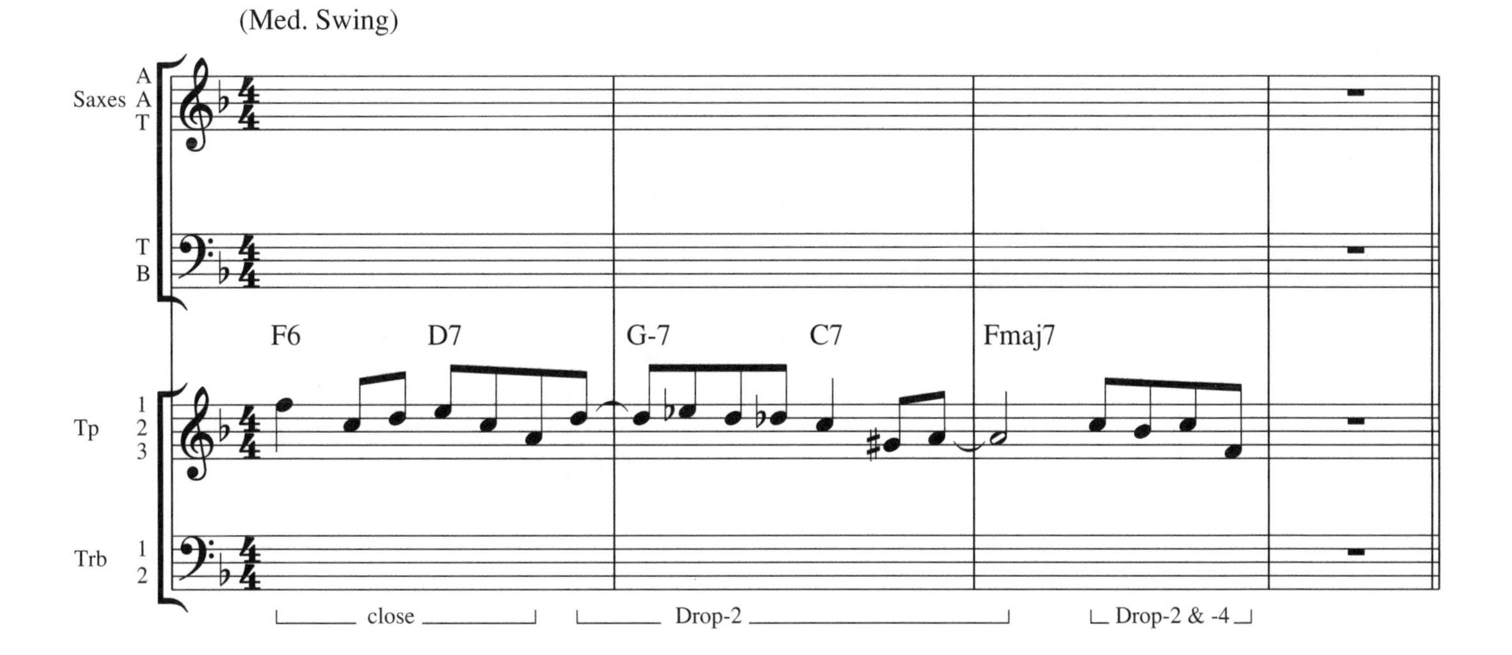

3. For a 5&5 ensemble, voice the brass section as indicated. Then, using a combination of constant and variable coupling, voice the saxophones in close or open position.

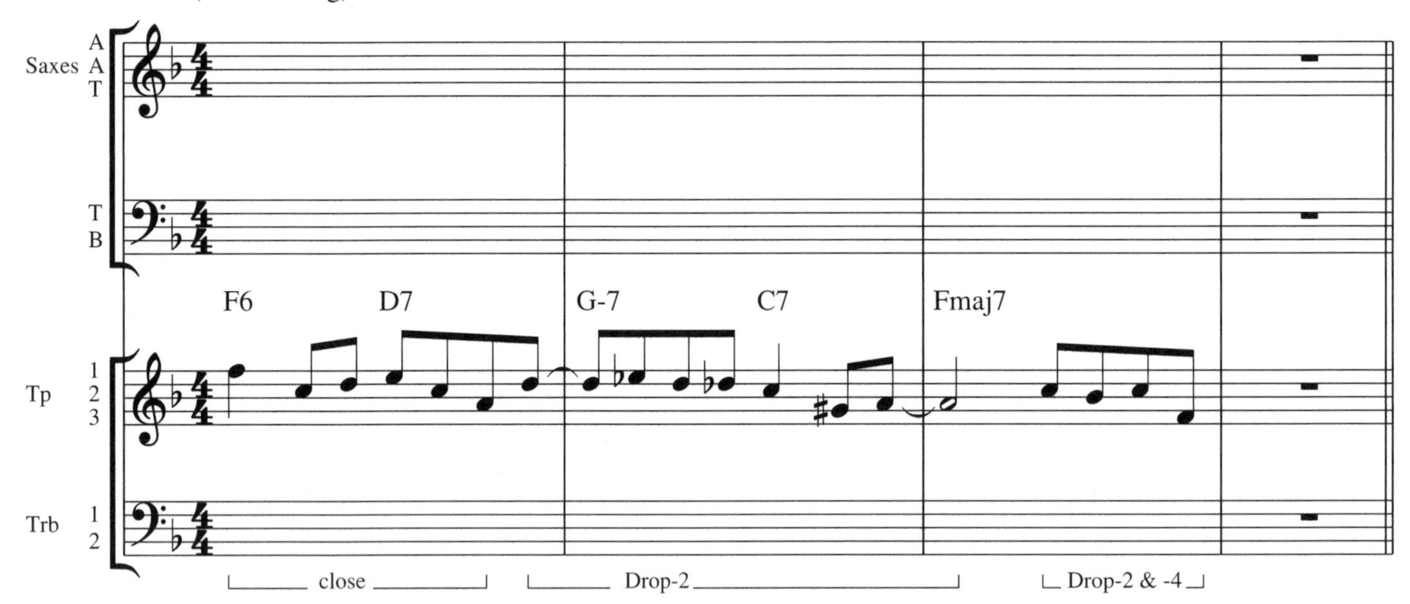

4. For a 7&5 ensemble, voice the brass in close or open position. Then add the saxophones using constant and/or variable coupling.

(Med. Swing)

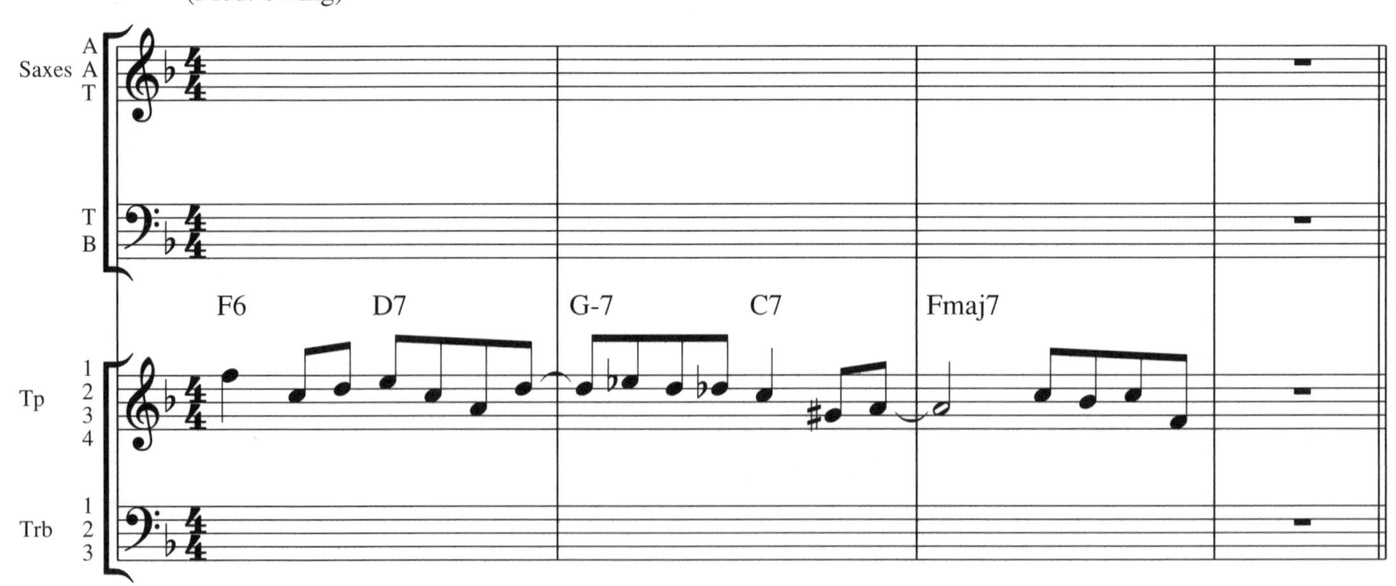

CHAPTER 4 Spread Voicings

IN THIS CHAPTER

4-1 Procedure

An arranger uses spread voicings, also known as pads, to add depth, fullness, or bottom to the sound of a big band. In contrast to mechanical voicings that are "hung" below the lead note, spreads are built up from the bottom note, which is always the root (or the note indicated, if there is an inversion) of the chord. Because "bottom" is a fundamental characteristic of spreads, the root is usually assigned to the baritone sax, bass trombone, or any other instrument that can play with conviction in the bottom of the bass-clef range.

The ideal range for roots of spread voicings is shown below.

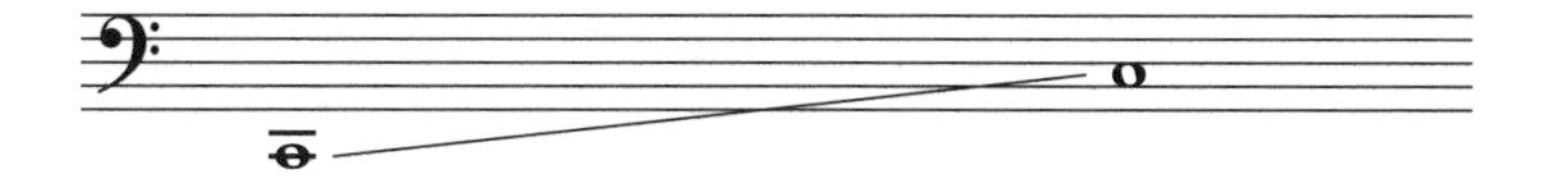

Spreads are often used to harmonize inactive or percussive melodies. Arrangers also use them frequently for backgrounds.

Before including spreads in your big band arrangements, you should know how to create and apply five-part spread voicings in smaller ensembles. For a full discussion of that subject, see *Modern Jazz Voicings* (Berklee Press, 2001).

In writing for large ensembles, the musical effect of a spread voicing is determined by:

- the number of different pitches
- the spacing of the notes
- the number of dissonant intervals
- the number of doublings (octaves or unisons)
- the distance from the top note to the bottom note
- the orchestration

We will look closely at each of these factors.

1. Number of different pitches

The greater the number of different pitches in the voicing, the greater the density.

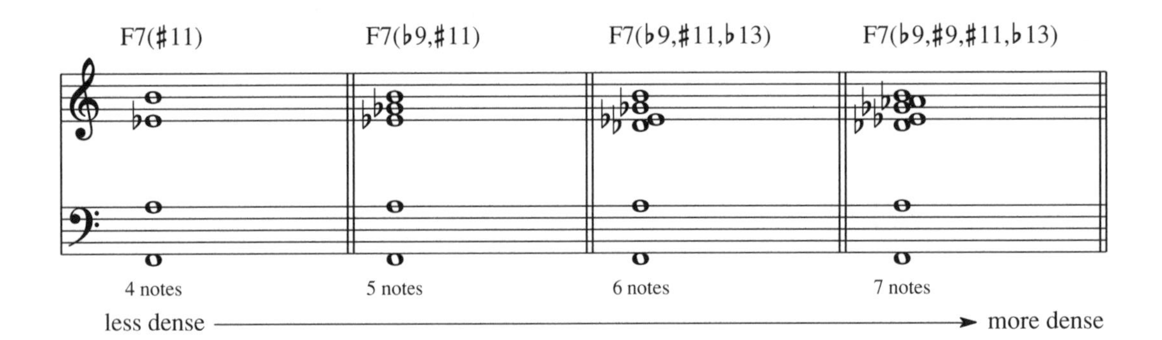

2. Spacing of the notes

The larger the intervals, the more open the sound. The smaller the intervals, the more dense the sound. The interval between the bottom two voices is critical: A tenth creates resonance; other wide intervals such as ninths, sevenths, sixths, and fifths may also work, but they are not as resounding.

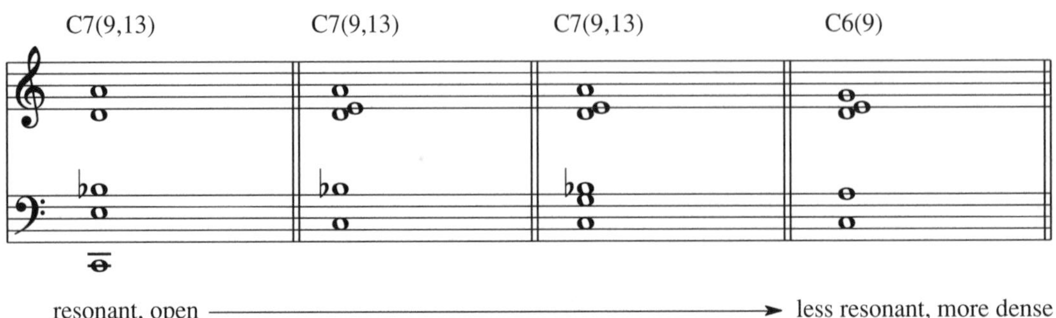

3. Number of dissonant intervals

The more ninths, sevenths, and seconds are used, the greater the dissonance and tension. The same is true for compound displacements of these intervals such as fourteenths, sixteenths, and so on.

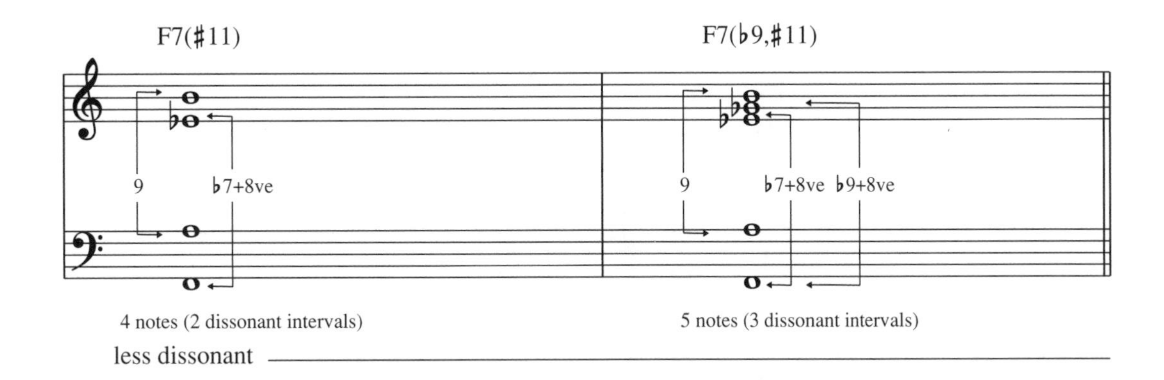

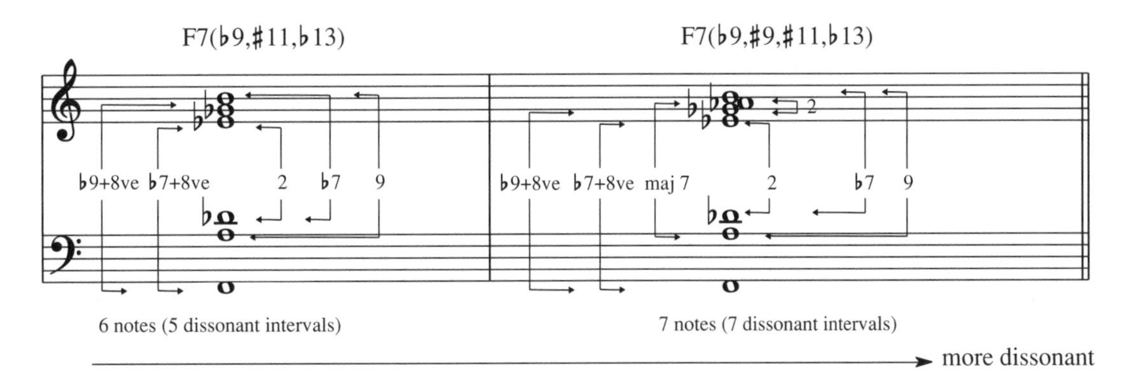

4. Number of doublings

The more doubling of notes (octaves or unisons) within the voicing, the fuller, heavier the orchestral effect. The thirteen-part voicing below includes nine doublings, creating a substantial sound.

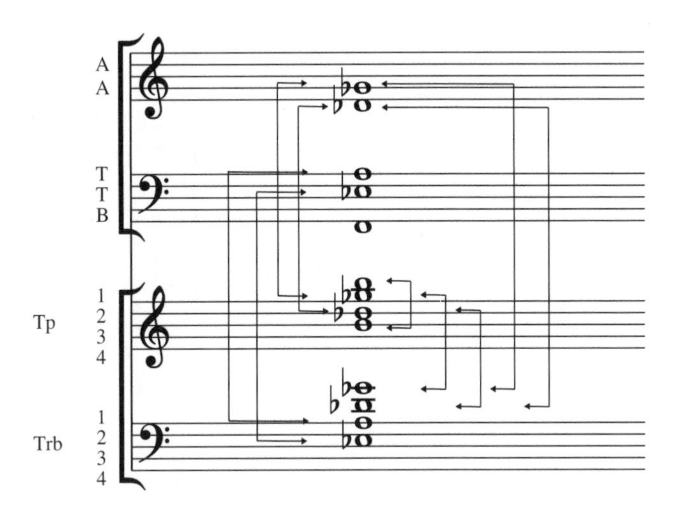

5. Distance from top to bottom

The greater the distance between the top and bottom notes, the more opportunity there is to include doublings and thereby create a powerful sound. A distance of three octaves and a minor sixth made it possible to include the nine doublings in the previous example.

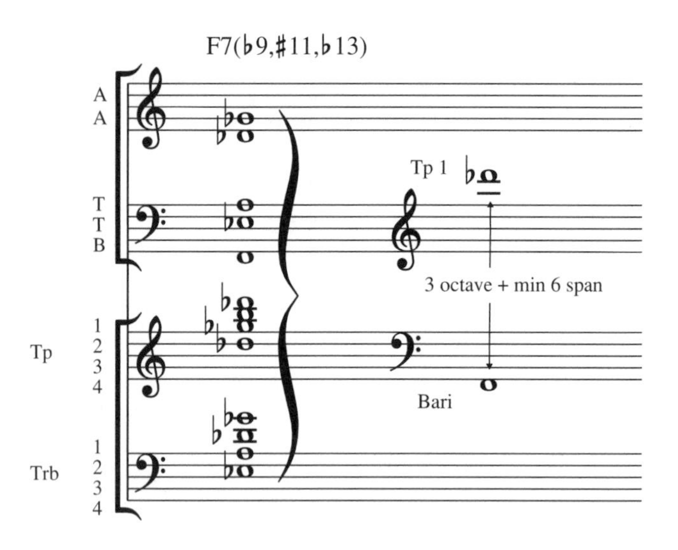

6. Orchestration

Because of each instrument's individual timbral characteristics and variations over registers, your choice of which ones to include and where to assign them within the spread will greatly affect the overall sound. Woodwinds will not be as strong as brass, for example, and low trumpets will not be as strong as high trumpets.

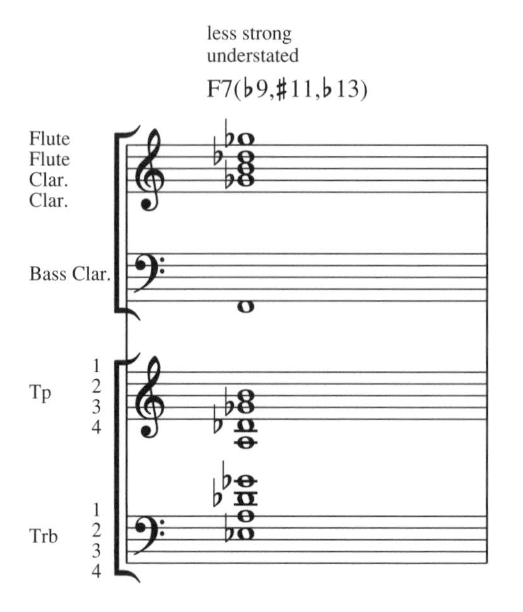

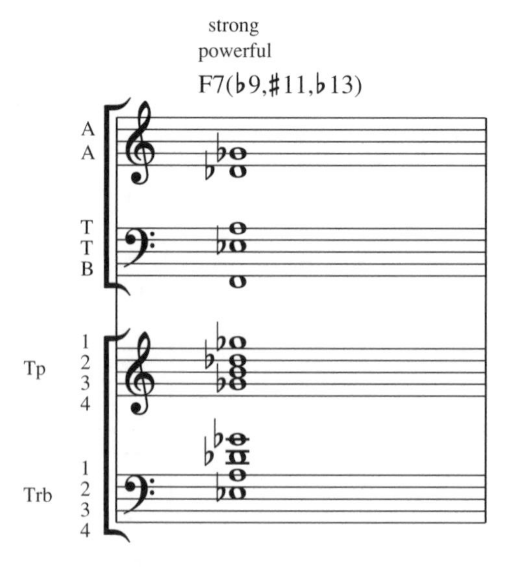

4-2 Spreads for 4&4 and 5&5

Five-Part Spread for 4&4 Under Unison Melody

In this example, we combine the trombone with the four saxes to create five-part spread voicings. Some of the spread lines are embellished slightly for more melodic motion between chords. The trumpets play the melody in unison.

28

Concerted Melody for 5&5 with Five-Part Spread

In this example, an inactive melody is concerted using five-part close voicings in the brass above a foundation of five-part spread voicings in the saxophones.

29

4-3 Tutti Writing Using Spreads

If you are writing a concerted passage for an active lead line with lots of eighth notes and sixteenth notes, spread voicings are impractical. Being full and bottom-heavy, they are not suited to quick movements.

The solution is tutti writing. In tutti writing, an active melody scored in unison and/or octaves is supported below by spread voicings arranged in a less active rhythm. The spreads align with the melody's rhythm at its strongest accent points, or "kicks."

Although we focus on spreads in this section, it is also possible to use supportive voicings other than spreads when writing tutti passages. Such voicings would play the same accenting role as spreads, but they would not supply the same depth. Once you have mastered all the voicing techniques discussed in this book, it is up to you to decide which one best produces the musical effect you want.

Five-Part Spread for 5&5

In this 5&5 example, the brass section has the melody in octaves and the saxophone section plays five-part spread voicings as support.

30

Eight-Part Spread for 7&5

In this 7&5 example, the alto and tenor saxophones play the melody in octaves while the baritone sax joins with the brass section in eight-part spread voicings.

31

Mixed-Timbre Spread for 8&5

In this 8&5 example, mixed-timbre combinations create a more complex orchestral sound, de-emphasizing the sectional role of trumpets, trombones, and saxophones.

32

Beyond Standard Orchestration

So far, our strategies for orchestrating voicings of all kinds have stressed scoring the brass first using complete chord sound and then adding the saxophones by doubling selected notes in the brass voicing. With this approach, the saxophone section simply reinforces the sound.

As an alternative, an arranger may score a voiced passage with a mixed group of saxes and brass, as we did in the example above. In this mixed-timbre approach, the saxes and brass have equal responsibility for producing the sound of the chord. Balance and blend are more difficult to control, but the resulting variety is worth the effort.

4-4 Exercises

1. Harmonize this percussive melody for the 5&5 instrumentation indicated using spread voicings.

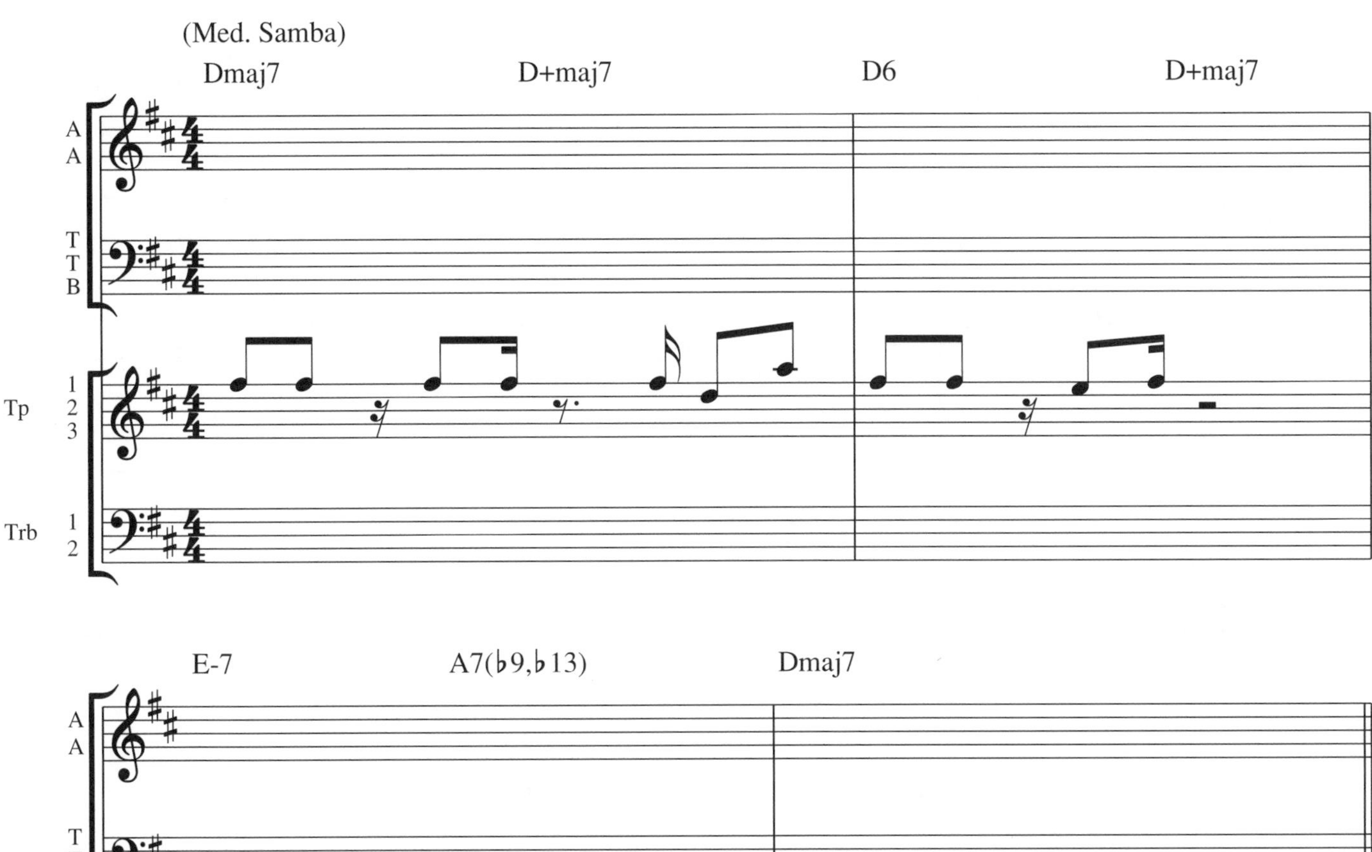

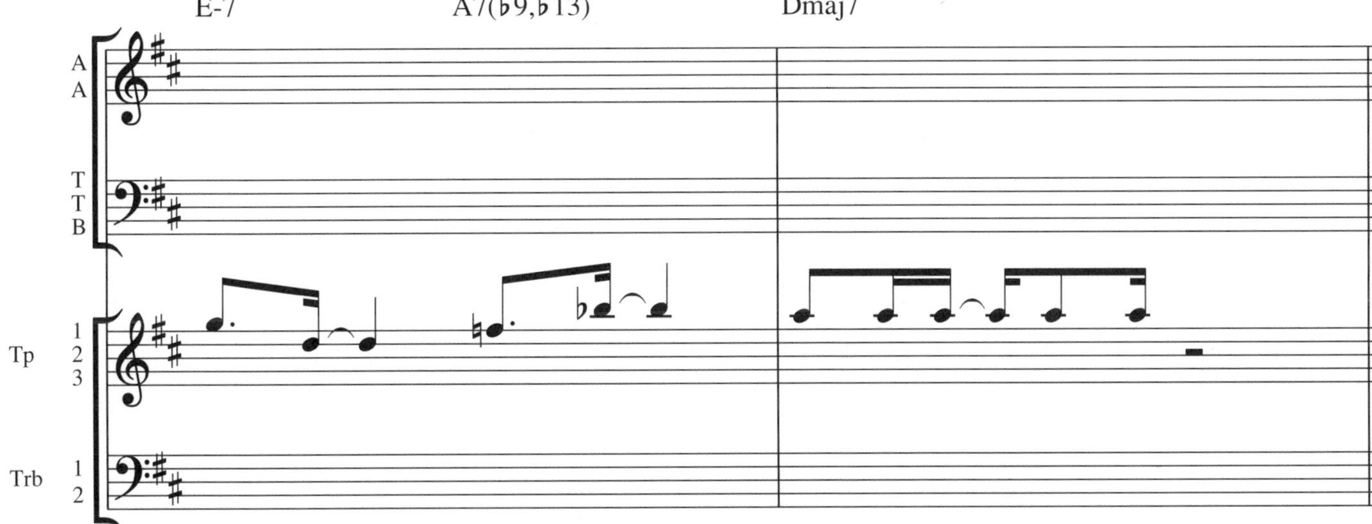

2. Support the alto saxophone solo line with sustained spread voicings. Embellish the spreads as appropriate and be sure to use all instruments indicated in this 7&5 ensemble.

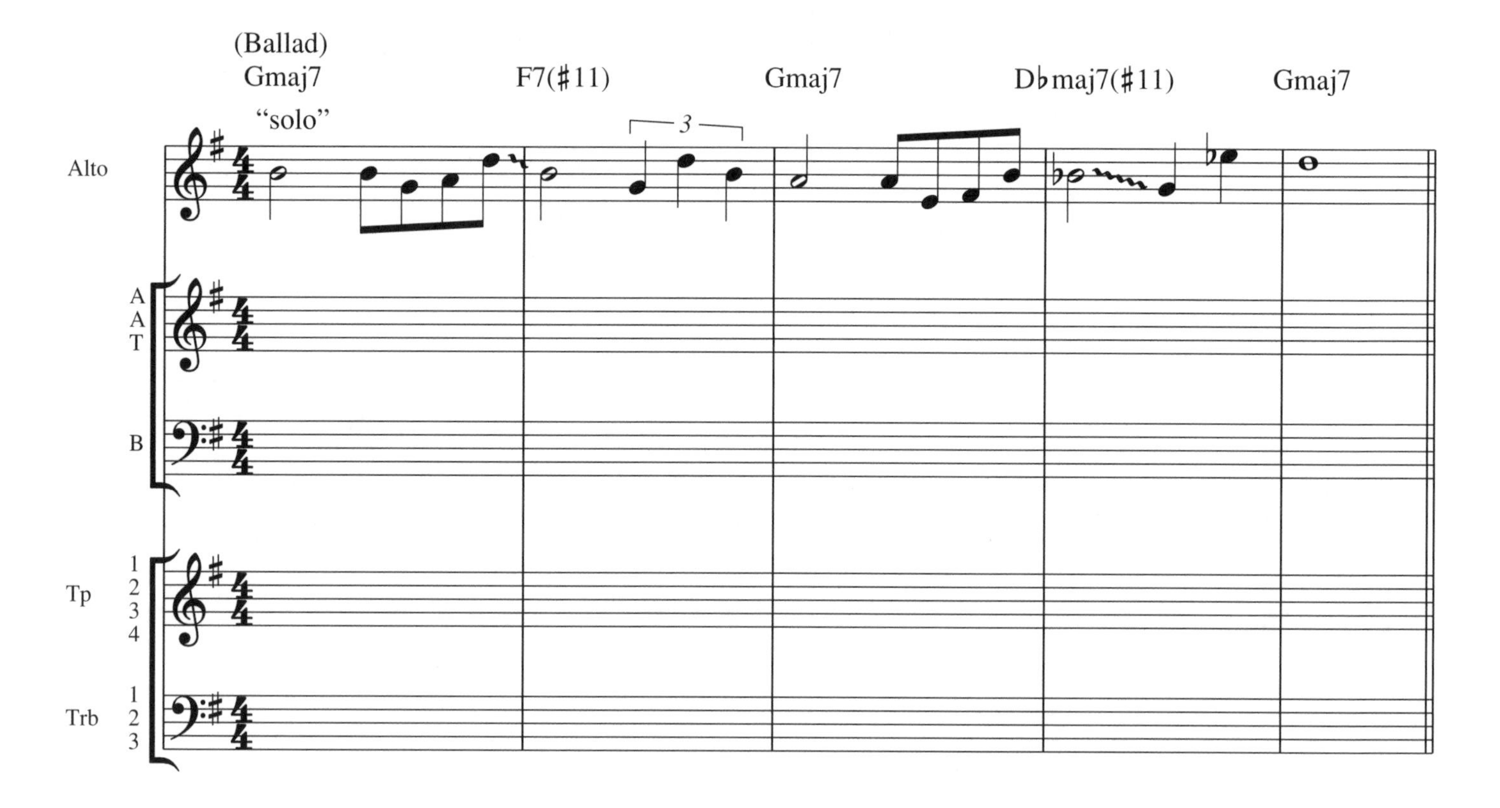

3. For this 8&5 big band, score the melody using tutti writing. Use spreads as the supporting voicings.

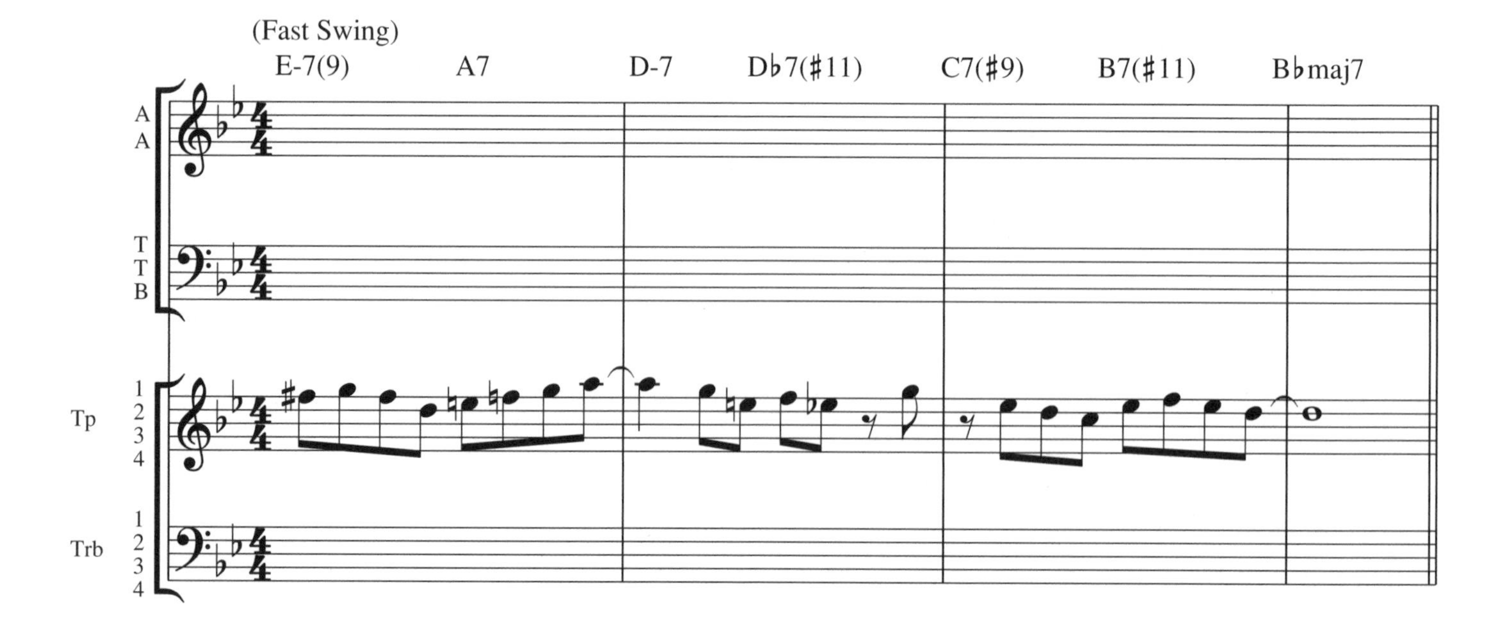

CHAPTER 5 Voicings in Fourths

IN THIS CHAPTER

In this chapter and the two that follow, we consider so-called non-mechanical voicings. Unlike mechanical voicings, whose spacing of notes rely on intervals of a third, these voicings are based on fourths, upper structure triads, and clusters (intervals of a second). They offer the arranger the opportunity to create sounds that are different from and potentially more colorful than the traditional, "tertial" quality of mechanical voicings. As with mechanical voicings, the choice of which notes to double in these non-mechanical voicings is an important consideration. This is especially true as the size of the ensemble expands to include eight horns or more. For a detailed explanation of constructing non-mechanical voicings and applying them to small ensembles, see *Modern Jazz Voicings* (Berklee Press, 2001).

5-1 Procedure for Voicings in Fourths

The predominant interval between adjacent notes in these voicings is a perfect fourth. The resulting even spacing and openness makes voicings in fourths resonant and mildly dissonant.

To construct a voicing in fourths for a large ensemble, begin by voicing the brass section down from the melody using notes of the appropriate chord scale and spaced a fourth apart. Be careful to keep lead instruments within suggested range limits. If the brass section is large (as in a 7&5) and fourths cannot fit in the lower part of the voicing, choose notes that support the chord sound—3, 6, or 7 of the chord.

(The airy nature of voicings in fourths raises special considerations for the trumpet section. Be sure to place the lead trumpet high enough so that the bottom trumpet parts are not forced too low in the register. Below the concert *b-flat* below middle *c*, the trumpet has difficulty projecting, which may throw off the section's balance.)

Next, before scoring the saxophones, consider how much "depth" you want in the voicing. The higher you place the lead alto within the brass voicing, the more high-register doublings you will create. This generates a high-timbre quality with relatively little depth. The lower you place the lead alto within the brass voicing, the more lower-register doublings will result, projecting a low-timbre quality with more depth. Score the saxophones in a spread voicing that contains fourths at the top of the spread. If the brass voicing is incomplete, have the saxophones complete the chord sound by filling in the defining notes, 3, 6, or 7.

The following examples show various ways to create voicings in fourths for big bands of different sizes. For each configuration, we recommend an appropriate range for the lead trumpet.

For 4&4

The suggested lead trumpet range is:

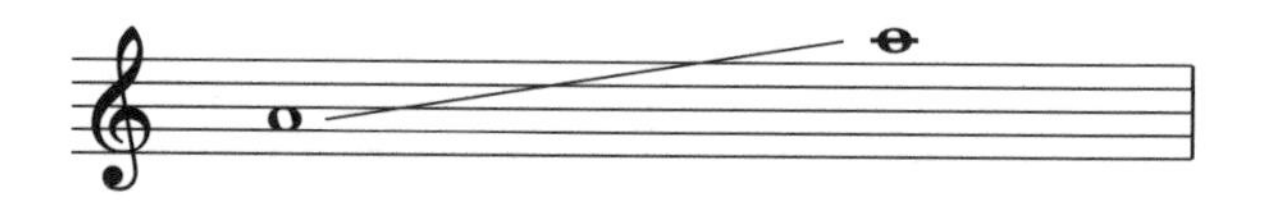

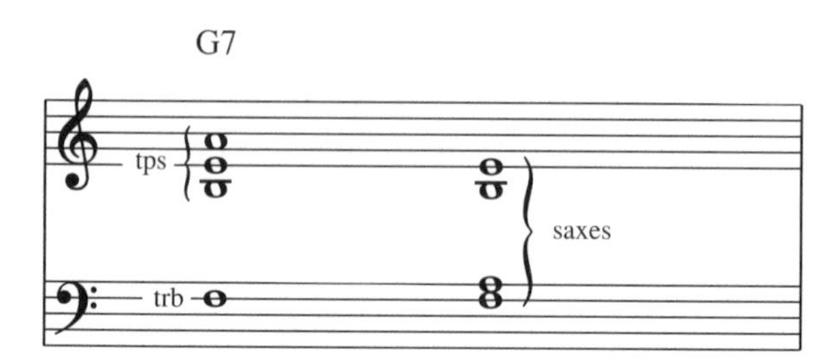

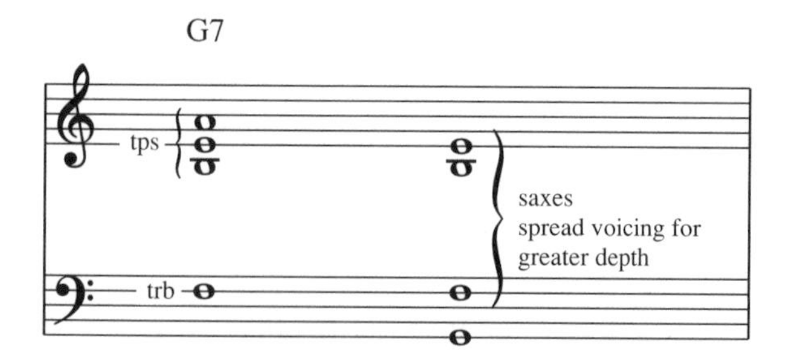

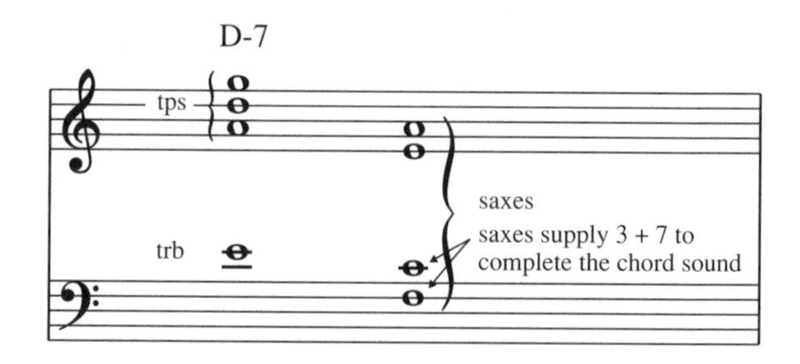

For 5&5

The suggested lead trumpet range is:

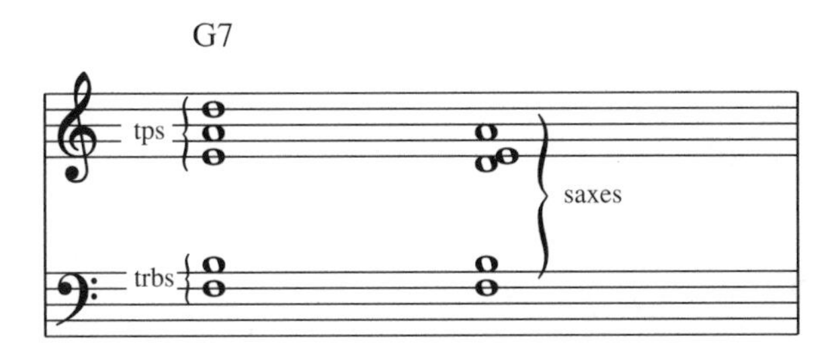

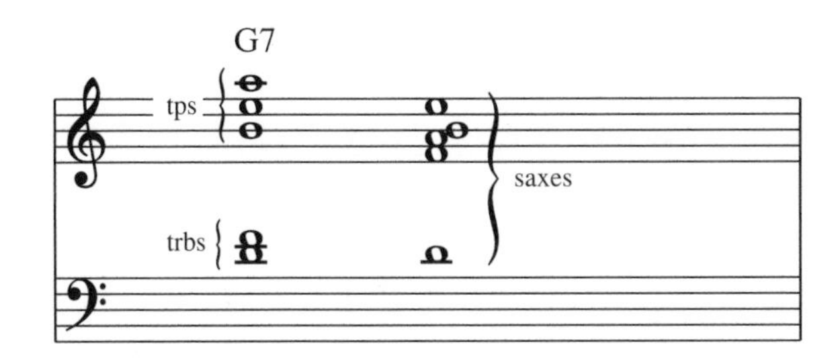

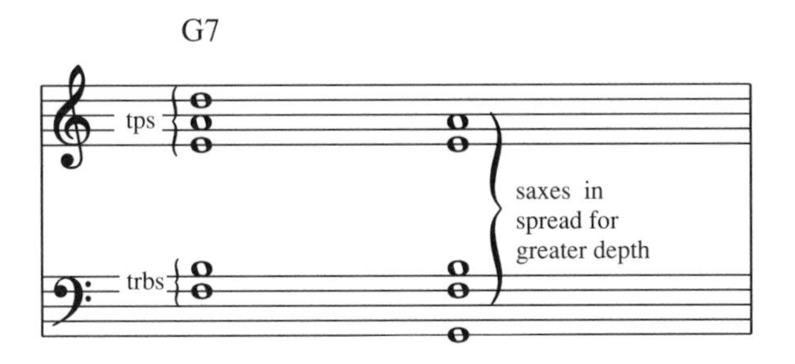

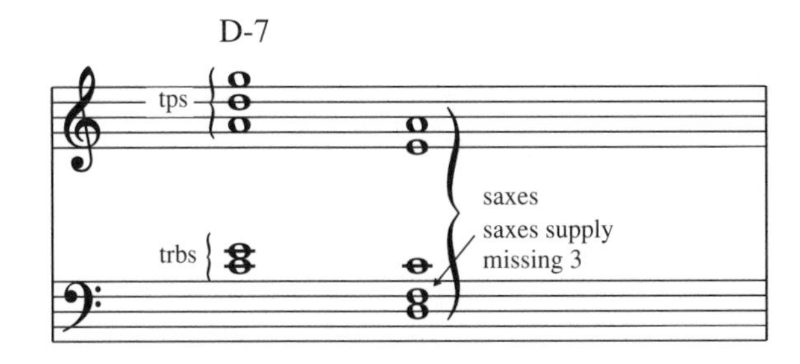

For 7&5

The suggested lead trumpet range is:

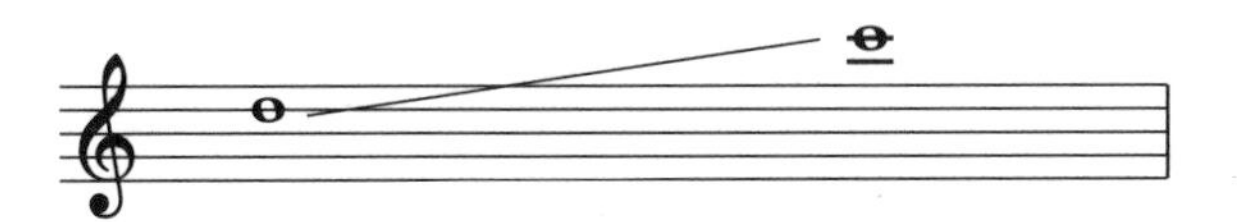

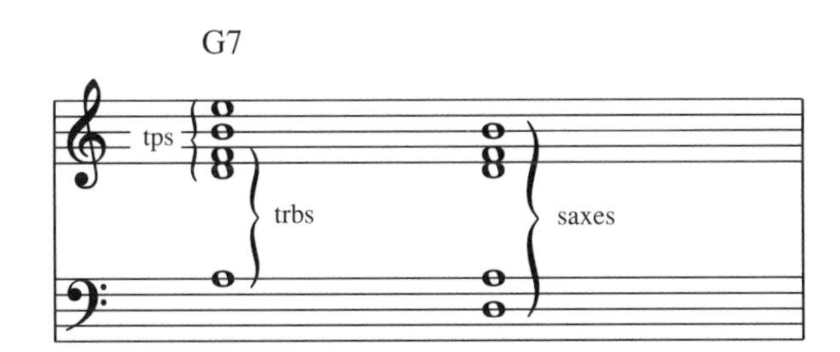

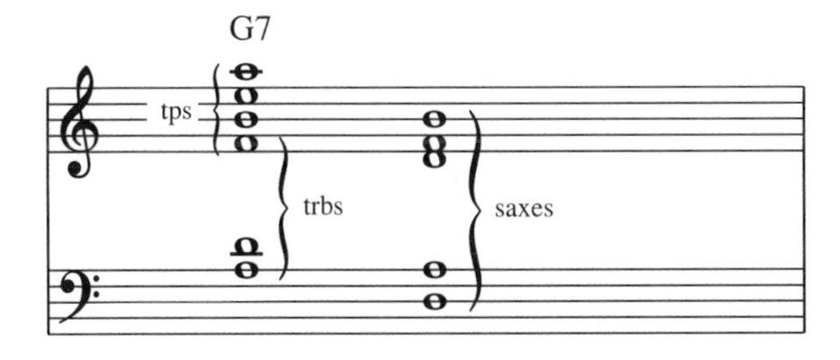

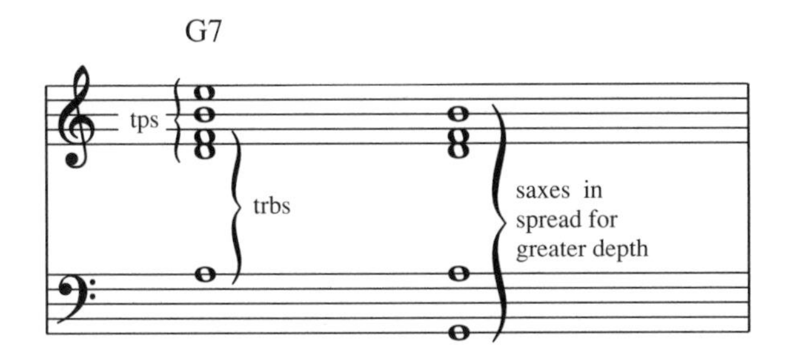

For 8&5

The suggested lead trumpet range is:

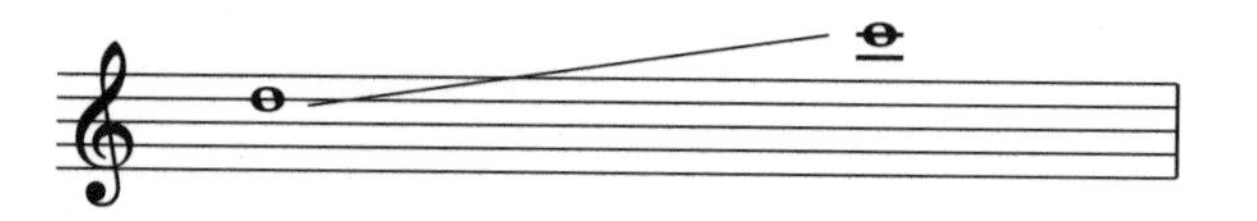

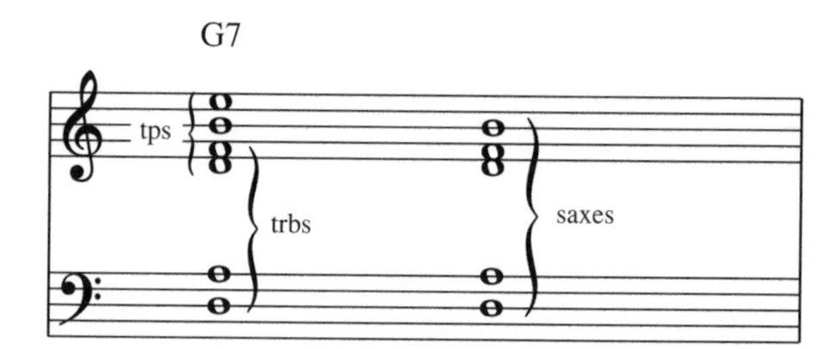

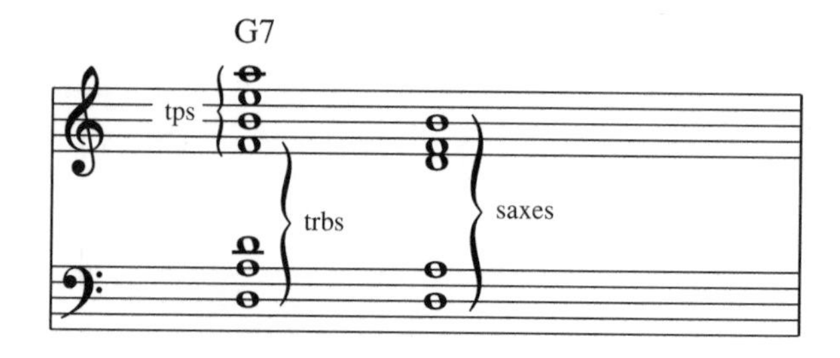

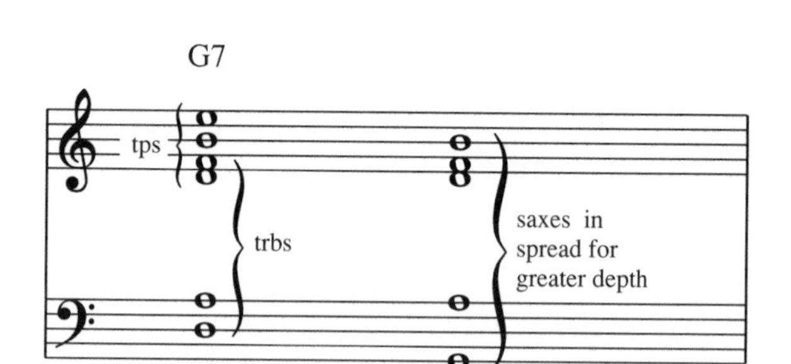

5-2 Sample Passages Voiced in Fourths

4&4 Concerted Writing Using Fourths

The following example shows a concerted passage voiced in fourths for a 4&4 ensemble.

33

5&5 Tutti Using Fourths

In this tutti passage for 5&5, the two altos play the melody in unison while the five brass and three lower saxophones are scored in supportive voicings in fourths.

34

7&5 Concerted Melody Using Fourths

35

In this example for a 7&5 band, the C Dorian melody is concerted using voicings in fourths.

8&5 Subdivided and Concerted Melody Using Fourths

In this passage for 8&5, the D Dorian melody is initially subdivided between the brass scored in fourths and the saxes scored in octaves. Then in the last measure, the melody is concerted using voicings in fourths for all the horns. Note that several of the brass voicings are incomplete—that is, missing the chord tones 3 or 7. When adjacent to complete voicings or when used in a modal phrase such as this, they sound fine.

36

5-3 Exercises

Write your own melody to the following chord progression, making sure it is suitable for voicings in fourths. That means you should be able to score emphasized melody notes in fourths while at the same time producing a complete chord sound. Refer to Chapter 5 of *Modern Jazz Voicings* (Berklee Press, 2001) for examples. Score the melody for 4&4, 5&5, 7&5, and 8&5 as directed.

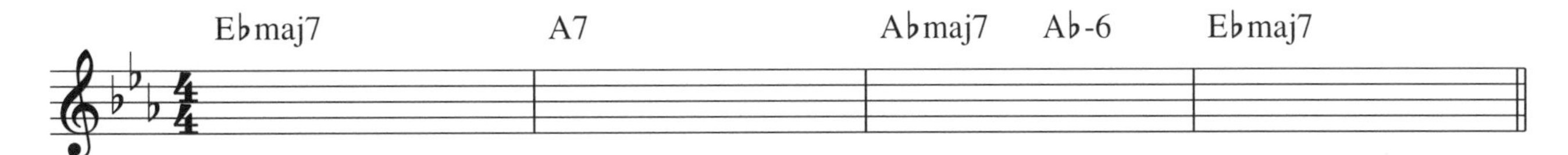

1. Score your melody using voicings in fourths for 4&4.

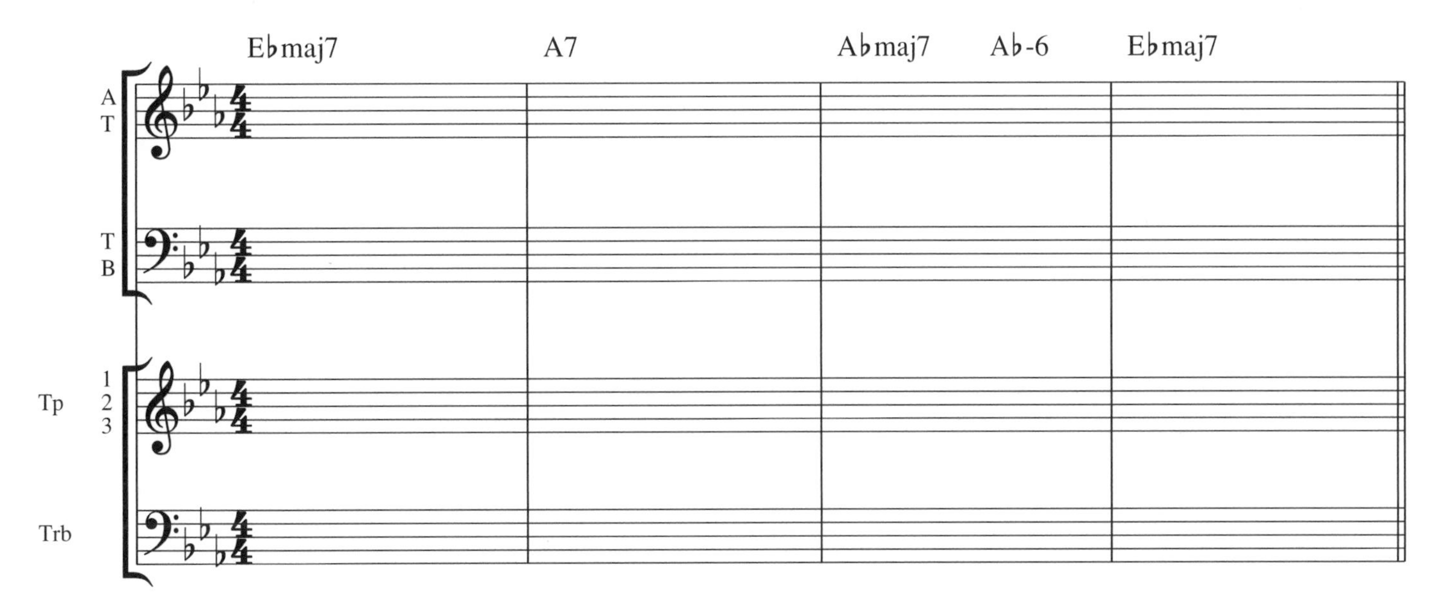

2. Score your melody using voicings in fourths for 5&5.

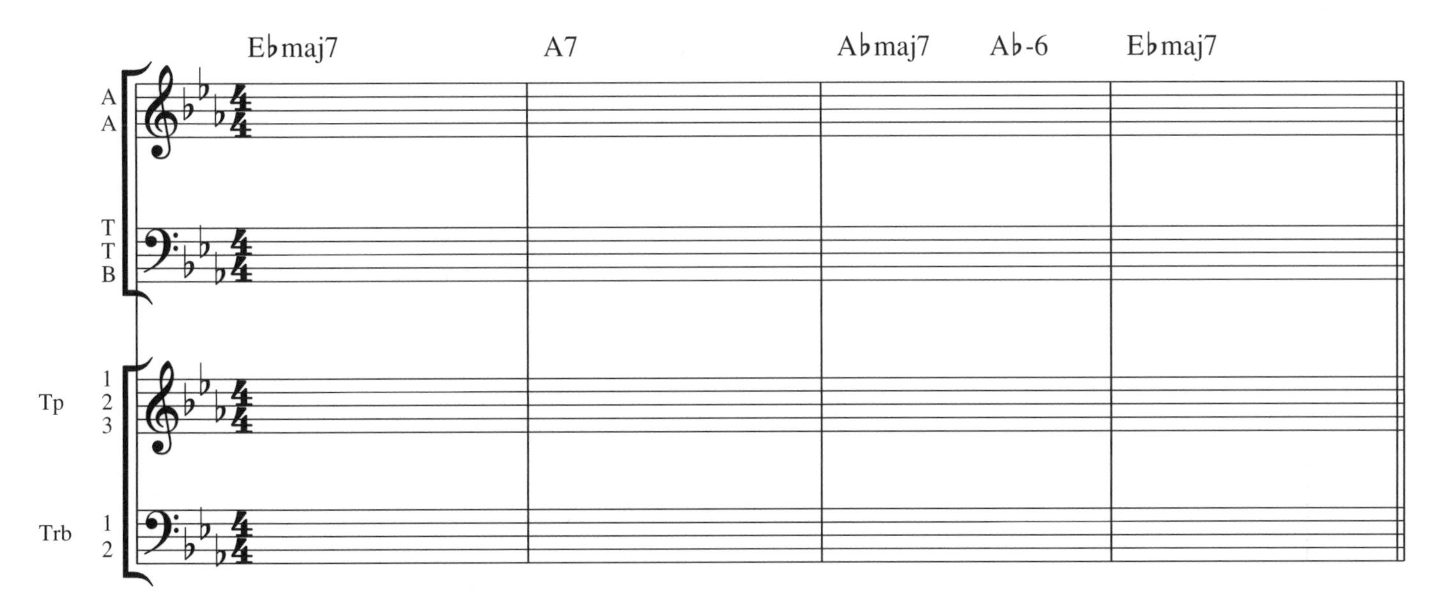

3. Score your melody using voicings in fourths for 7&5.

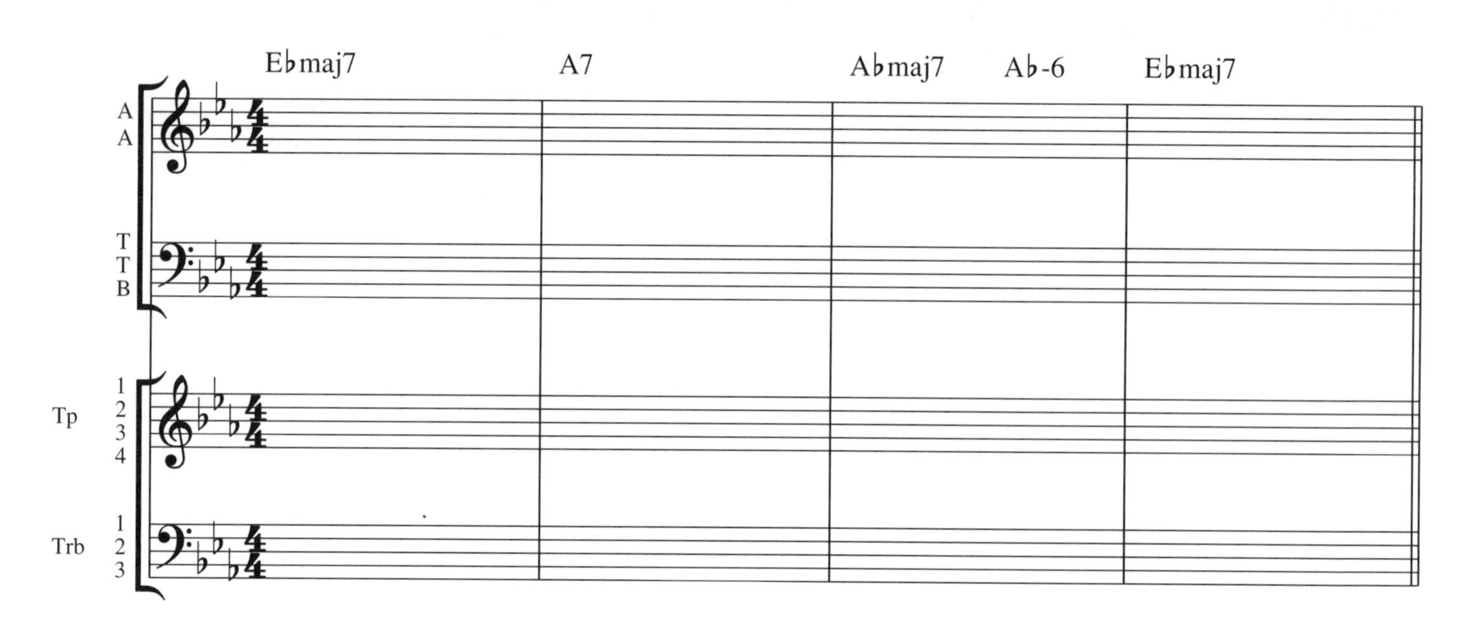

4. Score your melody using voicings in fourths for 8&5.

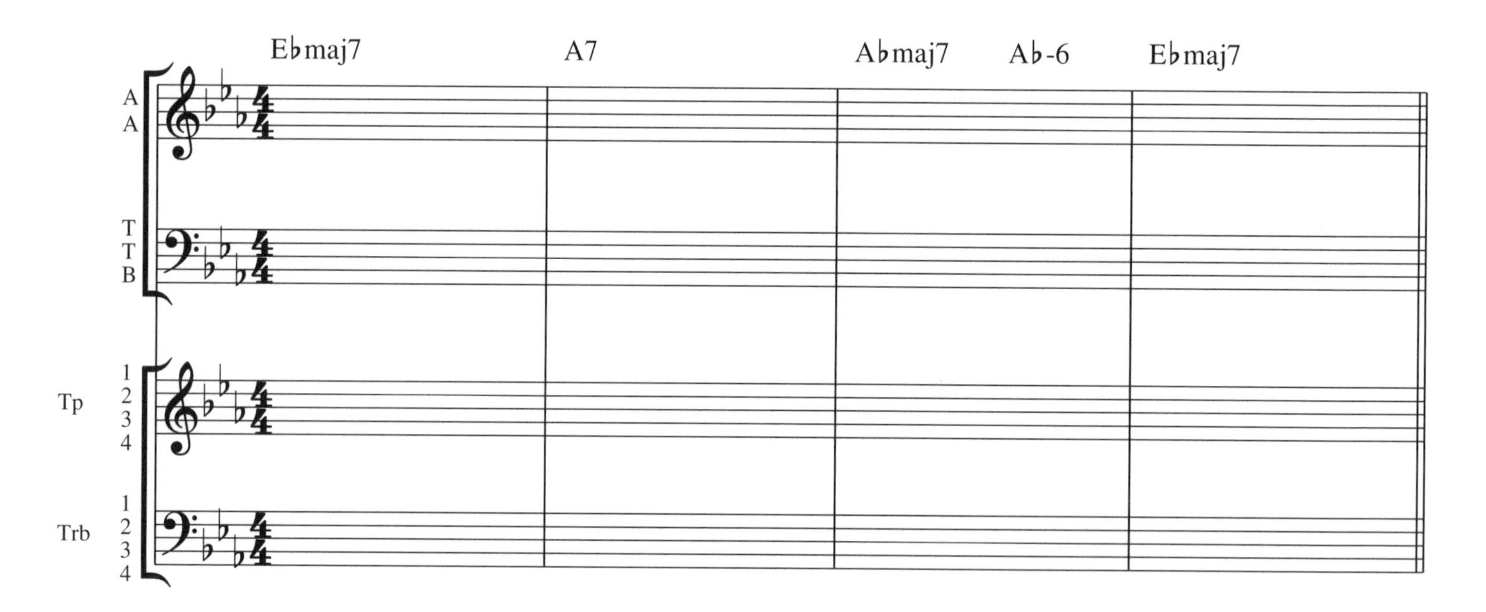

CHAPTER 6
Upper Structure Triad Voicings

IN THIS CHAPTER

6-1 Procedure

An upper structure triad voicing projects two personalities. First is the sound representing the given chord symbol. In addition, there is the harmonic quality produced by a distinct triad (or an inversion of it) at the top of the voicing. Use upper-structure triads when you want to create a powerful impression with considerable resonance. For basic principles and examples of constructing upper structure triad voicings for three, four, five, and six parts, see Chapter 7 of *Modern Jazz Voicings* (Berklee Press, 2001).

The following examples show how to construct upper structure triad voicings for big bands of various sizes, with suggested ranges for the lead trumpet in each case. The procedure varies slightly as the size of the band increases, but generally the trumpets are scored on the upper structure triad and the lower brass and/or saxophones provide chord-sound support.

For 4&4

In a 4&4 ensemble, the three trumpets play the upper structure triad in close position. The trombone provides chord-sound support by covering chord tones 3 or 7 (or 6 for sixth chords). Depending on the lead range and desired effect, the saxophones may be added either high or low in the brass voicing, doubling notes at the unison or octave. Alternatively, the saxophones may be scored with a spread voicing. If the chord sound is incomplete in the brass section (lacking the defining 3, 7, or 6), include the missing note in the sax voicing. The explanatory two-chord symbol in parentheses expresses the duality of the voicing; the upper structure triad is on top.

The suggested range for the lead trumpet is:

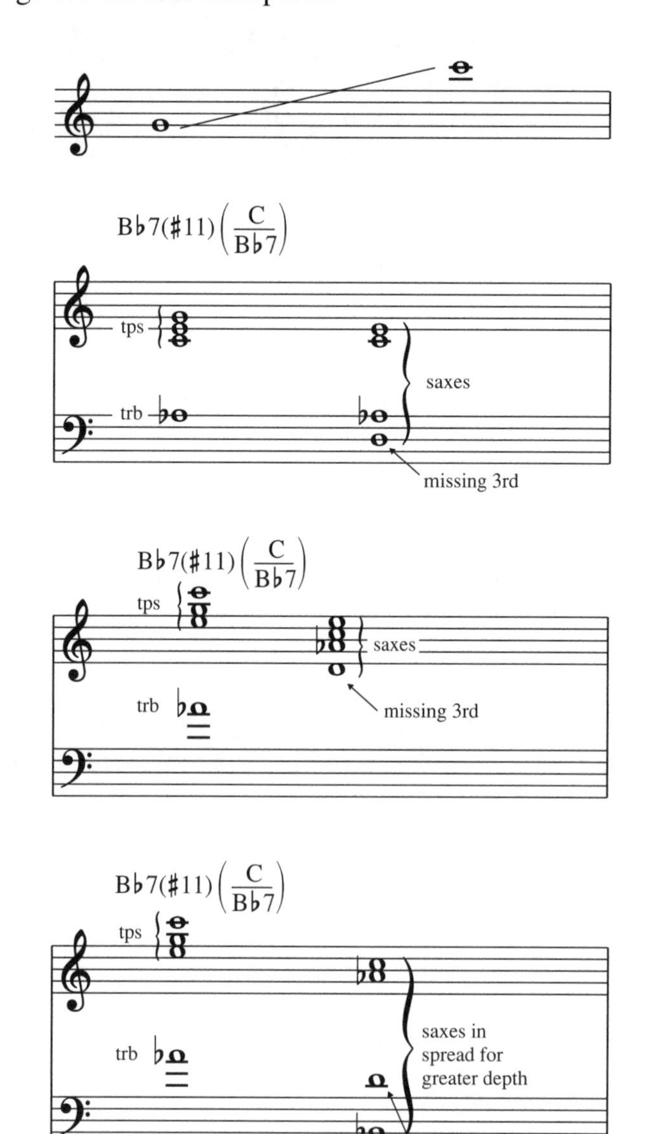

For 5&5

With a 5&5 group, the three trumpets have the upper structure triad (labeled as the top of the parenthetical chord symbol) while Trombones 1 and 2 define the primary chord sound by playing the important chord tones, usually 3 and 7. Depending on the lead range and desired effect, the saxophones may be added either high or low in the brass voicing, doubling notes at the unison or octave. Or they may be scored with a spread voicing.

The suggested range for the lead trumpet is:

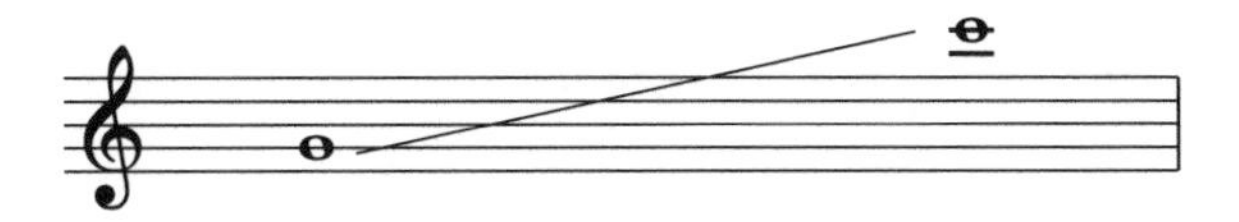

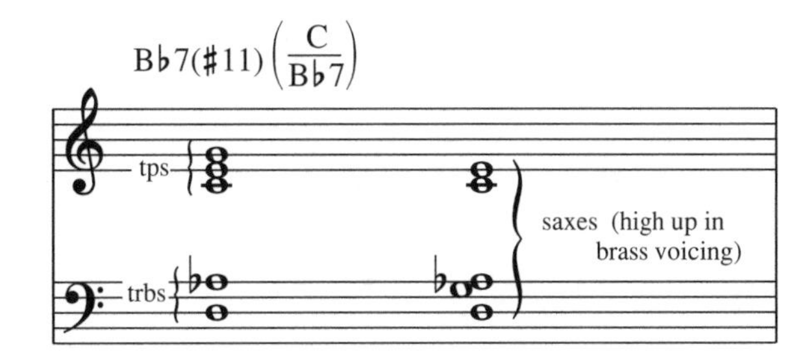

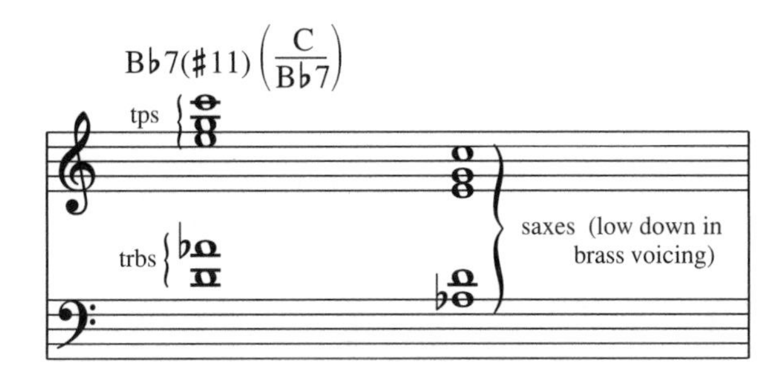

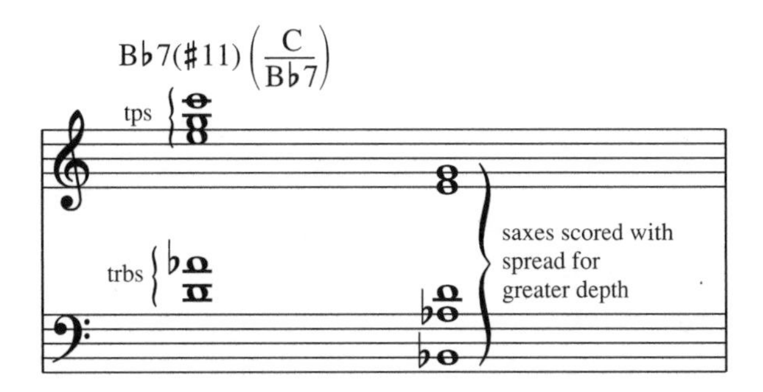

For 7&5

For a 7&5 ensemble, the top three trumpets play the upper structure triad in close position and the fourth trumpet doubles the lead an octave below. Depending on the lead range, Trombone 1 doubles one of the notes in the triad either in unison or an octave lower. Trombones 2 and 3 play defining chord tones, usually 3 and 7. Score the saxophone section with a spread voicing to provide strong harmonic support. With a group this size, it is not uncommon for the voicing to span four octaves.

The suggested range for the lead trumpet is:

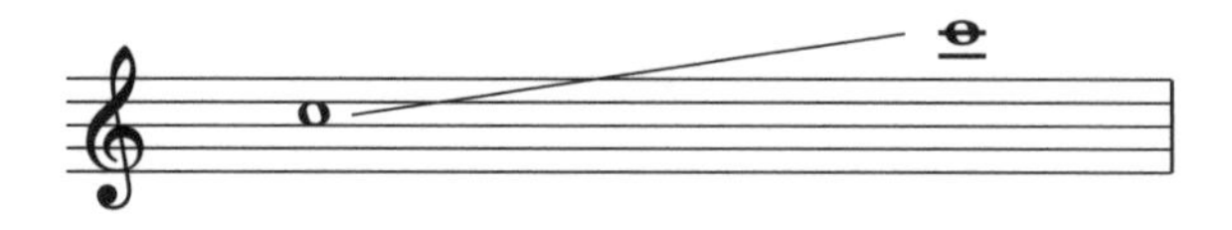

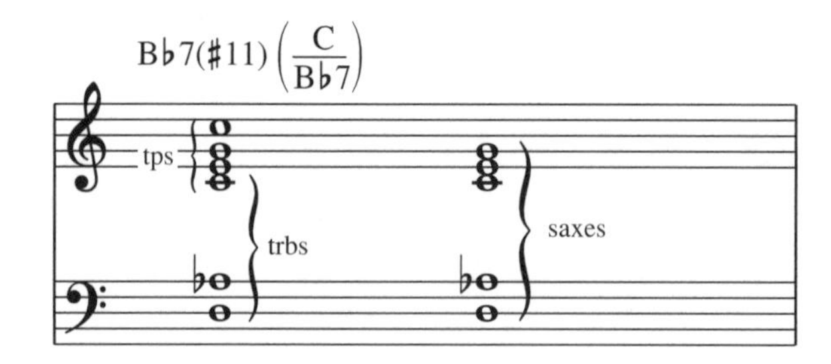

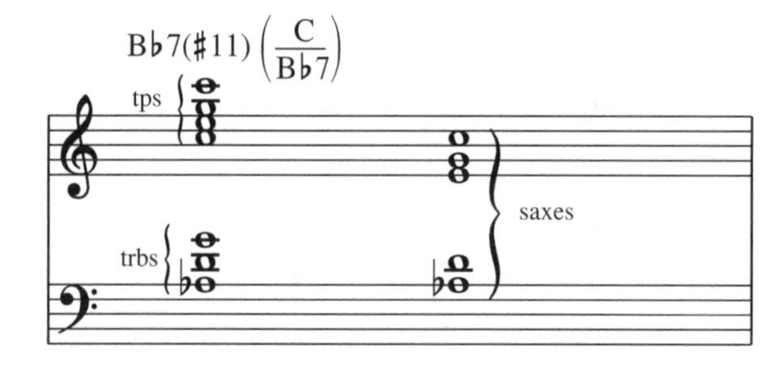

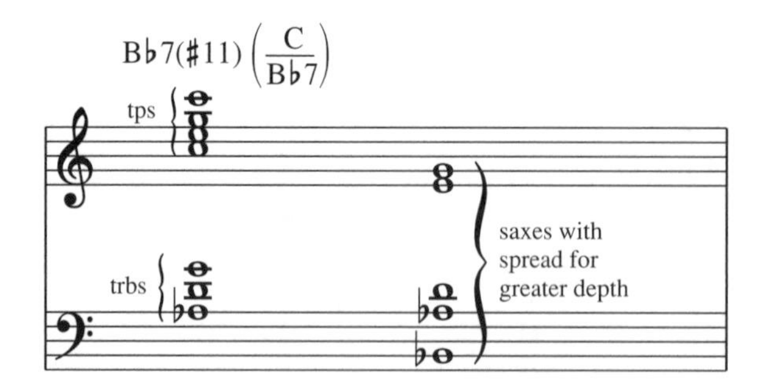

For 8&5

With an 8&5 band, you have more options. As in the 7&5 configuration, the top three trumpets have the upper structure triad in close position while the fourth doubles the lead an octave below. There are two possible approaches for the trombones. In the first case, Trombones 1 and 2 double two of the notes in the triad either in unison or an octave lower; Trombones 3 and 4 play defining chord tones. Alternatively, Trombone 4 (a bass trombone) may play the root, in which case Trombone 1 doubles one of the notes in the triad while Trombones 2 and 3 play the defining chord tones. The saxophone section usually has a spread voicing.

The suggested range for the lead trumpet is:

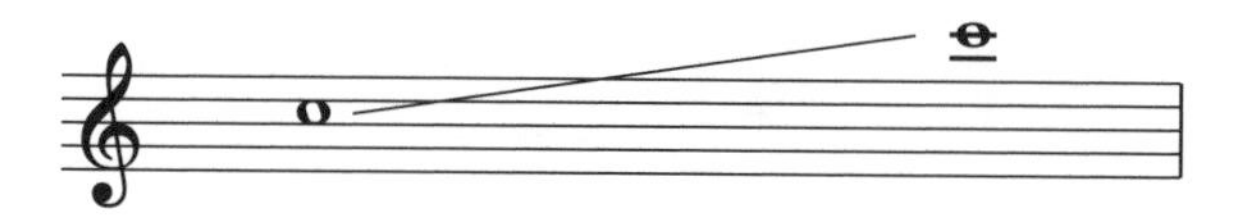

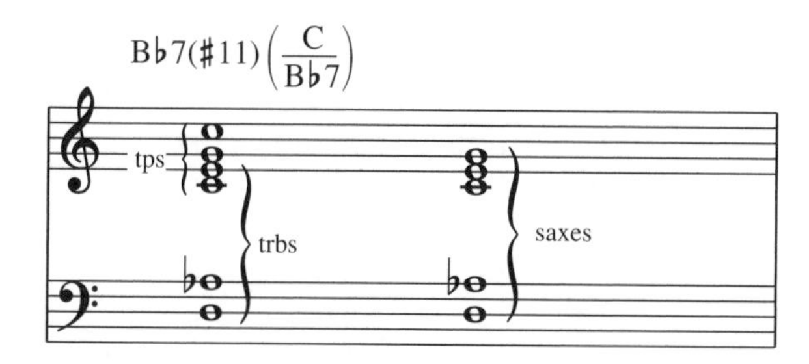

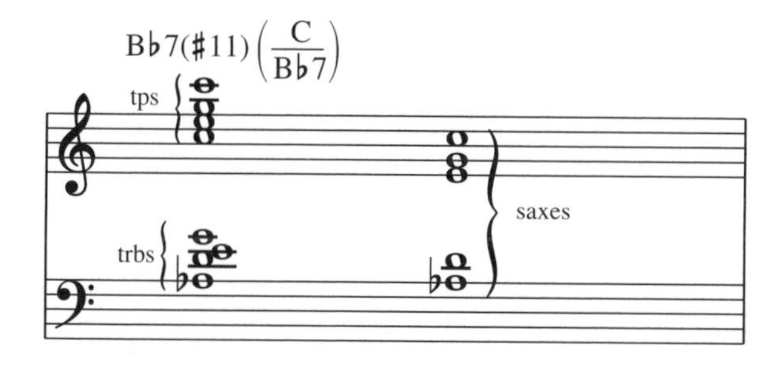

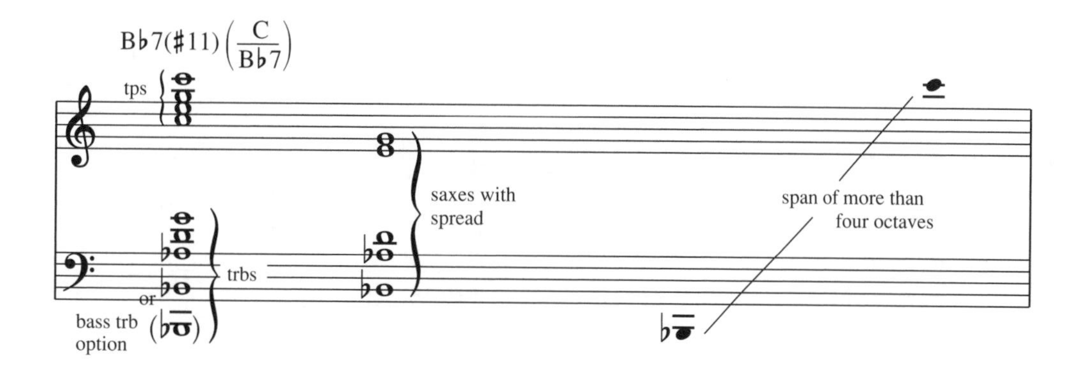

6-2 4&4 Upper Structure Triad Voicings

37

At the start of this 4&4 passage, an incomplete upper structure triad voicing in the brass sets up the saxophone melody, which is scored in octaves. The rest of the phrase, beginning in measure 2, is concerted using upper structure triads. Note how the baritone sax completes the chord sound—playing the 3 of F7 (*a*), the 7 of B♭7 (*a-flat*), and the 7 of F7 (*e-flat*)—while the other saxes double the triad.

(Medium funk)

A T T

B

Tp 1 2 3

Trb

Bass (sounding 8vb)

G/F7

Piano

A T T

B

Tp 1 2 3

Trb

Bass

C/B♭7

G/F7

Piano

6-3 5&5 Concerted with Supporting Spreads

In this 5&5 concerted passage, the top three saxophones and the top three brass play upper structure triad voicings, while the lower members of each section are scored in supporting spread voicings.

38

6-4 7&5 Reharmonized Melody

In the following 7&5 example, we embellish a portion of a melody from a lead sheet, then reharmonize it to include upper structure triad voicings.

Original lead sheet:

Embellished lead line, reharmonized using upper structure triads:

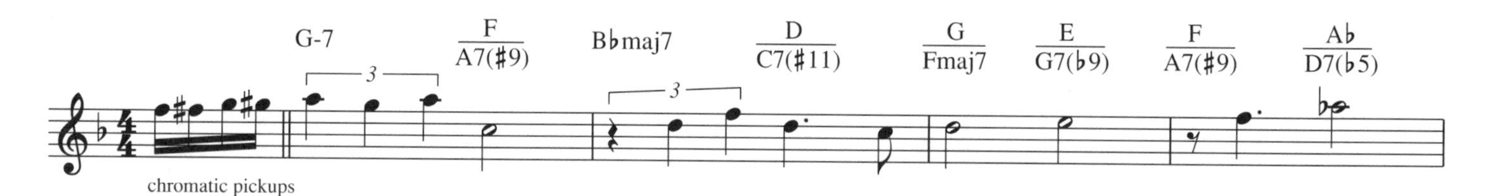

In the orchestration below, note the chromatic constant structure voicings for the pickups, the diatonic reharmonization in measure 1, and the voicing for the "and" of beat 4 in measure 2 that does not use an upper structure triad. This example uses both constant and variable coupling for the saxophone section.

39

6-5 8&5 Dominant Seventh Reharmonization

40

This 8&5 passage includes dominant seventh reharmonizations in measures 2 and 4. For each of these reharmonized chords, as for all the chords in this example, we use upper structure triad voicings. (See the following page for a closer analysis of measures 2 and 4.)

Notice that in measures 2 and 4, the dominant seventh reharmonizations result in the tritones (the intervals between 3 and 7 of the chords) being voice-led chromatically downward. This descending line creates motion independent from the melody.

Measure 2:

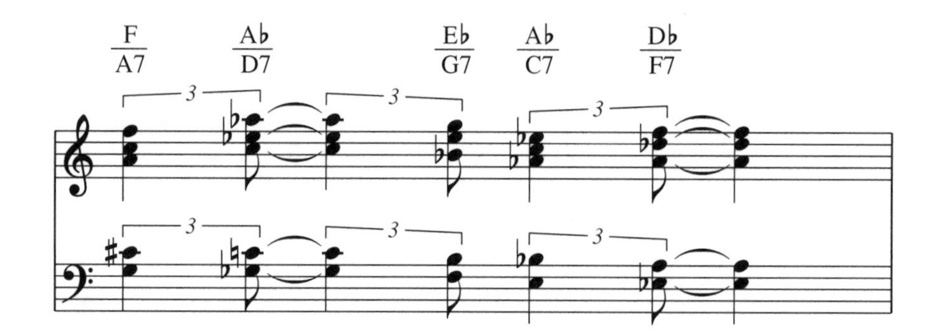

Measure 4:

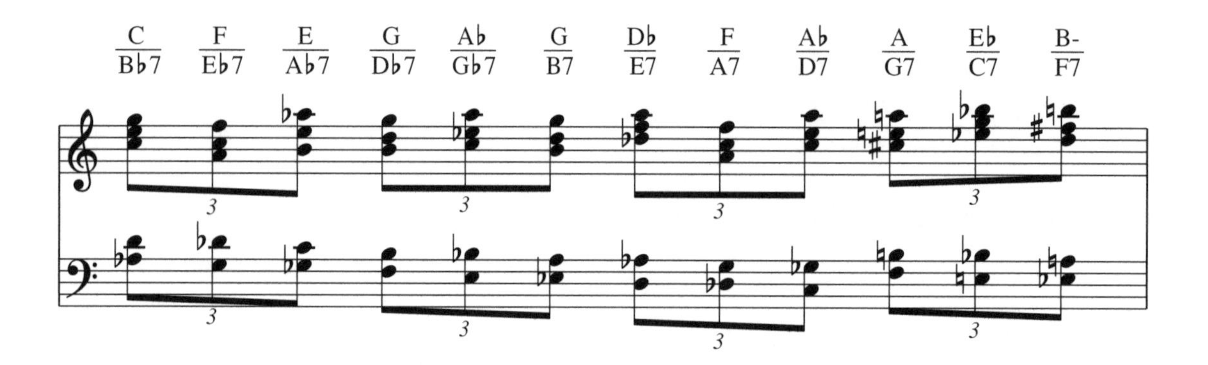

Note how the trombones and saxophones are aligned. Trombones 1 and 2 double two notes of the upper structure triad (in unison or octaves) while Trombones 3 and 4 play the descending tritones. Altos 1 and 2 and Tenor 1 double the triad (in unison or octaves) while Tenor 2 and the baritone sax double the descending tritones. Below we show each instrument's assignment on the downbeat of the fourth measure, where the primary chord is B♭7 and the upper structure triad is C.

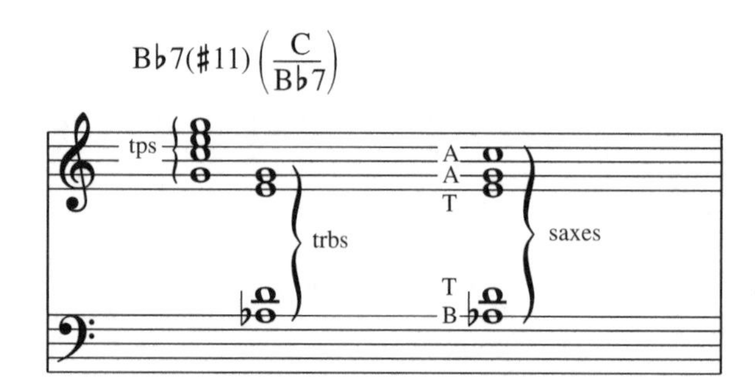

6-6 Exercises

1. Using the entire 7&5 instrumentation, score the following examples as indicated. ("UST" stands for upper structure triad.)

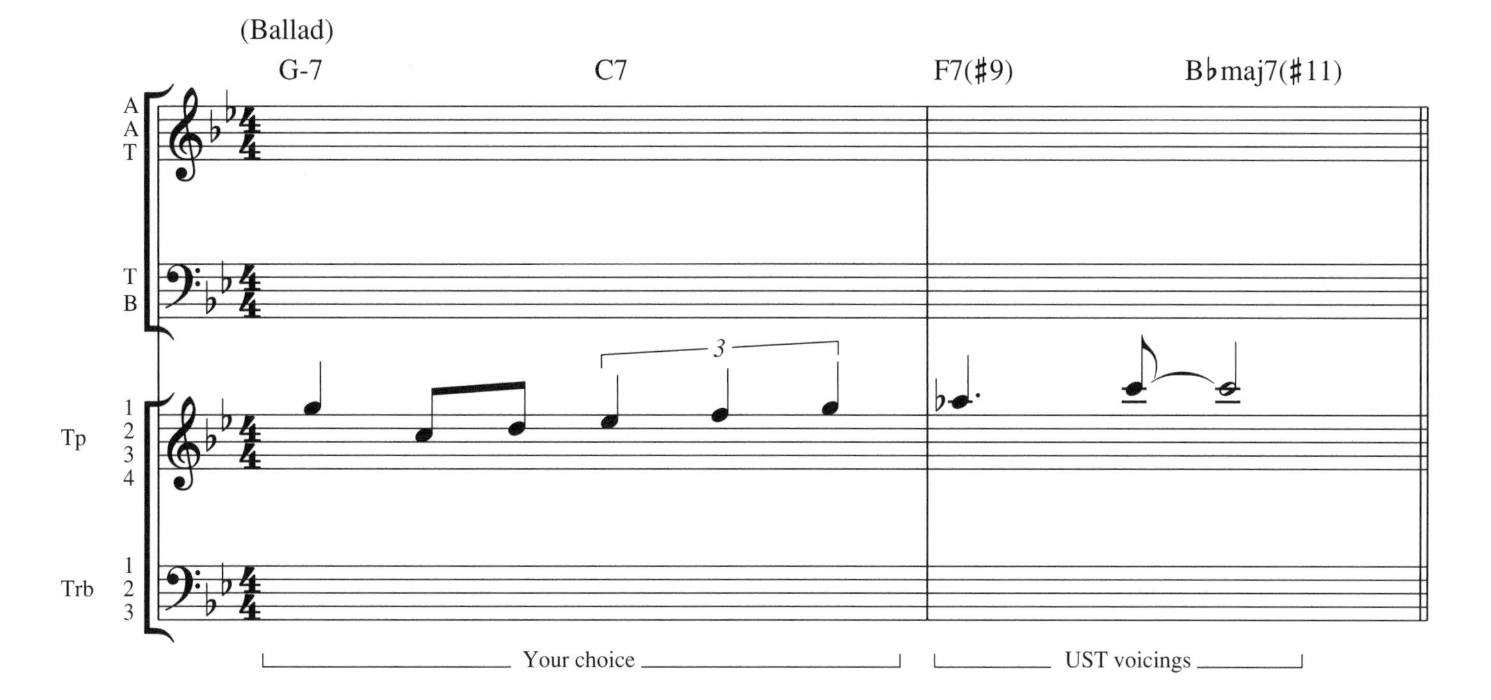

2. Using the entire 7&5 instrumentation, score the following examples as indicated.

3. Using the entire 7&5 instrumentation, score the following examples as indicated.

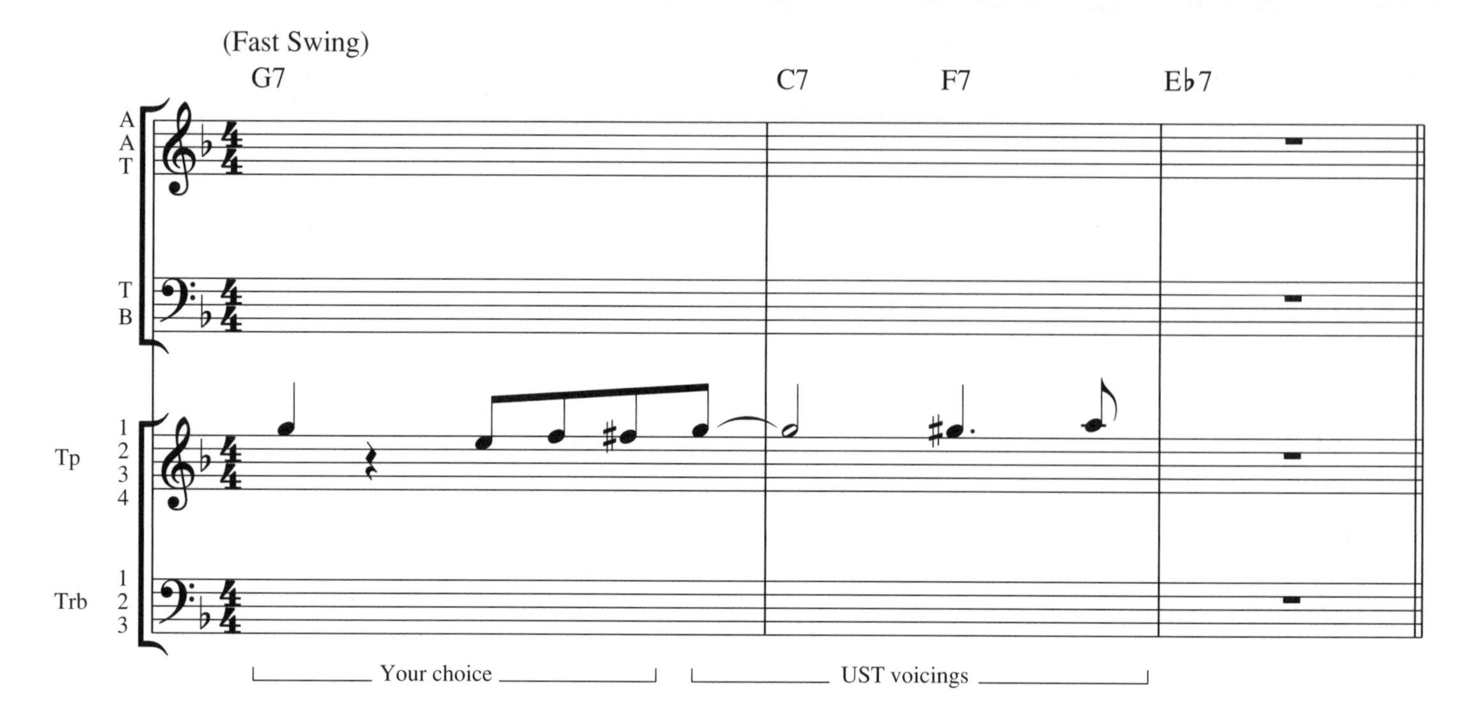

CHAPTER 7

Voicings in Clusters (Seconds)

IN THIS CHAPTER

7-1 Procedure

Cluster voicings are very dense and dissonant. The predominant intervals in cluster voicings are seconds. Minor seconds provide even more dissonance than major seconds.

For basic principles and examples of constructing cluster voicings in three, four, five, and six parts, see Chapters 6 and 8 of *Modern Jazz Voicings* (Berklee Press, 2001).

The following examples show how to construct cluster voicings for larger ensembles of various sizes, with suggested ranges for the lead trumpet in each case. You generally score the brass section in intervals of seconds using appropriate notes from the relevant chord scale and observing low interval limits. Then add the saxophones by either doubling notes from the brass voicing (coupling high for a bright sound or low for depth) or by continuing down in seconds below the brass for even more depth. Most cluster voicings fit within one octave, although some may be wider depending on how many instruments you include and how you assign the saxophone doublings.

When using clusters to score melody lines, separate the first and second voices by an interval of a third or fourth in order to keep the melody clear.

For 4&4

The suggested range for the lead trumpet is:

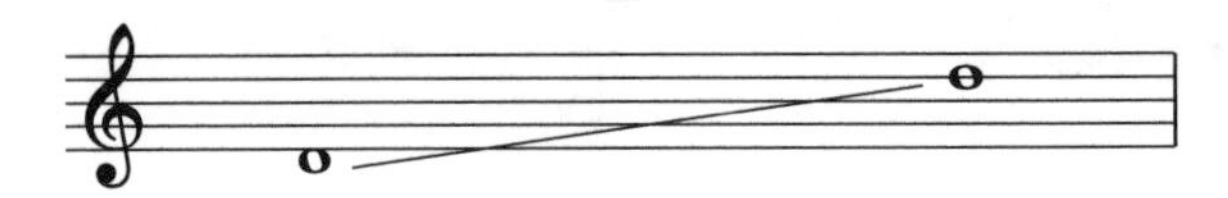

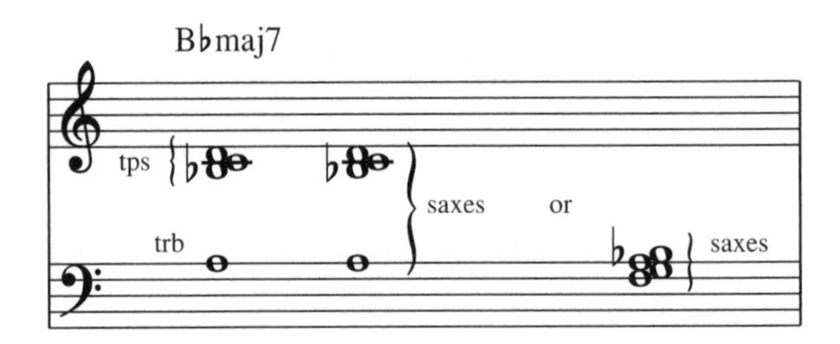

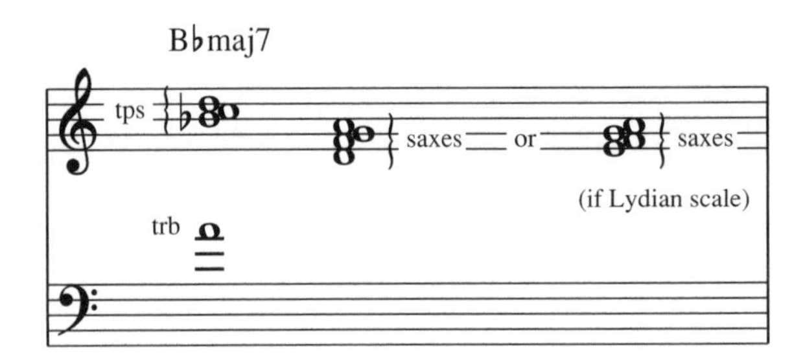

For 5&5

The suggested range for the lead trumpet is:

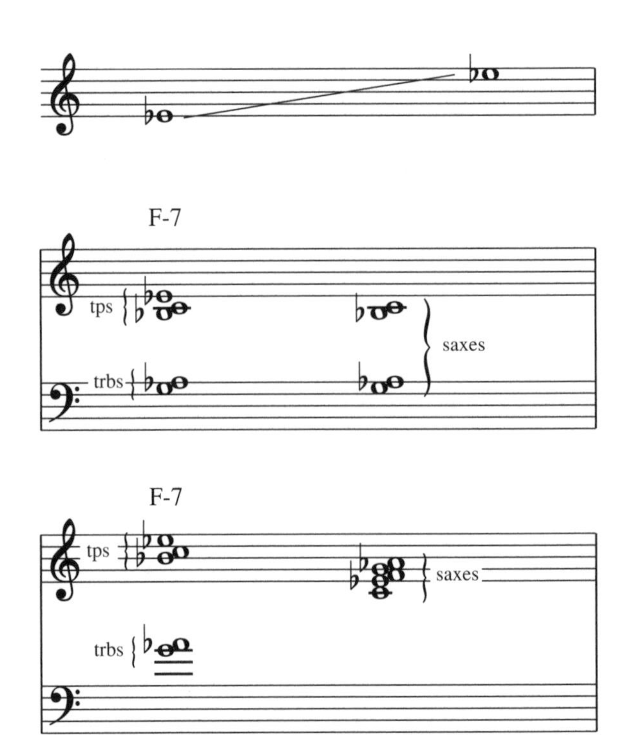

For 7&5

The suggested range for the lead trumpet is:

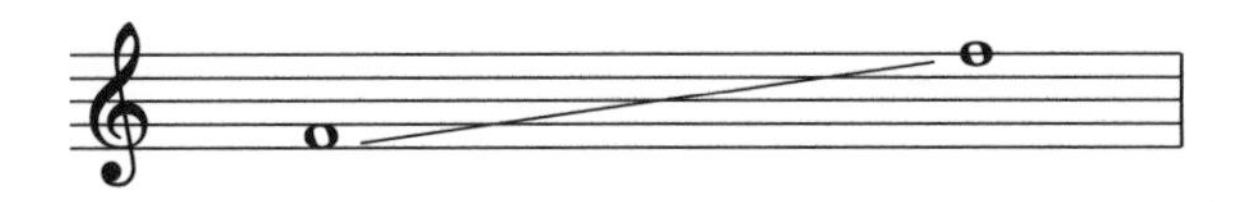

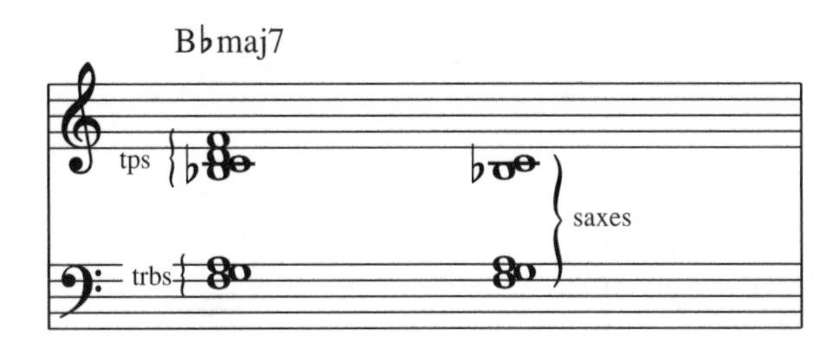

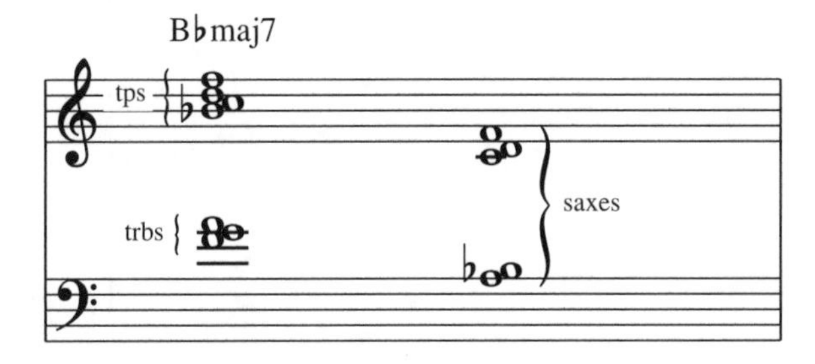

For 8&5

The suggested range for the lead trumpet is:

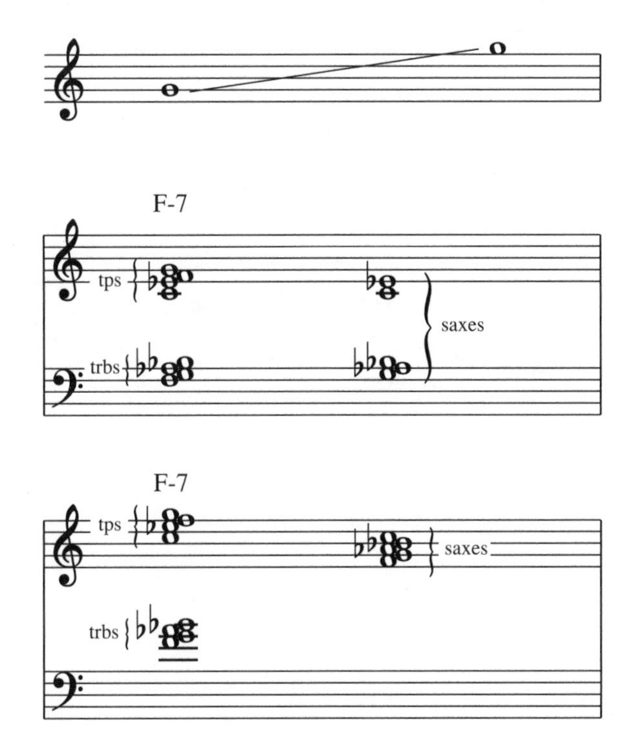

7-2 4&4 Using Clusters in Brass Counterpoint

In this 4&4 passage, the saxophones state the melody in octaves while the muted brass respond with a contrapuntal figure scored in clusters.

41

7-3 5&5 Saxophone and Brass Counterpoint

42

In the following 5&5 example, brass and saxophone counter melodies are scored in clusters. Although seconds make up the majority of these voicings, we use intervals wider than a second between each section's lead line and its second voice in order to emphasize melodic clarity.

7-4 7&5 Concerted Melody in Clusters

Here the melody is concerted using clusters through the entire 7&5 horn section. The saxophones double the bottom five brass parts, keeping the voicing depth within one octave. As in the previous example, we clarify the melody by using an interval larger than a second between the top two voices—in this case, a third. The third allows the melody to be distinct, but maintains the cluster voicing's quality of close spacing. (If the spacing of a third were to assign an avoid note to the second voice, we would use a fourth instead.)

43

7-5 8&5 Sustained Texture and Counterpoint

In this 8&5 example, we use cluster voicings in two very different ways. The sustained trill texture is scored in a five-part cluster for four muted trumpets and two flutes (Flute 1 doubling the lead trumpet and Flute 2 playing the second voice of the cluster.) The simple counterpoint line for two clarinets and three trombones is also scored as a cluster, this one in three parts with adjacent voices separated by intervals of a third and a second. The bass clarinet and Trombone 4 play the bass-clef melody in unison.

This page intentionally left blank.

7-6 Exercise

Write a simple background line to the given saxophone melody. Then use clusters to voice the background line for trumpets in harmon mutes and trombones in cup mutes.

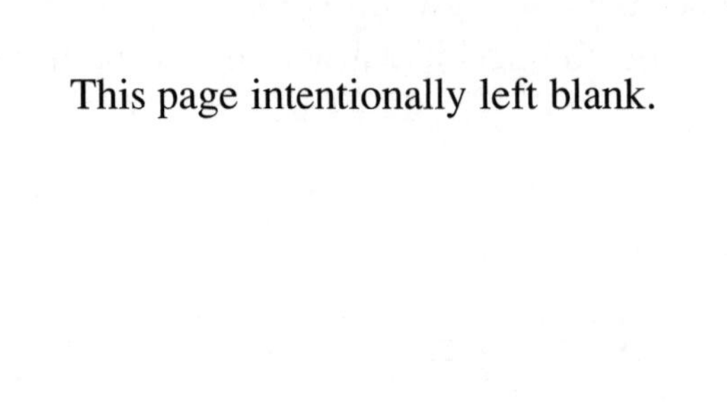

CHAPTER 8 Line Writing

IN THIS CHAPTER

8-1 Procedure

All the orchestration techniques we have considered up to this point build vertical structures using notes that are consistent with the chord of the moment, emphasizing chord sound and function. The resulting lines played by the inner voices are not the main concern of these techniques. Not surprisingly, these inner lines are often not very melodic.

Line writing is a more melody-driven alternative to these vertical approaches. In line writing, the arranger writes chord-based voicings for a relatively few target points in the melody, then connects these points with lines derived from the appropriate chord scales. Free of chordal imperatives, the arranger has more flexibility to make each connecting line melodically appealing, often using contrary motion in the lower lines to add interest.

Because the vertical sound is not the prime consideration, line writing can produce ambiguous, nonfunctional sonorities in the lines running between the more harmonically defined target points. For that reason, line writing works best at fast tempos, especially if the target points are far apart. At high speed the ambiguous moments are simply less apparent. Line writing is a challenging, advanced technique that requires experience and considerable ear-training.

Line writing is most often applied to four- and five-part writing, though it may also be used for three parts or for more than five parts.

Here is a step-by-step description of the line writing process:

1. Analyze the melody to determine the target points, those melody notes that are to be voiced as chord sound. These are generally notes of long duration, notes followed by a leap or a rest, notes that begin or end a phrase, and notes at the point of a chord change.

2. Determine the applicable chord scale and score the target points using a voicing technique suitable for the musical context. Voicings can be mechanical or nonmechanical, open or close, or a combination of open and close. The lead line's range and contour will influence your voicing decisions. You may use different depths of voicing and levels of dissonance to shape the dramatic content and flow of the phrase.

3. Connect the target voicings by writing lines derived from the appropriate chord scales. Use chromatic notes, those not in the chord scale, only when necessary; resolve them to the next note by step. Write one line at a time, making sure each line is as melodically interesting as possible. At the same time, do not allow these inner lines to overshadow the lead. Keep wide leaps to a minimum or, if possible, avoid them altogether.

As you construct your connecting lines, also keep these points in mind:

- Keep the spacing between lines even and no wider than an interval of a seventh, except between the bottom two voices. Wider spacing separates the sound into two groups of notes, undermining the blend.

- You can create contrary motion more easily by writing the bottom line first.

- Scan vertically to make sure there are no unintentional minor ninth intervals between any two lines. In the hands of an experienced arranger, the highly dissonant minor ninth sound may be used effectively, but less experienced writers should avoid it.

- Avoid repeating notes within a line. Try crossing voices (exchanging notes with an adjacent line) or using a chromatic tone to solve the problem.

- If problems arise as you are writing the last lines—unwanted doublings, unintended sonorities, a lack of space to fit the final lines in—revise your earlier lines and reconsider voicing decisions to find the best musical solution.

- Consecutive seconds in adjacent lines need special consideration. Because their dissonance can compromise melodic clarity and create intonation challenges in performance, you should try to avoid consecutive seconds. It is best to approach and leave a second by step in contrary motion.

8-2 Five-Part Saxophone Soli

The following example applies the line-writing procedure to create a five-part saxophone soli passage.

The soli will be based on this lead line:

Step 1. Determine which notes are to be the harmonic target points. We label each with an "X".

Step 2. Determine the appropriate chord scales and voice the target points with a suitable voicing technique. Here, we choose upper structure triad voicings, though many other approaches would work as well.

Step 3. Create the under parts from the given chord scale by connecting the target points with melodically interesting lines. Use chromatic notes (notes outside the chord scale) only when necessary. As you listen to the recorded demonstration and follow the written parts below, try to hear the melodic quality of each supporting saxophone line.

45

8-3 Line Writing in a 5&5 Concerted Passage

In order to apply line writing to concerted passages for large ensembles, follow these steps.

Step 1. Determine target points.
Step 2. Voice the target points for the brass section.
Step 3. Add the saxophones to the brass target points, in most cases doubling at the unison or octave, occasionally adding new notes.
Step 4. Write the connecting lines for each section.

Below we apply line writing to the same lead line, target points, and voicings as in the previous sax soli example, except that here we orchestrate the entire 5&5 ensemble. Note how the saxophones are aligned with the brass at the target points: altos and tenors doubling while the baritone adds a root to each of the brass voicings.

As we connect the target points, the primary concern is the melodic content of each player's line. Contrary motion, chord scale consistency, and chromaticism are all factored in to determining the final shape of the inner lines shown below. As you listen to the CD track, read each line and try to hear the melodic results.

8-4 Building from the Bottom for Contrary Motion

Contrary motion between the top and bottom voices gives a passage a sense of "breathing" and adds dramatic contour. As the melody goes higher, the bottom voice goes lower, offering more support. As the melody goes lower, the bottom voice ascends to the closely spaced target points. Arrangers need to choose voicings for target points that facilitate this effect. Most important, to create and emphasize the contrary motion, write the bottom line first.

Support the climax of such phrases with the deepest and/or most dissonant voicing. For target points at secondary climaxes, use voicings with less depth and less dissonance.

Five-Part Line Writing, Bottom First

In applying line writing to the following example for five mixed-timbre parts, we determine the bottom line first.

Lead line:

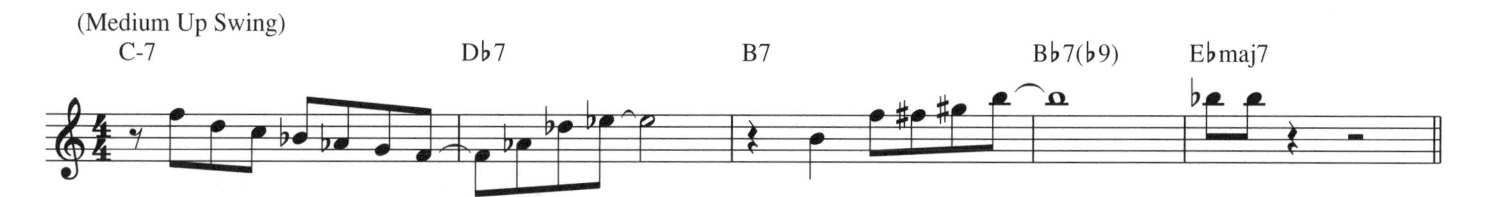

Step 1. Determine target points.

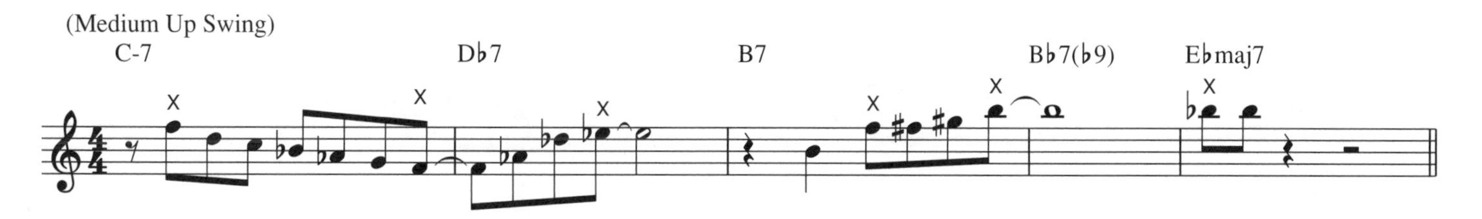

Step 2. Write voicings for the target points, keeping in mind which are the primary and secondary climaxes. Vary the spacing and dissonance of the voicings accordingly.

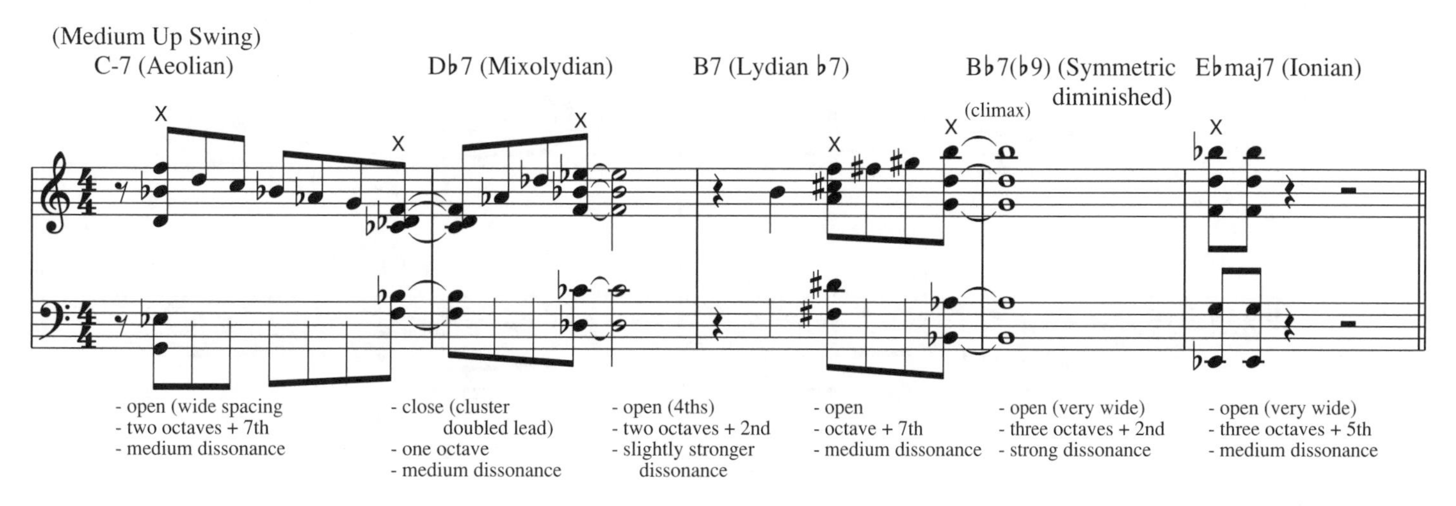

Step 3. Write the connecting lines using notes from the appropriate chord scales. Write the bottom line first, stressing contrary motion and connecting the target points in the most melodic manner possible. Note how our choices for target point voicings encourage contrary motion in the lines.

The breathlike expansion and contraction of this passage is easy to see in the condensed score layout below.

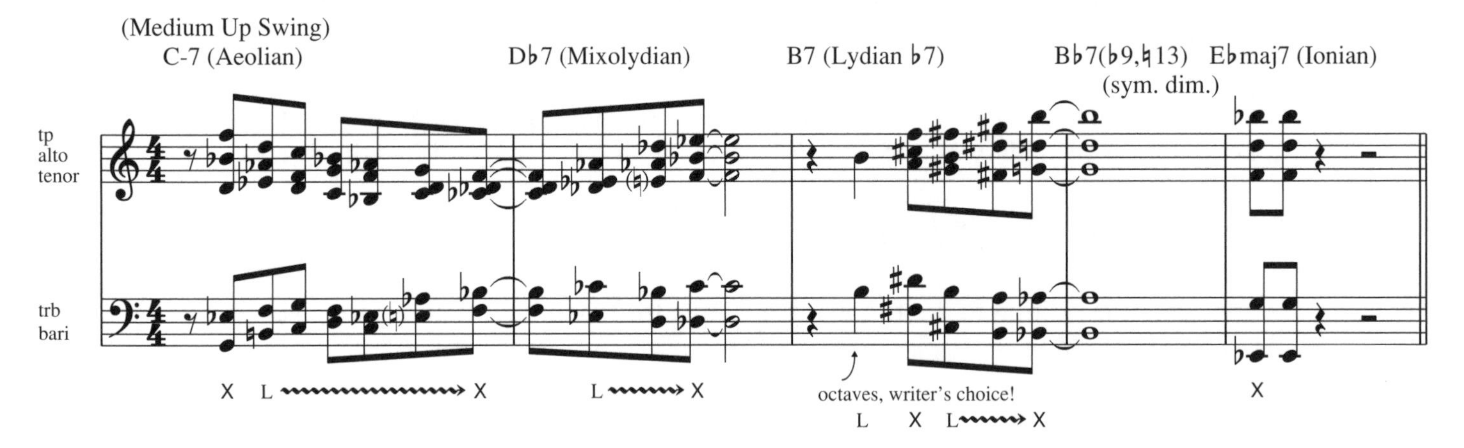

In this open score, each instrument's melodic line is clear.

Five-Part Line Writing in 7&5 Ensemble

Here we set the five-part line writing passage from the previous example within the context of a 7&5 ensemble. (When writing for large ensembles, you may choose to feature a smaller subgroup in this way.)

Trumpet 1, Alto 1, Tenor 1, Trombone 1, and the baritone sax make up the mixed-timbre, featured group. As you listen to the CD, follow the clear contrary motion between the upper and lower lines. Note also the deep, dissonant sound of the climax point voicing in the fourth measure. The remaining horns are scored to emphasize the stop-time effect.

8-5 Cascade Effect

Line writing can be used to create a cascade effect in which the melody "spills out" of a simple texture into a more complex sound. The cascade connects two target points, the simpler one scored in unison or octaves and the complex one fully voiced. In this application, all the standard principles of line writing apply.

In the first measure of the following 5&5 example, the saxophone texture changes from octaves to two, three, four, and five lines as we approach the target point, which is voiced in a hybrid CMaj7/F chord. Note the crossing of voices as Tenor 2 ascends to the third voice in the texture and Alto 2 changes from being the second of four voices to become the fourth of five. These kinds of decisions result from thinking melodically about each part.

The brass respond to the saxes, cascading in the second measure from octaves into the FMaj7 target voicing on beat 4.

In the final measure, both sections are concerted in a percussive figure. We use chromatic voice-leading from measure 2 to measure 3. Instead of having the saxes double the brass, we treat all instruments as equal components. The freely aligned ten-part voicing, with the root doubled at the unison and the 3 and 7 doubled at the octave, contains all seven notes of the Lydian chord scale.

48

Listen to the sound of each line "peeling off" into additional lines and ending in a fully voiced climax.

8-6 Exercise

Score each of the first three target points (marked with an X) using voicings in fourths. Score the last three with upper structure triad voicings. Then apply the strategies of line writing to compose the connecting lines. Use the entire 5&5 instrumentation.

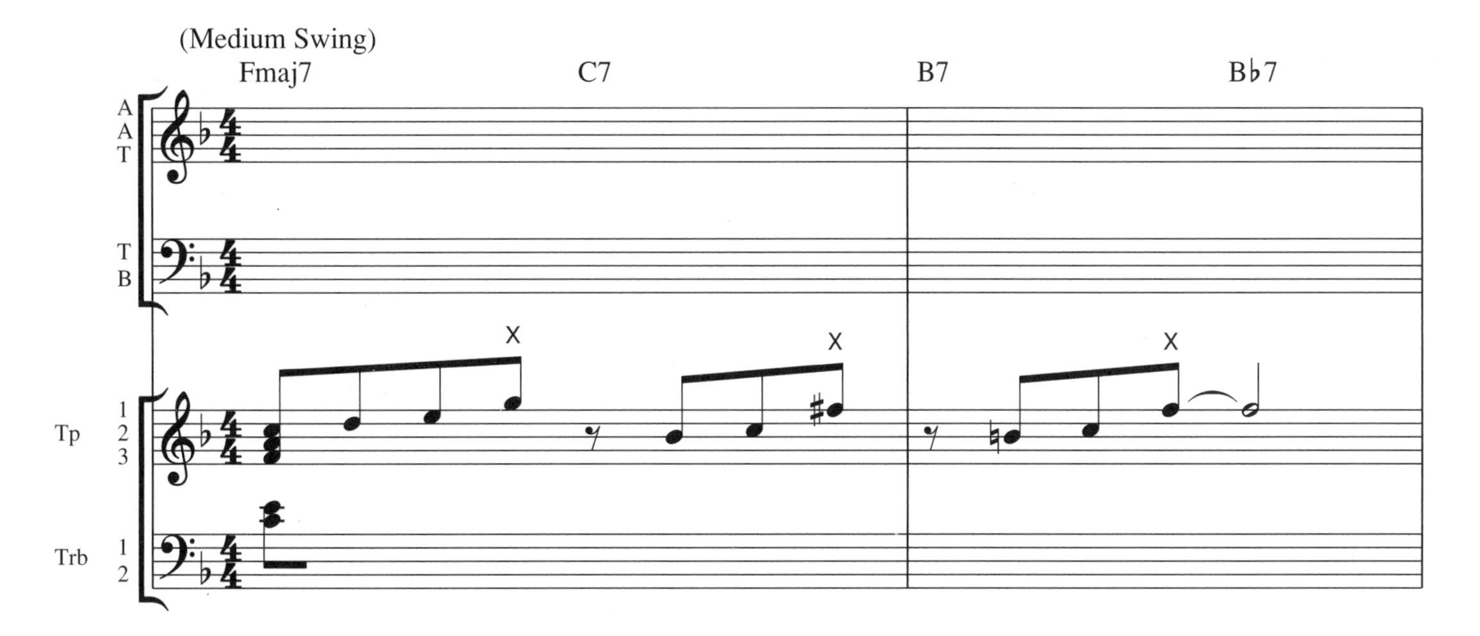

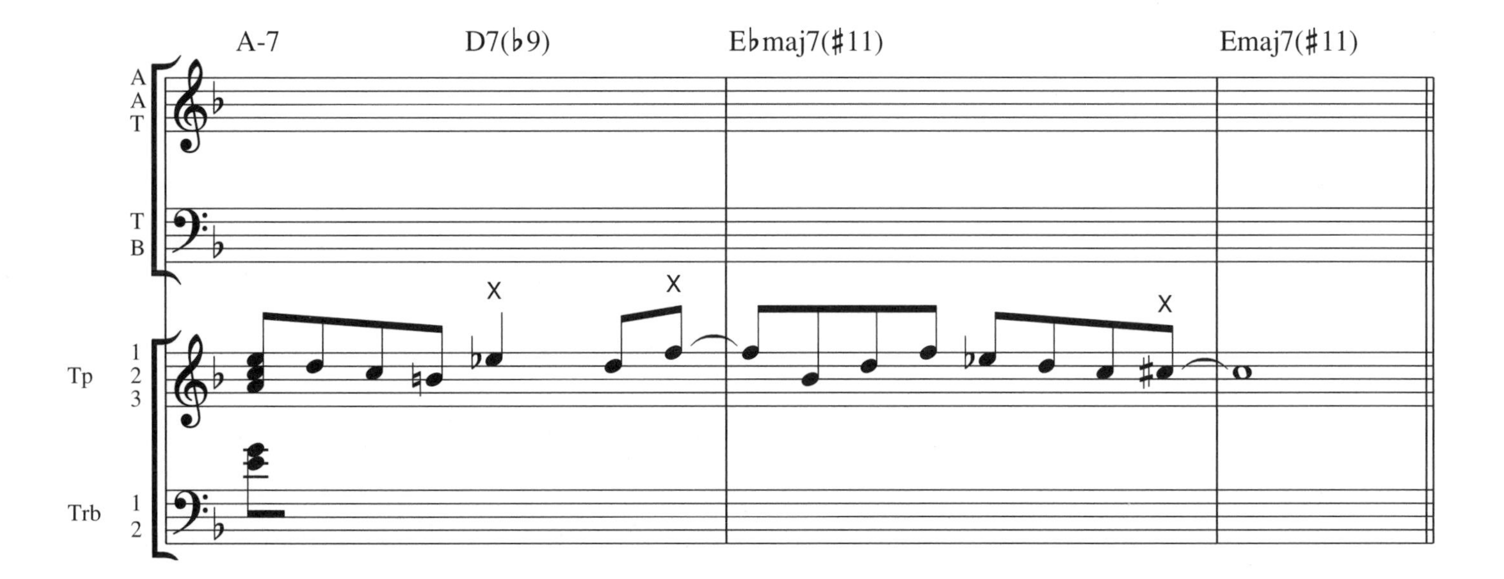

CHAPTER 9 Woodwind Doubling and Muted Brass

IN THIS CHAPTER

- 9-1 Which woodwind instruments saxophonists commonly double, and how to write for them.
- 9-2 Five different brass mutes, how they sound, and practical considerations in writing for them.
- 9-3 Standard applications: unison and octave combinations, voiced woodwind solis in two and five parts, and a 5&5 passage demonstrating various orchestral colors.
- 9-4 Exercise.

You can greatly increase the spectrum of orchestral colors available to you as an arranger by having the saxophonists play woodwind instruments and by having the brass players use mutes. This approach offers an alternative big band sound quality that might be described as cooler, subtler, and, in some cases, darker.

9-1 Woodwind Doubling

The standard woodwind doublings in a big band are as follows:

- the altos play flutes
- the tenors play clarinets
- the baritone plays bass clarinet

Of course there are many other possibilities depending on the capabilities of the instrumentalists involved. In addition to soprano saxophone, more exotic instruments such as alto flute may be used. But you should always check in advance which doubling instruments are owned by each saxophonist and what ability each has on these secondary instruments. In the past it was safe to assume solid doubling, but in the last twenty years or so saxophonists have concentrated less and less on developing these skills. Consequently, it is a good idea to write conservative woodwind parts for the doubling saxophonist.

Remember to list the doublings in the instrumental identity section of the score (see Chapter 1) and to write it on the saxophone parts as well. Show players which instrument to start on, and be sure to give them enough time to switch—no fewer than four bars, if possible. Place the instruction to change instruments ("To Flute," "On Alto," and so on) above the staff.

Doubling woodwind players can usually control the bottom register of their instruments more skillfully than the higher register. For best results, write conservatively, keeping technical demands to a minimum and observing these suggested range limits. (Ranges are shown in concert pitch.)

Flute

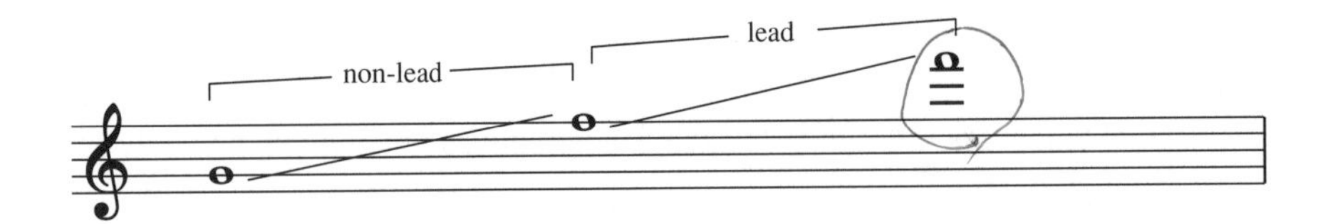

B♭ Clarinet

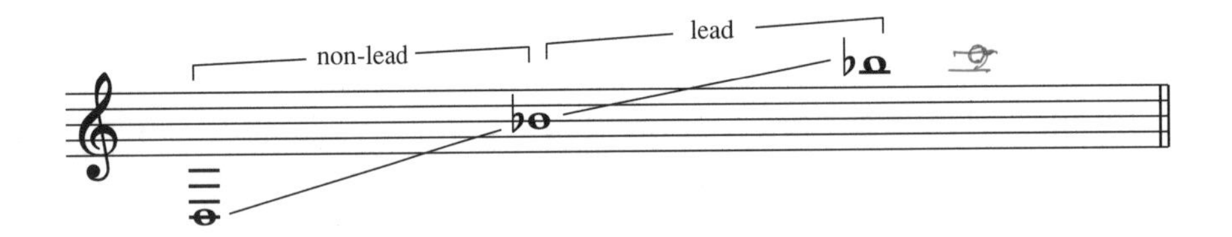

B♭ Bass Clarinet

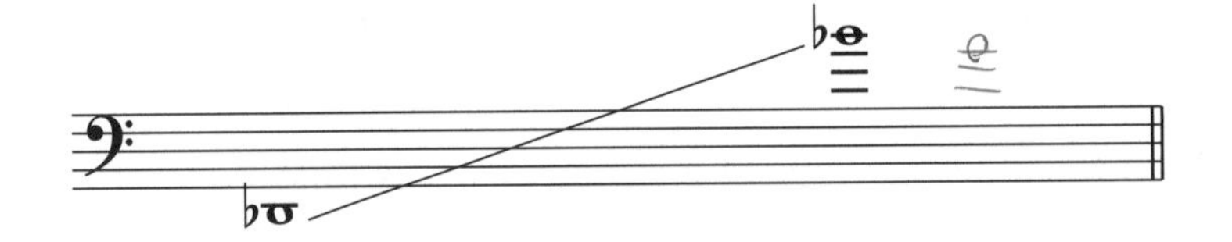

9-2 Muted Brass

A mute changes the sound of a brass instrument in two ways. First, it reduces the instrument's capacity to project its sound. Second, it changes the instrument's timbre. Both effects enable the arranger to create a variety of orchestral colors.

The three most popular mutes—harmon, cup, and straight—are inserted into the bell of the instrument. (Many of the CD tracks referred to in this chapter provide a good demonstration of the sound quality of harmon and cup mutes.) Two other mutes, bucket and plunger, remain outside of the bell.

Characteristics and Range Limits for Five Mutes

Because they drastically change the air flow, mutes make it harder for trumpeters and trombonists to play reliably well at either end of the normal range. Muted notes in the low register are difficult to control and to project. Similarly, at the high end some mutes make it difficult to project or stay in tune. For these reasons, in the discussion below on individual mutes, our suggested lead ranges are more limited than those for general section playing.

Of course, a strong lead player can extend above these upper limits. Notes below the lower end of the ranges shown may be used for a special effect—a dark, distorted, or ambiguous sound, for example. But for the best, consistent results, we suggest you follow these guidelines. All range suggestions are in concert pitch.

Harmon Mute: With a one-piece cork collar that keeps it snugly in the bell, this mute allows no natural sound to escape. It filters the low frequencies and allows some highs to pass, but mixes them inside the mute before letting them out. The result is a metallic, "buzzy" sound. A harmon mute cuts sound projection by about eighty percent. It is used primarily for trumpet.

The harmon mute has an adjustable stem extending from the front. With the stem in place, it produces a nasally "toy trumpet" sound. A player can create a "wah-wah" effect by covering and uncovering the end of the stem with the left hand. Most jazz writing, however, does not require the stem to be in the mute. With the stem removed, the mute creates what might be called the Miles Davis sound: The trumpet becomes stuffy and hard to play in tune in the low register (below concert *d* above middle *c*). Ascending to *f* on the top of the treble clef, the buzzy, metallic sound becomes more focused. Above *f* it gets progressively more difficult to produce a full sound as the back pressure increases.

Although there is a harmon mute for the trombone, few trombonists have one. The characteristics are the same as for the trumpet, but occurring an octave lower.

For best results, keep harmon-muted trumpets in the following range (bearing in mind, as always, that strong lead players may be able to go higher):

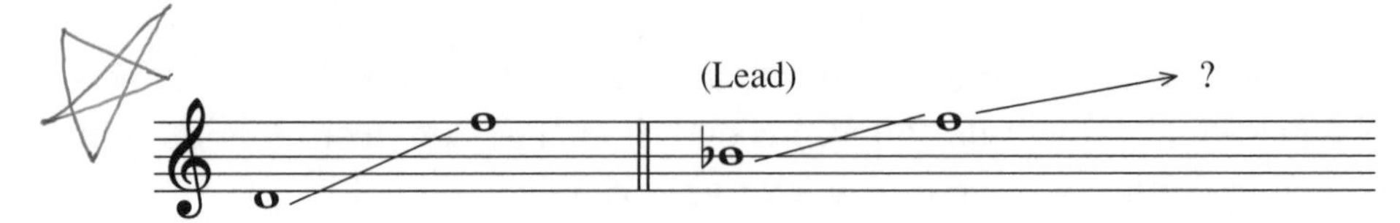

Cup Mute: Held in the bell by three small cork strips, the cup mute allows some of the natural sound to escape. But that sound is reflected backward by an attached bowl-like deflector, which also filters out the highs. The result is a mellow sound. A cup mute cuts sound projection by about fifty percent.

Cup mutes are easier to play in the low register than harmon mutes. In the low register, the sound is very mellow and easy to control. Ascending to the higher register, the sound becomes less mellow and more penetrating; controlling intonation becomes difficult.

For best results keep cup-muted trumpets and trombones in the following ranges:

Trumpet

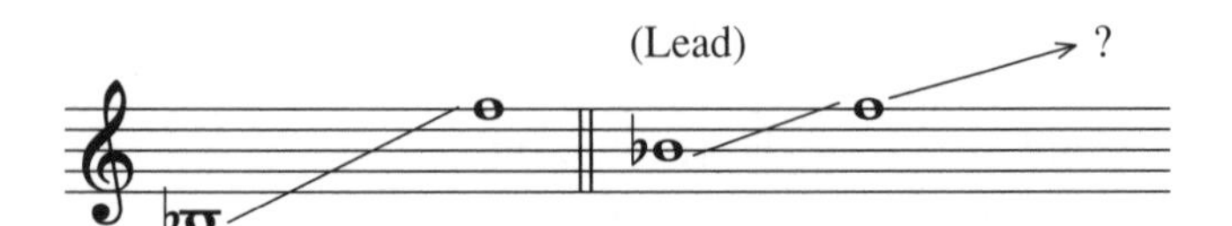

Trombone

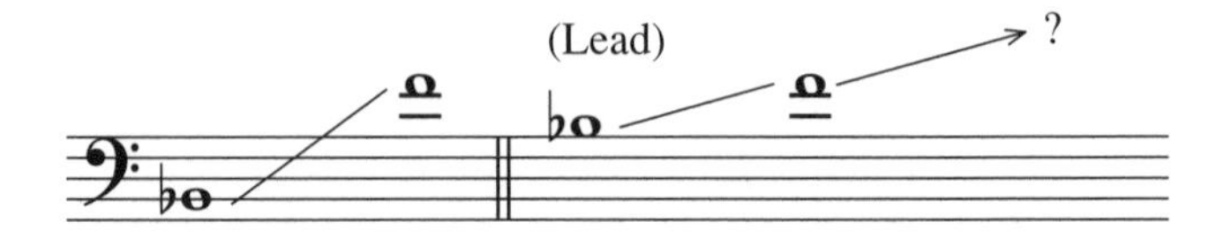

Straight Mute: Like the cup mute, the straight mute is held in the bell by three small cork strips. The resulting space allows some of the natural sound to bypass the mute. With no attached deflector (as on the cup mute), it filters out the lows and allows the highs to pass, creating a piercing sound that is stronger and closer to a natural, unmuted sound than that produced by either the harmon or cup mute. The straight mute is used more in classical settings than in jazz. It cuts sound projection by about twenty-five percent.

The straight mute is more effective and easier to play in the high register. It projects less in the low register, but it is not as stuffy as the harmon or as mellow as the cup. Ascending from low to high, the straight mute allows a fuller, more penetrating sound than a harmon mute. Because it is easier to control, players can go a little higher while maintaining good intonation and balance.

For best results, keep straight-muted trumpets and trombones in the following ranges:

Trumpet

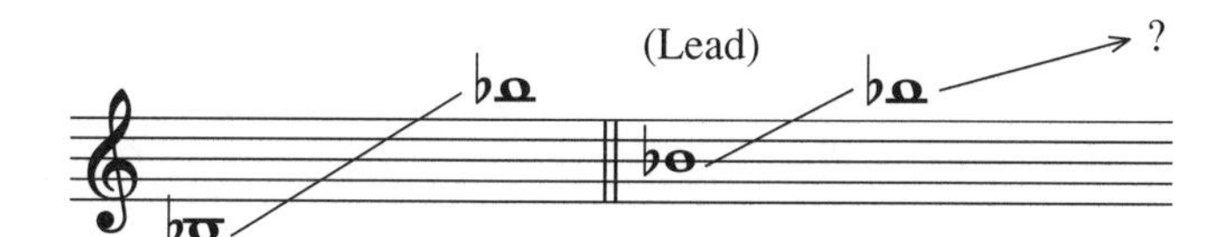

Trombone

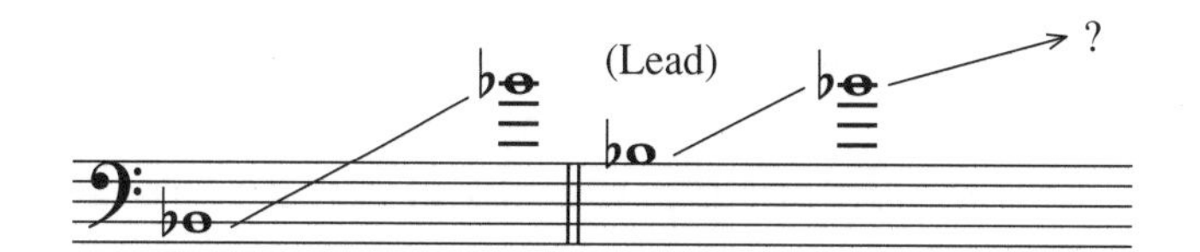

The following two mutes are not inserted into the bell. Held in front of the bell, they filter highs out of the natural sound by deflecting it backward.

Bucket Mute: This mute is not inserted into the bell, but clipped onto it. It deflects the horn's natural sound with a gauze-like material that filters out the highs. Bucket mutes create a very mellow sound with very little edge, similar in quality to a flugelhorn, that is just a bit louder than that produced by cup mutes. A bucket mute cuts sound projection by about forty percent. Players can simulate the sound of a bucket mute by playing directly into their stands (write the instruction "Play in Stand" on each part).

Because it does not actually go inside the bell, this mute creates a sound that is closest to the natural open sound. It is easy to play in all registers.

For best results, keep bucket-muted trumpets and trombones in the following range:

Trumpet

Trombone

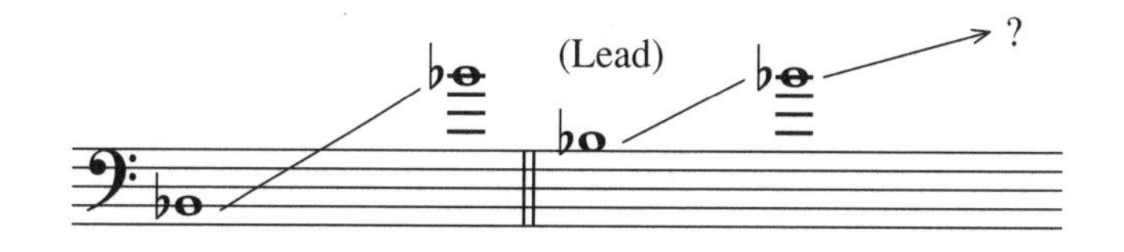

Plunger Mute: This mute does not attach to the bell in any way, but is held in the hand. A player can use it to close off the sound completely or to allow different levels of natural sound by changing the angle of its open position. By going from closed to open position on the same pitch, a player can create a "wah-wah" or "doo-wah" effect. A player with advanced plunger skills can mimic vocal inflections.

Because this mute is held in front of the bell, it can be used in any part of the instrument's range to alter timbre and projection. It requires no specific range limitations, although, as with all mutes, it is best to avoid extreme highs and lows.

For a very special effect, usually for a solo, a trombonist may use a plunger in conjunction with a pixie mute, a small straight mute designed to go deep into the bell. The resulting voice-like effect (associated originally with Joe "Tricky Sam" Nanton of Duke Ellington's band) was perfected by Quentin "Butter" Jackson, who was featured in recordings he made with Duke Ellington, Charles Mingus (*Black Saint and Sinner Lady*), and Thad Jones.

In writing for the plunger mute, indicate the closed sound with a "+" and the open position with a "0."

Practical Considerations for All Mutes

Before deciding to use mutes in a passage, visualize the physical movements needed to insert and remove a mute. You must give a player enough time to reach for the mute and put it in the horn before playing the passage. Usually, a rest of two to four measures is adequate; for slow pieces, one measure may suffice. For bucket mutes, which have to be clipped on to the bell rather than simply inserted, you might provide another measure or two. Give the player the same amount of time to remove the mute before going on to an "open" passage. You will gain the respect of your players if you give them enough time to make these switches.

Write your muting instructions on brass parts above the stave containing the muted passage: "With Cup Mute," "With Harmon Mute," "Remove Mute," and so on. Following a muted passage, use the instruction "Open" to remind players that the next section is to be played without mutes. The traditional Italian terms are *con sordin* (with mute) and *senza sordin* (without mute).

You can generally expect trumpet players to have harmon, cup, straight, and plunger mutes with them. Trombonists normally have only cup, straight, and plunger mutes. When organizing rehearsal and recording sessions, always remind the brass players to bring the mutes called for in your arrangement.

9-3 Applications of Woodwinds and Muted Brass

Woodwinds and muted brass can be used in unison or octaves and can also be voiced in concerted passages. In addition, you may apply various combinations to color passages that also contain saxophones and open brass. Personal taste, along with experimentation and listening, will determine which approaches work best.

Be especially aware of instrumental balance when using this subdued instrumentation. In the lower register, the overall dynamic level must be soft if the woodwinds and/or muted brass are to be heard. In the higher register, they can project more effectively over the rhythm section.

Unison and Octave Combinations

The following examples show some of the most common unison and octave combinations:

49

1. Trumpet in harmon mute with flute in unison

50

2. Trumpet in cup mute with clarinet in unison

3. Trumpet in cup mute with flute an octave higher

51

As with any of these combinations, you may choose to assign more than one player to a part. The following example has two trumpets in cup mutes and two flutes an octave higher.

4. Clarinet with trombone in cup mute an octave lower

52

The following example again assigns two players to each part, two clarinets and two trombones using cup mutes an octave below.

Voiced Woodwinds

When writing for woodwinds, you can use any voicing technique. Because woodwinds have a relatively softer sound than saxophones, you should use them in their strongest and clearest registers. The following examples show two standard techniques for featuring voiced woodwinds.

1. Two-part soli in thirds and sixths

53

A common strategy for harmonizing a woodwind line in two parts is to use intervals of a third and a sixth. To increase the presence of a woodwind passage within the ensemble, you may assign two or more players to each line. Here, two flute players have the melody and two clarinet players have the harmony.

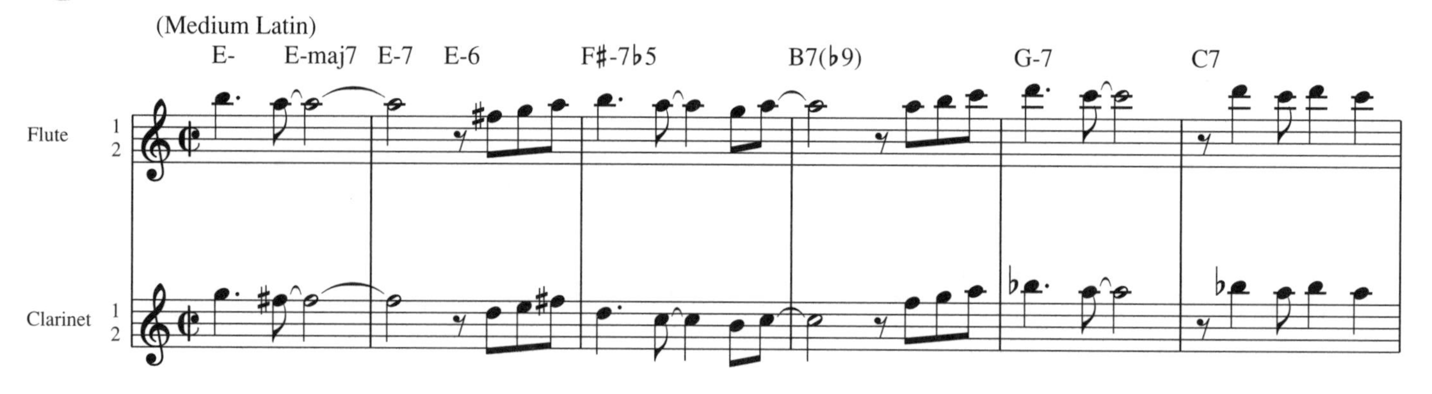

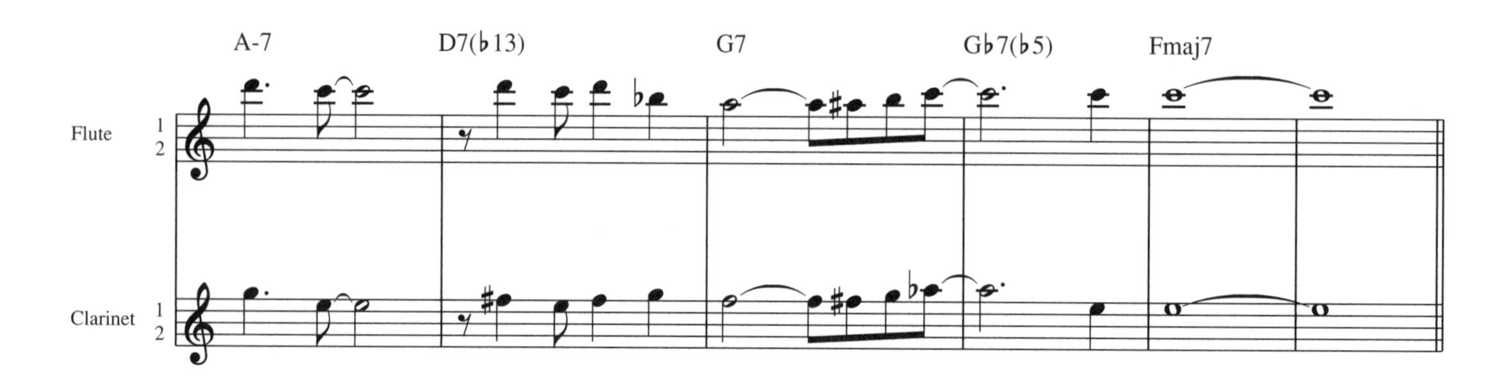

2. Five-part soli (mixed techniques)

This woodwind passage includes a variety of open and close voicing techniques, including four-part/double lead voicings with and without tension substitutes. Note the treatment of approach notes using both traditional and nontraditional strategies.

54

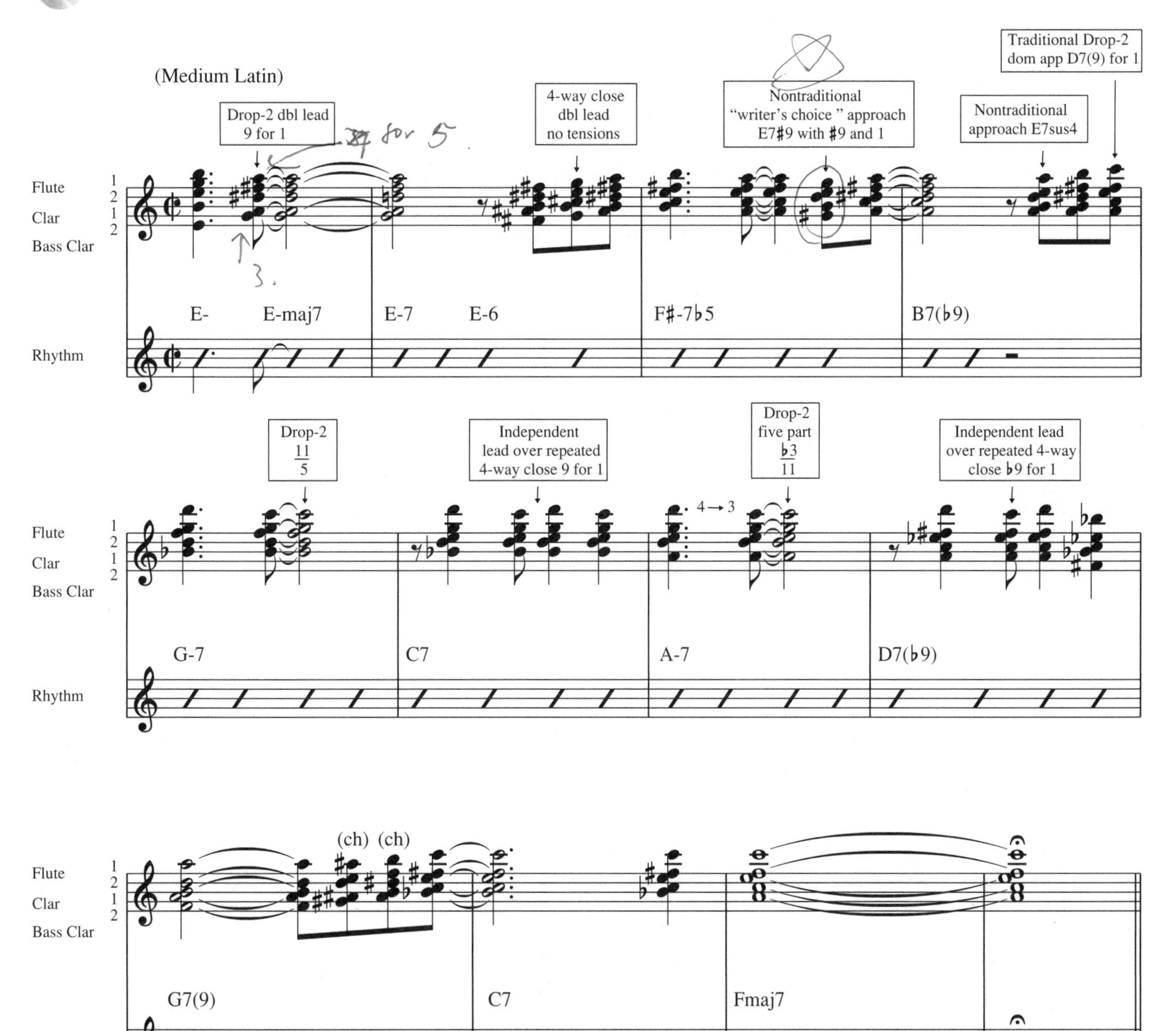

Large Ensemble, Various Woodwinds and Muted Brass Effects

The following 5&5 example uses a variety of textures to demonstrate the wonderful orchestral colors possible when woodwinds and muted brass are combined. Listen to the recorded track repeatedly, first to pick out each effect individually, then to appreciate the overall sound within the ensemble.

The different sound qualities and textures include:

- Dense cluster voicings played by woodwind and muted brass (measures 1 to 4)
- Solo lines by the bass clarinet (measures 1 to 2) and bass (measure 4)
- Bass clarinet aligned with trombones as bottom support (measures 3 to 12)
- Counter lines in flutes and clarinets using both unison and octave doubling (measure 8)
- Piano doubling of flute line to add color (measures 7 to 8)
- Varying mutes:
  - —Trumpets start with harmons (measures 1 to 4), then change to cups (measures 6 to 12)
  - —Trombones start open (measures 1 to 8), then change to cups (measures 9 to 12)

55

Fl 1 2
a2
Cl 1 2
a2
B Cl
Tp 1 2 3
Trb 1 2
(to cup mutes)
(cup mutes)
Bass
Piano
Dbmaj7 Bb-7
G-7
Gb/C7
D-9
D-9
Drums
(time)
8
9
10
11
12

This page intentionally left blank.

9-4 Exercise

Choose one of these AABA ballads:

- "In a Sentimental Mood"
- "You Don't Know What Love Is"
- "Chelsea Bridge"
- "When I Fall in Love"

Working with the ballad of your choice, complete the assignment below using two flutes, two clarinets, bass clarinet, three trumpets (with straight, cup, or harmon mutes), two trombones (with straight or cup mutes), piano, bass, and drums.

1. Compose a four-measure, thematic introduction.

2. Score the first two A sections, treating each one differently. Include and feature mixed-soli voicings for combined muted brass and woodwinds. Also include woodwind counter lines in unison or octaves.

3. Compose a two- to four-measure ending.

4. Produce an open score showing these elements.

This page intentionally left blank.

CHAPTER 10 Soli Writing

IN THIS CHAPTER

10-1 Procedure

As part of developing a large ensemble piece, and to contrast those moments that feature individual soloists, you may include soli passages. These passages allow you as the arranger to "take a solo." You do this by constructing a lead line that emulates the sort of improvisational paraphrasing of a given melody that a jazz player might create spontaneously. You then score the line in concerted fashion for a section of the band.

The most common of these soloistic passages features the saxophone section. You may also write soli passages for the entire brass section, or for the trumpet section or trombone section separately. Solis may feature a mixed group of saxes and brass, as well.

Any kind of scoring technique—mechanical voicings, nonmechanical voicings, line writing—can be applied with great results. Concerted sectional writing is the most common texture for soli passages, but even contrapuntal soli passages can be effective.

Suggested Lead Ranges for Soli Writing

For the most consistent balance and blend, observe the following guidelines for lead instruments.

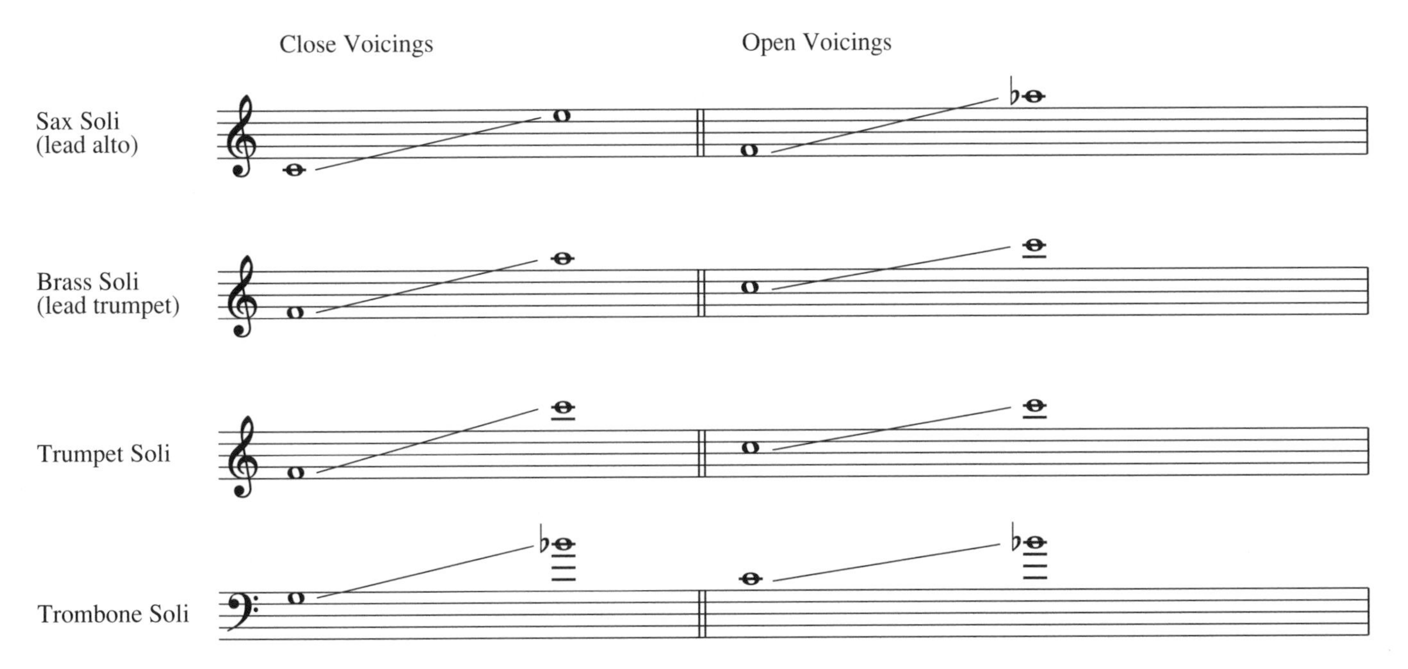

Creating the Lead Line

To construct a soli lead line, paraphrase a given melody line in the style of a jazz improviser. In this example we begin with a melody and harmony taken from a lead sheet, as shown below.

Lead sheet:

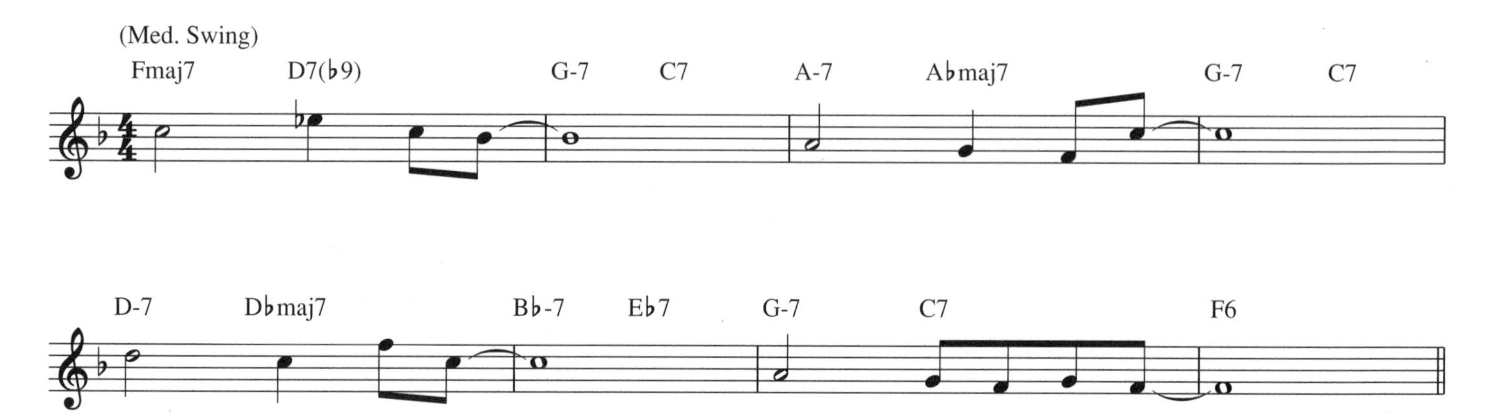

Here is the resulting soloistic paraphrasing that will serve as the lead line for the soli:

To create the soli passage, harmonize the soli lead line for the chosen instrumentation using any technique that suits the musical context. In the following sections, we show examples of various solis based on this and other lead lines.

10-2 Saxophone Solis

Four-Way Close, Double Lead

56

Here we harmonize the lead line to create a saxophone soli using four-way close, double lead voicings. Note the reharmonization of approach notes, labeled in parentheses.

Line Writing

Here we construct another soli by scoring the lead line from the previous example using the line writing technique (see Chapter 8). First we identify the target points, usually notes at the point of a chord change, and mark them with an "X." Then we voice the target points using upper-structure triad voicings, represented by the stacked chord symbols in parentheses.

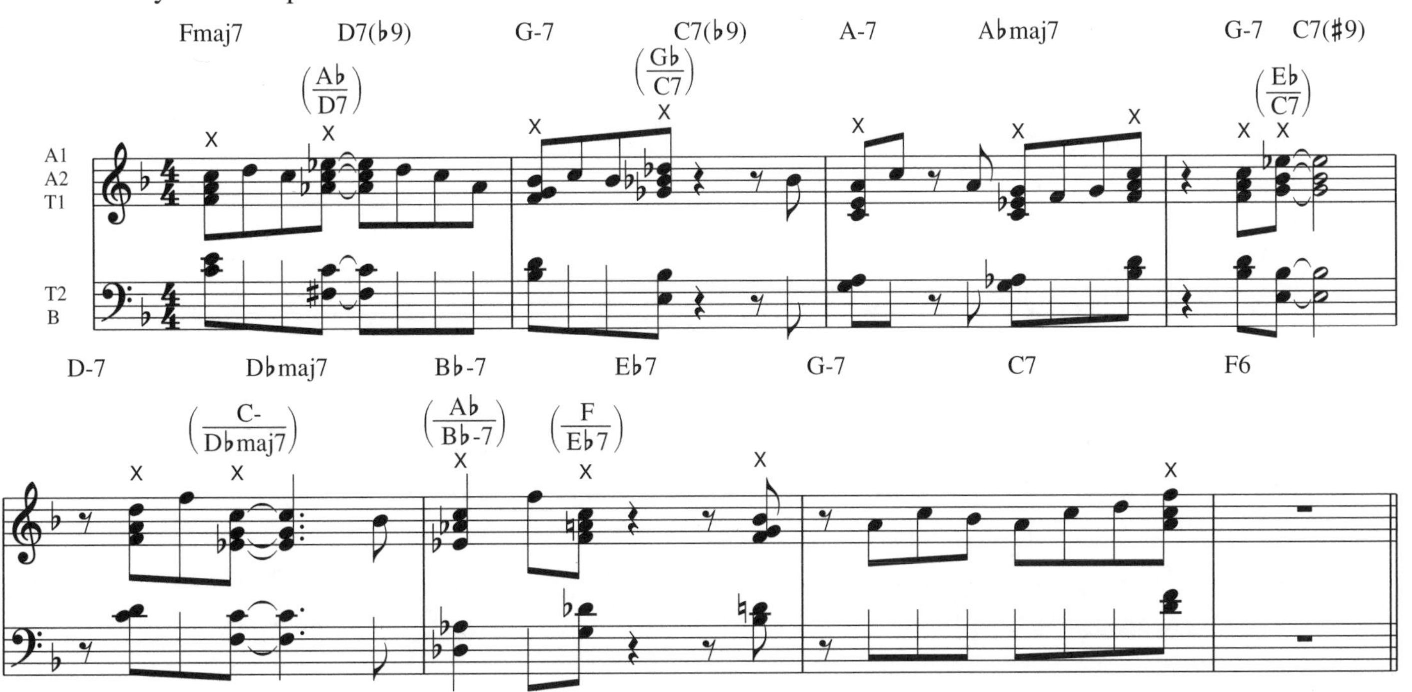

Next, the target points ("X") are connected with melodic lines ("L"). Listen for the difference in voicing depth, compared to track 56. Hear the contrary motion in the lower voices.

10-3 Brass Solis

For Four Trumpets, Three Trombones

Based on a different lead line from that of the previous examples, this soli passage for four trumpets and three trombones uses upper structure triad voicings. With all players relatively high in their registers, note the bright, powerful impact of this passage.

58

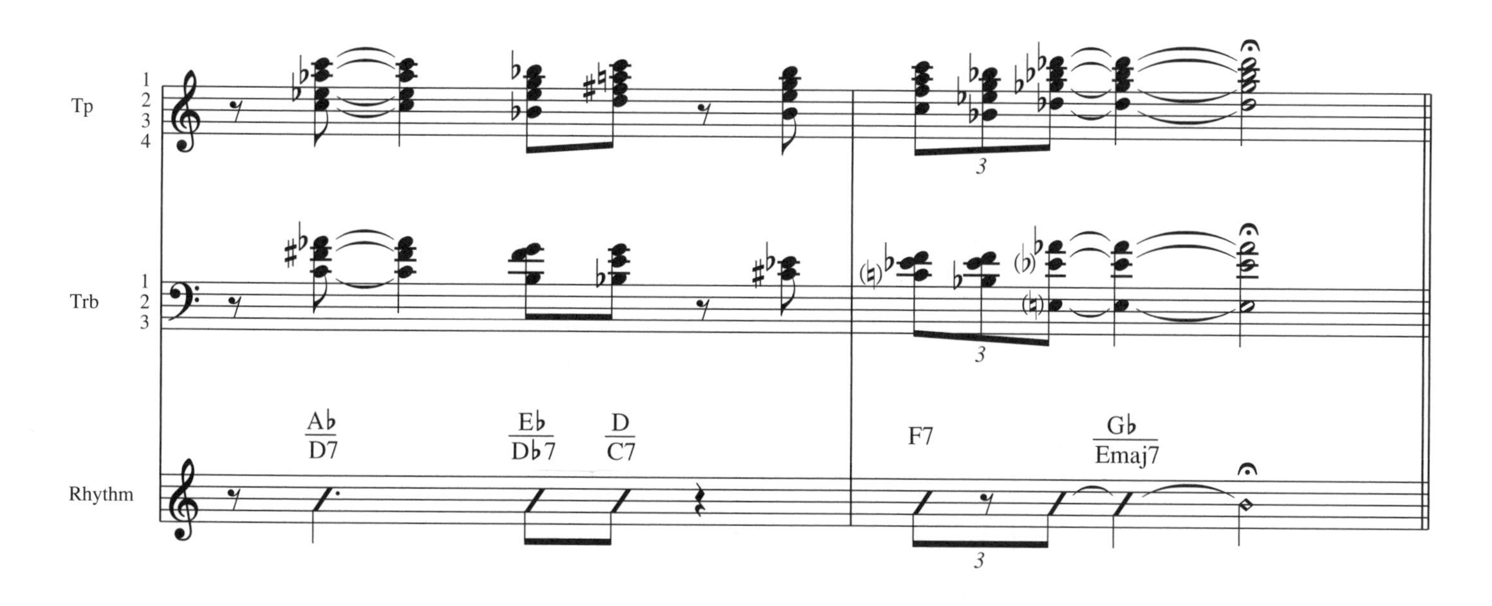

For Four Trumpets

This soli for four trumpets is orchestrated using voicings of constant structure: from top to bottom, the lines remain separated by intervals of a minor third, a minor third, and a minor second. You can hear the lower voices moving in parallel motion under the melody. The rhythm section responds with stop-time figures.

59

For Three Trombones

This three-trombone soli applies a variety of close voicings, some of which we have not discussed. Try analyzing the structure of these unfamiliar voicings, while listening to the musical effect they create in this soli.

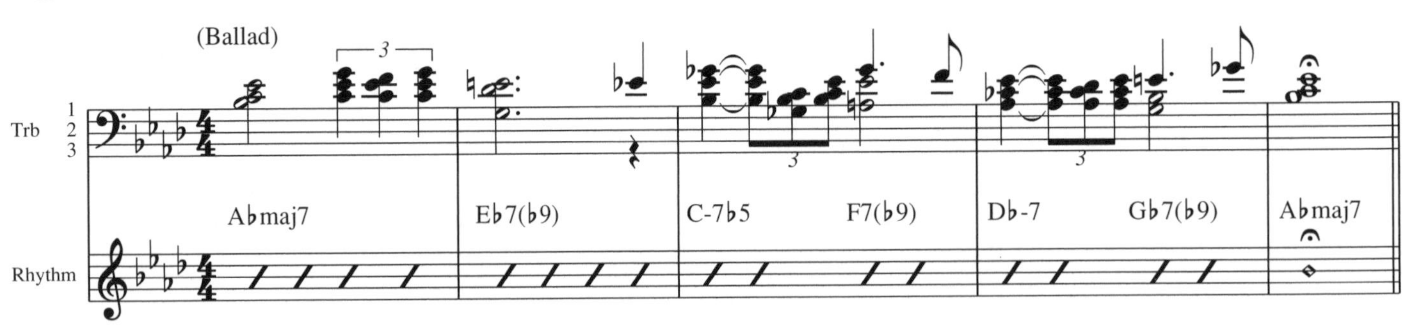

10-4 Exercise

Write a saxophone soli for two altos, two tenors, and a baritone based on the melody and harmony shown in the lead sheet below. First, create an alto lead line by paraphrasing the melody in a style emulating an improvised solo. Then harmonize the lead with the rest of the saxophones. Use whatever voicing techniques you feel are appropriate.

Lead sheet:

Sax soli:

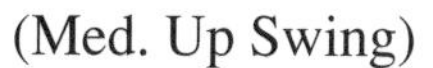

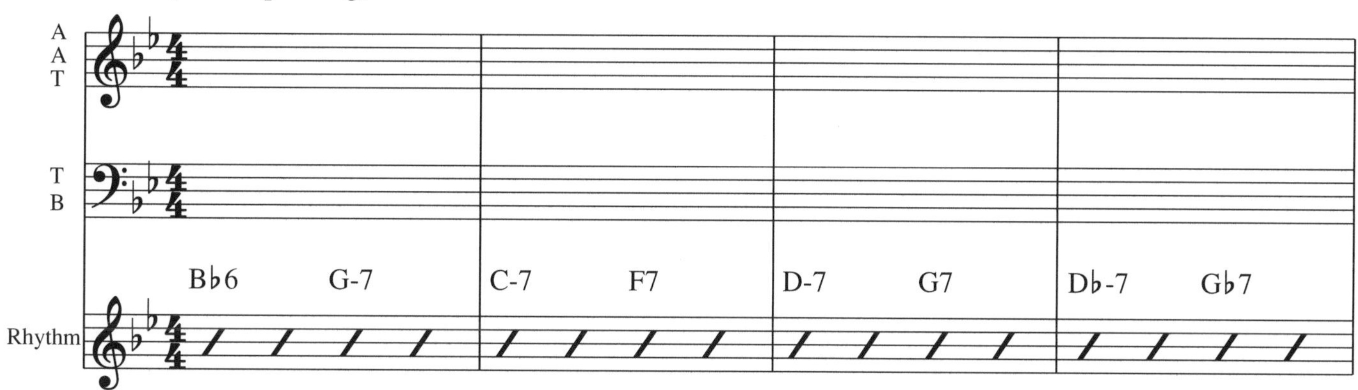

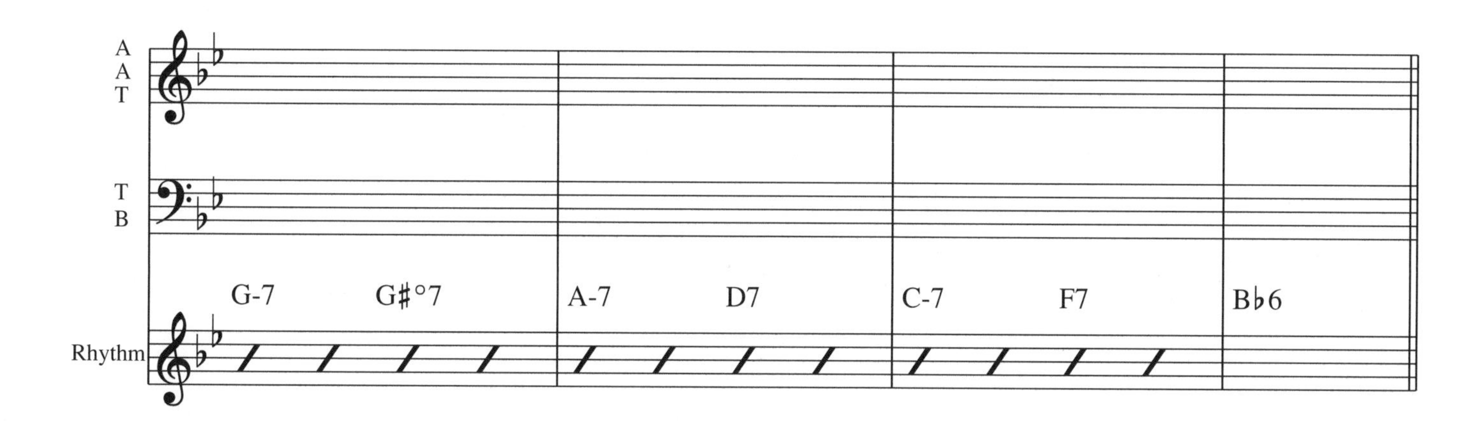

This page intentionally left blank.

CHAPTER 11 Background Writing

IN THIS CHAPTER

11-1 Riff Background

The concept of written backgrounds behind soloists comes out of the "riff" tradition started in the early days of organized jazz ensembles. A riff is a short melodic statement, usually bluesy in flavor, that is improvised by a single player or section. Once the riff starts, other players or sections harmonize it or answer it in call-and-response fashion. This usually builds to a climax, at which point the next section of the chart begins.

This is still how bands improvise backgrounds to support soloists and create "head arrangements." But as the art of arranging became more sophisticated, arrangers began to include written background figures and passages so that they could create specific compositional effects and better control the form, flow, and musical impression of the arrangement.

In general, write sparsely when creating backgrounds. A good background usually allows the soloist to remain in the foreground. There may be occasions, however, when you want a texture to share the foreground with the soloist. You may try to shape the direction of the phrase with composed texture and have the soloist respond, rather than lead, as the solo is developed. While some soloists may consider this approach an obstacle, it can be very dramatic when an exciting background inspires the soloist to ascend to a more intense performance.

Background writing should not last for an entire solo. For example, in a thirty-two-measure solo, an appropriate background might support just the second sixteen measures; for a two-chorus solo, you might include backgrounds in the second chorus only. You can encourage a call-and-response dialogue with the soloist by leaving space in your background passages. A background is also effective toward the end of a solo. It can help establish a point of climax and release in your arrangement and at the same time serve as a transition to the next section of the piece.

Choose instruments so as to distinguish the background's sound from that of the soloist. If a saxophone is soloing, for example, use the brass for backgrounds; if a brass player is soloing, create a sax background. Consider also the timbral contrasts among instruments in different registers. Behind the bright, penetrating timbre of a trumpet or alto, for instance, you might use the darker, mellower-sounding trombones and/or tenor saxes. It is difficult to prevent backgrounds from overwhelming rhythm-section soloists (piano, bass, and guitar); for these soloists, backgrounds should be sparse or not used at all.

The following sections describe three of the most common background techniques and present examples of each.

Although riff backgrounds are often based on improvised figures that are then memorized in a "head arrangement," they can also be part of written arrangements, as shown in the music that follows.

In this passage, Tenor 1 solos over three choruses of a blues. Alto 1, Alto 2, and Tenor 2 play a simple blues-based riff background during the first chorus. In the second, the sax riff is answered by a related figure played by the trombones. Such call-and-response ideas are often "layered in" this way, the call starting in the first chorus, the response joining in when the call is repeated in the second chorus. In the third chorus of this example, the trumpets and baritone sax add yet another line, lending a percussive feel to the background.

61
Med. Blues
(play 3x)
Alto 1
mf
Alto 2
coll' Alto 1
(Solo)
F7
Bb7
Tenor 1
Tenor 2
mf
coll' Alto 1 8vb
Baritone
coll' Tenor 2
(play 3rd x only)
Trumpet
f
(play 2nd & 3rd x)
Trombone
mp
coll' Trombone 1
(walk)
Bass
coll' Piano
Drums
F7
Bb7
Piano

Alto 1
Alto 2
coll' Alto 1
F7
Ab7
G7
C7
F7
Tenor 1
Tenor 2
Baritone
Trumpet
f
ff
Trombone
mf
ff
Bass
Drums
fill
F7
Ab7
G7
C7
F7
Piano

11-2 Backgrounds Based on Guide Tone Lines

Another common type of background is based on guide tone lines. Guide tones are the notes that define the sound of a chord: the 3 and 7. Used most often for II–V progressions, a guide tone line is created by voice leading, by step or common tone, from the 3 or 7 of one chord in a progression to the 3 or 7 of the next chord. Because 3 and 7 so clearly identify the sound of a chord, they provide a clarifying effect when played as a scale line through a progression. The smooth, linear motion does not distract the listener, thereby keeping attention on the soloist. Guide tone background lines may be scored in unison or in octaves or they may be harmonized. They may ascend or descend.

Basic Guide Tone Line

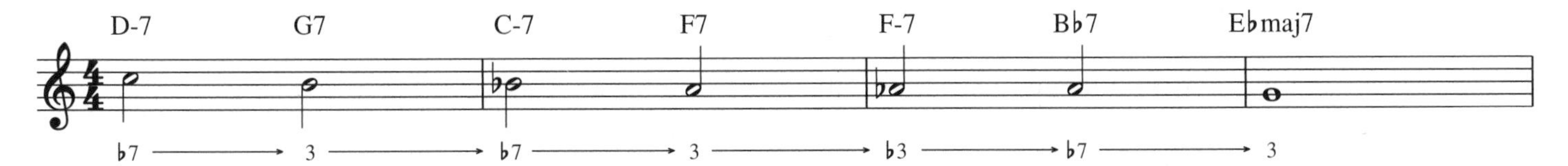

Embellished Guide Tone Line

An arranger may embellish a basic guide tone line to create a background that suits the given tempo and style. Here we alter the basic guide tone line for a medium swing feel.

Expanding the Concept

We can create additional backgrounds by generalizing the strategy of guide tone lines. This approach creates lines by voice leading, via step or common tone, from any chord tone or available tension in one chord to any chord tone or available tension in the next chord. Here are four background lines created by applying this approach to the progression from the previous examples.

11-3 Compositional Approach

With this strategy, the arranger becomes a composer, taking a motive from the thematic material in a piece and developing it into a background passage. We used this approach in creating the backgrounds for the arrangement of "1625 Swingerama Ave.," presented in the final chapter of this book.

The discussion that follows is an analysis of how we conceived and constructed the background phrases for the B chorus of "Swingerama," which features a tenor solo. Look over the lead sheet on page 185 to familiarize yourself with this tune. We also suggest you listen to CD track 68 a few times from the beginning up to the end of the B chorus. And keep the B chorus cued up so that you can replay it as needed. You will find it between 0:50 and 1:45 on the track.

Before writing, an arranger needs to decide where the backgrounds start and stop and how best to apply contrast and variety. In "1625 Swingerama Ave.," because the B chorus immediately follows a full-band scoring of the melody, we decided to keep the first eight-measure phrase free of backgrounds. This would enable the soloist to establish his or her presence. The first background appears at B9, the second eight-measure phrase. It is a simple unison line played by the trombones. For contrast, the background in the bridge (beginning at B17) has all sections of the band playing percussive voicings. In the last eight-measure phrase that begins at B25, the background returns to the idea of a simple unison line for the trombones.

Now we examine the process of adapting a melodic motive to create the specific background lines.

Creating the Background Line

The background line at B9 uses motives drawn from the melody of the tune. Our general idea was to keep it simple and out of the way of the tenor soloist.

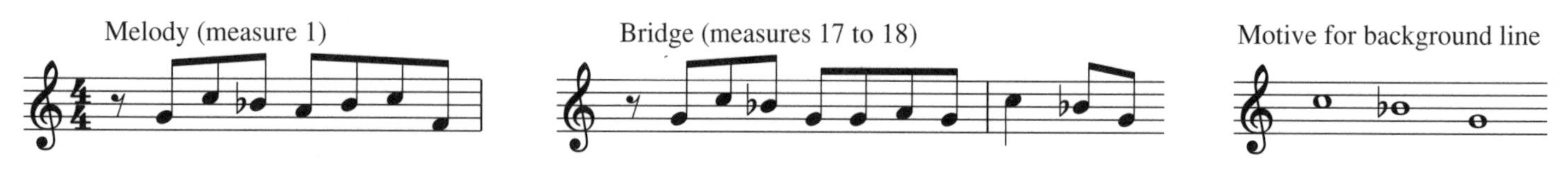

Next we transpose our original motive down a fifth:

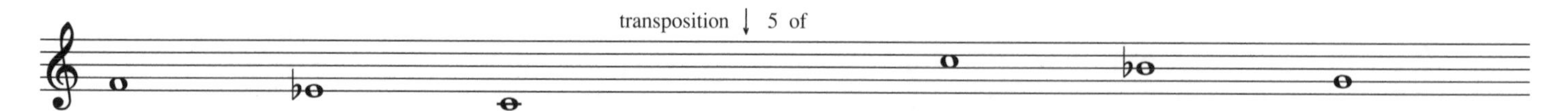

Here we use our transposed motive to build an unembellished framework for the first four measures of the background line starting at B9:

Then we embellish the framework to suit the medium swing feel and tempo:

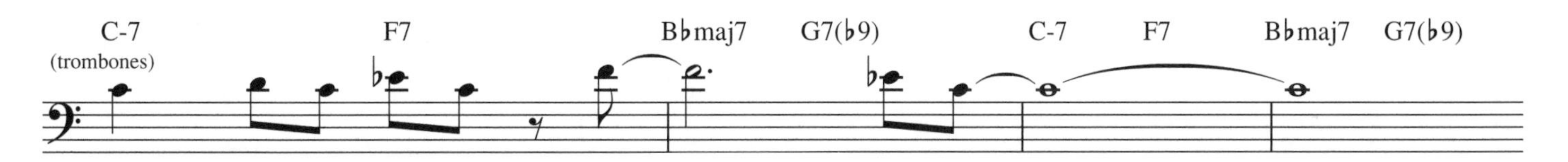

The next four measures repeat the riff but with some variation so as to create a "response" to the first four-measure "call":

Below, we show the full eight-measure phrase in unembellished form. It is easy to see its four-measure call-and-response structure (also know as question/answer or antecedent/consequent structure).

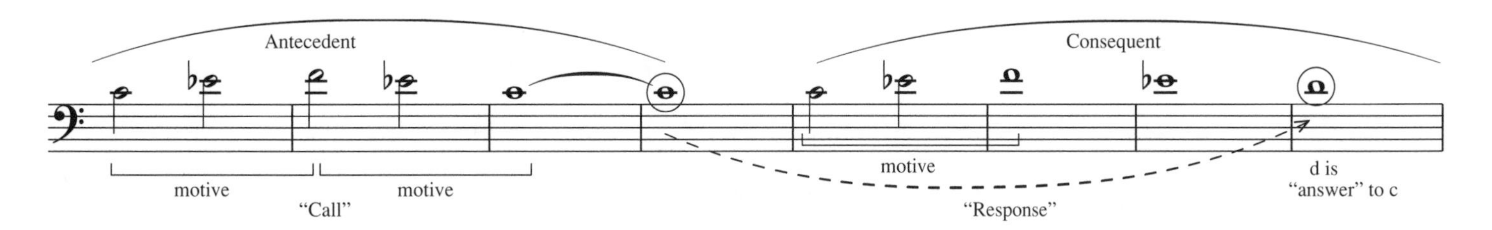

At B17, we create a percussive harmonic background in which the horn section becomes a "comping" unit behind the soloist. It is a dramatic contrast to the linear backgrounds at B9 and B25. The B17 background is discussed in further detail by the text accompanying the full score in the last chapter of this book.

For the background starting at B25, we revisit the B9 motive but develop it further. You can still see (and hear) the significance of the *c*, *e-flat*, *f*, and responding *d*, but the notes are reordered slightly and the phrasing is fragmented into four two-measure statements. In the first six measures, stepwise connection of chords is still the predominant strategy.

Here is the unembellished framework for the six measures starting at B25:

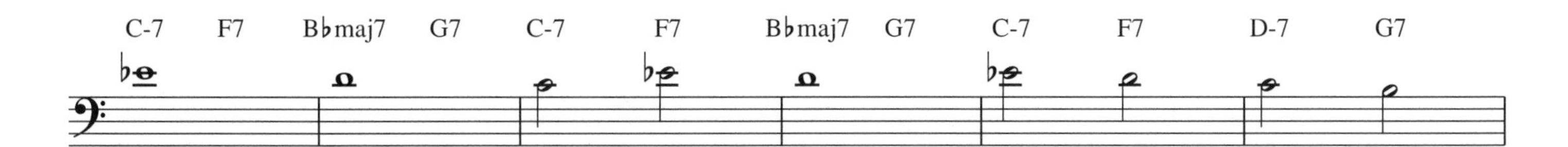

Here is the embellished, final version of the six measures starting at B25:

In the last two measures (B31 and B32), Trombone 1 refers to the rhythm and shape of the first measure of the melody:

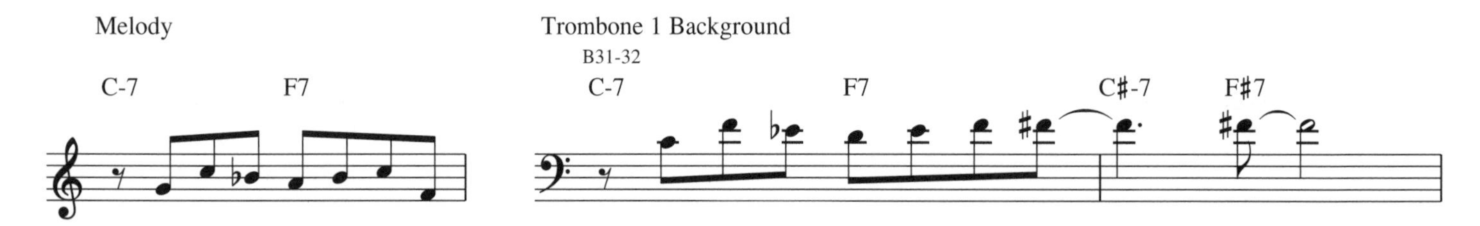

Note how the dramatically different final note of that trombone line (*f-sharp* versus the melody's *f*) adds to the bluesy flavor of our original three-note motive. It also provides a good climactic release into the interlude.

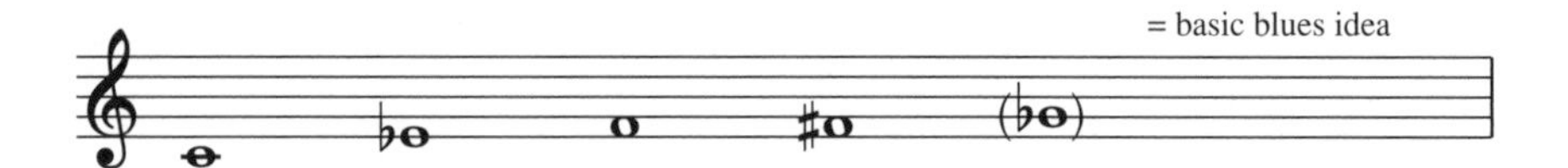

Now that you know how the backgrounds were created and appreciate how they reinforce the basic compositional material of the tune, listen to track 67 again from the beginning up to the interlude. Concentrate on how the compositional continuity feels and flows. You should hear a lot more than you heard in your earlier listening.

Investigate the backgrounds in the C chorus of this arrangement and read the accompanying text to learn how they were created. Then listen to the track from sections B to D (from 0:50 to 2:50). Be aware of how all the background writing supports the soloists, develops motives, and provides transitions from one part of the form to the next.

11-4 Exercises

Score three different backgrounds as specified to support a tenor saxophone solo on the chord progression of the phrase shown below. Use the melody as a motivic resource. Indicate which instruments are playing.

1. Use an embellished guide tone line in unison, octaves, or harmonized.

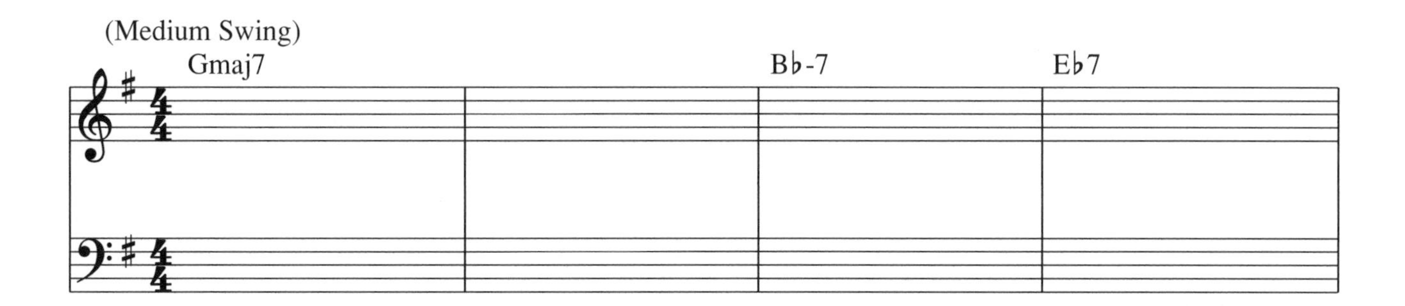

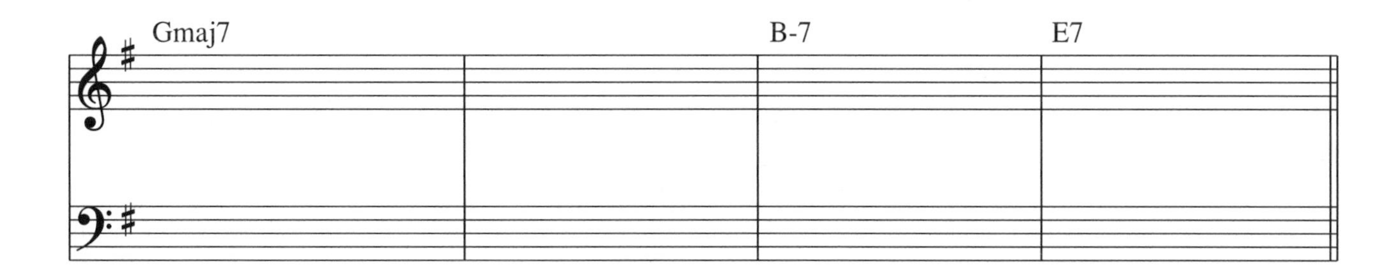

2. Use percussive voicings.

(Medium Swing)

Gmaj7 B♭-7 E♭7

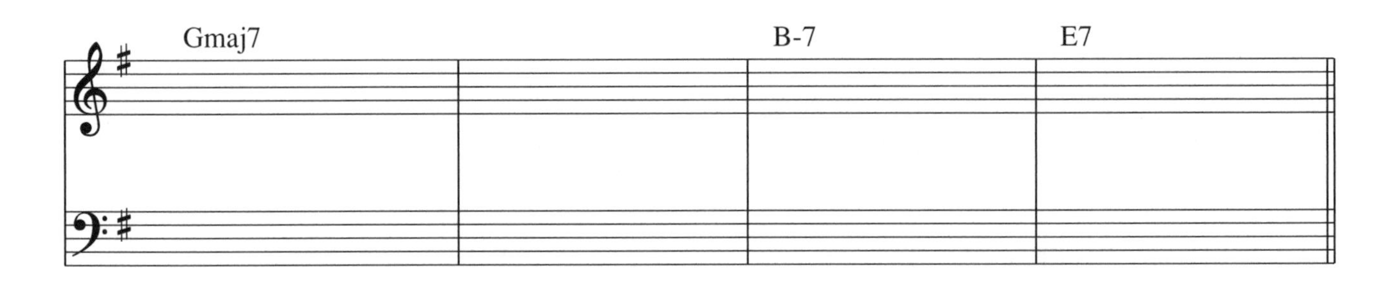

3. Use a riff scored in unison, octaves, and/or voicings.

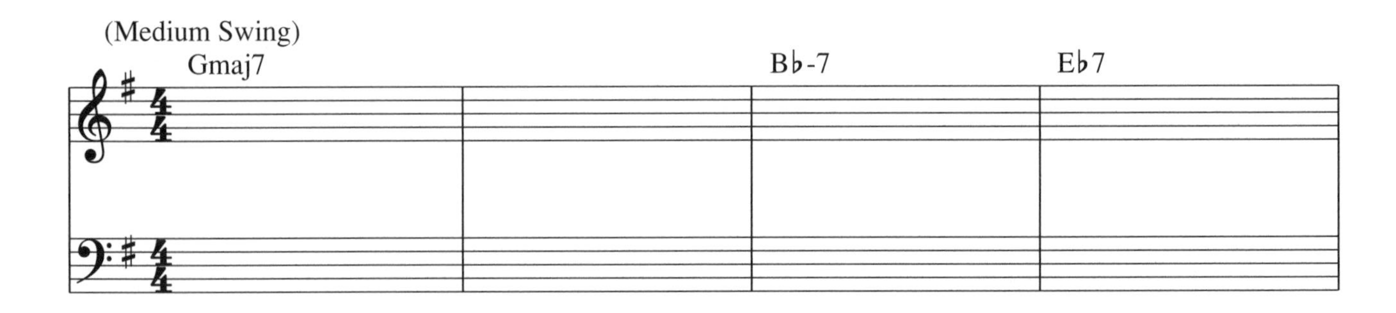

Gmaj7 B-7 E7

CHAPTER 12
Shout Choruses

IN THIS CHAPTER

12-1 Characteristics

The shout chorus is a climactic section at or near the end of a big band arrangement during which the entire band plays. It very often replaces the recapitulation of the melody with new material. Sometimes a shout chorus occupies only a part of the tune's form before the melody (or a section of the melody) returns as a final statement. Or, just as often, the last part of the melody is replaced with a shout phrase. The texture can be concerted, contrapuntal, or a combination of both.

Shout chorus characteristics include:

- percussive lead lines, often using no more than three or four attacks per measure
- repeating riffs
- lead trumpet in the high register
- loud dynamic level
- extensive reharmonization and/or development of the melody
- call-and-response exchanges between the horns and the drums or between the saxes and brass.
- concerted texture, with the entire band scored under the lead trumpet
- special effects in the brass, including shakes, falls, and flips
- contrapuntal texture, with each section of the band playing its own line (see the Holman-style version of the birthday song on page 171 in chapter 13)
- dense voicings, typically six or seven different pitches with doublings
- wide voicings, often three to four octaves

There is no specific technique or procedure that can be used to create a shout chorus. As with background writing, the arranger must become a composer and manipulate thematic material from the tune to create a dramatic climax. The best way to learn about shout chorus writing is to listen to examples from the big band repertoire.

12-2 Recommended Listening

Find as many of the following recordings as you can and listen to the suggested pieces. The more examples you listen to, the more ideas you will be able to extract and possibly apply in your own writing.

For each recommendation below, we list the piece, the band, the arranger, the album with its catalog number, and brief suggestions for what to listen for.

1. "In a Mellow Tone" (Basie Band, arrangement by Frank Foster), *Count Basie at Birdland* (*The Complete Roulette Live Recordings of Count Basie and His Orchestra*, Mosaic Records, CD ♯ 135-DISCS I-IV). The shout chorus is the last chorus of this six-chorus arrangement. Note the drum setup and the concerted, loud, sustained, and percussive voicings. The drummer fills and responds to the figures. Note also the use of brass shakes and falls.

2. "Days of Wine and Roses" (Woody Herman Band, arrangement by Nat Pierce), *Woody Herman Encore 1963* (Philips PHM 200-092). The shout chorus in this arrangement comes after the second chorus, a trumpet solo. It occupies only the second half of the chorus. Note the modulation, drum fills, and the percussive paraphrasing of the melody.

3. "Satin Doll" (Harry James Band, arrangement by Bob Florence), *Harry James Today* (MGM E3848). This arrangement plays with the form of the tune. The second chorus, featuring a trumpet solo, is really only half a chorus: AA of the form. The shout chorus then follows, covering the first two A sections again. The full chorus form is completed by a piano solo on the bridge and a restatement of the melody in the last A section. The shout writing is concerted, loud, and percussive with a high lead trumpet, brass shakes, and exchanges with the drummer.

4. "Basically Blues" (Buddy Rich Band, arrangement by Phil Wilson), *Swingin' New Big Band* (*"Live" at the Chez*) (Pacific Jazz CDP 8 35232 2 1). The shout writing in this arrangement evolves gradually in the three choruses that follow the piano solo. It starts with a band soli of moderate volume that eventually builds into a louder climax. It features sustained and percussive concerted textures with brass shakes and drum fills and setups. It ends with the "punch" on beat 4 that prepares the recapitulation.

5. "Frame for the Blues" (Maynard Ferguson Band, arrangement by Slide Hampton), *A Message from Newport* (Roulette Birdland Series R-52012). In the third chorus, the setup of the trombone solo features the typical high, hard, loud, and concerted texture characteristic of shout writing. The next to last chorus is the real shout chorus. It features the extreme high register trumpet and wide shakes associated with the Maynard Ferguson band.

6. "Shiny Stockings" (Count Basie Band, arrangement by Frank Foster), *Count Basie in London* (Verve CD♯833 805-2). The last chorus of this arrangement is shout writing at its best. The classic climactic elements include percussive and sustained concerted textures, brass shakes, and exchanges with the drummer.

7. "Stompin at the Savoy" (Stan Kenton Band, arrangement by Bill Holman), *Contemporary Concepts (Stan Kenton: The Complete Capitol Recordings of the Holman and Russo Charts*, Mosaic CD♯136-Disc IV). The shout writing occurs mainly in the next-to-last chorus, following the sax solo. Loud and concerted, it creates a strong climax that leads to a partial recapitulation of the melody before ending with the shout idea one last time.

8. "And We Listened (Maynard Ferguson Band, arrangement by Bob Freedman), *A Message from Newport* (Roulette Birdland Series R-52012). The last chorus of this arrangement is a classic shout chorus. Note the two-part counterpoint in the first phrase, the melodic paraphrasing with drum breaks, and then the screaming trumpets in the concerted last phrase.

9. "Splanky" (Basie Band, arrangement by Neil Hefti), *E=MC²=Count Basie (Count Basie/The Complete Atomic Basie Roulette* CDP 7243 8 28635 2 6). This is a simple but powerful 12-bar blues arrangement. Following the two choruses for tenor sax are two choruses of shout writing. Note the drum setup, the concerted and percussive figures with strong lead trumpet, and the loud dynamic level. After a one-chorus recap, the shout chorus is repeated for a climactic ending.

10. "Diminuendo and Crescendo in Blue" (Duke Ellington Band), *Duke Ellington at Newport 1956* (Columbia/Legacy C2K 64932). In the last two choruses, screech-trumpeter Cat Anderson's screaming responses on top of the concerted band create one of the most memorable shout moments on record. The whole last section of the arrangement, following the extended tenor solo by Paul Gonsalves, is one continuous buildup to the climactic shout ending.

12-3 Analysis of a Shout Chorus

Let us look closely at the shout chorus from the Dick Lowell arrangement of "1625 Swingerama Ave.," which appears in the last chapter of this book. Take a moment to familiarize yourself with the written music for the shout chorus; it begins at D25 in the score. We also suggest you listen to the full arrangement on CD track 68, paying special attention to the shout chorus, starting at about 3:28 in that track.

Inventing the Shout Melody

The tune, a variation on "rhythm changes," has the form AABA. In this arrangement, the shout chorus occupies just the last A section. The original melody is shown here in lead-sheet form. The shout melody appears below it as the lead trumpet line in the abbreviated shout-chorus score. Compare the two themes, noting how the original was altered to create the shout melody.

Original melody from lead sheet (final A section of "1625 Swingerama Ave."):

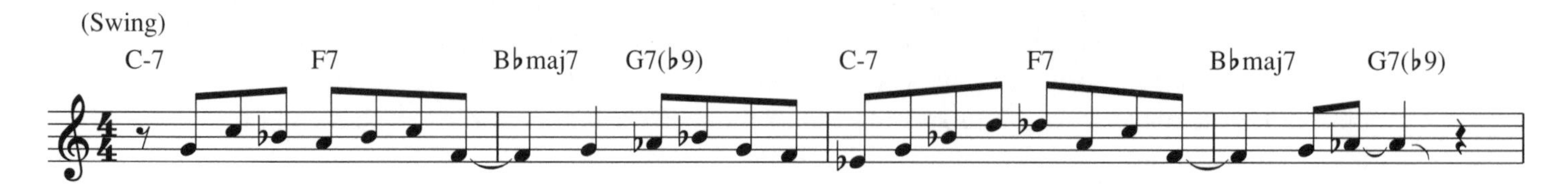

62 Shout melody, fully scored:

Now we look more closely at process of inventing the shout melody.

We used no reharmonization in creating the shout phrase. We did, however, construct an entirely new melody from ideas occurring in the last A section of the original melody. Our aim was to create a primary climax for the arrangement.

In the first two measures, emphasized notes from the melody are used to create a simpler lead line for the shout.

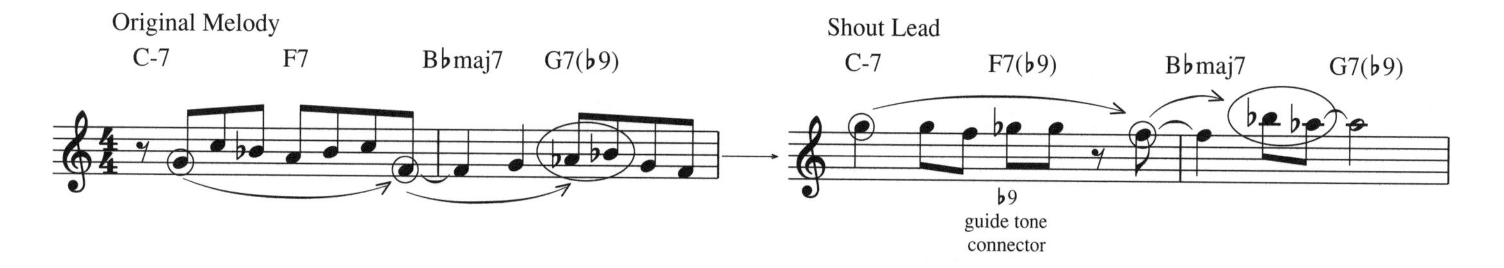

Notice how the shout phrase's second measure is nearly the same as measure 4 of the melody.

The third measure is a percussive melodic statement typical of shout sections. As in the first two measures, *g* and *f* are extracted from the tune's original thematic material. The six beats of rest in measures 3 and 4 enable the drummer to respond and set up the next four-measure phrase.

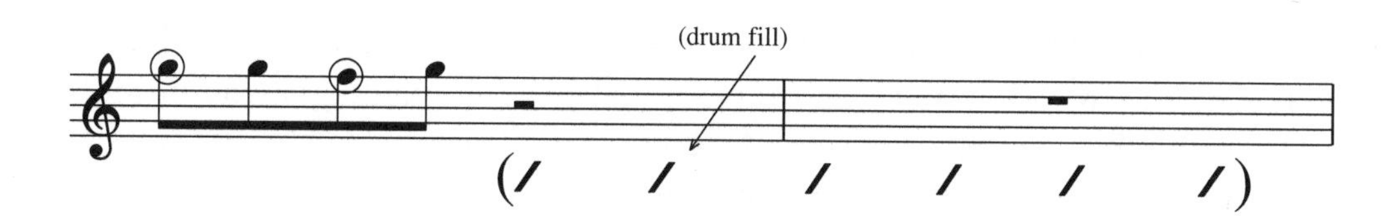

In measures 5 and 6, a rhythmic, chromatic "guide-tone" line continues the typical percussive melodic style of shout writing. As it ascends using only two notes per measure, it builds nicely to the climactic ending statement in measure 7.

In measure 7, note the reference to the tune's first three melody notes and the repeat of the ascending chromatic line (in an altered rhythm) from measures 5 and 6. These are good compositional decisions that establish motivic continuity for the shout phrase.

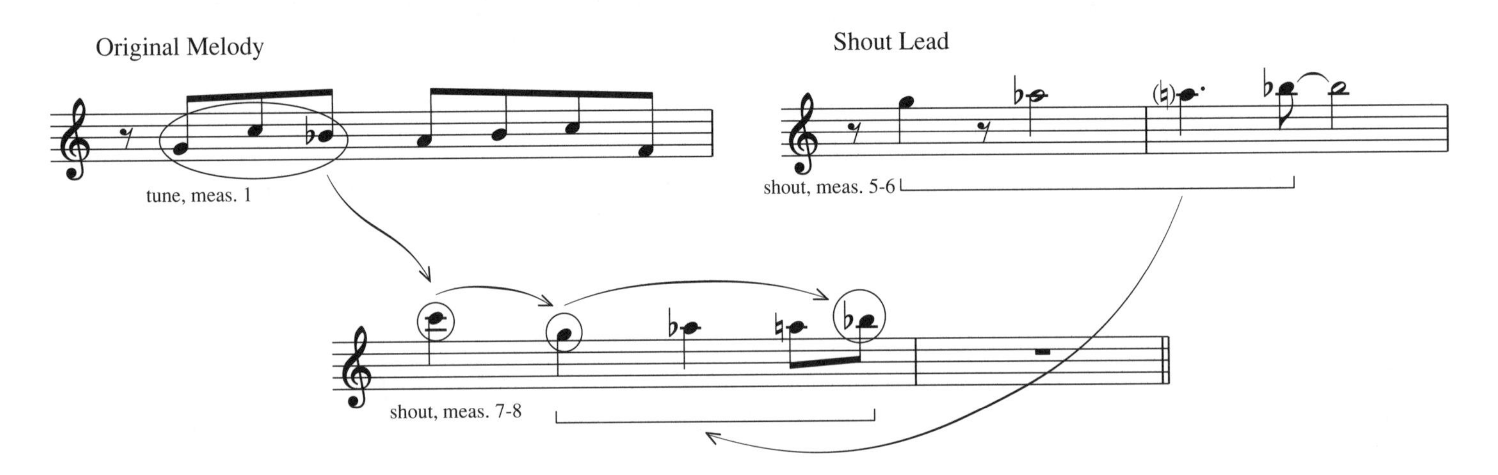

The horn's full rest in measure 8 is another opportunity for the drummer to respond and to set up the arrangement's ending phrase.

The Big Picture

Listen once more to CD track 68 to appreciate the role of the shout chorus in the overall arrangement. Notice how the shout phrase is set up by the scoring at the end of the bridge (D17), and then how it establishes the climactic release of the chorus. Note also how many of the typical characteristics appear in this shout chorus:

- lead trumpet in high register
- the whole band concerted under the lead trumpet
- loud volume level
- percussive melodic design
- call and response between horns and drums
- wide span—three octaves or more—of the voicings (measures D29 to D31)

12-4 Exercises

1. Replace the existing shout section of "1625 Swingerama Ave." with one of your own design for an 8&5 ensemble. Refer to full chart in Chapter 14; the shout chorus begins at D25.

2. Write your own shout chorus version of the birthday song for a 7&5. Refer to the lead sheet at the start of Chapter 13 and to the shout choruses (letter B) in that chapter's Basie-style and Holman-style arrangements.

This page intentionally left blank.

CHAPTER 13 Style

IN THIS CHAPTER

Exploring classic styles through five arrangements of the birthday song.

- 13-1 Early jazz.
- 13-2 Count Basie's cool, relaxed, swinging style.
- 13-3 Duke Ellington's "Pep Section," call and response, and symmetric diminished sounds.
- 13-4 Bill Holman's reinvented melodies, unison and counterpoint lines, and conventional harmony.
- 13-5 Gil Evans' orchestral approach.

Every arranger strives to create his or her own musical personality. In the history of large ensemble writing, certain recognizable styles have become models to be appreciated, studied, and emulated by aspiring writers.

In this chapter we present five versions of the birthday song. These arrangements, created by faculty of the Berklee College of Music, parody the work of famous arrangers in order to demonstrate their main stylistic characteristics.

Refer to the lead sheet below as the melodic and harmonic starting point for each arrangement. (Although the tune is usually sung in 3/4, we present it here in 4/4 so that it will swing.)

The Birthday Song

13-1 Early Jazz Style

Arrangement by Bill Scism

The first eight-measure chorus demonstrates the origin of soli writing using four brass (three trumpets and one trombone) in the general style of Don Redman. The voicings are largely triads voiced down from the melody, with the trombone doubling the melody an octave lower. The rhythmic style is a 1920s two-beat, "boom-chick" pattern written for the piano and drums. The bass part would just as often have been played by tuba.

The second chorus shows a typical 1930s swing style with the saxophones doubling the brass parts to create a thicker texture. This is reminiscent of the early concerted style of Fletcher Henderson. The baritone sax plays the roots of the chords while the bass animates the changes by "walking four to the bar" in early swing style. The piano comps in a slightly freer style than in the first chorus. The drums play more in the style of an early four-beat swing pattern.

Note the reharmonization of approach notes in both choruses. Measures 1 and 5 illustrate chromatic approach and measure 7 uses a diminished approach.

63

B
♩ = ♩ (1930s, 4-Beat Swing)
Alto
coll' trumpet 3
Tenor 1
coll' trumpet 1 8vb
Tenor 2
coll' trumpet 2 8vb
Baritone
Trumpet 1
Trumpet 2
Trumpet 3
Trombone
C
G
C
C D-
C
Piano
Bass
Drums

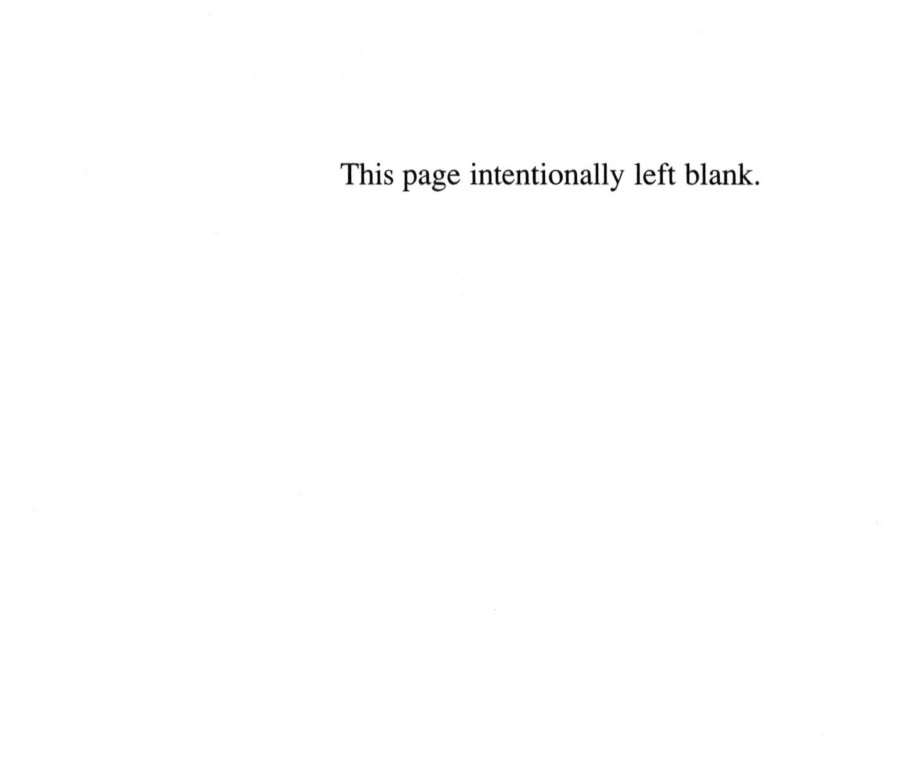

This page intentionally left blank.

13-2 Count Basie's Style

Arrangement by Scott Free

There is great intensity in the way the Basie band swings, but the underlying feeling is cool and relaxed. In order to get that balance, the band has to be accurate without rushing, and lyrical without losing its edge. The Thad Jones/Mel Lewis band was the modern reflection of this outlook. (Thad played trumpet and wrote for the Basie band).

The introduction—a sparse piano solo delivered as the rhythm section lays down the time—is the first of many Basie characteristics in this arrangement. The melody uses sharply articulated figures with accents on the syncopated attacks. Concerted voicings get the optimum power from the brass and reeds. Note the reharmonizations using substitute dominants from above or chromatic dominants from below the target chords.

The start of the second chorus heightens the excitement by modulating from the key of F to G♭. The melody notes in the sax soli are shortened, leaving space for the syncopated brass responses as punctuation. The arrangement closes in classic Basie style: a *d-flat* pedal point at the final cadence, followed by the piano's well-known "Basie tag" (using the ♯II°7 passing diminished chord between the II–7 and inverted I6).

64
Swing (♩ = 116)
(Intro)
A
Alto 1
Alto 2
Tenor 1
Tenor 2
Baritone
Trumpet 1
2
3
4
Trombone 1
2
3
Bass Trombone
Guitar
Piano
Bass (sounding 8vb)
Drums
coll' trumpet 2
coll' trumpet 3
coll' trumpet 1 8vb
coll' trombone 2
coll' trumpet 1 8vb
mf
f
F6 D7 G-7 C7 C/Bb A-7 Ab7 G-7 C7 Gb7 E7(#9) F6 Db7 C7(9) C7(b13)
Light solo fills
light fill
brushes (play time)
(sticks)
play time

Alto 1
(coll' trumpet 2)
mf
Alto 2
(coll' trumpet 3)
mf
Tenor 1
(coll' trumpet 1 8vb)
mf
Tenor 2
(coll' trombone 2)
mf
Baritone
sfz
mf
Trumpet 1
sfz
ff
f
2
sfz
f
mf
3
sfz
f
mf
4
sfz
f
mf
Trombone 1
(coll' trumpet 1 8vb)
2
sfz
3
sfz
Bass Trombone
sfz
B7(♯9) C7 E7 F6 G♭7 F7 B7 B♭7 B°7 F7 D7(♯9) D♭7
Guitar
light fill
F6 G♭7 F7 B7 B♭7 B°7 F7 D7(♯9) D♭7
Piano
Bass
(time) (kicks)
Drums

B
(bend pitch)
Alto 1
Alto 2
Tenor 1
Tenor 2
Baritone
coll' trumpet 1 8vb
coll' trumpet 2 8vb
coll' trumpet 3
coll' trumpet 4
coll' bass trombone
Trumpet 1
2
3
4
Trombone 1
2
3
Bass Trombone
8vb
Guitar
Piano
Bass
Drums
Gb7
D7
Db7(13)
Db7
Ab-7
Gb6(9)
G7
C7
"Hard swing"
(play time)
mf
fp
f
ff
(mf)

Alto 1
(coll' trumpet 1 8vb)
Alto 2
(coll' trumpet 2 8vb)
Tenor 1
(coll' trumpet 3)
Tenor 2
(coll' trumpet 4)
Baritone
(coll' bass trombone)
Trumpet 1
2
3
4
fp
Trombone 1
2
3
Bass Trombone
8vb
Guitar
Cb7 C°7 Gmaj7 Gbmaj7/Db Db7 Gb6
Piano
mf
mp
Bass
Drums

This page intentionally left blank.

13-3 Duke Ellington's Style

Arrangement by Jeff Friedman

Duke Ellington's career spanned nearly fifty years, stylistically encompassing early jazz from the 1920s and 1930s, swing from the late 1930s and 1940s, and the more modern approaches represented by bebop, modal jazz, and even so-called free jazz. This arrangement represents some of the characteristics and devices found in Ellingtonia from around the mid 1950s through the 1960s.

The first chorus features the melody played by the saxophone section in unison and octaves. A three-part harmonic accompaniment is played by Trumpets 3 and 4 and Trombone 1 using plunger mutes. Note the "doo-wah" sound of the plungers. This muted brass trio, dubbed the "pep section," was a mainstay of Ellington's orchestral vocabulary. The pep section can be heard in the second and last choruses of the blues "Such Sweet Thunder," from the suite of the same name, *Such Sweet Thunder*, Columbia COL 4691 40 2 or Columbia/Legacy CK 65568.

After modulating from F to B♭ via a dissonant, bluesy symmetric diminished voicing, the second chorus features a saxophone soli "in conversation" with the brass. This call-and-response phrasing, and the many strident symmetric diminished voicings found in the saxes and the brass, are typical Ellingtonian devices.

In a final gesture characteristic of Ellington, the last chord leaves the arrangement with an ambiguous, unfinished feeling.

65
Medium Swing
A
Alto 1
Alto 2
Tenor 1
Tenor 2
Baritone
coll' alto 1
coll' alto 1
coll' alto 1 8vb
coll' alto 1 8vb
Trumpet 1
2
3
4
(Plunger)
(open)
Trombone 1
2
3
Bass
(walk)
F6
C7
F6
F7
B♭6
B°7
F/C
C7
F6
F7(♭9,13)
Drums
Ride (play time)

B
Alto 1
Alto 2
Tenor 1
Tenor 2
Baritone
coll' alto 1 8vb
Trumpet 1
2
3
4
Trombone 1
2
3
Bb6(9)
F7(b9)
F7(b9)
Bb6(9) Bb°
Bb6 Bb7(b9)
Eb7
E°7
Bb/F
F7
Bass
Play time
Drums
mp

This page intentionally left blank.

13-4 Bill Holman's Style

Arrangement by Ted Pease

Bill Holman's arranging style is characterized by unison lines and counterpoint. He also likes to recompose familiar melodies so that they are disguised to casual listeners but interesting and challenging to musicians and jazz fans. Thus his lead lines often take on the quality of improvised solos, as demonstrated in this arrangement.

Holman's voicings are usually conventional big-band block chords, typical two-handed piano voicings in thirds that contain little tension. Occasionally, to create harmonic variety, he surprises the listener with powerful dissonance. Most of all, his music swings.

66

Medium Up Swing (♩ = 180)
♩ = 180
Intro
A
Alto 1
Alto 2
Tenor 1
Tenor 2
Baritone
Trumpet 1
2
3
4
Trombone 1
2
3
4
Piano
Bass
Drums
coll' trumpet 1
coll' tenor 1
coll' trombone 2
f
mf
mp
light fill to time
(Play time, light ride cymb.)

Alto 1
Alto 2
Tenor 1
Tenor 2
Baritone
(coll' tenor 1)
Trumpet 1
2
3
4
coll' trumpet 1
coll' trumpet 1
coll' trumpet 1
Trombone 1
2
3
4
coll' trombone 1
coll' trombone 1
Piano
Bass
Drums

B
Alto 1
Alto 2
Tenor 1
Tenor 2
Baritone
Trumpet 1
2
3
4
coll' trumpet 1 8vb
coll' trumpet 1 8vb
coll' trumpet 1 8vb
Trombone 1
2
3
4
coll' trombone 1
coll' trombone 1
Piano
Db-7 C-7
F7(b9)
Bb6
Bb7sus4(9)
Bb13
Bass
Drums
(time)

Alto 1
Alto 2
coll' alto 1
Tenor 1
coll' alto 1 8vb
Tenor 2
coll' tenor 1
Baritone
Trumpet 1
2
coll' trumpet 1
3
coll' trumpet 1
4
coll' trumpet 1
Trombone 1
2
(coll' trombone 1)
3
(coll' trombone 1)
4
Eb
Ab7
Bb6 (high fill)
Piano
Bass
Drums

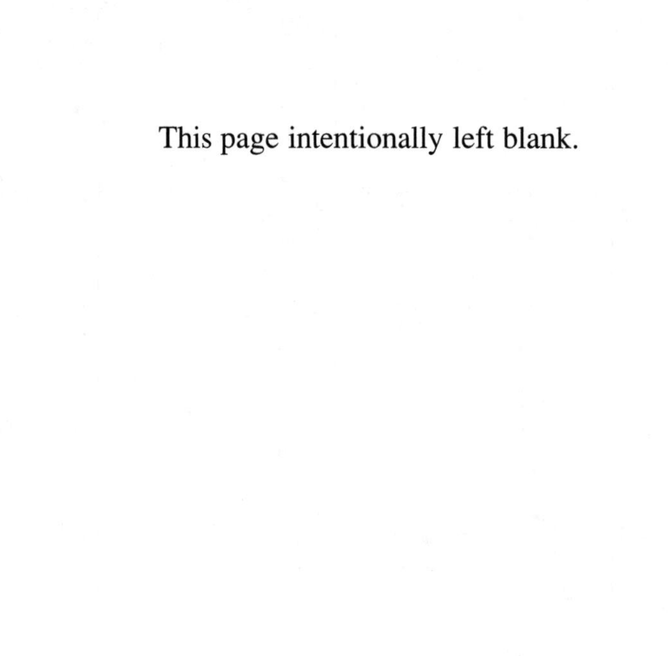

This page intentionally left blank.

13-5 Gil Evan's Style

Arrangement by Greg Hopkins

Gil Evans represents the orchestral school of arranging. He most often dealt with material from other writers but he would always develop and alter it to suit his own values as a composer and orchestrator.

This arrangement demonstrates the Evans approach in several ways. The tune has been reconceived in the context of Evans' own harmonic vocabulary. The melody has been elongated, and a great deal of space separates each melodic statement. And the piece is written for an expanded, orchestral instrumentation: The brass section includes a solo flugelhorn (which adds solo fills ad lib in a manner reminiscent of Evans' collaborations with Miles Davis), two French horns, and a tuba; woodwinds replace the saxophones.

In the introduction, a rhumba ostinato figure establishes the C tonal center but uses both major and minor chromatic colors, creating a mysterious, unsettled quality. The first two measures present the rhythmic and harmonic motive upon which the entire arrangement is based. This idea is developed by repetition, harmonic variation, and contrasting orchestrations. Note that the rhythm section does not comp changes but instead plays a specific, composed texture.

The melody starts at measure 9, a modal and bluesy alteration of "Happy Birthday's" given melody. A composed texture reharmonizes the normal tonic/dominant harmony of the tune. The climax, from measures 31 to 34, features an exotic reharmonization of the altered melody. It is emphasized by concerted scoring for nearly all members of the band.

The 6/4 section beginning at measure 37 develops the idea from the introduction's first two measures, creating a descending cadential pattern that resolves to the open fifth (*c* to *g*) at 41. Trumpets in mixed mutes and woodwinds offer one last motivic statement, voiced in dissonant clusters. (Note the alternating placement of woodwinds and trumpets through the cluster voicing; within each section, adjacent instruments are separated by thirds, which makes it easier to maintain good intonation.) The final chord resolves to the C tonal center, but with no defining 3 or 7 in the chord, a dramatic Aeolian ambiguity prevails.

67
Slow Rhumba (♩ = 96)
9
(Solo) 2nd time
Solo Flügelhorn
Flute 1 2
a2
Clarinet 1 2
Bass Clarinet
Trumpet 1
2
3
4
French Horn 1 2
Trombone 1
2
3
4
Tuba
Guitar
Piano
Bass (sounding 8vb)
Drums
Slow Rhumba (Play time)
(TT's)
Play time (simile)

Solo Flügelhorn
Flute 1 2
Clarinet 1 2
Bass Clarinet
Trumpet 1
2
3
4
French Horn 1 2
Trombone 1
2
3
Tuba 4
Guitar
Piano
Bass
Drums
sfz
mf
(Harmon)
(Harmon)
(Harmon)
(open)
(open)
(lead)
sfz
sfz
sfz
mf
2
mp
3

21
Solo Flügelhorn
Flute 1 2
Clarinet 1 2
Bass Clarinet
Trumpet 1
2
3
4
French Horn 1 2
Trombone 1
2
3
4
Tuba
Guitar
Piano
Bass
Drums
a2
coll' trumpet 1
(time)
(Play time)
f
mf
mp

31
Solo Flügelhorn
Flute 1 2
Clarinet 1 2
Bass Clarinet
Trumpet 1
2
3
4
(coll' trumpet 1)
coll' trumpet 2
French Horn 1 2
a2
Trombone 1
2
3
4
Tuba
Guitar
Piano
Bass
Drums
mp
mf
f
ff
decresc.

Solo Flügelhorn
C- (Aeolian)
Bb-
Flute 1 2
a2
mf
sf
Clarinet 1 2
a2
mf
sf
Bass Clarinet
mf
mf
decresc.
Trumpet 1
mp
2
mp
3
mp
sf
4
mp
sf
French Horn 1 2
a2
mp
sf
mf
decresc.
Trombone 1
mp
sf
mf
decresc.
2
mp
sf
mf
decresc.
3
mp
sf
mf
decresc.
4
Tuba
mf
sf
mf
decresc.
Guitar
Piano
Bass
Drums
(more relaxed)
(Play time)
3
3

Rit. . . . . Slower
Ab-
G-
(optional)
Solo Flügelhorn
Flute 1 2
Clarinet 1 2
Bass Clarinet
(harmon)
(harmon)
(cup)
(cup)
Trumpet 1
2
3
4
French Horn 1 2
Trombone 1
2
3
4
Tuba
Guitar
Piano
Bass
Drums
mp
p

CHAPTER 14 Analysis of a Complete Arrangement

IN THIS CHAPTER

In this final chapter, we consider the complete arrangement of "1625 Swingerama Ave." as a vehicle for demonstrating all of the techniques discussed in this book.

14-1 Schematic of the Arrangement

The diagram below gives an overview of the structure and major elements of this arrangement. When you listen to CD track 68 the first few times, use this schematic to help you follow the "big picture" of the arrangement through its four choruses (A, B, C, and D).

As we noted when we first examined this schematic in Chapter 1, the arrangement contains the kind of variety and contrast that any good arrangement should have. Its primary components include:

- an introduction and matching ending, in the bookends style
- an interlude
- various contrasting written textures
- three modulations to new keys
- space for soloists
- a shout chorus

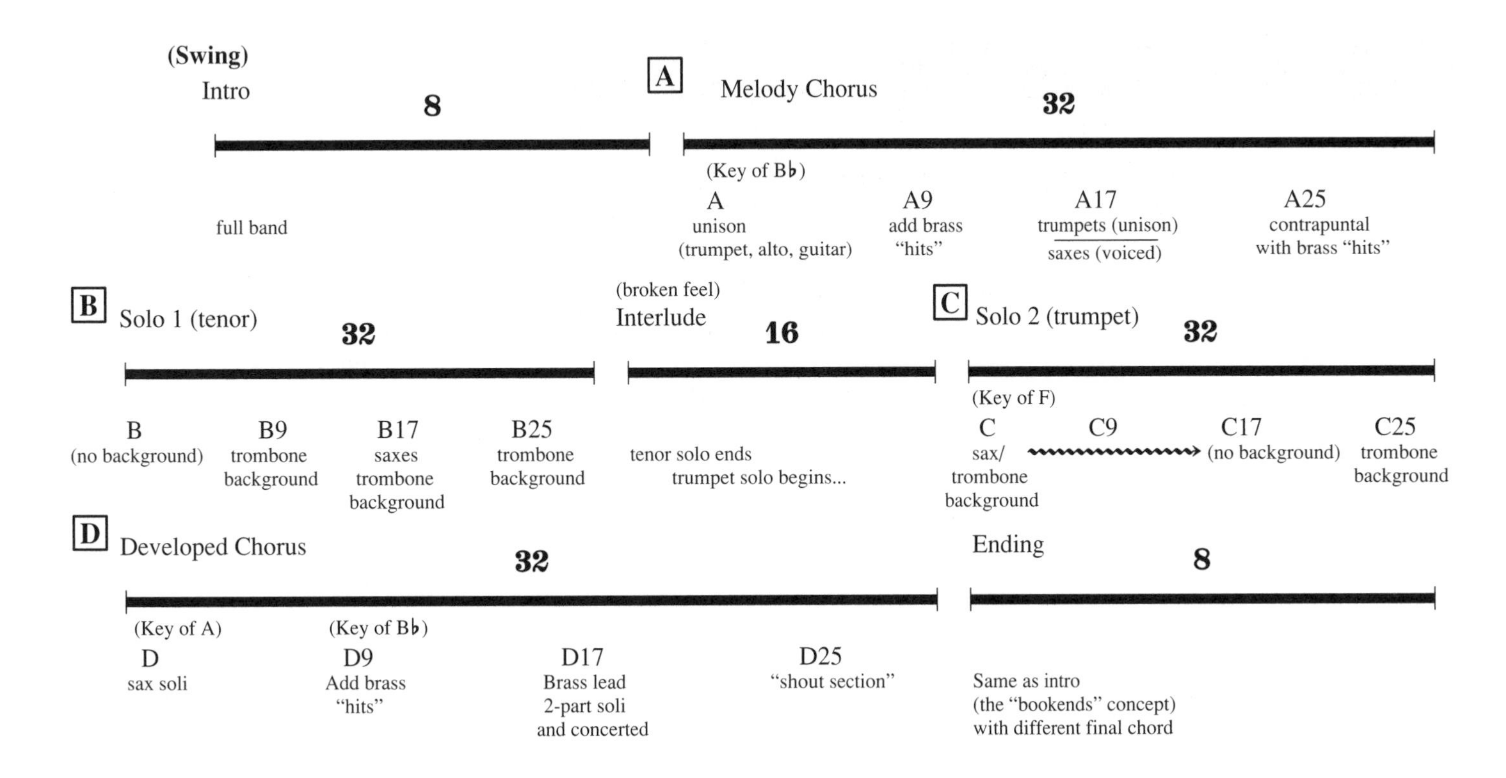

14-2 Lead Sheet

"1625 Swingerama Ave." is an AABA tune based on a variation of the "rhythm changes" chord progression. Its primary key center is B♭. Refer to the following lead sheet as you listen to and analyze the complete arrangement of this tune.

1625 Swingerama Ave.

14-3 The Score and Commentary

The score that follows is in concert pitch. (The bass is shown up an octave, as it will be written on the bass part.) Because of the chromatic nature of the lines and the shifting key centers, the arrangement is written in open key, showing no key signature.

After you have listened to the complete arrangement several times, follow along on the score. Each page shows eight measures of the full score accompanied by analytical comments. Studying the details of each phrase will give you a better understanding of how to apply the various arranging strategies discussed throughout this book.

68

The introduction begins with stop-time, voiced "hits" in the brass and rhythm sections. This sets up the sax line in octaves during measures 1 to 2 and the answering of this line by the trumpets in octaves during measures 3 to 4. A tutti passage in measures 5 and 6 has the trumpets and trombones subdividing the melody while the saxes emphasize the chord sound. Observe how the brass lines "cascade" from unison or octaves to voiced texture. The passage ends with concerted spreads. In measure 8, the climax of this introduction uses a concerted upper structure triad voicing, an E♭ triad over the primary G7 chord.

In the first A section, the melody is scored lightly with a mixed high-timbre unison of Alto 1, Trumpet 2, and Guitar. This repeats for the second A section (starting at A9), while the brass provide harmonic support. Note the first "hit" in A9, which is scored using mechanical voicings: Trumpets 1, 3, and 4 with Trombone 1 use a drop-2 voicing; Trombones 1, 2, 3, and 4 are in a four-way close voicing. At A11 and A12, the brass are voiced in spreads. Notice how the last two accented brass voicings not only respond to the melody's first four-measure phrase but also set up the melody's second phrase.

At A17 the orchestration changes. The melody is now scored in unison for Trumpets 1, 3, and 4. The saxophone section provides harmonic support and a simple contrapuntal reaction to the trumpet melody. (The saxes are inactive when the trumpets are active, then active when the trumpets are inactive.) From A17 to A19 the voicings are spreads; they change to drop-2 double lead at A20. Examine the dominant and chromatic approach-note reharmonizations in measure A20 and the crossing of voices in A22 that avoids repeated notes in the saxophone lines. At A23, all the horns play the same accented rhythm, providing a good medium-level climax. The altos, tenors, and trumpets are in a two-part soli while the trombones and baritone are voiced in supporting spreads.

A25 features a lightly scored two-line counterpoint. Alto 1, Trumpet 2, and Guitar provide a high-timbre, unison melody over a medium-timbre, unison counter line played by Tenor 1 and Trombone 1. Note the trombone's register: The trombone is easy to play and blends well when scored between *g* above the staff and *g* in the fourth space in the staff. The brass section provides voiced kicks in response to the counterpoint. Note the drop-2 voicings with octave doublings. The phrase ends abruptly at A31 with a concerted B♭6 voicing on the up-beat of beat 4. This sets up the stop-time solo break for the tenor solo.

The B chorus is a solo for Tenor 2. Notice that Tenor 2 has an eight-measure rest at A25 to prepare for the solo. Wise arrangers try not to involve a soloist in the phrase that immediately precedes the solo. This gives the player time to stand, adjust the music if necessary, and get comfortable. It also makes the entrance of the soloing instrument a more dramatic event. Here, the first eight measures feature just the soloist and rhythm section. (The guitar lays out as the piano comps). At B9, Trombones 1, 2, and 3 play a unison background line. Note both the bluesy quality and the guide-tone linking of the chords. The background rhythm is inactive so as not to get in the way. It also has a clear call-and-response structure that propels the phrase forward. It is common practice to distinguish the soloist by having a contrasting section provide the background. Here, the low brass background sets off the saxophone solo effectively.

As the tenor solo continues, the background writing changes its orchestration and approach. Now the saxophones play percussive voicings scored in four-way close from B17 to B19. At B20 and B21, the saxes move to upper structure triad voicings. To give more climactic impact to the G♭7 chord at B21, the trumpets overlap the sax background with a four-way close voicing. Just before B22, the trombone's "fp" attack and quarter-note anticipation emphasize their four-way close background (which also could be interpreted as a cluster voicing). This figure sets up the trombones' last three attacks: bluesy and rich voicings for B7 and D7. Moving from the first chord to the second, the intervals within the voicings remain constant: minor third/major second/tritone. The note functions change, however, from 13/♭5/3/♭7 for the B7 to ♯9/1/♭7/3 for the D7.

B25, the last "A section" of the B chorus, has Trombones 1, 2, and 3 providing a unison background line for the tenor solo. This time, the line is more active than the earlier trombone background at B9. Compare these two sections and examine the lines for compositional consistency and development. At B31, Trombone 4 enters and strengthens the line by doubling it an octave below. Note how the four lines then cascade out of the octave/unison doubling into four-part voicings. At B32, a II-V reharmonization (C♯–7 to F♯7) modulates the key center up a half-step from B♭ to B.

The interlude furnishes a contrast in texture, harmony, and time feel. At first, B major is felt as the new key center, as the harmonic rhythm becomes more elongated. The trombones are voice-led into the first measure of the interlude to smooth the transitional flow. Now a new soloist, Trumpet 2, enters while the tenor solo continues. As the dialogue between the trumpet and tenor progresses through the interlude, the tenor becomes more passive and fades out while the trumpet intensifies to start its solo for the C chorus.

The implied key shifts to D♭ Lydian, followed by the IV7 chord (G♭7). Note how the feel is "stretched out" to prepare for the return of the swing groove and chorus form at C. There is no better way to renew a swing time groove than to contrast it with a floating, broken, or stop-time passage. While this interlude provides useful contrast and also supports some improvisational fun between the tenor and trumpet, it serves another important function. Its harmonic framework, especially the last two chords, triggers a modulation to the key of F and a resumption of the tune's chord progression at the start of the next section. (D♭Maj7♯11 [♭VI] and G♭7 [SubV] connect to G–7, C7, FMaj7 D7, and so on.)

The C chorus is scored for a trumpet solo in the newly established key center of F. The guitar takes over as the primary comping instrument. Background support starts immediately with Alto 1, Alto 2, and Tenor 1 playing a four-measure unison line based on the melody. At C5, Trombones 1, 2, and 3 answer the saxes in call-and-response fashion. The scoring of this background line could also be considered an example of melodic subdivision with no dovetailing.

From C9 to C16, the background continues to alternate between the saxes and the trombones. But now the scheme of melodic subdivision is as follows: two measures for the saxes, two measures for the trombones, and a final four measures for the saxes. And in contrast to the unison sound of the background played from C1 through C8, the texture has now changed to two-part writing, using a pair of instruments on each part.

For a contrast, and to give the trumpet soloist a bit more room, there are no backgrounds during the bridge, from C17 to C25. The rhythmic ideas for the piano, played behind the guitar's comping, recall ideas from the interlude.

The trombone background line starting at C25 develops the linear ideas of the earlier trombone background played behind the tenor solo, from B25 to B32. This reference to the previous chorus establishes a continuity between the two solo sections. In fact, the voicings for the chords C♯–7 and F♯7 in B32 and C32 are exactly the same. These chords, which in B32 resolved to the interlude's BMaj7, now resolve to the B–7 in the first measure of the D chorus, creating a modulation to the key of A for the upcoming sax soli.

The D chorus is the recapitulation, which gains extra distinction by starting in the newly established key of A. The first A section of the tune is a sax soli. Because the original melody is already soloistic, very little embellishment is used. The voicings are mostly four-way close, double-lead with occasional drop-2 voicings sprinkled in for contrast. Note how the double lead changes from Tenor 2 to baritone in the first four bars as crossing of voices is used to avoid repeating notes and to create more interesting lines. Analyze the techniques used to reharmonize approach notes throughout this eight-measure phrase. In the last measure, D8, the brass entrance in octaves builds a link into the next phrase as the D♭–7-to-G♭7 progression moves chromatically to C–7 and F7. This prepares a return to the key of B♭ for the second A section, which starts at D9.

The second A section is back in the original key of B♭. The sax soli continues but uses a simplified version of the original melody. Percussive brass "kicks" set up and respond to the saxes. These kicks are primarily scored in four-way close voicings in the trumpets doubled an octave lower in the trombones. Note also the two upper structure triad voicings that are used for contrast.

Beginning at D17, climax is the goal. The brass section presents the melody in a two-part soli texture with each line doubled at the unison or in octaves. From D17 to D20, note the reharmonization and the specific scoring for the rhythm section. The saxophones' response to the brass at D20 is voiced in clusters. In D21 and D22, all the horns are scored in a two-part soli texture, with the "highs" in unison and the "lows" in octaves. The lead trumpet has an independent part that moves up to an octave doubling of the last note in D22. This passage ends emphatically with the brass section's concerted voicings in support of the sax's embellished melody. The last note is scored in a powerful upper structure triad voicing for the D♭7(♯9) chord.

In the final A section, the climax escalates with a loud shout chorus, a concerted scoring of a new variation on the melody played by the entire band. In D25, the lead alto line uses variable coupling to the brass. In D26, notice the doubling choices for the concerted, close voicings that lead up to the two upper structure triad voicings for the G7. In D27 the horns are once again in concerted close-position voicings, setting up the solo drum fill in D28. From D29 to D31, spread voicings emphasize the climax. Notice the variation in spacing and color achieved in these spreads by using four-way close, drop-2, upper structure triads, fourths, and the related doubling choices, while maintaining the root and chord sound in the bottom of the voicings. The drummer responds to the climax with a solo fill to set up the ending.

Following the "bookends" approach, the ending is identical to the introduction, except for the last voicing. The G7, which was on beat 2 of the last measure of the introduction (as a setup for the C–7 at letter A) is replaced with a D♭maj7 voicing. Note the quarter-note anticipation and upper structure triad voicing that make the D♭maj7 (♭IIImaj7) a strong and dramatic ending. The drummer ad libs a solo fill as the band sustains the final chord.

AS SERIOUS ABOUT MUSIC AS YOU ARE

Berklee Press DVDs are a great way to keep growing and stay creative by tapping into the energy and expertise of successful musicians. With each DVD, you'll get a 30- to 90-minute lesson with top Berklee College of Music teachers, alumni and high-profile professional artists.

DVD VIDEO

Shred Metal Chop Builder
Featuring Joe Stump

Improve your technique, increase your speed, and take your guitar chops into the stratosphere.

$19.95 HL: 50448015 ISBN:0-87639-033-5

Building Your Music Career
Featuring David Rosenthal

Get detailed, practical advice on how to network, adapt to different musical settings, take full advantage of opportunities, and be a successful musician.

$19.95 HL: 50448013 ISBN: 0-87639-031-9

Modal Voicing Techniques
Featuring Rick Peckham

Bring new colors and voicings to your playing with inventive demonstrations that will expand your musical vocabulary, no matter what instrument you play.

$19.95 HL: 50448016 ISBN: 0-87639-034-3

Beginning Improvisation: Motivic Development
Featuring Ed Tomassi

Build compelling improvisations from just a few notes with a method that's easy to understand and practice.

$19.95 HL: 50448014 ISBN: 0-87639-032-7

Jim Kelly's Guitar Workshop

Improve your playing by studying and emulating the techniques of great players like Jeff Beck, Stevie Ray Vaughn, Pat Metheny and more.

$29.95 HL: 00320168 ISBN: 0-634-00865-X

Basic Afro-Cuban Rhythms
Featuring Ricardo Monzón

Learn how to play and practice the classic rhythms of the Afro-Cuban tradition.

$19.95 HL: 50448012 ISBN: 0-8679-030-0

Turntable Technique: The Art of the DJ
Featuring Stephen Webber

Learn to play the turntable like your favorite Djs and create your own style!

$19.95 HL: 50448025 ISBN: 0-87639-038-6

Berklee Press DVDs, videos and books are available at music stores, book stores, or www.berkleepress.com. Call 617-747-2146 for a free catalog.

WWW.BERKLEEPRESS.COM

Distributed By HAL•LEONARD®

More Fine Publications from Berklee Press

berklee press

As Serious About Music As You Are.

Prices subject to change without notice.

GUITAR

VOICE LEADING FOR GUITAR
▸ by John Thomas
50449498 Book/CD $24.95

THE GUITARIST'S GUIDE TO COMPOSING AND IMPROVISING
▸ by Jon Damian
50449497 Book/CD $24.95

BERKLEE BASIC GUITAR
▸ by William Leavitt
Phase 1
50449460 Book $7.95
Phase 2
50449470 Book $7.95

CLASSICAL STUDIES FOR PICK-STYLE GUITAR ▸ by William Leavitt
50449440 Book $9.95

A MODERN METHOD FOR GUITAR 123 COMPLETE
▸ by William Leavitt
50449468 Book $29.95
Also available in separate volumes:
Volume 1: Beginner
50449404 Book/CD $22.95
50449400 Book $14.95
Volume 2: Intermediate
50449410 Book $14.95
Volume 3: Advanced
50449420 Book $14.95

MELODIC RHYTHMS FOR GUITAR
▸ by William Leavitt
50449450 Book $14.95

READING STUDIES FOR GUITAR
▸ by William Leavitt
50449490 Book $14.95

ADVANCED READING STUDIES FOR GUITAR
▸ by William Leavitt
50449500 Book $14.95

COUNTRY GUITAR PICK STYLES
▸ by Michael Ihde
50449480 Book/Cassette $14.95

JIM KELLY GUITAR WORKSHOP SERIES

JIM KELLY'S GUITAR WORKSHOP
00695230 Book/CD $14.95
00320144 Video/booklet $19.95
00320168 DVD/booklet $29.95

MORE GUITAR WORKSHOP
▸ by Jim Kelly
00695306 Book/CD $14.95
00320158 Video/booklet $19.95

BASS

THE BASS PLAYER'S HANDBOOK
▸ by Greg Mooter
50449511 Book $24.95

CHORD STUDIES FOR ELECTRIC BASS
▸ by Rich Appleman
50449750 Book $14.95

READING CONTEMPORARY ELECTRIC BASS
▸ by Rich Appleman
50449770 Book $14.95

ROCK BASS LINES
▸ by Joe Santerre
50449478 Book/CD $19.95

SLAP BASS LINES
▸ by Joe Santerre
50449508 Book/CD $19.95

KEYBOARD

HAMMOND ORGAN COMPLETE
▸ by Dave Limina
50449479 Book/CD $24.95

A MODERN METHOD FOR KEYBOARD
▸ by James Progris
50449620 Vol. 1: Beginner $14.95
50449630 Vol. 2: Intermediate $14.95
50449640 Vol. 3: Advanced $14.95

DRUM SET

BEYOND THE BACKBEAT
▸ by Larry Finn
50449447 Book/CD $19.95

DRUM SET WARM-UPS
▸ by Rod Morgenstein
50449465 Book $12.95

MASTERING THE ART OF BRUSHES
▸ by Jon Hazilla
50449459 Book/CD $19.95

THE READING DRUMMER
▸ by Dave Vose
50449458 Book $9.95

Berklee Press Publications feature material developed at the Berklee College of Music. To browse the Berklee Press Catalog, go to www.berkleepress.com or visit your local music dealer or bookstore.

SAXOPHONE

CREATIVE READING STUDIES FOR SAXOPHONE ▸ by Joseph Viola
50449870 Book $14.95

TECHNIQUE OF THE SAXOPHONE ▸ by Joseph Viola
50449820 Volume 1: Scale Studies $14.95
50449830 Volume 2: Chord Studies $14.95
50449840 Volume 3: Rhythm Studies $14.95

TOOLS FOR DJs

TURNTABLE TECHNIQUE: THE ART OF THE DJ ▸ by Stephen Webber
50449482 Book/2-Record Set $34.95

TURNTABLE BASICS ▸ by Stephen Webber
50449514 Book $9.95

BERKLEE PRACTICE METHOD

Get Your Band Together

BASS ▸ by Rich Appleman and John Repucci
50449427 Book/CD $14.95

DRUM SET ▸ by Ron Savage and Casey Scheuerell
50449429 Book/CD $14.95

GUITAR ▸ by Larry Baione
50449426 Book/CD $14.95

KEYBOARD ▸ by Russell Hoffmann and Paul Schmeling
50449428 Book/CD $14.95

ALTO SAX ▸ by Jim Odgren and Bill Pierce
50449437 Book/CD $14.95

TENOR SAX ▸ by Jim Odgren and Bill Pierce
50449431 Book/CD $14.95

TROMBONE ▸ by Jeff Galindo
50449433 Book/CD $14.95

TRUMPET ▸ by Tiger Okoshi and Charles Lewis
50449432 Book/CD $14.95

BERKLEE INSTANT SERIES

BASS ▸ by Danny Morris
50449502 Book/CD $14.95

DRUM SET ▸ by Ron Savage
50449513 Book/CD $14.95

GUITAR ▸ by Tomo Fujita
50449522 Book/CD $14.95

KEYBOARD ▸ by Paul Schmeling and Dave Limina
50449525 Book/CD $14.95

Distributed by
HAL•LEONARD®

IMPROVISATION SERIES

BLUES IMPROVISATION COMPLETE ▸ by Jeff Harrington ▸ Book/CD
50449486 Bb Instruments $19.95
50449488 C Bass Instruments $19.95
50449425 C Treble Instruments $19.95
50449487 Eb Instruments $19.95

A GUIDE TO JAZZ IMPROVISATION ▸ by John LaPorta ▸ Book/CD
50449439 C Instruments $16.95
50449441 Bb Instruments $16.95
50449442 Eb Instruments $16.95
50449443 Bass Clef $16.95

MUSIC TECHNOLOGY

ARRANGING IN THE DIGITAL WORLD ▸ by Corey Allen
50449415 Book/GM disk $19.95

FINALE: AN EASY GUIDE TO MUSIC NOTATION ▸ by Thomas E. Rudolph and Vincent A. Leonard, Jr.
50449501 Book/CD-ROM $59.95

PRODUCING IN THE HOME STUDIO WITH PRO TOOLS ▸ by David Franz
50449526 Book/CD-ROM $34.95

RECORDING IN THE DIGITAL WORLD ▸ by Thomas E. Rudolph and Vincent A. Leonard, Jr.
50449472 Book $29.95

MUSIC BUSINESS

MIX MASTERS: PLATINUM ENGINEERS REVEAL THEIR SECRETS FOR SUCCESS ▸ by Maureen Droney
50448023 Book $24.95

HOW TO GET A JOB IN THE MUSIC & RECORDING INDUSTRY ▸ by Keith Hatschek
50449505 Book $24.95

THE SELF-PROMOTING MUSICIAN ▸ by Peter Spellman
50449423 Book $24.95

THE MUSICIAN'S INTERNET ▸ by Peter Spellman
50449527 Book $24.95

REFERENCE

REHARMONIZATION TECHNIQUES ▸ by Randy Felts
50449496 Book $29.95

COMPLETE GUIDE TO FILM SCORING ▸ by Richard Davis
50449417 Book $24.95

THE CONTEMPORARY SINGER ▸ by Anne Peckham
50449438 Book/CD $24.95

ESSENTIAL EAR TRAINING ▸ by Steve Prosser
50449421 Book $14.95

MODERN JAZZ VOICINGS ▸ by Ted Pease and Ken Pullig
50449485 Book/CD $24.95

THE NEW MUSIC THERAPIST'S HANDBOOK, SECOND EDITION ▸ by Suzanne B. Hanser
50449424 Book $29.95

POP CULTURE

INSIDE THE HITS ▸ by Wayne Wadhams
50449476 Book $29.95

MASTERS OF MUSIC: CONVERSATIONS WITH BERKLEE GREATS ▸ by Mark Small and Andrew Taylor
50449422 Book $24.95

SONGWRITING

THE SONGWRITER'S WORKSHOP: MELODY ▸ by Jimmy Kachulis
50449518 Book $24.95

THE SONGS OF JOHN LENNON ▸ by John Stevens
50449504 Book $24.95

MELODY IN SONGWRITING ▸ by Jack Perricone
50449419 Book $19.95

MUSIC NOTATION ▸ by Mark McGrain
50449399 Book $19.95

SONGWRITING: ESSENTIAL GUIDE TO LYRIC FORM AND STRUCTURE ▸ by Pat Pattison
50481582 Book $14.95

SONGWRITING: ESSENTIAL GUIDE TO RHYMING ▸ by Pat Pattison
50481583 Book $14.95

1/03